Crest of the Forgotten

Johnna Dee

Book 3 in Ascelin Series

Hardcover: 978-1-959356-20-2|
Paperback: 978-1-959356-21-9|
EBook: B0DVLQ5STB

First Paperback Edition: October 2025

Edited by: Alstroemeria Publishing
Cover Art by Shirleane Santos and Johnna Dee

Physical books printed by
Ingram spark and
Hero and Villain Designs.
www.alstroemeriapub.com

For those looking for a male who is rough around the edges and whose favorite drink is their blood, this book is for you.

TRIGGERS

- Vampires
- Blood/Biting
- Fighting
- Cuss words
- Abuse Emotional and Physical from an ex
- War
- Open Door

- **Mantua** [MAN-tyoo-ah]- Was a gown inspired by the clothing of the Middle East. A mantua was fuller than the old style but could be belted for a neat fit. Pleated versions that featured pleats in front and back made for a dressier, more traditional look. As with skirts of earlier years, the front skirt area could be draped back. Underskirts featured decorative elements like embroidery, ruffles, and pleating. Necklines rose and squared with the decorative edges of the corset visible. Some necklines were perfectly horizontal. Women continued to wear stomachers that were tied or pinned to the front of the bodice. Embroidered stomachers changed the look of an outfit. **Chapter 1**
- **Shu** [SHoo] - god of air **Chapter 2**
- **Tefnut** [tef-n-ut] - goddess of moisture **Chapter 2**
- **Geb** [Gebeb] - was the Egyptian god of the Earth. He could also be considered a father of snakes. It was believed in ancient Egypt that Geb's laughter created earthquakes and that he allowed crops to grow. Geb was both Nuit, husband and brother. **Chapter 2**
- **Osiris, Set, Isis, and Nephthys** - Children of Geb and Nuit. **Chapter 2**
- **Susinum** [sak-se-num] - a perfume based on

lily, myrrh, and cinnamon. **Chapter 2**

- **Matteuccia de Francesco** - She was an alleged witch and nun, known as the "Witch of Ripabianca" after the village where she lived in Italy. In 1428 she was put on trial for being a prostitute, having committed desecration with other women and of the selling of love potions. She confessed to having sold medicine and of having flown to a tree in the shape of a fly on the back of a demon after having smeared herself with an ointment made of the blood of newborn children. She was judged guilty of sorcery and sentenced to be burned at the stake. **Chapter 3**
- **Seshat** [Sheh-shaht] - was the ancient Egyptian goddess of writing, wisdom, and knowledge. She was the daughter of Thoth. She was seen as a scribe and record keeper; her name means "female scribe". **Chapter 6.**
- **Tengu** [ten-gu] - are supernatural beings from ancient Japanese religions. They are often depicted as forest goblins. They have the ability to shape-shift into a variety of human or animal forms and can teleport instantly from place to place. They gained a reputation for being skilled in the art of war and proud mischief makers. **Chapter 6**
- **A mhuirnín** [uh WUR-neen] - Meaning "Darling" **Chapter 6**
- **Mo shíorghrá** [muh HEER-ggrawh] - Meaning "My Eternal Love" is a more modern translation of the concept of fated mates. **Chapter 48**
- **Is ceol mo chroí thú** [Is cyoal mu khree who] - Meaning "you're the music of my heart". **Chapter 48**
- **Pankuketsubichi** [PAN-ku-koe-chi-bi-chi] - パンクケツビッチ meaning punk ass bitch. **Chapter 6**
- **Tale of the Genji** [genn-Jees] - The Genji Monogatari Emaki (源氏物語絵巻), also called The Tale of Genji Scroll, is an illustrated handscroll of Japanese classic literature, produced

during the 12th century authored by the court lady Murasaki Shikibu. However, only 20 of the 54 chapters are known today, and the original scroll was about 450 feet long with over 100 paintings and 300 sheets of calligraph. **Chapter 7**

- **Zythus** [Zy-tHəs] - a malt beer made in ancient Egypt. The earliest existing records of brewing relate to the production of zythum by ancient Egyptians, c. 2000 BCE. The principal ingredient was malted grain, either emmer wheat or barley or both together. **Chapter**
- Vulcan's Mirror - Vulcan (Hephaestus) was the Roman god of the fire. He was a master of the forge. In myth he forged a magical mirror that could show him the past, present, and future. He gave it to his wife, Venus who used it to hide her affair with Mars. **Chapter 22**
- **Cailleach Bheag** [cal-hahh breg] - little witch in Gaelic. **Chapter 28**
- **Futhark** [footh-ark] - The term for a runic alphabet that follows a Germanic order is Futhark. **Chapter 30**
- **"Praecipe eis, alliga eos ad hanc locum."** Translates to "Command them, bind them to this place." **Chapter 30**
- الماء الساطع بعمق يجلب لي الإجابات التي أسعى إليها. [kebdana al-satea bamaq yaglab lee al-ijabat al-tay asaa eliha.] - Water shining water deep bring me answers that I seek. **Chapter 34**
- **St. Januarius** - The blood is kept in two glass ampoules. The dried blood of St. Januarius, who died around 305 A.D., is preserved in two glass ampoules, one larger than the other. The Church believes that a miracle occurs in response to the dedication and prayers of the faithful. When the miracle occurs, the mass of reddish dried blood, adhering to one side of the ampoule, turns into completely liquid blood, covering the glass from side to side. **Chapter 41**

Young Feya, a fae, survived a vampire attack on her village, but not unscathed—a vampire's bite marked her. Inter-species relations were forbidden; discovery meant death. She fled with the help of her best friend, Elwyn, only to be found by Aethelredd Ascelin, another vampire, bleeding out in the forest. He saved and raised her. With Aguya, Leo, and Brady, she found a family. Growing up, she joined their work, taking odd jobs the church assigns.

Years later, Elwyn's arrival stirs up Feya's past. He seeks her family's aid in uncovering his would-be assassin and the queen's enemies. Redd refuses, fearing discovery by the fae queen of what Feya is, but disobeying her father, she secretly joins Elwyn.

Feya joins Elwyn on a flight to the fea vale, stepping into an unfamiliar world that terrifies her. Fear grips her as she uses her magic to aid Elwyn, battling alongside burgeoning feelings for him. Surrendering at last, she falls for Elwyn's charm as they uncover the attacker: Olette, Elwyn's mother.

While capturing Olette, the Fea queen, Casada discovered Feya's secret. Instead of execution, she bound

Feya to her will with a celestial contract.

Crest of the
SCORNED

Aguya, a fire witch, was framed by her sister, Alse, for their stepmother's murder when she was young. To escape execution, she fled, lost and alone, until she found refuge with Aethelredd Ascelin and his family. She quickly became one of them.

Years later, her sister's return throws everything into chaos. While desperately trying to free Feya from her celestial contract, Redd sends her to refuge with an unexpected person—her ex. After a bitter breakup, she'd sworn never to see Alvero again. Yet here she is, hiding in his tiny forest cabin, alone with him and his demonic barghest, Bobo. Alvero, a healing fairy bearing the marks of past battles, both physical and emotional, offers her shelter. Amidst their bickering, Aguya rediscovers lingering feelings for the one male she could never truly forget.

The forest's hushed peace, shared with Alvero, shattered by the attack of her old coven. Thrown into a frigid icebox, the chilling dampness seeps into her bones, stealing warmth. Alone in the suffocating dark, the fear is a tangible weight, her fire magic useless against the bone-deep cold. She repeatedly attempted to summon her fire magic, with minimal success. Time passes and with no sense if she was there days or hours, she heard fighting and, with a final, desperate surge of magic, finally sparked enough power to break free. Emerging from the icebox, she saw the battle raging above and joined the fray, but days without food left her exhausted, and she fainted. Her sister, Alse, escaped during the chaos of the battle.

Aguya, abandoning her hiding place, returns home. A fight erupts with Alvero; he refuses to leave the forest; she refuses to stay. Overwhelmed by sadness, she flees, tears blurring her vision as her sister approaches unseen. A gunshot rings out; Aguya falls, bleeding. Redd, Leo, and Brady rush her to Alvero for healing. In a dreamlike limbo, she encounters her deceased mother, gaining the strength to persevere. Recovered, she and her family return home.

Alvero recalls a gift from the old queen's maid—a magically locked box. Its contents remain a mystery, only that Queen Casada desperately wants it hidden. He reveals the box to the queen, hoping to secure Feya's release, but Casada threatens him. Alvero refuses to yield, and with his animal companions, escapes the fae realm. At its edge, he encounters Alse before returning home.

At home, she confronts her feelings. She goes to Alvero and tells him how she truly feels finally.

REDD

Chapter 1

Aethelredd Ascelin's gaze remained transfixed on the woman seated across the dimly lit tavern. The soft flickering of the candlelight accentuated her ethereal beauty, highlighting her porcelain skin that seemed to radiate a gentle glow. Her flowing blonde locks cascaded down her shoulders, dancing with the faint whispers of the breeze drifting in from the open door. As their eyes met, her piercing pale blue gaze studied him intently, like a painter observing her subject. A warmth enveloped him, causing a smile to spread across his face. However, the glimmer in her eye sent an ominous shiver crept down his spine, a warning hidden. Despite this unease, he dismissed it, convinced that this delicate woman held no threat to a robust soldier like him.

He debated for a minute, his heartbeat pounding in his chest, if he should approach her as he ran his calloused hand through his brassy red hair, feeling its coarse texture. Maybe she was looking at someone behind him. He turned his amber eyes to glance behind him. No one was there. Turning back, he could practically feel her eyes piercing through him, a tingling sensation crawling up his spine.

Standing up, he ambled over, the soft rustle of his clothing blending with the faint piano music in the background, his eyes never leaving those hypnotic blue eyes. As he got closer, he saw the finery of her mantua gown, the vibrant hues of blue and golds catching the light. Her expensive jewelry sparkled in the candlelight, the twinkling reflections dancing. Jewelry that probably cost more than a year's worth of his soldier salary, a stark reminder of the vast difference in their worlds.

His mind wandered aimlessly as he wondered why such a fancy lady would be in an English pub tucked away in the depths of nowhere. The dimly lit room, filled with the aroma of aged wood and freshly poured pints, echoed with the lively chatter of patrons engaged in jovial conversation.

"Wha' a lass like ye doin' 'ere?" He smiled his most charming smile as he looked down at her. The scent of her perfume, a delicate floral fragrance, wafted towards him.

Laughing, her soft, lilting voice said, "Is that how you approach a lady?"

Feeling a wave of self-consciousness wash over him, he furrowed his brow and nervously shifted his weight from one foot to the other. With narrowed eyes, he carefully examined her, questioning whether he had misinterpreted the situation.

"Grab my cloak and follow," she said, standing and turning to walk away. "You shall do fine."

He stood there, completely astonished, his eyes wide and mouth agape, before hastily snatching the cloak and hurrying after her. Exiting the bustling tavern, he trailed behind her until they reached a waiting coach. As he approached, he hesitated for a moment, uncertain. A cool breeze drifted around him as he looked at the elegant coach. The coach emanated a faint scent of leather and polish. In the soft moonlight, the coach's dark wood and gold trim gleamed. The deep, velvety red curtains gently danced to the rhythm of a cool night breeze, accompanying the coachman's gesture as he graciously swung open the door. He looked over at the horses, as dark as midnight, tethered to the front of the carriage.

His gaze locked with hers, and he found himself captivated by the intensity in those eyes, momentarily taking his breath away. It felt as if she could consume him with just one glance. Shaking off the thought, he dismissed it from his mind. After all, she was petite, barely reaching half his height. Even her coachman appeared to be of diminutive stature. There was no way they could take him on. He needed to get these bizarre thoughts out of his head.

Smiling, he climbed into the coach with her. He sat in the soft padded blue velvet seat, his wide torso taking up almost one entire seat as he sat across from her. She looked so tiny across from her. He rested his elbows on his knees as leaned in towards her.

"Ain't ye a pretty lil lass," he smiled beguilingly. He reached his hand out and brushed a strand of silky hair out of her face.

Sighing, she uttered. "You need a bath. Please sit back."

He reluctantly obeyed, his gaze fixed on her enticing figure. His narrowed eyes, barely open, reflected his inner conflict as he weighed his options. A part of him still yearned to explore the pleasures hidden between her thighs, while another part questioned if it was worth all the effort. With a nonchalant shrug, he conceded he was already inside the carriage and decided to indulge in some amusement. Besides, he couldn't ignore the undeniable need for a thorough bath after enduring the arduous journey of the past few days. Lacking the rank or wealth to gain a horse, he had been marching for days and sleeping on the cold, hard ground. He reasoned that if he had to cleanse himself to enjoy a passionate encounter with the fancy lass, so be it.

"Aye, then," he stated, a smirk on his face as he crossed his arms across his chest.

The road was bumpy as they traversed the dirt roads. Soon there came the sound of gravel crunching as the coach came to a halt. The door swung open as the coachman opened it.

He stared at the lassie, waiting for her to leave.

She rolled her eyes. "You need to leave first. Your legs are blocking the way."

"Alrighty den," he laughed as he stood up.

The roof, barely reaching his height, forced him to hunch over as he climbed out. He wiped his calloused hand on his dusty pants, then extended it towards her. Her lip curled up slightly, her fingers hesitantly intertwining with his. A surge of resentment coursed through him, fueled by her subtle disdain. He grew weary of the haughty upper class, looking down on soldiers like him.

His steps faltered, his breath caught in his throat as he stood before the awe-inspiring manor house. The ancient gray stone house rose high, casting long shadows in the moonlight. Numerous pristine windows shimmered with a reflective glow. A massive wooden door, adorned with intricate ironwork, stood high and inviting. Above, the conical tower roofs soared towards the starry night, a silent testament to the grandeur within.

He had not seen many places this grand, having grown up in a small farm town. He was the youngest of eight siblings. It had been years since he had last seen any of them. He had left home hoping to make his fortune, instead he was following one order after another, trying to climb the ranks and stay alive.

A butler, wearing a crisp black suit, opened the door with a quiet creak. His dark, piercing eyes sparkled like polished obsidian, reflecting a glimmer of excitement. As he extended his arm, his fingers gracefully gestured for them to step inside.

"My lady." The butler bowed.

She handed him her cloak as she entered. He followed behind her, every hair on his body standing on end as an eerie feeling filled his soul.

He entered the dimly lit entryway. His eyes scanned as he tried to see everything.

"Take our guest... umm... What's your name?" she sighed.

"Aethelredd Ascelin," he bowed. "An' ye name, lassie?"

"Sophine Rathmore. Draw a bath for him and find something for him to wear." She snorted as her eyes went up and down his body. "Once the bath has been accomplished, bring him to me. I'll be in my chamber."

Effortlessly, she ascended the stairs, her graceful movements accompanied by a faint whisper of her flowing dress.

Meanwhile, a frown etched itself on his face as he towered over the male, standing tall at 6'4". The glint of annoyance shimmered in his cat-shaped amber eyes. His jaw, sharp and triangular, accentuated the feline allure that emanated from him. He straightened his back as his muscular arms crossed firmly over his chest.

"This way," the butler said in a raspy voice.

Aethelredd emerged from the warm bath, the

droplets clinging to his muscular frame as he swiped them away with a thin linen cloth. The rough texture of the fabric glided effortlessly across his skin, leaving a tingling sensation in its wake. Standing at the door, the butler patiently waited for him to finish. The copper tub had provided him with a rare moment of luxury.

Glancing at the clothes carefully arranged on the table, he observed the navy blue Spanish breeches adorned with delicate silver filigree, accompanied by a matching coat and waistcoat. A crisp white shirt, collar, cravat, and white stockings lay neatly beside them. As he surveyed the finery before him, he hesitated. Adorned in such extravagant attire, he would become a peacock, a spectacle he never wished to be. He frowned as he donned the clothes, the fit snug having been meant for someone smaller than himself. He adjusted himself, trying to get comfortable in the stiff clothes.

The butler raised an eyebrow as he spoke. "Ready?"

Nodding, he figured he was as ready as he was going to be. Plus, hopefully, the clothes would be on the floor soon.

He followed the butler as he led him up the stairs. He opened a door, gesturing him in.

He walked into Sophine standing in front of the fireplace as it flickered. Her long white dressed gown appeared sheer as he took in the delicate curves.

"Yooehr a pretty lettle one," he whispered as he kicked the door closed in the butler's face.

"Come here," she whispered as she glanced over her shoulder.

"If a lass want, den I abide," he whispered.

Walking over, he brushed the satiny strands off her shoulder as he planted a kiss there. "Ye are one o' de

prettiest lasses I've ever seen."

Laughing, she turned around. "Lay down on the floor."

His brow furrowed, creating deep lines on his forehead as he obediently followed her command. The rough texture of the coarse blanket underneath him offered little solace, causing discomfort as he laid down. The sound of her tongue lightly grazing her lips echoed in the air, heightening his senses. With her feet straddling him, she gracefully knelt down, her long hair cascading around his head like a curtain. A sense of foreboding enveloped him, sending shivers down his spine. His heart pounded in his chest, the rapid beats reverberating through his entire body as he gazed up at the captivating beauty.

Her fingers traced a line down his neck. "Your heart is racing."

"Joehst excited," he said, uncertainty tinging his voice.

Laughing, she bent down and smelled his neck. Her nose gently brushed against his throat. "Much better. You are stronger than I thought you would be."

"Is a lassie needin' a strappin' yooehng man?" he whispered, as his hand came up tangling in her hair, as he dragged her mouth towards his.

"No kissing," she whispered.

He released her as his thoughts swirled. The room filled with a thick silence. What was she wanting of him if not this?

The glint of the firelight danced on her teeth as she smiled. Something about her teeth seemed different as he stared at her, so subtle he could not put his finger on it. She brought her mouth to his neck, gently sucking the flesh in, her breath tickling his skin.

He smiled, a flicker of relief as maybe they were back to what he thought this was about. He closed his eyes as his hands went down to her hips, digging into the flesh as he pressed her onto his engorged cock. Pleasure raced through him for a moment before a flash of pain as her teeth sunk into his neck, a sudden jolt that caused him to suck in his breath. Soon, the pain was gone as numbness washed over him. A hazy cloud appeared in front of his eyes as she sipped from his life force. He grew cold as she continued to drink his blood, a chilling sensation that spread through his veins. He wanted to fight, to snap her pretty little neck, but his head felt drunk, his thoughts muddled, and his limbs refused to obey. She pulled back, her lips stained crimson as his blood dripped down her chin.

As she grabbed a dagger, the metallic glint of the blade caught the firelight, a sharp contrast to the darkness that was enveloping him. He tensed, waiting for her to stab him, but she did not. The blade sliced across her hand as blood poured from the cut. She dropped the dagger as she gripped his chin, pouring her blood into his mouth, the warm liquid pooling on his tongue. The coppery taste made him gag, the bitter tang overwhelming his senses as the warm liquid slid down his throat, an intense sensation that burned through his veins. An intense pain coursed raked through his body, his head spinning, his vision narrowing as darkness crept at the edges. He felt his world slipping as the darkness consumed him.

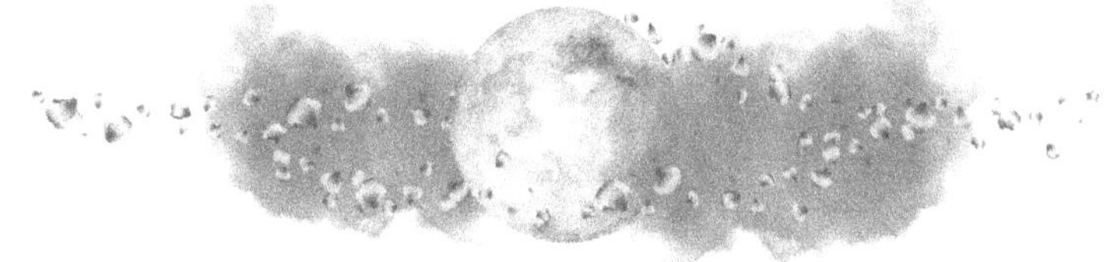

Gradually, Aethelredd emerged into the land of the living. His eyelids fluttered open, revealing a world blurred and shrouded in darkness. As he blinked away the haze, a gritty sensation filled his eyes, as if sand had infiltrated them. A dryness enveloped his mouth, a coppery taste tainted it. A dull ache throbbed within his skull, pulsating with each heartbeat.

Raising his hands to his head, he attempted to massage his temples, but his movements were abruptly halted. Confusion clouded his mind as he tried again, only to be met with the clinking sound of metal. Startled, he sat upright, his eyes adjusting to the pitch-black darkness that surrounded him. Peering down, he discovered cold metal shackles tightly encircling his wrists. He tugged at them, his gaze following the chain that led to the unyielding stone wall. The chains were not budging an inch.

Memories flooded his consciousness, reminding him of the events from the previous night. He realized he was fortunate to still be breathing. Yet, his luck seemed tarnished, as he found himself imprisoned in this dark, dank cell. His eyes roamed the prison, taking in his surroundings as he rose from the bedroll and stood up on unsteady legs. For a moment, his head swam as he tried to get his bearings, amplified tenfold by the blood loss he had suffered.

Drawing closer to the wall to which he was tethered, he carefully explored his neck with his limited freedom, searching for any signs of the bite marks. To his surprise, there were no cuts, scratches, or bites. Perhaps he had been too intoxicated to recall, or maybe she had slipped something into his drink, but he could swear that she had sunk her teeth into his neck and drank his blood.

A faint thudding noise echoed through the chamber, drawing his attention towards the door. It resembled the rhythmic beat of a low drum, two distinct drums approaching the cell door.

The heavy wooden door creaked open, allowing a sliver of dim candlelight to spill into the room. The metallic scent of blood wafted through the air, mingling with the musty undertone of aged books. In the flickering glow, the butler stood, gripping a diminutive male whose neck bore a shallow, oozing wound and a lone candle. A gnawing hunger clawed at his insides, causing his stomach to emit an audible growl. Tremors coursed through his trembling hands, as if echoing the desperate need to satiate the all-consuming craving. His brows furrowed in a valiant struggle against the relentless hunger coursing through his veins.

"I see you're awake, Sir Aethelredd," the butler tipped his head as he shoved the bleeding man into the room.

The smell of that blood filling his senses as an intense hunger growled through his core. With every bit of his willpower, he fought the urge. Donning his most charming smile, he said. "Call me Redd. Ye dink ye can loosen dese shackles?"

"After you feed and come to terms with what you are now," he whispered. Slamming the door shut.

His eyes fixated on the door, his gaze unwavering as the hunger within him grew more intense. The air was heavy with the scent of blood, infiltrating his nostrils and igniting an insatiable craving to feel and taste. His breaths became ragged, matching the rhythm of his pounding heart as he pressed his body against the unforgiving coldness of the stone wall. Confusion coursed through his veins, battling against the overwhelming hunger that gnawed at his very core. His fists clenched, his nails digging into the flesh of his palms, desperate to anchor himself in this maddening moment. The steady drumbeat reverberated in his ears, steadily growing louder, and he realized with a jolt that it emanated from the male before him. He fought to calm his racing heart, to steady his erratic breathing, drawing upon the memories of his soldier training. But all rational thought fled his mind, consumed by the primal desire to taste the warm, life-giving blood that oozed from the male's veins.

"It's alright," the male sighed. "I am ready to die."

"Sahrry. I dahn't know what de foehck ye are talkin' abooeht," Redd growled. He clawed at the chains, trying to get them off.

The male stepped closer to him. "She left me for her cousin. So it's alright. They said she would be blamed when they find my body. She will pay for leaving me."

The drumbeat got louder the closer the male got.

"What de foehck is dat noise?" he said, raising his hands to his ears.

Inches separated the two males. He stared at the bleeding male. His eyes, unaffected by the cloak of night, marveled at his own clear vision. A fleeting thought of how he could see so vividly was abruptly interrupted by a sharp pang of hunger, causing him to hunch over in pain. The metallic tang of blood overwhelmed his senses, eclipsing all other scents. The male advanced, his breath hot against his face. Resisting became futile, and with a firm grip on the male's hair, he twisted his head. His mouth descended upon the exposed neck, teeth piercing the skin. The taste of coppery blood flooded his mouth, satisfying his insatiable appetite. The crimson liquid cascaded down his throat, a heavenly sensation. Gradually, the hunger waned, and he released the male, only to be confronted with the horror of the lifeless body slumped at his feet.

Chapter 2

There was a time she, Nuit Gamal, was worshiped as the goddess of the sky. Her father Shu, god of air, and her mother, Tefnut, goddess of moisture, would spoil her. The sweet scent of incense and the soft murmurs of prayers as her believers left sacrifices of food, incense and gifts at her temples still filled her memories. She and her family had helped build a kingdom in the desert thousands of years ago. The golden sand shimmered under the scorching sun, but her kingdom had crumbled and her family had all scattered to the wind. She had been alive for centuries, yet she could not remember the last time she saw any of her old family. She couldn't help but feel a pang of loneliness creeping in, as she realized that everyone she had once known had long ago forgotten about her and moved on.

The emptiness in her heart was a constant ache, like a never-ending desert wind that whipped through her soul. She had walked this earth for eons just floating through one pretend human existence after another. She could not even tell how many identities she had over the years. The memories of each life were like fleeting mirages, fading in and out of her mind. Fifteen years was her limit in any one place; then she'd move on, just long enough for people to not see that she doesn't age. No social media presence, no friends to get her through the hard times. She only had herself to rely on.

Loneliness, like a heavy fog, settled around her, obscuring her from the world. The humans would fade in and out, dying with their short life spans. Going through that over and over again had been so painful, so she stopped letting humans into her small world. She had a few magicals as friends, but she rarely saw them. The rare moments of connection were like drops of rain in a vast desert, rarely quenching her thirst for companionship.

Every once in a while, she would look back and reflect on her family and what might have been. The distant sound of laughter and the warmth of familial love would briefly fill her senses before dissipating into the void. Those thoughts were fleeting, and the longer she lived, the less she remembered. Those that survived the war had abandoned her, so there was no point in dwelling on thoughts of them. The bitterness of betrayal clung to her, reminding her of the pain of abandonment.

Now she stood here, enveloped in the lingering scent of aged paper and musty books. The dimly lit shop echoed with the sounds of a human car salesman's voice, his words filled with frustration and disappointment. As he spoke, he absentmindedly tossed a weathered book from one hand to the other, the rhythmic thud creating an anxious knot in her stomach. With each toss, her heart skipped a beat, as if it could leap out of her chest at any moment.

The one constant in her life had always been books. Shelves lined with colorful spines, neatly stacked, offered a comforting, familiar sight. The sound of pages turning, the gentle rustling echoing through the cozy bookshop, created a symphony of knowledge and imagination. Nostalgia and history filled the air, heavy with the scent of aged paper and ink. Books were her constant companion over the years. In a book she knew she would find a friend, an adventure, love, and most important, it would never abandon her.

She had opened the bookshop in the 1800s. It had become her sanctuary, a place where she found solace amidst the chaos of the world. It was here that she spent countless hours immersed in the written word, finding a respite from the outside world.

She would stay for fifteen-year intervals, the passage of time marked by the changing seasons that painted the landscape with vibrant colors. Inside her cozy apartment that was above the store, she would spend the evenings curled up with a book by the fire. The soft touch of the pages of the book against her fingertips brought a sense of comfort as she would curl up in her favorite armchair, immersing herself in the stories that unfolded before her. During the day, she worked in the bookstore. Offering the wandering clientele an assortment of new and old books.

In this familiar place, she found solace and purpose, knowing that she was a part of something greater, connecting people through the magic of literature. But at this moment, she didn't feel so magical. All she wanted to do was snatch the book out of the dunce's hands.

"So, is there any wiggle room on the price?" he said with his thick southern accent.

"Unfortunately, no," Nuit sighed as her hands itched to grab the book.

She delicately brushed away a stray strand of midnight hair that had escaped her neatly arranged bun, the soft touch of her fingers grazing against her face. As she huffed, her bangs fluttered across her forehead. Her eyes, as dark as obsidian, remained fixed on the book, following its swift movement from one hand to the other. A subtle glow seemed to emanate from her honey-colored skin, casting a warm radiance from within. As she moved behind the counter, the faint scent of a sweet rose fragrance wafted through the air. An aquiline nose, wrinkled in a frustrated snort, showed a touch of annoyance. She tilted her angular chin down, thinking the human would drop the book.

With a forceful thud, the human slammed the book on the polished wooden counter, causing a sharp echo to reverberate through the quiet room. Grimacing, she winced as she gingerly picked it up. Turning it over, she scrutinized every inch of the book, her eyes scanning for any signs of harm. To her relief, the spine and pages appeared to be unscathed.

"I guess I'll just have to buy it elsewhere," he sighed, turning and walking out the door. The doorbell chimed softly as he left.

"Good luck with that. Since there are less than 1000 of this book worldwide," she muttered to herself.

Clutching the book to her chest protectively, she walked through the store, her fingers glided across the spines of her familiar friends. Flecks of dust floated, reminding her of the stars at night. The last words of her mother floated through her mind as she paused, watching the dust float in a ray of light. "Be fearless, sweet star, because you sparkle brighter than even the sun." She had not known those would be the last words she would hear her mother say ever. It had been almost 2,000 years since she had heard those words, yet she could still hear the sweet cadence of her mother's voice.

Stopping, she gingerly replaced the old, weathered book on the dusty wooden shelf. The faint scent of aging paper and dust tickled her nose as her fingers lightly brushed against the worn cover. Her mind wandered to the dusting, knowing the entire store could use a spring cleaning.

Suddenly, the deep, resonating chime of the grandfather clock reverberated through the air, announcing 6pm, signaling the end of another day as the sound echoed throughout the quiet bookstore. With a sigh, she turned, her footsteps creating a soft, muffled sound against the creaking wooden floorboards.

Heading towards the front of the store, she reached for the key. She turned the key in the lock, sealing off the world outside and embracing the solitude within.

Walking towards the back of the store, she closed her eyes, her fingers gliding against the spines until she stopped and grabbed a book, feeling the rough texture of the cover. Pulling it towards her chest, she never looked at the title. She just knew this would be tonight's friend.

Climbing the creaky stairs, she went up towards her apartment. The scent of lilacs filled her nostrils as she opened the door, the sweet floral aroma enveloping her senses. From the open window, a soft breeze gently swayed the petals of the vibrant lilacs sitting in a vase on the antique wooden coffee table, their bright splash of color catching her eye. The sounds of bustling traffic wafted in, making her feel less alone. The polished hardwood floors gleamed under the soft glow of the evening setting sun as she slipped off her shoes and placed them on the shoe rack.

The antique grandfather clock, standing tall against the wall, emitted a gentle ticking sound that resonated throughout the room, its rhythmic cadence becoming a soothing background melody. A vibrant, ruby-red round rug adorned the center of the room, its plush texture inviting her toes into its softness. The absence of a television was noticeable, but it only enhanced the tranquil atmosphere of the space. Instead, a collection of paintings, carefully curated over centuries, adorned the walls and hung above the fireplace. A cream-colored sofa, invitingly plush, stood against one wall, its soft fabric practically beckoning to be touched.

Setting the book next to the bouquet, she went to the tiny kitchen to brew a cup of chamomile tea, the comforting aroma of the herbal tea filling the air as it steeped. With a tea cup in hand, she went back to her favorite chair, a wingback with a floral pattern. Sipping her tea, she sat down and opened the book, the sound of the pages rustling as she delved into the story.

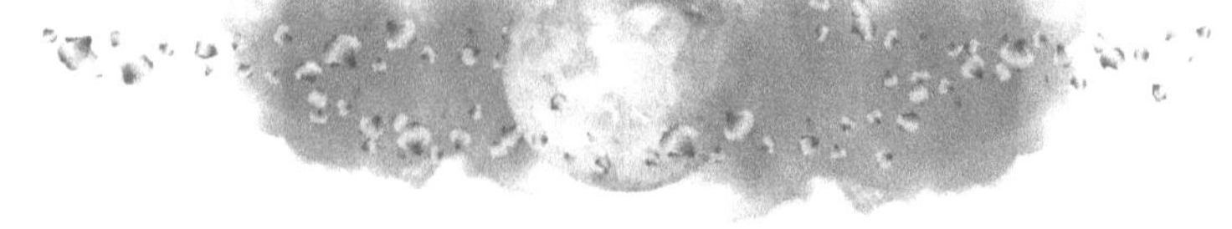

As she floated through a fitful slumber, haunting nightmares swirled around her like ethereal specters, as if the war's weight had lingered after all these centuries. Tears cascaded down her cheeks, leaving a salty trail that mingled with the faint touch of her mother's gentle hand as she tossed and turned. In the dim candlelight, the shadows danced upon Tefnut's tan face, casting an intricate tapestry of light and darkness, highlighting the radiant glow of her sun-kissed skin.

"Momma," Nuit whispered. "I am scared. I can't fight like my brothers."

"Sweet star," Tefnut whispered calmly. "You will not need to fight because you are going to run. Isis and Nephthys will join you, while Geb, Set, and Osiris will stay back to fight."

"What about you?"

"My place is next to my husband. Your place is protecting your daughters from harm."

"I wish I could fight like you."

"No, you don't. You need to make sure our family is safe. Take them and run to safety."

"But—"

"Do not fight me on this. Do as your mother says."

Nuit her eyes downcast, filled with melancholy, reflecting the weight of her inner turmoil. The sound of her racing heartbeat drowned out all other noise, echoing in her ears like a persistent drumbeat. With a heavy heart, she debated the futility of fighting her words, the taste of defeat lingering on her tongue before she had even spoken. Finally, with a resigned nod, she turned to leave, her sandaled footsteps echoing softly on the cold floor.

"Nuit, wait."

Turning, she looked back at her mother, the woman who had fought for her, raised her and loved her unwaveringly. "Yes."

"Be fearless, sweet star, because you sparkle brighter than even the sun," Tefnut whispered. Tears sparkled at the corner of her eyes like tiny diamonds.

With a quick, determined stride, she sprinted towards her mother. As she reached her, she embraced her tightly, feeling the softness of her mother's back against her hands. The sweet scent of her mother's susinum perfume enveloped her, adding to her overwhelming feeling of love and sadness. In that moment, she absorbed the strength and courage that her mother exuded effortlessly, like a warm embrace on a chilly day.

She walked down the dimly lit corridor, the muffled sound of shouts carrying on the air. Turning one last time, she watched as her mother walked down the hallway towards the great hall.

"Do we really just leave?" Nephthys said, drawing her eyes.

Nodding, she tried to exude the fearlessness her own mother had. As she approached Isis and Nephthys, their small figures seemingly shrinking in the face of fear, their wide, dark eyes reflecting their trepidation. Grabbing their hands, she hastened towards the secret passages. The sound of their hurried footsteps echoing through the stone walls seemed to be louder than thunder to her own ears, as she prayed the Greeks would not hear them. Behind them, two loyal human guards and a human priest trailed anxiously, their heavy boots thudding against the floor. Suddenly, the sharp clash of steel hitting steel pierced the silence, causing her breath to catch in her throat. She turned back briefly, her heart sinking as a fresh wave of tears streaming down her face. The cacophony of battle cries and the metallic scent of blood hung heavily in the air, signaling the arrival of the Greek Gods. This was just the beginning of a brutal and fierce battle.

"Come." A hand tugged her as she turned to look at Isis.

Nodding, she followed them down a dimly lit corridor, the air heavy with a musty scent of dust and dirt. Each step she took on the stairs echoed in the eerie silence, reverberating through the narrow space. The darkness seemed to stretch endlessly, making her feel a sense of unease. Suddenly, a deafening explosion shattered the stillness, causing the walls to tremble violently as rocks flew around them. Amidst the chaos, she lost sight of them, their figures swallowed by the engulfing darkness. Alone and disoriented, she ventured forward, her fingertips brushing against the cold, crumbling walls as she navigated her way through the unknown. The cool stone guided her further into the darkness that encompassed her.

Startled, she woke up, her body drenched in perspiration, the tangy smell of fear lingering in the air. As her phone rang, its shrill tone cutting through the silence, she glanced at the screen. A smile slowly spread across her face, knowing that the vampire was oblivious to the fact that he had just roused from slumber.

REDD

Chapter 3

Redd felt the tension in his shoulders, aching from the weight of his world crashing around him. The living room was dimly lit, casting long shadows that danced across the walls as Father Cassius paced back and forth. Only the soft creaking of the wooden floor broke the silence, emphasizing the gravity of the situation. The church rarely made house calls, but it seemed today they decided he needed a stern talking to.

He shifted his gaze to his phone; the screen illuminating his face in the dimly lit room. Puzzled by his own actions, he knew he should concentrate on Cass and the chaos of his life. Yet, against his better judgment, he found himself typing a message to Nuit.

As he glanced around, he tried to avoid making eye contact with the Father. The worn Persian rug caught his gaze with its rich maroons and browns. Positioned in an 'L' shape around the crackling fireplace, the dark brown sectional offered comfort as he leaned back. Someone had casually tossed an off-white quilt over the brown leather recliner chair across from him. The shelves that adorned the walls held a treasure trove of sights, from vibrant paintings and cherished trinkets to the well-loved books that lined each shelf. Moonlight filtered through the picture window, casting a gentle glow upon the room.

As the soft brown blackout curtains billowed with the breeze, the sweet scent of roses from the garden wafting in.

"You went off course and now we are dealing with the fallout," Father Cassius sighed dramatically while he paced. Cass was a fae. He didn't know whether he had left his kind to join the church or whether they had exiled him; he only knew that the Father had exasperated the hell out of him.

Raising a fiery red eyebrow, he shot a piercing glare at the Father. The Father's brown hair, glistening with gel, was meticulously slicked back, catching the light as he turned his head. His piercing baby blue eyes seemed completely unaware of the intense glare Redd shot his way.

After the devastating loss of his clan in the deafening chaos of the great war of the 1700s, he reluctantly joined forces with the church. Taking missions primarily revolved around tracking down stolen relics and precious artifacts.

But when his daughter, Feya, a halfling who is part vampire and fae, dared to entangle herself with a member of the fea court, it was as if a whirlwind of emotions swept through him. A storm that stirred the depths of his soul as he remembered the dangers she had put herself and their family in. At that moment, he withdrew from his duties with the church and since then Cass had been pressuring him to come back.

"We have been turning a blind eye for centuries to your disobedience, but—" Father Cassius started.

"I think you have me confused with a lap dog there, Cass," Redd growled.

"Do you not understand what is going on in the Fae court?" Cass threw his hands up in exasperation.

Shrugging, Redd glanced out the window. The soft, silvery moonlight bathed the rose garden, casting an ethereal glow on their delicate, velvety petals, which seemed to shimmer like drops of blood.

"There are skirmishes breaking out all over the place," Cass continued. "We have been fighting hard to keep this off the internet, but one such fight was already on it. Do you know how much work goes into making humans believe this is fake?"

"Was I on the video?"

"No, but—"

"Then, I am confused about what it has to do with me. I have managed to not get myself exposed online. So maybe you should take it up with the idiot who got exposed," Redd snickered.

"That is not the point," Cass said, exasperated. "This war is spilling into the human world, and we need to stop it."

"We?"

"Yes, we."

Redd rolled his neck to release his tense muscles again. An ache lingered in his stomach as he tried to ignore it.

"If we do not stop this, the hunt for our kind will start all over again," Cass pleaded. "We barely survived the first war as they hunted us down. They outnumber us, and we cannot fight them all. So we need to nip this in the bud before it goes any further."

"I did nothing to cause this," Redd stated as he ran a hand through his red hair. "I simply helped out in finding the person who was trying to start a revolution in the fae court. So, maybe instead of lecturing me, you should go talk to those people."

"We both know you and your family are knee deep

in this mess," Cass snorted.

Shaking his head, a million sarcastic retorts came to his mind, but he held them back. "I am not sure why you think I started this mess, but I didn't. So, we can keep going back and forth or you can let me do my job."

"And what exactly is that job?" Cass crossed his arms across his chest.

Shrugging, Redd stared at the ceiling. *How can I explain to a male who has no family that my family is my primary focus and not some greater good the father keeps preaching about? I have to break the celestial contract spell on Feya, find Aguya's sister before she hurts someone else I love again, and now I am to blame for a pansy ass war I didn't start.*

Remembering the spell the fea Queen Casada had put on Feya renewed his anger. He had spent centuries protecting his one and only sire for her to get mixed in with fea court drama. Now he was knee deep in the mire and trying to fix the mess made. Then he had Aguya's sister, Alse, to deal with. Aguya had almost died from the attack Alse did and now here he sat listening to Father Know-It-All preaching to him like he was some wayward choir boy.

"I think there is some kind of miscommunication," Redd snarled. "My job is whatever mission I take. My loyalty is to my family. So, I have taken a break from *jobs* to tend to my family."

"What we need—" Cass started.

"Doesn't matter," Redd interrupted.

"Again, what we need—"

"Is to find someone else or be patient."

"Maybe, if you let me finish, our paths might align," Cass stated while his brow furrowed.

Sighing dramatically, Redd said, "Fine, tell me this damned message you're so impatient to relay so I can go have my breakfast."

"Damned vampires," Cass muttered under his breath.

"I mean, if you want to volunteer a vein, I won't complain," Redd sneered.

Sighing, Cass stopped pacing and stared at Redd, his brow furrowed. "You can be quite impossible. And no that will never happen. We need you to find out who is the usurper who is after Queen Casada's throne."

"Maybe we should just let them have it," Redd rubbed his temple.

"Have what?"

"The throne. What does it matter to us who is in charge?"

Shaking his head, Cass sighed deeply. "Is that because of the celestial contract on Feya?" Cass smiled sweetly.

The urge to bite down on Cass's neck and drink every ounce of blood if it wiped that dumb ass smile off the Father's face crossed through his mind. The celestial contract binds Feya to the Queen. Whenever the Queen wanted Feya, she was bound to come calling like a lapdog. The spell could not be broken by any means that they had found yet. He had debated just killing the Queen, but the spell would just be inherited by the next in line of her lineage.

"We both know that to be true, so why bring it up?" Redd growled.

"Instead of our usual pay scale agreement," Cass paused, his eyes locked with Redd's. "We can make other arrangements."

"Other arrangements?" Redd said as his attention focused fully on the Father.

"What if we have something that can break the spell?" Cass said in a hushed tone.

Redd searched the Father's face looking for answers. In all the years he had known Cass, he had always shot the truth out straight as an arrow. A heavy silence enveloped the room. The silence was so overwhelming that even the faintest creak of the floorboards or the rustle of leaves would have been deafening.

"Is that an if or an actual?" As he spoke, his words cut through the silence like a sharp arrow, the sound echoing in the space.

"It could be an actual if you help us out," Cass whispered.

Nodding, Redd mulled over the words. *If I do whatever job they need from me, it could end in two ways. I can free Feya or at the very least get them off my back for a while.*

"If I find out you're sending me on a fool's errand..." Redd let the sentence die as he glared at the Father.

He could not remember how many people that the church had assigned them over the years, the constant ebb and flow of various priests and fathers seemed to blur over the years. This time, however, marked a significant departure from the ordinary. For the first time, they found themselves in the company of a non-human assigned to them, a fae.

Uncertain of Cass' true intentions, he wondered whether this would work out in their favor or unleash a tempest of unforeseen complications that he did not know if he could handle right now. Nonetheless, he decided to fulfill the task assigned to them, all the while doing what was most important: taking care of his family first.

He took a long, slow breath. The intoxicating scent of the Father's blood wafted into his nose, a delicate blend of strawberries, jasmine, and plums. The scent had his mouth salivating.

Intently listening, he focused on the rhythmic thumping of Cass's heart. Each beat resonated in his ears, echoing through the silence. The steady cadence of the heartbeat gave him a faint assurance that perhaps Cass was speaking the truth. But he knew better than to rely solely on that sound. Memories flooded his mind, reminding him of those who had deceived him before. The sound of a steady heartbeat could be misleading, and he knew better than to let his guard down.

It crossed his mind to use his abilities to see if the priest would give him more information, to glamor him, but knew Cass would get upset if he did. The thought of having the church more angry with him did not sound so appealing in the long run.

"This won't be a fool's errand, I assure you," Cass nodded. "We have been extremely patient with you during all this. We are supposed to work together as a team. So, if you do this for us, we can then help you out. I need you to get the Grimoire of Matteuccia de Francesco."

"Wait, what?" Redd said as the crease between his brow deepened. "You want to send me to find some dumb book?"

"No," Cass sighed. "I am sending you to find a book we need. This is not just any book. It belonged to a very powerful witch. There is also one other task we need from you. We need to find out who Olette was working with. These are the two things I need from you while we try to negotiate a peace treaty in the fae community and to get the celestial contract spell broken."

"So, I am just twiddling my thumbs and tracking down an ancient book, while you guys supposedly fix everything?"

"And find Olette and who she was working with. Yes, we will negotiate to get everything back to normal before anyone else gets hurt or humans get any more eyefuls."

Redd's brows furrowed, a deep frown etching lines on his face as he fought to conceal the knowledge that Olette was dead. He knew that unmasking the truth of who she worked for would only come directly from the source, which he was already trying to figure out with little success.

"You want me to find a dumb book and the woman who hired someone to kill my daughter?" Redd growled.

"Umm," Cass paused as crimson crept across his face. "I would like you to find an important grimoire and the person who was the catalyst to the problems facing the magical community."

"That's exactly what I said," Redd snorted.

"No, you said the woman who hired—"

"I don't think you understand still," Redd shook his head, his red hair shimmering in the moonlight streaming in. "We don't have the same problem, but our problems came from the same source. Olette dragged my family into this bullshit."

Cass's eyes fixed on Redd. Redd slowly squinted his eyes as he noticed the anxious tremor in Cass's hands. Listening, he noted the unsteady cadence of Cass's heartbeat, and knew the Father was nervous.

"You'll bring us, Olette, safe and sound." Cass said, his eyes moving to stare at Redd's feet.

"Is that a command or a question?"

"Please, just try to work with us on this one issue."

He remembered the first time he met the Father

thirty years ago. Their old human priest contact, George, was growing frail and was retiring, so they had assigned them another contact. When the old priest had brought Father Cassius by to introduce him, it had surprised him once he saw the fae. There were few magical beings in the church. It was mostly human beings. A lot of creatures lost their faith after centuries of living. Cass had been quieter, more reserved than the old priest, which was a pleasant change. Sometimes, he got the impression that the Father feared him, as if sensing his power. It was the way the Father's heart rate spiked whenever his temper snapped. Sometimes, he would mess with Cass and let loose with a blustery storm of fake rage.

"Fine, I will search for her and this dumb book. What details do you have on it?" Redd shrugged.

With shaky hands, Cass pulled a folder out of his satchel. He handed over the file filled with papers. *Amidst a chaotic situation, he's wasting my time.* He took the stack as he glared up at Cass. Flipping it open, he glanced at the words on the pages. Nothing caught his eyes, as his mind was elsewhere. Annoyance filled him as his mind raced. Then a thought hit him. There is someone who can look for this book for me. A slow smile spread across his face.

"Ok, you can leave now," he snorted as he raised an eyebrow at Cass.

Nodding, Cass turned and left.

Rolling his shoulders to relieve the tension, he listened to the Father's departure, the sound of footsteps echoing in the hallway before the front door opened and closed. Pulling his cell phone out from his pocket, he weighed his options. The cool glass of the screen against his fingertips gave him a sense of uncertainty. He had not talked to her in months. *Would she even reply to me? Should I text or just show up? I mean, it would make sense to bring her the papers to review the history.*

Chapter 4

Sitting at the counter stool, Nuit gently turned the delicate, yellowed pages of the antique book. The musty scent of aged paper filled her nostrils as she immersed herself in the haunting tale of a nanny tormented by a vengeful spirit. Lost in the eerie narrative, the soft, melodic chime of the bell above the door interrupted her reverie, prompting a wistful sigh as she reluctantly lifted her gaze.

"Open a little late," he smirked.

As she closed the book, her fingers grazed the cover, reminding her of how engrossed she had been in it. As she shifted her gaze, her eyes fell upon the grandfather clock standing in the corner, its rhythmic ticking filling the silence. With a start, she realized that she had lost track of time. The clock's hands pointed to 9 p.m.

"Oh my," she sighed.

Her eyes darted back to Redd, scanning his rugged appearance. The strands of his red hair tousled in the gentle breeze of the open door, his baggy jeans swaying with each confident step he took towards the door. A faint scent of citrusy cologne wafted towards her. His white, skin-tight shirt hugged his muscular frame, emphasizing the contours of his physique. A mischievous smirk played on his lips, captivating her attention. There was an enigmatic allure about him that kept her captivated every time she saw him. She struggled to decipher why his image randomly danced through her thoughts, like an elusive puzzle waiting to be solved. Her ears perked up, catching the faint sound of a lock clicking shut. A knot formed in her stomach, tightening with anticipation, as she observed the fluidity and grace with which his long, strong fingers performed the task. He effortlessly tucked them into his pocket, concealing them from her view, leaving her with a lingering sense of curiosity of what they would feel like.

"How..." she cleared her throat as a lump had formed. "How can I help you?"

"How have you been?" he asked. His long strides made short work of the distance as he stopped in front of the counter.

"I guess good," she sighed.

His gaze intensely roved over her face, his eyes darting from feature to feature. Curiosity and uncertainty filled the atmosphere, as if he desperately sought a hidden answer in her face. She couldn't help but feel a tingling sensation creeping up her spine, as if his searching eyes were leaving an invisible trail on her skin.

"Do you miss it?" he whispered.

"Miss what?" she asked.

"The adoration of the throngs of followers for Nuit, the goddess of the sky, stars, and cosmos," he smiled.

"Not really," she paused as memories flooded her mind. Gazing upon the Sphinx, the sun-bleached pyramids stretching to the horizon, a breathtaking panorama of ancient wonders. The roar of the crowd, a wave of adoration washing over her, countless faces upturned in love and awe. Then, the sickening crack, the dust and debris, the cold, harsh reality of utter loss that was left after war. "But sometimes..."

Laughing, his eyes sparkled as the smile spread across his face. "Oh, sometimes?"

She inhaled, breathing another whiff of his intoxicating cologne while it filled her senses. A warm flutter, like trapped butterflies, stirred in her stomach as she gazed into his warm, amber eyes, their depths shimmering like a polished stone.

Laughing, she smiled up at him. "Like who wants to do chores? Laundry and scrubbing toilets are just something I'd rather let someone else do." She shrugged as her smile turned self-deprecating.

"Alright," he laughed, running his fingers through his hair.

A silence stretched between them, stretched between them. The scent of polished wood and old coffee hung in the air. His fingers, cool and deliberate, traced slow circles on the worn, smooth wooden counter. *I wonder what those fingers would feel like on my skin.*

"Did you come all this way to ask me that?" she murmured.

"No." He shook his head.

"Alright," she laughed nervously. A captivating aura surrounded him; she couldn't explain it as it drew her in.

Maybe he came to ask me on a date. Her breath hitched, his mesmerizing amber, held hers; her heart hammered a frantic rhythm against her ribs. A shiver, a mixture of fear and anticipation, traced its path down her spine as she waited for his reason to be here.

"I am looking for a book," his deep voice said as it seemed to trail down her spine leaving gooseflesh in its wake.

Fool. The thought raced through her mind. *I haven't been with a male in a while. This is just a normal reaction to wanting attention. I should go out and mingle at a bar, maybe meet a stranger for a one night stand. He is obviously not interested in me.*

"A book?" she asked, hiding her disappointment. Turning, she waved at the rows of books. "I have tons available. What genre are you looking for?"

"Not any of those." His head snapped toward the maze of spines. Reaching behind him, he produced a rolled stack of papers from his back pocket. With a soft thud, he dropped a worn folder on the counter, the sound of the papers rustling as they settled. She had not noticed the roll in his pocket, she had been so distracted by his mere presence.

Frowning, her fingers grazed the rough edges of the folder as she gingerly opened it up. Scanning the pages, she immersed herself in the history of the Grimoire of Matteuccia de Francesco, absorbing the words as if they were etched onto her retinas. The story unfolded before her, revealing the tale of a nun who possessed supernatural powers, earning her the infamous title of the "Witch of Ripabianca". Matteuccia wrote the grimoire throughout her life. She made the last entry days before her execution in 1428, when they burned her at the stake. The files meticulously traced the journey of the grimoire, its whereabouts carefully documented until the early 1900s, when it had last fallen into the hands of Aleister Crowley. However, that's where the mystery began, as there was no trace of the book's existence beyond that point. Upon Crowley's death the book had vanished.

"So you want me to find this grimoire?" she exhaled as disappointment washed over her as the realization hit her. *He only came here for a job, not to see me.* "I can start searching. It might take me a few months to track it down. I will—"

"I don't have a few months." He cut her off.

Her brow furrowed as she studied the grim frown on his face. "When do you need it?"

"A week."

Her mouth dropped open as she gazed at him. A charmingly disarming smile spread across his face. A wave of excitement coursing through her, causing her heart to flutter like a delicate hummingbird's wings. Those piercing eyes seemed to penetrate the depths of her soul, creating an electric current inside her. As she opened her mouth to speak, she felt a sudden dryness, like the desert sand clinging to her tongue.

Swallowing, she took a second to find her voice. "I don't think that's possible."

His hand glided up, his fingers grazing her cheek with a feather-light touch, sending a tingling sensation through her skin. The warmth of his touch compared to the coolness of his fingers against her flushed face, causing a gentle blush to bloom further. Their eyes met. The intensity in his eyes caused her to struggle to articulate her thoughts and explain to him the immensity of the task he was asking. His captivating eyes sparkled with a seductive gleam, exploring every inch of her face, silently urging her to do as he wished. Finally, his lips parted, barely making a sound as he whispered a single word, sending a shiver down her spin. "Please."

Her heart melted as she whispered back, "Yes." As soon as the word left her lips, she could feel the weight of regret settling heavily in her chest. The room fell silent, and a deafening stillness filled the air, punctuated only by the faint sound of her racing heartbeat. The scent of tension permeated the room, its sharpness lingering in her nostrils. She could feel the heat rising even hotter on her cheeks, as she knew she could not possibly go through hundreds of years of records in a mere week.

"Thank you," he whispered as he leaned forward.

Her breath caught in her throat, a mix of anticipation and nervousness. The dim lighting cast gentle shadows on his face. She could hear the soft rustle of fabric as he leaned in closer. She inhaled his breath, a warm wave that filled her lungs. But just as she closed her eyes, ready for the anticipated touch of his lips, he suddenly withdrew. Losing the warmth from his hand on her cheek sent a shiver down her spine, mingling with the cool breeze of the overhead fan. Confusion swirled in her mind, fogging her thoughts like a thick, hazy mist.

As she opened her eyes, the scene came into focus before her as he took a step back, the sight of his retreating figure causing her heartbeat to pause. A rosy blush of embarrassment was painting her honey colored skin. The self-consciousness she felt was like a wild stallion, racing through her veins, making her pulse quicken. Despite the inner turmoil, she summoned all her strength to put on a facade, stretching her lips into a forced smile. Her gaze rose to meet his, searching for any sign of what he was feeling.

I just want to get this over with. I was a fool to think this brash and virile vampire would be interested in a nerdy bookworm like me.

Her back stiffened as she stood taller. "Anything else?" she asked in as dismissive of a tone as she could muster.

"Well," he shrugged as he tucked his hands back in his pockets.

She observed him intently, her gaze lingering on his face as he slowly averted his gaze. As his eyes fixated on the rows of books, they appeared to shut down as all emotions seemed to vanish. While her eyes scanned his profile, she noticed the faint scars marring his neck, remnants of the transformation that had turned him into a vampire. Absent-mindedly, he pulled a hand out and ran his fingers through his hair; the strands appearing velvety and inviting as her fingers itched to run through them.

I wonder if he feels the same about me or if it's all in my head. I probably just imagined that look and only saw what I wanted to see. She wondered as her eyes continued to sweep across him. *It's just in my head. My books have kept me isolated from contact with anyone for a long time.*

"Yes?" she said after he had not spoken for a while.

"Nothing," he shrugged, turning back to her. "I just need the book. It's an emergency. I can pay you whatever you need."

"No worries," she sighed. As she looked into those piercing amber eyes, she couldn't help but feel a wave of defeat wash over her. The coolness in the air seemed to match the disdain emanating from those eyes. The weight of her disappointment settled in her chest, making her feel heavy and deflated. "We can discuss the cost after I have found the book. It is usually based on time, resources, and cost of obtaining the book. I will talk to my contacts and let you know what I find."

"Thanks," he said, shifting his weight from one foot to the other. "You have my number. Just text me when you find anything out."

He began to turn and walk away, but then hesitated. As he turned, she felt her heart quicken, her eyes fixated on his. The intensity of the fire within them seemed to dance, like flames licking at the edges of her soul.

"I wanted to thank you for the help you gave us the last time we met," he said as the cocky grin came back.

"No need to thank me," she muttered uncertainly. "I just cast a simple spell."

"It wasn't a simple spell to me. It helped me find someone important to me."

The atmosphere seemed to crackle with unspoken words. With a last glance, he turned away. Leaving her alone and confused.

REDD

Chapter 5

Stepping out of the shop, his loins throbbed, a traitorous chorus of whispers and curses. In his head, a cold, clear voice, insisted on the rightness of his decision to leave, but the memory of her beauty, a vibrant splash of color against the greyness of life, was very potent. He snorted, a harsh sound swallowed by the city's low hum, then slid into the cool, black leather of his BMW.

He glanced at the clock face of his watch, its tick-tock a tiny hammer against the silence, realizing he had only a few hours until the pale light of sunrise touched the horizon. A frantic rush of thoughts–a whirlwind of anxieties–assaulted him; he simply didn't have the time to chase the alluring scent of her and still make the drive home before dawn. The cold plastic casing of his car keys felt heavy in his palm.

"Put them in the ignition, dumbass," he mumbled to himself.

His thumb, a warm weight, glided across the smooth, cool plastic. His fingers, tracing the familiar contours of the keys, felt the subtle texture beneath their pads. A low hum vibrated faintly in his hand. His brain, a frantic drumbeat in his skull, urged him towards reason.

"The best way to get someone off your mind is to get them out of your bed," he muttered to himself.

A deep sigh escaped his lips as he fought to banish the image of her obsidian eyes, dark with desire triggered by the ghost of a touch on her cheek. The way her hand clenched into a fist when his hand touched her. He could almost feel the hitch in her breath, the quickening of her pulse as he leaned closer, the tang of her blood filling his senses.

"Fuck it," he growled as he jumped back out of the car. "I can blow off some steam. It's not like anything is going to get resolved tonight."

He circled the car's hood, pausing. An icy dread, sharp as shattered glass, pricked his mind; too many unseen dangers lurked around every corner right now. Queen Casada's voice, a venomous whisper in his thoughts, could summon Feya at any moment. The chilling knowledge that Aguya's sister, Alse, a wraith of unhinged violence, remained free after the near-death struggle Aguya had faced not too long ago against her.

"I should head home," he muttered as responsibilities to his family won out. "My heightened senses are because of my need to feed. So, maybe I should eat something instead of trying to seduce a pretty little goddess. Fuck."

The car door slammed shut with a clang, frustration a heavy weight in his chest as the engine coughed to life. Her image, vivid and sharp, haunted him; a persistent ache behind his eyes as he pressed the accelerator. The memory of Sophine, a ghost shadow and a whisper of rosy perfume, had kept him firmly anchored in solitude, avoiding the treacherous waters of romance in all these centuries and he knew Nuit would be a dangerous path.

The moment Sophine transformed him, a fiery passion had ignited in him for her, yet her restless heart always sought more attention, more affection. She would often bring a new lover home only for them to vanish not long later. Their clashes echoed with the sharp sound of broken glass and raised voices. She sculpted him, a painstaking process; vocal coaches smoothed his rough-edged accent and tutors filled his mind with words as he learned to read and write. Even after their tumultuous years, watching her fall, moonlight glinting on the blood blooming from the stab wound on her heart while on the battlefield, shattered him.He had barely survived that battle, finding a small hollow to hide in from the sun's searing rays. Alvero Thiten, a grumpy fae, found him there, his healing magic healing his physical wounds. Their unlikely friendship began there, amidst the shadows and decay of war.

He swore he would let no one in again or transform someone into what he was. Not long after, someone from the church had approached him, asking if he wanted to do odd jobs for them. They were using various magical creatures for odd jobs the church needed done, like hunting down items and people. He had been good at it, so it became his full-time job, something that chased the monotony away. The thrill would get his blood rushing, plus it made it easier to find some asshole to drink dry.

Years later, he had been walking through the forest because he had heard there was a vampire horde that had attacked a fae village. The church had asked him to find help for his jobs, so he had followed the rumor looking for a fae who might have lost his family or something. When he got close, a little slip of a fae child was wounded and bleeding to death. He had broken his own cardinal rule and gave her his blood. Raising her had been his salvation. He had felt like a zombie walking through life until those misty green eyes looked up at him. She was his one and only sire. Soon he had brought others into his found family, Leo a wolf shifter, Aguya a fire witch, and Brady a fae. They helped him feel more human again.

Now everything he built—his empire, his life—crumbled, leaving a sickening sensation in his gut. The steering wheel bit into his palm as his knuckles turned white. Every path he took, a brick wall seemed to loom in front of him. Darkness gnawed at him; the engine's low growl mirroring the turmoil within. No closer to breaking the Celestial Contract binding his daughter, no trace of Aguya's sister. Only the cold, unyielding weight of the unopened box remained–a prize the Queen craved, a bargaining chip insufficient to save his child as of yet.

The moonlit, soaked road stretched endlessly before him as he left London behind, its clamor fading into a distant hum. His stomach growled, a hollow ache, as he debated one of Alvero's animals–a tempting, juicy distraction. Stealing one wouldn't quench his thirst, but it might postpone the agony a little longer until he could find a fresh source.

Silver moonlight washed over rolling hills and shadowed valleys, painting the scene before him as he approached the manor. The long drive, a ribbon of pale gravel under his wheels, did nothing to soothe the frantic thrumming in his chest. Each mile that separated him from her only amplified the restless unease that gnawed at him, an icy agitation clinging to his skin.

Pulling into the driveway, the low-hanging moon cast a silvery sheen on the gravel. The gray stone manor, cool and imposing, stood proudly, its silhouette stark against the inky sky. Moonlit windows glimmered, ethereal behind open shutters, a soft light beckoning. The massive, dark wood of the front door stood heavy with intricate ironwork. Above, the tall, conical towers pointed like accusing fingers at the star-dusted night.

The old carriage house, repurposed as a garage, stood open. He pulled into his spot; the gravel crunching under his tires. Jumping out, he headed towards the kitchen. A faint, rapid thump-thump-thump reached his ears before he saw it—a tiny brown rabbit, its heart beating like a hummingbird's. He knelt, the rough ground pressing against his knees, waiting patiently. His eyes fixed on his target. Then, a flash of brown fur, and it darted towards him, tiny claws scrabbling on the ground. With a swift movement, he caught the rabbit, its soft fur surprisingly warm against his hand as it struggled. He continued his walk, the rabbit's frantic thumps muffled against his firm grip.

As he stepped into the kitchen, a wave of comfort enveloped his soul. The familiar sights of his sanctuary brought calmness. He closed his eyes and absorbed the surrounding sounds. The gentle hum of his family's presence filled the air - Aguya's footsteps upstairs, Alvero, Brady and Leo's movements downstairs, and Feya and Elwyn chattering in the living room. Feeling at ease, he cherished the quiet moment, grateful for everyone's safety.

He scanned the bright kitchen. White wood cabinets gleamed, reflecting the light off the white granite counters, their gray streaks as subtle as a whisper. Warmth radiated from the white-washed brick walls, their texture rough against the fingertips. Stainless steel appliances shone, their surfaces cool and smooth under the bright overhead lights.

Walking to the porcelain sink, he held the thrashing rabbit above it, its tiny claws scrabbling for freedom. He opened his mouth, the scent of blood already filling his nostrils amplified by the rabbit's fear, ready to sink his fangs into the soft fur, when a piercing scream sliced through the air.

"Don't you dare!" Alvero yelled.

A slow breath whooshed out as he pivoted. The scent of fear soaked blood, and the earthy fae filled the air. Alvero's approach was a thunderclap of frustrated footfalls on the hardwood floor. The rabbit, snatched from his grasp, Alvero pulled it to his chest. Alvero's fingers, tangled in his dark brown fur, were a blur. His chestnut eyes, blazing with annoyance, burned into him.

"Were you really going to eat one of my friends?" Alvero's words hissed, a viper's strike, as a chilling death glare, sharp and cold as glacial ice, pierced Redd.

Bobo came in, sniffing the air. His glowing red eyes darted to the rabbit. In the kitchen lights, his black fur gleamed. The massive three-foot tall barghest, a demon dog, came up and brushed against his hand. The soft fur glided against his fingers as he reached down and scratched his head.

Snorting, Redd looked at Alvero, stating, "It's just a damn rabbit and I need to eat."

Alvero's brow furrowed, a deep crease etched above his hawk-like eyes as he looked down at the small, trembling rabbit. "Ignore Redd, he's an idiot." Alvero's eyes shifted to Bobo, annoyance shining brightly. "Bobo, don't encourage him."

"I am not an idiot," Redd growled. Redd's hand caressed Bobo's soft fur. Looking down, he wondered what Bobo had said. He knew Alvero and Bobo talked telepathically. A wave of irritation, sharp and bitter, washed over him as he strode from the room.

I can't even have one meal in peace in my own kitchen for fucks sake.

The old house creaked softly under his feet as he walked into the dimly lit living room. A flickering TV above the stone fireplace blared a melodramatic scene; Feya and Leo, completely engrossed. Feya's black hair, escaping its messy bun, framed a face illuminated by the screen's soft glow, her misty green eyes glued to the unfolding drama. Beside her, Elwyn, his blue eyes unfocused on his phone, rested his arm around her shoulders. His brown hair, partially swept back in an unfinished gesture, fell across his forehead. The newest addition to his family was a thought that brought a familiar, bitter taste to his tongue. He silently reminded himself, again, that he couldn't choose his daughter's mate, no matter how strongly he wished he could. Leo, a 6'8" giant, reclined in his worn leather recliner. His intense blue eyes, mirroring the flickering screen's drama, held a faraway look. Wild gray hair tumbled around his face. Redd inhaled, the sharp tang of aged whiskey stinging his nostrils from the glass in Leo's hand.

"Still here, boy?" Redd sarcastically asked.

"Can't get rid of me, old man," Elwyn snorted. "No matter how hard you try."

"Oh, why would I bother? Knowing how much joy you bring us," Redd paused before continuing. "That is when you leave."

"Father!" Feya exclaimed. "Can you just play nice?"

"Little one," Redd sighed. "I am being nice. The boy needs to just toughen up. He hasn't had a man to do that since he had that little bitch of a—"

"Father!" Feya exclaimed.

Misty green eyes, blazing with intensity, glared at him as he rolled his own eyes. Her raven-black hair falling out of the bun onto her shoulders. The blush on her rosy cheeks was a sharp contrast to her porcelain-pale skin. A frown etched across her diamond-shaped face, revealing her frustration. Those same brilliant, almond-shaped eyes shone with an almost painful brightness as he let out a long, weary sigh.

Elwyn's bright blue eyes, sparkling with mischief, smirked up at him. He ran a hand through his brown hair, the scent of sandalwood faintly clinging to it. A newly grown, bristly stubble softened the sharp angles of his rectangular jaw.

The boy thinks he's won some kind of battle. I just want to smack that stupid grin off his face.

Redd glanced at Leo, his eyebrows shooting up. The snicker that rumbled from Leo was accompanied by a flash of bright blue eyes, sparkling with playfulness.

Redd's gaze swept over the group. This was Leo, his oldest, dearest friend, known since soon after he sired Feya. A bond forged in shared secrets, a silent understanding that promised unwavering loyalty, a steadfast companion in any coming storm, and many battles fought together.

"What are we watching?" he asked as he dropped between Feya and Elwyn forcing them apart.

"Father," Feya said as she elbowed him. "Sit somewhere else."

"I just wanted to sit next to my daughter. Is that a crime?" he replied.

"We both know that's not what this is," she laughed, shaking her head causing more strands of hair to fall out.

Standing up, he rose from the couch. He shuffled down the long sectional, making room for Feya to snuggle with Elwyn. A secret smile played on his lips; he couldn't deny the quiet pleasure of taunting Elwyn.

"Thank you, father," Feya sighed as she cuddled back up to Elwyn.

The worn couch cushions sunk under him as he tried to focus on the brightly lit, swirling figures on the TV. But the image flickered, replaced by the memory of midnight-black eyes, wide and intense, gazing up at him.

Chapter 6

The warm glow of the phone screen illuminated Nuit's face as she scrolled through contacts, her fingers brushing the cool glass. Barely making a whisper, her flats glided across the polished hardwood while she paced. Her gaze stopped, a familiar name sparking a wave of anxiety, a tight, icy knot forming in her stomach.

Why am I helping that brash asshat? I should tell him to go fuck himself. Pushing me to hurry and help him out. Who does he think he is? The instant the idea sparked in her mind, a warmth bloomed in her chest, a silent affirmation echoing the decision: she would help. *Three months. Three months until I move again. I can do this one thing before I vanish again. At least for another fifteen years.*

Nuit sank into her favorite floral wingback chair, the plush cotton yielding to her weight. The vibrant pink blossoms and deep green leaves of the chair, usually a cheerful sight, failed to lift her spirits today. Her gaze glued to the cool glass of her phone, she swung her feet up onto the soft, mossy green footstool as she puffed out a soft sigh, her bangs fluttering. Pulling her gaze away, she looked around the room.

The stark emptiness of the fireplace, usually warm

and inviting, mirrored her mood. Above it, the sun-drenched canvas depicting the pyramids beckoning to happier times. She could almost feel the scorching desert wind whipping across her face, the fine sand stinging her cheeks–a vivid memory. She had found it at a flea market years ago. The tan couch, softened by plush vibrant throw pillows, sat turned towards the coffee table. Despite the hours she'd poured into creating this haven, tonight, the calming scene of the room couldn't stop the turmoil within.

Inhaling deeply, she looked back down at her phone. Tapping the cool screen, initiating the call. The sharp ring sliced through the quiet as she pressed the phone to her ear.

"Nuit?" a sweet voice picked up.

She tried to remember the last time she heard that voice, but could not remember. "How have you been, cousin?"

"Oh, I have been well," Seshat's sweet voice rang with laughter. "I seem to land in a different port every few months these days. How have you been?"

"I have been good just trying to keep busy." Nuit exhaled, feeling the anxiety drift away. She did not know what she expected of this call, but it was not the pleasantries she was getting now.

"We really should meet up and catch up one of these days. Where are you at now?"

"I'm in England. You?"

"I just landed in Amsterdam now. The weather is wonderful."

"Well, if I am up that way, I will have to stop by. I have not been there in ages."

"It's always worth the visit. The best place to get

poffertjes. Then, of course, there is the cheese." Seshat made kissy noises.

"Yes, true." Nuit laughed before the laughter died. "Umm..." Nuit paused nervously as she tried to figure out how to ask her this favor.

"What is it?" Worry filled Seshat's voice.

"I hate to ask a favor of you, but," Nuit sighed. "My search for a very specific book has led me to several dead ends. I was curious if you knew anyone who could track it down without having touched it?" The barely there lie, a whisper of deceit, brushed past her lips, smoother than expected.

"Oh," Seshat gasped. "What book are you trying to find?"

"It's just," Nuit paused, frowning. "It's just an old grimoire someone commissioned me to find. If you don't, I completely understand." Her mind raced, a whirlwind of thoughts, each one a frantic hummingbird against her skull. The ticking of a grandfather clock in the hall echoed the frantic beat of her heart. *I don't know how else to speed this search up*. Her shoulders slumped as she leaned back into the chair.

"Well," Seshat stated. "I know of someone, but he is..."

Nuit's heart, a trapped bird, stilled as a fragile hope, like a butterfly's wing, stirred. A hush fell, heavy and expectant, as Nuit waited, the silence pressing in for Seshat's next words.

"Not a very nice person," Seshat huffed. "You probably should look elsewhere if you can."

"I can deal with not nice," Nuit laughed.

"No, I mean, he is dangerous."

Nuit debated her next words. *Should I look the old-fashioned way which can take months if not longer or just go deal with this dangerous person?*

"Give me the contact information, please," Nuit asked. *It's best to get this over with, then I can move on from a male who is not interested in me whatsoever. Maybe once I put some distance between us, I can stop thinking about him so much.*

"He is a black market dealer of stolen magical items," she hesitated. "Dante Reaper is not a male you want to mess with. He can help you, but the price will be high. He is a tengu and can take many forms."

"That's fine. I can handle him," Nuit said with as much confidence as she could muster. "Just text me the details so I can reach out to him."

"He will ask for a steep price for his work. Most people cannot meet his demands. Are you sure you want to get tangled in that mess?"

Nuit felt the weight of unspoken words, a pressure in her chest while she debated what she should do. Finally, she spoke, her voice a soft rustle in the quiet. "Yes."

Sighing, Seshat replied, "Alright. I'll text you the information."

"Thank you, cousin," Nuit said, grateful as her mind raced with what kind of payment this tengu would ask for. *Maybe I should study up on his kind before I go.*

"Before I go, there is one bit of information I can offer you that might help," Seshat stated.

Nuit heard Seshat's deep breath, a rustling sigh before the insightful words flowed, a warm rush of information. The line clicked dead, leaving a heavy silence. Her mind, a whirlwind of possibilities, raced; the cost, a tangible weight in her chest, a knot tightening with each passing second.

The soft tick-tock of the grandfather clock, a comforting rhythm against the quiet hum of the house, filled the air as she debated. A sigh escaped her lips. With a light touch, her fingers flew across the cool glass screen of her phone, composing the text.

I have a lead I will follow up on tomorrow night.

She waited as three blinking dots appeared. At least she knew he saw her message.

Want company?

Eyes glued to the glowing screen, a thousand thoughts swirled like a flock of starlings, their wings a blur against the fading sunlight. The ghost of his aloofness settled on her skin, a stark contrast to the warmth of the room. His casual disregard, a bitter taste lingering on her tongue even after the hours that had passed.

"Maybe it's better I avoid him. I don't want to catch a case of the feels," she whispered to herself.

Typing away, she replied.

No, thank you. I can handle this.

Her gaze lingered on the stark digital words, a moment stretching into a small eternity before her finger, hesitant, tapped send. Doubt, a cold weight in her chest, gnawed at the bravado of her typed message; the unknown future stretched before her, a shadowy, daunting path. She was not sure if she could handle any of what she was about to face.

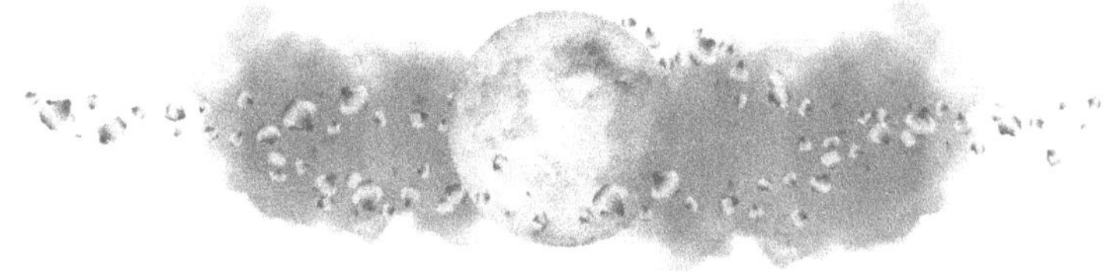

Nuit's car tires crunched on the gravel as she pulled up, the address a nondescript brick warehouse, smelling faintly of dust and decay. The rusted metal door, a dull, grey expanse, was unremarkable except for a tiny, almost invisible symbol etched into the doorbell—a subtle glyph barely disturbing the peeling paint. It was a deliberate camouflage. She felt it, a chilling sense of its power blocking even her own abilities. *That means when I go in, I am going in defenseless.*

Her fingers, tracing the worn leather of the shoulder bag, felt its familiar weight. Inside, nestled amongst the soft velvet lining, was the item she hoped to trade for the tengu's services. She had held this precious item safe for centuries, but lately it had sat in a safe. The thought of relinquishing this treasure brought a fresh ache to her chest. Perhaps the tengu would keep it just as safe and cherish it as well as she had.

A cold shiver, like icy fingers, traced her spine as she summoned the courage to press the button. I can do this without my magic. *I am a smart woman who can talk herself through this situation, right?* She paused, waiting for her own internal voice to reply, but no reassurances came. She inhaled deeply, her breath catching in her throat while her hand trembled.

"Are you going to take all day?" a husky voice said from behind her.

The sudden sound of his sent a jolt through her. She leaped, a dizzying spin, her heart hammering a frantic rhythm against her ribs. Redd's amber eyes, gleaming like polished stones in the dim light, seemed to taunt her.

"N... N... No," she sputtered as her eyes darted around.

I didn't even hear him approach. How did he know where to find me? Are we playing a game I don't know the rules of?

"Then push the button and we will enter," he smirked.

"What are you doing here?" she muttered, her eyes as big as saucers.

"I figured I'd come help you retrieve the book."

"I did not come to retrieve the book. To talk to someone about the location is why I'm here," she growled, temper flaring as fear subsided. "I told you I could handle this."

"Never said you couldn't." That infuriating, cat-like smile spread across his face.

Her breath hitched, a ragged sound in the still air, as she glared up at him, eyes blazing as they narrowed. Straightening her shoulders, she could almost feel the tension in her muscles as she tried to exude as much intimidation as possible.

"You need me to ring the bell for you?" His eyes twinkled as she realized she was not intimidating him.

Turning back to the door, she inhaled deeply. Her hand, trembling slightly, reached out, fingers brushing the cold, smooth surface of the button as she pressed. A fresh wave of nervous energy surged through her.

A gravelly male voice, amplified and distorted, echoed around them. She craned her neck, eyes scanning the brick wall and surrounding area; yet she found no visible source of where the voice came from. "What do you want?"

Inhaling, she screwed up her courage and spoke, "I am here to see Dante Reaper. Seshat sent me."

A sharp metallic click, followed by the groan of metal hinges splitting the silence, announced the door's opening. Her hand, hesitant, brushed the cold metal of the knob, pulling the heavy door open the rest of the way. Stepping inside, the air hung heavy and still, thick with the scent of dust. A single, stark beam of light sliced through the gloom, illuminating a descending staircase, a pale finger pointing into the warehouse's shadowy depths. The vast space felt cavernous and empty, save for the echoing silence; unseen corners held their breath as if waiting. A chill prickled her skin as she started towards the light, a knot of apprehension tightening in her chest.

Maybe it's best he came along after all, she thought. Swallowing, she took the first step in, trepidation filled her as she walked towards it.

Walking, her heels clicked sharply on the cool, grey concrete, each tap echoing slightly in the cavernous space as she headed towards the staircase. With as much bravado as she could muster, she stated, "Let me do the talking."

Redd snorted, a harsh, guttural sound, but remained silent otherwise, his footsteps echoing softly behind her. The cold wooden handrail bit into her palm as she perched on the top stair, its worn wood gritty beneath her fingers. A tremor ran through her as her gaze plunged into the inky blackness below.

"Maybe I should take the lead," Redd stated as his hand brushed down on her hip.

Golden warmth radiated from his touch, jolting her senses awake. She gulped, a dry rasp in her throat, shaking her head, the scent of his cologne filled her nostrils. Each step forward echoed faintly in the oppressive silence of darkness as she descended the seemingly endless stairs. Then a distant, shimmering light pierced the suffocating darkness. Her breath hitched; she hurried towards it, her heart pounding a frantic rhythm against her ribs as she was unsure if she was running to something good or bad. She just knew she wanted out of the darkness with this vampire behind her.

Redd's hand grabbed her hip. "Slow down," he whispered.

She paused a few steps from the bottom of the staircase. A sliver of warm, golden light outlined the slightly ajar door as dust motes danced in its beam. His breath feathered across her skin as he stood close behind, his presence a tangible warmth against her back.

"What?" she whispered, looking over her shoulder. She could barely see the outline of his face.

"Slow down," he stated. "We don't know what we are going into."

"What makes you think I haven't been here a million times before?"

"Now's not the time to play games, a mhuirnín," he murmured, the faintest whisper of a touch from his nose sending shivers down her spine. A jolt, sharp as a sudden sting, pierced her at the brush of his nose.

She thought about asking what he said meant, but knew this was not the right time. Inhaling deeply, the dusty air filled her lungs while she continued at a slower pace.

He's probably right, I don't know what I am walking into.

He placed his hand, cool against her skin, on the small of her back. A wave of warmth bloomed from that spot. She tilted her head, puzzled by the paradox—his touch, so cool, yet igniting such internal heat. The faint scent of cigar smoke mingled in the air wafting from the room as she lifted her hand to rap on the heavy oak door.

Turning, she saw him—a Tengu—at the desk. Her gaze locked on his crimson, scaly skin, the rough texture almost visible in the dim light. Black, demonic eyes burned into her, the sharp, pointed nose seeming to pierce the air. Large fangs glinted, catching the dim light. The stench of the cigar he smoked hung heavily, creating a swirling cloud around him. She'd never seen anything like it.

The crimson of his skin shifted and faded, the rough texture of scales smoothing into warm tan flesh. A whisper of sound accompanied the change, like dry leaves rustling. His obsidian eyes dulled to a soft, light brown, the transformation rippling from right to left, a visible wave. His long, pointed nose shortened. Only the menacingly sharp ivory tusks and the lingering deathly glint in his eyes remained. A chilling grin stretched his lips, the sharp points of his fangs catching the light, sending a shiver of icy dread down her spine. The black suit strained and rippled, a silent testament to the change occurring beneath the fabric.

Two identical guards stood beside him, their white sleeves rolled up, revealing corded forearms. Crisp black slacks, holsters snapped into black belts against the fabric, and polished black shoes reflecting the light; their blonde hair plastered back, menacing grins stretched across their faces—a mirror image of uniformity. Neither glanced at her, ignoring Redd completely; the silence was heavy with their unspoken threat.

"Hello," the deep voice of Dante spoke. Her ear caught the subtle Hakata-ben accent, placing his origin near Fukuoka City, Japan.

Her eyes darted around the dimly lit room. Dante sat in a worn leather chair before a massive, dark wood desk. A laptop and notebook rested on its surface in front of him. Behind him, two steel filing cabinets stood sentinel beside a vibrant explosion of artwork, a riot of color against the white walls. On the other walls, glass shelves nestled in alcoves displayed treasures from his homeland–the gleam of pottery, the carved wood statues–a tangible history. An icy dread pinned her to the spot, preventing her from turning to see the door they'd just passed, too afraid to look away from the three males.

Her gaze, a slow drift, returned to Dante. He puffed his cigar again, releasing a plume of smoke. She had no experience with Tengus, their customs a foreign landscape to her experience. She'd always steered clear of the magical underworld's shadowed corners, a place where secrets festered and rotted and shadows danced in the corners, each a potential hiding place for unknown horrors.

"It's a pleasure to meet you," she said as she walked up and extended her hand. "My name is Nuit, and this is Aethelredd. I–"

Dante looked at her hand and snorted. "Just state your business."

Nodding, she opened her mouth, but before she could speak, Redd spoke. "We are looking for a book and were told that you might know where it is."

A sharp jab to Redd's gut, but his body remained still. The smell of sweat and exertion hung heavy in the air. Speaking, she corrected him. "No, we heard no such thing. I am here for a spell."

"I don't know if I can help you since there seems to be a conflict," Dante shrugged.

"You will–" Redd started.

"There is no conflict," she said, cutting him off. Glaring up at Redd, her eyes pleading silently, a desperate plea for quiet so she could talk.

"Are you sure?" Dante said as his shoulders shook.

"We're here to find a–" Redd stated.

"Yes," she cut him off.

"Ah, pankuketsubichi," Dante laughed, his eyes drifting up and down Redd. A long, crimson tongue, slick and thick, snaked from his mouth, a wet, rasping sound accompanying its movement while he licked his lips.

"I suggest if you are going to insult me, you at least say it so I can understand it." Redd stated. The threat of violence radiating from that voice sent gooseflesh across her skin.

"It would not take much to insult a low life blood sucker as yourself," Dante snickered.

Laughing, Redd shook his head. "You have a life-time to be an idiot. You might want to take today off since this blood sucker is a lot smarter and stronger than a low life demon could ever imagine."

Dante's eyes were mere slits as he said, "You are outnumbered. As soon as you take one step, it will all be over."

Chapter 7

Redd opened his mouth to reply, but before he could, Nuit's elbow jabbed into his gut again. The unfamiliar language that the other male spoke only fueled Redd's frustration, making him clench his fists in readiness to extract the information through force if need be. He could sense the tension rising in the room, the air thick with the promise of impending conflict. Despite the chaos, Redd's keen senses picked up on the faint sound of Leo's heartbeat descending the stairs, a reassuring presence in the midst of the brewing storm. Leo's silent footsteps spoke volumes about his stealth, a trait that seemed lost on their oblivious adversaries. *Now, I just need to make sure Nuit doesn't get hurt.*

The morning text message he received from her had sealed his resolve; he wouldn't let her face this alone. Despite her protestations, he put up no fight via text. Leo chauffeured them in the limo, to stake out her place. He'd spent the day hidden in the back, hiding from the sun, while Leo watched her working away in the book shop. He did not want to wait around while Leo got all the fun, just because the sun was out. He'd breathed a sigh of relief at her decision to go at nightfall then he could go with her. Now, they stood in front of the twat and his two goons, her diplomatic attempts felt like a thin veil that was going to take forever to get what they needed. Plus, she was taking what little enjoyment he got out of these church dealings.

Things would get done faster if she just moved out of my way and let me handle this my way, he thought.

"That is neither here nor there, Mr. Reaper," Nuit chimed in. "I know we can come to a resolution that will please all parties."

He dug his fingers, rough and calloused, into her hip, the warmth of her skin a stark contrast to the chill of his own. He wanted this ridiculous goose chase for the book over with. He wanted to focus on his family, the image of their faces sharp in his mind. Images of Aguya and Feya swirled in his mind, the weight of their safety pressing down like a physical burden, mirroring the savage thirst clawing at him. A burning thirst, acrid and metallic, that coated his tongue. The taste of animal blood, unsatisfying, left him itching for more, a phantom itch he couldn't scratch yet. He needed a real meal. The hunger, a gnawing emptiness in his gut, was growing.

His mind wandered back to the males before him. His eyes darted between the three. The scene was alive with anticipation. The aroma of Japanese cuisine hung in the air, tantalizing his senses. The tengu's blood carried a sweet fragrance of mandarin oranges and pear, making his mouth water. The serpent shifters exuded an earthy scent, hinting at a savory potential dessert.

Nuit's hands, trembling like hummingbird wings, brushed his leg. A jolt, like static electricity, shot through him at her light touch. He heard her heart hammering against her ribs, a frantic drumbeat. The scent of her fear, sharp and metallic, filled the air. His fingers, rough against her silk blouse, offered a clumsy comfort, rubbing her back. Yet, her pulse, a frantic fluttering, remained a wild, erratic rhythm.

"I need a spell to track an item I've never touched and have nothing tied to it," Nuit said as she smiled sweetly, a smile that did not reach her eyes.

"Well, well, well," Dante laughed. "That will cost you a pretty penny. Maybe even more since you brought in this..." he flicked his hand in Redd's direction. "Trash. So, how much are you willing to pay for the spell?"

"I have one of the original scrolls from the Tale of Genji," she demurred. "One that no one has seen in thousands of years. You create and cast the spell, then I will give you the scroll as payment. Do we have a deal?"

The rhythmic tap-tap-tap of Dante's hand on the polished mahogany desk punctuated the tense silence, a counterpoint to the erratic thump-thump-thumping of surrounding hearts. His fingers, shifting subtly from tan flesh to his crimson scales, betrayed a practiced ease that unnerved Redd. A faint tremor ran through the notebook with each tap, a physical manifestation of the unspoken tension. Dante's own pulse remained a steady drum against his ribs, a stark contrast to the right twin's sudden, betraying spike of adrenaline before their rhythm settled back into a deceptive calm.

"What would I need with an old scroll?" Dante finally broke the silence that had stretched on.

"Oh, please," Nuit laughed.

He felt her muscles soften beneath his touch, her warm laughter a honeyed wave washing over him. The sound, a delicious torment, made his lips twitch; his gaze remained locked on Dante. Dante recoiled, a visible flinch at her mirth. With a sharp intake of breath, he transformed into his true form, the pretense dissolving as rage contorted his features. His black eyes blazed, twin embers of furious dark fire. He glanced down at the crown of her head, her dark, braided hair catching the dim light, enjoying the way she'd ruffled the tengu's feathers.

"We don't need to play games," Nuit smiled. "Take my offer and create the spell for me. We both know you have been searching for items from your culture. I am here to offer a rare item that will be quite the boon for your collection."

Dante seemed to mull over her words as he sat quietly. "You have a deal."

Nuit stepped forward, Redd's fingers digging into her waist, applying pressure in hopes she would not step closer to the demon. She brushed his hand away, throwing a side eye glance filled with frustration. His fingers itched to grab her and drag her back to his side, to keep her safe.

She extended her hand to the demon, asking, "Do we shake to seal the deal?"

"How do I know you have an actual scroll?" With a rustle, the tengu shifted, his demon form devolving into human shape. He leaned heavily on his elbows, his huge fangs glinting in the light as they did not shift.

Redd's eyes, narrowed in concentration, watched as she reached into the worn satchel. Her hand slid into the bag, emerging with a pair of pristine white gloves. A soft rustle accompanied the delicate action of slipping them on. Next, she withdrew a stainless steel tube. A faint scent of dust and aged parchment wafted from the tube. Redd's gaze darted around the room, a silent vigilance in his eyes, alert to any movement the goon squad might make. With meticulous care, she unrolled onto the desk an ancient scroll, its faded yet vibrant colors—a breath-taking scene of a Japanese garden. Unfamiliar characters, precise and elegant, lined the parchment. The scroll looked impossibly fragile, paper-thin and brittle, its edges worn and incomplete. A hushed breath escaped Dante's lips as his fingers stretched out to touch the delicate arti-fact.

"Don't," Nuit whispered with urgency. "Never touch it without special gloves. It is very delicate and can crumble if not properly taken care of. I have a document I attached to the outside of the tube that tells you how to maintain and take care of the scroll."

Dante's hand, trembling slightly, hovered over the ancient scroll, his eyes darting across the script. He felt the weight of history in the air. She carefully rolled it back up, the brittle paper creaking softly, and slid it back into its protective tube.

"I ask again, do we have a deal?" She extended her hand across the desk again.

The thud-thud-thud of Leo's heart drummed a steadfast rhythm on the other side of the door. His gaze, sharp and watchful, scanned the males before him— searching for any sign they might hurt Nuit.

"Fine, we have a deal," Dante said as his hand grasped hers and shook. "Let's get this over with. Tell me the book you're looking for."

"Thank you," Nuit said, smiling as she pulled her hand back. She pulled a picture of the book out of the bag and set it on the desk. "I am looking for Matteuccia de Francesco grimoire."

Dante's wrist flicked; the right twin nodded before silently gliding to a shelf. The twin retrieved a map from a small, intricately carved wooden box. Next came a black stone bowl, followed by a chaotic array of herbs and potions, laying each item on the desk carefully. He inhaled deeply, trying to figure out what they were grabbing, the sudden assault of pungent, acrid smells—a sickeningly sweet undertone masking something bitter and rotten— forcing a harsh cough from his lungs.

Holding his breath against the fetid stench, his eyes darted to Nuit. Her honey-colored skin shimmered in the dim light. Her long black braid, a silken waterfall, trailed down her back, igniting an urge to wrap that braid around his fist and drag her close. The gentle sway of her hips as her hands rested upon them, long fingers bare of any jewelry. The loose black slacks against the crisp white shirt—a tantalizing contrast that whispered of a forbidden, naughty librarian fantasy that was playing out in his mind.

Dante's voice, a low rumble that sliced through the quiet, dragged him from his thoughts. The words blurred, a mumbled rush like wind chimes in a storm as he stirred the thick, fragrant broth. Only "Matteuccia de Francesco grimoire" pierced the confusion, sharp and clear. He stole a quick glance at the two guards; one remained a statue of stillness, the other back in his post. The thrum of Leo's barely contained impatience vibrated through the door, a tangible pulse of frustrated energy as his heartbeat spiked up and down. Disappointment, a cold wave, washed over him; the fight he craved, the clash of fists he had anticipated and a reason to feed, remained elusive. Neither he nor Leo would get their wish today.

He inhaled again, the acrid bite of brimstone and something indefinably foul stinging his nostrils. A burning sensation filled his lungs. Dante poured the viscous blue liquid into the map box. It sat as a shimmering orb for a moment before flowing like a blue serpent streaming across the map. Stepping closer, Redd felt the slight chill of the damp air as he peered down; the liquid swirled, a hypnotic dance, before coalescing into a single point.

"Go here," Dante said, pointing at the map.

Chapter 8

Nuit's gaze traced the map's faded lines, a chill seeping into her bones as she watched where the mark landed. Her heart, a trapped bird, fluttered against her ribs, a cold dread constricting her breath.

Why there and why him? Her thoughts, a frantic whirlwind, raced as she knew Redd had seen the location; the chill that traveled throughout her veins screaming at her. *I need to ditch Redd, otherwise he'll never give me the book. I'll be lucky to escape his wrath unscathed as it is.*

"Thank you so much, Dante," Nuit said as she pulled the tube with the scroll back out. With a sigh, she delicately placed the scroll in Dante's hands, each touch a fresh stab of sorrow. Years of memories, carefully preserved, swirled within her—a bittersweet kaleidoscope of vibrant silks, hushed temple gardens, and laughter echoing in the moonlit night. This scroll, a relic from a life lived centuries ago, from one of the few times she had taken a human lover, was given to her as a gift. The last piece of that sweet time of her life now left her grasp. Its absence felt like a hollow ache in her heart, and all to help this boorish male next to her who acted like a bull in a china shop everywhere he went.

"You're welcome," Dante uttered as he held the scroll. His fingers lovingly caressed the tube. "You can leave now."

Dante shifted back to his true form, delicately cradled it in his hands, the sight of his demon form contrasting with his gentle touch. A faint feeling of relief echoed through her, pushing a small piece of the lingering ache of sadness away.

As she turned, the glint of dim overhead lighting on Redd's fangs caught her eye just before he opened his mouth. Her fist, a tight ball of knuckles, connected with his gut, a dull thud echoing in the stillness. Disappointment, a cold wave, washed over her as his expression remained unchanged, his eyes unwavering. *He didn't even feel it*, she thought.

With a snorting breath, Redd followed, the door creaking open. A gasp, sharp as shattered glass, escaped her as a hulking figure loomed in the dim hallway. It took a moment for her eyes to adjust to realize it was Redd's shifter friend. Redd's gentle nudge sent her stumbling into the darkness of the stairwell. A solid thwack echoed as the door slammed shut.

"Let's go," Redd muttered.

Her eyes, dark pools reflecting the dim light like tiny stars, darted over her shoulder to look at him. Only fleeting shadows hinted at his presence as she glanced at him.

"You realize," she murmured. "I don't have the same night vision you guys do?"

She felt Redd's gaze like burning coals on her skin, a silent pressure against her back. His hand, a warm, rough graze, ignited the familiar fire that spread through her, a heat that bloomed with each touch, leaving a tingling warmth in its wake.

"Don't worry. I'll guide you," Redd's deep voice

reassured.

Nodding, she followed the shifter's broad back up the dimly lit stairs, each step echoing faintly in the cavernous space. Dust motes danced in the weak light filtering from the dim swinging light far above. The upward climb felt endless, a slow, silent ascent. She felt Redd's nearness, a warmth at her back, his hand occasionally brushing her hip, a light pressure guiding her. Relief filled her as they reached the landing of the main floor of the warehouse. Leaving the musty-smelling warehouse, the cool night air hit her face as she walked toward her car, the males' footsteps a steady rhythm behind her. The urgent need to lose them, to get the book, tightened in her chest, but the how remained elusive. A whirlwind filled her as excuses, reasons, filled her, but none seemed to land as an option to get the book.

"I know the book dealer who holds the book," she lied, taking out her car keys and unlocking her honda civic. "I can have the book in a day or two. So, you guys can head to your home. Just text me the address and I'll bring it to you as soon as I have it."

Her fingers brushed the cool chrome of the car door, but a firm, freckled hand, rough as sunbaked bark, stopped her. She glanced up at the smattering of red hair and graceful, long fingers on his hand.

"We need to talk," Redd whispered so close she could feel the strands of hair that had come loose shifting under his breath. She had not realized he had come up behind her, he had been so mute.

"About?" she asked, frozen to the spot. Her heart raced in her chest as she tried to figure out how to move without touching him.

"Several things," Redd whispered.

Leo walked to the other car climbing in. She heard the car door shut with a soft thud.

"I'll meet you at the bookstore," Redd said, before releasing her hand. He walked to the passenger seat of her car and climbed in.

"Well, I guess we're talking on the way to the bookstore," she whispered, pulling the door open.

"Yes, we are."

She climbed into the seat. The engine coughed to life, a sputtering sound that vibrated through the compact car. Beside her, his presence pressed close, making the already cramped space feel suffocating. A nervous swallow caught in her throat before she managed, voice trembling slightly, to speak. "What do you want to talk about?"

"First off, how much do I owe you for the scroll?" He broke the tense silence with his words.

"I don't know," she shrugged, turning down the long, dimly lit road. "It technically is invaluable and so, therefore, I can't put a price on it."

"How am I to pay you for your services if I don't know the cost?"

"Umm..." she debated as her mind shifted back and forth between worry about going to get the book and an attraction to the male next to her. "$500."

"That seems low for something so... invaluable."

She could practically hear the silent snap of his eyebrow as her gaze remained glued to the asphalt ribbon before them. "$1000."

"Come now," he laughed. "Tell me how much you paid for it."

"Paid for it?" she laughed as her eyes darted for a split second off the road to him. His eyebrow was arched just as she thought. "The price I paid was the life of someone I once knew. You can't even begin to understand that."

"Do you think I have never lost someone?" That deep voice, a rumbling tremor that came from his chest, was so level and low, a smooth, dark river giving no emotion away.

Laughing, she could not begin to tell this male even a tenth of the loss she had been through in the eons she had lived. "Have you ever been forgotten by those you loved?"

Shrugging, he said, "Of course, I have."

"No, I mean really forgotten," she growled.

"I feel like you want me to understand something you're not telling me."

With a snorting, ragged breath, a rush of emotions—a tempest in her veins—choked her words. She inhaled deeply, the crisp air filling her lungs, a momentary calm before a forceful exhale. "We live such a long life that we forget some of those who touch our lives. That scroll is a reminder of a life I left behind that I had fond memories of. It was the last piece of that life and now it is gone forever. So if you want me to put a price on that, how about $50,000?"

"Alrighty then. I'll get that to you as soon as possible," he said, the words a little rushed. A moment of silence, punctuated only by the rhythmic tap-tap-tap of his fingers drumming on the cool, hard car door handle. "So, umm, I guess onto the next subject."

She waited patiently for him to continue. "Just spit it out."

Laughing softly, he said, "Rather impatient, aren't you?"

Turning, she glared at him.

"I will take that as a yes," he said as the drumming of his fingers stopped. "When are we heading over to that spot on the map?"

"We?" she laughed self-deprecatingly. "I think it best I go alone, so I don't listen to you try to start a fight with my... contact. You can be a bit... Umm... Brash? Last thing I need is to watch another pissing match between males."

"So, I take it you know whose place that little bleep on the map is."

Teeth sinking into her lip, a sharp, sudden pain, she realized, with a sickening twist in her gut, that she'd revealed too much. "I don't know what you mean."

"Don't lie, it's unbecoming."

A flutter of nerves, like a trapped bird, stirred in her stomach. The scent of his cologne, sharp and clean, hung in the air as she considered a witty retort, a tempting lie dancing on her tongue. To let him know she did not care if she was *becoming* to him or not. But no witty retorts came to her. "What makes you think I'm lying?"

"Your heart rate. I can hear it. It changes when you lie. So, would you like to go back and tell the truth?"

"I know who it is and I will have the book by tomorrow night, if you let me do the job you paid me for."

"There it is again."

"There what is?" she frowned.

"That spike. So, we can leave later tonight after the sun has gone down," he stated.

She sat quietly, not wanting to voice any thoughts for fear she'll give too much away again. As his words settled in her mind, a sense of clarity washed over her, the weight of realization sinking in, and the idea of what she needed to do. *I need to go when the sun is up to ensure he can't follow me.*

A slow breath escaped her lips, a silent sigh of relief as tension eased from her shoulders. The weight of her plan felt lighter now, a palpable shift. The car bumped gently over the cracked asphalt of her minuscule parking lot as she pulled into her parking spot.

"I guess this is where I leave you," she said as she smiled at him. "We can meet up tonight after the sun goes down, then go wake him up."

"You think I'm going to let you get away that easily?"

Chapter 9

Redd watched her dark eyes, pools of night reflecting the moonlight, widen. Her stiff posture was a silent scream, betraying her attempt to mask her feelings. Her expression alone confirmed the feeling she was trying to get rid of him. He felt a prickle of amusement; she seemed to think she was some enigma that he could not solve, but she was easier to read than a child's book.

A dull, gnawing ache, like a cold stone settling, pulsed through his stomach. Shaking his head, he pushed past the pain, trying to ignore it.

"Wha... Wha... What do you mean?" she stammered.

"I mean Leo and I can just crash at your place till sundown, and then we can head out together." He smiled a catlike grin, watching annoyance flicker like a candle flame across her dark eyes. Those expressive dark pools reflected a storm of emotions: annoyance, a quick flash of frustration, then the slow surrender of resignation, leaving a quiet darkness in their depths.

"Oh," she muttered as disappointment flashed in those eyes.

"Here, I thought you'd like it if I spent the day with

you," he whispered as his hand came up and cupped her cheek. His thumb, tracing the curve of her cheek, felt the silken warmth of her skin. His eyes devoured her, a feast for his gaze; he watched her dark pools of night deepen with desire, the heat radiating from her like a silent hum.

"Why..." She swallowed, her throat bobbing with the motion. "Why would you think that?"

"Sorry if I was mistaken," he whispered, as his fingers stroked her cheek more. His hand slid down, trailing to her throat. Hearing the hitch of her breath as his fingers stroked. The frantic thump-thump-thump of her pulse vibrated faintly against his fingertips. A slow smile stretched his lips as he gently withdrew his hand.

"Yes," she muttered, turning away. "I... I... I don't care if you stay or go."

"That's fine," he sighed over dramatically. "But..."

"But?" she asked.

"The sun will be up soon." Squinting, his eyes looked at the horizon, the faintest blush of rose and gold painting the eastern sky. He still had time. He could also lock himself in the limo, but she did not need to know that. "I need to find a place to stay before it comes up. Do you think we could stay with you?"

His eyes moved to her mouth, watching as her tongue flicked out and licked them. "I guess you can stay," she mumbled.

"That's so kind of you," he said as he leaned over the center console. His warm breath mingled with hers, and a subtle wave of mint filled his lungs. The faintest whisper of her exhale brushed his skin, a fleeting touch as light as a summer breeze. "As soon as the sun goes down, we will head to your friend's house."

"Do you think you could let me do all the talking if you go?"

"Of course I can." He smiled at her. "We should head inside before that darn sun comes up."

"I guess so," she grumbled, climbing out of the car.

He leaped out, landing on the cobblestones, and glanced over his shoulder. Leo approached, his footsteps echoing faintly. Turning, he trailed Nuit, his eyes glued to the rhythmic sway of her hips as they hurried down the path. The scent of London filled the air, a mix of exhaust, dust, trees and humans. A brutal, twisting pain clawed at his stomach, the thirst a searing brand. He gulped in the dusty air, fighting the overwhelming, metallic tang of his bloodlust.

Stepping onto the street, he inhaled deeply, searching for a snack to tide him over till his next meal. The hunger gnawed at him, its nails digging into his guts. Looking at Leo, he nudged his head towards Nuit. His gaze fixed on the alley where he could smell a mix of dirt and blood pumping through veins. There, amidst over-flowing bins and the reek of stale urine, lay a homeless man, asleep. A deep breath revealed no trace of disease in the coppery scent clinging to the air. Thirst clawed at his insides, a searing pain, as his mouth watered. Bending, he saw startled blue eyes open, staring up at him. An irresist-ible itch pulsed in his fangs, a primal urge to sink them into the offered flesh.

Calling for his power, he spoke coolly. "Stay calm. I am going to pay you for a job. All you have to do is hold your wrist out towards me."

The homeless man lifted his wrist, the rough dirty skin a stark contrast to his trembling fingers. Redd seized it, the pulse a frantic drum beneath his teeth. Warm blood flooded his mouth, a rich, savory tang that ignited a primal craving. A fierce battle against the desperate urge to not stop feeding, to drink every last ounce of blood he could suck out. The blood rage roared in his ears, a deafening symphony of need. He pulled away, the taste lingering, a cruel mockery of satiation. His hands shook, a tremor mirroring the internal struggle as he gently replaced the wrist. The scent of blood, thick and cloying, clung to the air. He recoiled, the weight of his hunger pressing down; the thought of killing an innocent to quell it was a bitter burden.

"Thank you," he whispered. Fingers fumbling with worn leather, he snatched all the bills out, around $100. He pressed the wad into the other man's outstretched hand. "Go back to sleep. Use the cash to buy yourself a hot meal."

He stood, hand sweeping across his lip, the coppery tang of blood thick on his tongue. Looking at his hand, he saw crimson smeared across his palm as he shoved it into his pocket. *That small amount will have to do for now until I can find more.* With head bowed, he hurried towards the shop. He could feel the sticky warmth on his chin slowly drying, a reminder that he needed to remain unseen.

Entering the shop, its bell chiming a faint welcome, he locked the door with a click. Stopping, he listened, the rhythmic thump of footsteps and heartbeats echoing from the floor above. The musty scent of old wood and dust filled his nostrils. Walking around, he found a small, dimly lit bathroom. The cool porcelain felt soothing against his skin as he washed the blood from his face and hands, the crimson staining the water a pink before running clear. Leaving the bathroom, he jogged up the creaking wooden stairs to the apartment above. The cozy warmth of the small apartment enveloped him like a blanket. He looked around, his eyes searching. Finding Nuit in the kitchen, he stepped across the worn wooden threshold of the archway.

"What took you so long?" Nuit asked as she put a kettle on the stove.

"Nothing much," Redd shrugged. *I know she knows what I am, but would it turn her away to know what I did?* The thought circled around in his head before he shrugged it away. *I don't have time for a dalliance.*

Turning, he glanced back at Leo, sitting on the couch, looking like a giant in a child's seat, his discomfort palpable as he shifted. Redd, rubbing his mouth, fought back a smile.

"I am making you guys some tea," she said as she hummed a little ditty.

"I don't drink tea," he said, watching her flit around the kitchen.

Cool, white-tiled counters gleamed under the lights, a stark contrast to the vibrant floral wallpaper bursting with vibrant color.

"That's rude," she said, turning to frown at him. Disappointment, a thick fog, clouded her expressive eyes, their usual sparkle dimmed. The idea of eating a meal hung heavy in the air, a stark contrast to the tightness in his chest as he fumbled for words, a desperate search for a way to explain that he would get sick if he ate food.

"I guess I can try some," he muttered as he gave in. *A small bite won't kill me.*

"That's sweet of you." She turned back to the cupboards as she went through them, her hands moving and shuffling things around. "You go have a seat and I'll bring the tea out. I think you'll love this one. I got the tea leaves from this little shop in China. It is one of my favorites. Plus, I made some blackberry lavender scones yesterday. They are one of my favorites."

"Alright."

Turning around, he walked over to Leo and settled down next to him on the couch. The two big males almost took up the entire couch. The sweet scent of roses from a nearby candle filled the room. As they sat there, the sound of Nuit's melodic voice filled the air, singing a lullaby that was unfamiliar to him.

Lowering his voice, he looked at Leo. "We will head out after sundown to where the map says the book is." Pausing, his ears perked up as he heard the clink of dishes. "Nuit isn't wanting to tell me who has the book, but I am pretty sure she fears whoever it is. So we will need to be on guard."

"Did you feed?" Leo whispered.

"Enough to tide me over for now. But I'll need to feed again soon."

Leo nodded. "Maybe you can have a sip of whoever she's scared of. We will come back with the book and if they threaten her, we will..."

"You read my mind," Redd laughed softly. "We will get the book and not let Cass know we have it for a month or two. Just let him think we are on a merry little chase for a..." He stopped talking as Nuit entered the room with a tray filled with tea cups and scones.

Inhaling deeply, he caught the sweet scent of blackberries mingling with the delicate floral of lavender from the warm scones. If he actually ate food, he thought he might actually like those pretty little scones, their golden-brown tops glistening with white chocolate on the white plate. She handed him a steaming cup; the warmth radiating through the thin china. He took it, his fingers brushing hers briefly. Leo grabbed the other cup and took a deep sip of the fragrant liquid before breaking off a piece of a flaky scone.

"This is delicious," Leo said, reaching for another scone.

"Oh, those." Nuit smiled sweetly. "I made those yesterday. They are Blackberry Lavender White Chocolate Scones. I just warmed them up for you guys to munch on. I can make a care package so you can take some home when you leave."

"That would be great, ma'am." Leo said, reaching

for a third one.

Redd tried to hide his smirk, *if there're any scones left.* He inhaled the rich spices of the tea, as the swirl of steam wafted up, filling his nostrils.

"Take a sip," Nuit said as those dark eyes stared into his. A part of him wondered if she could see into his soul, the warmth of her smile fading like a sunset, the corners of her mouth drooping slightly. A subtle shift in the air, a silence heavy with unspoken things.

"I... Umm..." he started, but then he saw her frown grow deeper and put the cup to his lips. He took a small swig as her eyes lit up. "Yummy."

He knew he could not drink anymore since his stomach was already starting to revolt from just the little sip. The teacup felt surprisingly heavy before it slipped, a dull thud echoing as it hit the floor. A nauseous wave crashed over him; even a tiny sip was too much. His head swam, a dizzying fog swirling behind his eyes. He shook his head, the world tilting precariously. A heavy weight pressed against his ribs—Leo slumped against him, breathing slowly and even, eyes closed. The scent of stale alcohol hung heavy in the air. He glanced back at Nuit; the darkness creeping in at the edges of his vision, a cold pressure building in his chest.

"Why?" His voice was ragged as he tried to fight the darkness creeping into his vision.

"I know you won't let me go there without you," she sighed. "This is something I need to do alone."

He fought the overwhelming urge to sleep, a heavy tide pulling him under. He tried to rise, but his leaden legs refused to obey, rooted to the floor. His arm, a dead weight, lay useless in his lap. The soft brush of Nuit's hand against his cheek was cool, a gentle pressure guiding his head to the softness of a throw pillow.

"If I take you to see him, he will never give me the

book," she whispered. "I am not even sure he will either way."

He opened his mouth, trying to voice the words that swirled on his tongue, but they could not leave his lips.

"You just rest. I will make sure the sun doesn't hurt you. I will be back..."

Her words drifted away as his eyes drifted closed.

Chapter 10

Nuit listened to the soft, rhythmic snores of her guests, a gentle rasping sound as both were in deep slumber. The air hung heavy with the sweet, slightly bitter scent of the spilled tea. She had laced the tea with a sleep tincture. A prickle of guilt grazed her conscience at the drugged tea, but the steady rise and fall of their chests confirmed its efficacy–and her necessity.

The sharp "of course" had sliced through the air, a lie clear in its haste when Redd had said it. So she decided a different approach was needed; escape before sunrise was impossible with him there, watching her every move. He would never leave let her leave alone. Then she remembered the sleep tincture–her only recourse. His initial refusal to drink the tea was a cold splash of despair that hit her, but quickly replaced by relief as he finally drank some. She had worried he had not drunken enough. Unlike Leo, who had chugged the tea. She'd made it strong, a double dose for the two large males. Whispering a silent prayer against them awakening before she could leave. Their rapid descent into slumber was unexpected, a heavy, silent fall which lead her to believe she may have overdone the amount.

Walking to each window, she placed blankets over the glass and curtains, muffling the faint morning light. A hushed silence settled in the house, broken only by the gentle rustle of snoring. If they woke, she thought, they'd have the entire house to explore, shielded from the day's harsh sunlight.

I hope he isn't too upset with me. Shaking her head she tried to shove the thought away. *Like I care what he thinks.*

The question, a persistent fly, buzzed in her mind. *Why was I helping him? I could have vanished, slipped into a new life.* A glance over her shoulder; Redd's chest, a slow, rhythmic rise and fall beneath the taut shirt. The soft rasp of his snores, a gentle, even rhythm, filled the air. She moved closer, the floorboards cool beneath her bare feet. Her eyes darted around his handsome face, taking every angle, every curve, every inch in. A frustrated sigh escaped her lips. *I have no time for such idle musings.* Turning, she double checked the windows to make sure no light would creep in. Quietly she crept to the door and down the stairs. The morning chill surrounded her as the sun rose in the horizon.

The car seat yielded slightly as she climbed in, steadying her breath, her gaze fixed on the dashboard. White knuckles gripped the steering wheel. A century since she'd last seen him. Had the whiskey rotted him further? The collapse of their world had broken him; she remembered the burning rage in his eyes, the hatred a searing brand as he stared at her. Those cold, black eyes still haunted her sleep, icy visions piercing the darkness. Her trembling hand turned the key. The engine coughed to life, a low rumble vibrating through the car. Beneath the asphalt, the tires blurred; the road stretching before her, shrinking the distance. With each mile, a chilling dread mixed with a heavy sadness that settled deep in her chest.

Chapter 11

A buzzing, insistent vibration, like a frantic bee trapped in a glass jar, shook him awake from his drowsy stupor. He rubbed sleep-crusted eyes, feeling the dull ache in his stiff neck and the unfamiliar weight on his hip. With a shove, he removed the weight. A muffled thud and a grunt—a pained, guttural sound—filled the air. He rubbed his face, sitting up, and the blurry world sharpened into focus. He'd pushed Leo onto the floor; the shifter groaned, pushing himself onto his elbows, his face contorted in pain.

"Wake up, old man," Redd grumbled as he realized where they were. He gently nudged Leo with the toe of his shoe.

His phone vibrated fiercely against his thigh, a buzzing that seemed to resonate in his bones. A low growl rumbled in his chest as he snatched the phone from his pocket, the rough denim scratching his skin. A searing rage flooded him; the bitter taste of betrayal coated his tongue. He'd been a fool, letting that dark-haired woman, with her shy smile and silken voice, lure him into drinking the tainted tea.

"What?" he growled into his phone.

"We have a situation," Aguya abruptly said.

Rubbing his temple, he tried to clear the fog that was still rolling in his head. "What situation?"

"Feya is acting weird."

"Weird?" The words swam before his ears, a blurry, indistinct tide of sound washing over him. His mind felt thick with fog, each syllable a muffled thud against the inside of his skull.

Leo sat up suddenly. "Where are we?"

"Give me a minute." Redd told Leo.

"Weird as in weird," Aguya hissed, her voice tight with frustration, the Lithuanian lilt thick. Whenever she had high emotions, her Lithuanian roots would come out in her voice. Her fingers drummed a restless rhythm on a table, a staccato beat against the low hum of the throb in his head.

"Do *you* think that means something to me?" Redd said, leaning back on the couch. His head struck the wall with a sickening thud. A sharp pain shot through him, the sound echoing in the sudden silence.

"I mean, she is not acting like herself. How is that so hard for you to understand?" Aguya growled.

Inhaling deeply, the crisp, lavender-scented air filling his lungs, he weighed his next words carefully. He knew he was safe enough distance from the fire witch's immediate wrath, and would not get burnt for his sarcastic reply. "Is it that time of the month?"

A pregnant pause on the phone told him he'd asked the wrong question. He sighed, the sound a warm rush against his skin, reminding himself that at least he was far enough away she could not exact revenge by burning his britches or collar. He could almost feel the phantom heat of her fire magic, a phantom warmth that did not quite reach his skin.

"Is that a no?" he exhaled. "I'm having trouble focusing, so I am going to need you to be very specific. Leo got us drugged."

"Me?" Leo croaked as he leaned onto the couch.

"Wait, what?" Aguya said, astonished.

"Leo accepted some tainted tea," Redd said, not wanting to admit his part in falling for the ploy in those dark eyes.

Laughing, Leo shook his head before groaning, a low, rumbling sound.

"If Leo took tainted tea, how did you get drugged?" Aguya slowly asked.

Redd's brow furrowed, a deep crimson line etched against his pale skin. The silence hung heavy, thick with the unspoken accusation; he felt the prickle in his stomach, the taste of dryness in his mouth. He couldn't answer; the words felt like lead in his gut at the idea of implicating himself.

"Tell her the truth," Leo sighed.

As he rolled his eyes, a dull throb receded like distant thunder, replaced by the normalcy of his quick healing. "I may have taken a small sip of the tea."

"But you don't drink tea," Aguya stated. "Or anything besides blood, for that matter."

"Apparently, I do," Redd muttered.

"Tell her how all she had to do was bat her little eyelashes at you and you drank it down like a good lil' lap dog," Leo laughed.

"A pretty woman asked you to drink drugged tea, and you... Just did it?" Aguya snickered. "Neither of you thought maybe to smell the tea first?"

"Again, that was Leo's fault. He should have smelled the drugs," Redd said as he glared at Leo. "He's the one with a super powered sniffer there."

"There was nothing to smell," Leo snorted. He shook his head. "It smelled just like any ordinary tea."

His eyes, narrowed in disbelief, searched his friend's face, the lines etched by worry, a contrast to the look of innocence and shock in Leo's eyes as he realized the truth. He couldn't fathom how Nuit, that sly whisper of a woman, had managed it. She was off to the man whose presence radiated a palpable threat to her while they waited for the sun to go down.

"Is the sun still out?" Redd asked, looking around the room as he searched for any sign of sunlight. Thick blankets muffled the window. No light peeked through, but a prickling unease told him the sun was still out.

"Yes," Aguya said as her voice turned serious again. "Back to the reason I called you, you idiot. Feya is acting strange. She will sit there talking to us, and then her eyes glaze over. She'll stop talking mid-sentence, then start back up as if nothing has happened."

"Does Alvero think this is because of the celestial contract?" Redd stated. An icy dread, a burning rage, clashed within him as his focus returned to his daughter.

Aguya hesitated before speaking. "He thinks so, but he is not sure what is happening."

Nodding, thoughts filled his head like a storm raging. "Alright."

Aguya's voice shook as she spoke. "I am scared the queen is going to call her away again."

He buried his face in his hands, remembering. His daughter, vanishing through a shimmering, iridescent portal—no warning, just a silent whoosh of air as she stepped into the pulsing orb of light, then gone. The celestial contract bound Feya to the fae queen's whim, a chilling whisper in the back of his mind. The queen could summon a portal, and Feya would walk through without a second thought, her will dissolving into the queen's chilling control.

For a moment, he'd forgotten his priorities. He'd been chasing a vision of honey-skinned beauty, a goddess, for a seemingly useless book. Now, trapped within this house, he felt useless, his skin prickling with the fear of the sun's touch outside, so he sat here in the dark.

Gulping, he swallowed his pride. He would just have to let Nuit get the book alone. "I'll head back as soon as the sun goes down."

"Sooo," Aguya dragged the word out. "Who was it that got you to drug yourself again?"

Snorting, Redd ignored the question. "Was there anything else you needed?"

"Nuit," Leo muttered as he pushed himself back onto the couch.

With a sharp shove of his foot against Leo's leg, he spat out the words, "Can you butt out of our conversation? Damn wolf's hearing."

"Oh, so is this that pretty Egyptian Goddess? Alvero's little friend?" Aguya said, her voice tinged with a sarcastic undertone.

"That is neither here nor there," Redd snapped. "Stay on topic."

"Yes, the one he has been giving goo-goo eyes at," Leo laughed. The couch shuddered, springs groaning under Leo's shaking laughter. Redd's hand shoved him hard as his brow furrowed.

"That explains a lot," Aguya snickered.

"I have never and never would give anyone goo-goo eyes," Redd snapped. "Do none of you have boundaries?"

Aguya's laughter roared through the phone line. "That's fresh coming from the king of dancing over people's boundaries."

With a click, Redd ended the call, his phone cool against his palm as he shoved it into his pocket. His gaze met Leo's, where fresh tears glistened in the dim light. Leo's lips were pressed together, his shoulders trembling with barely suppressed laughter, a soft, rumbling sound.

"Fine, get it all out now," he snorted, rubbing his forehead. "That way, we can get back to what's important."

"You have to admit, it's kind of funny that we both fell for her little trick," Leo said as the laughter died out. "Do you think she intends to harm us?"

"Yes, that was completely hilarious," Redd shook his head. "And no, I don't think she wants to harm us. She thinks I'm too brash and would piss her friend off so they wouldn't give us the book."

"I mean..." Leo shrugged as he stood up and stretched.

"Shut up," Redd said, playfully socking Leo on the arm.

"So, what are we going to do now?" Leo asked.

"Find a damn TV and see what's on," Redd laughed boisterously as he stood up and started walking around the apartment. Opening doors as he went to see what was in each.

Chapter 12

The gravel crunched under Nuit's tires as she pulled into the driveway. She knew this house, though years had blurred the memory of him. When he first moved here, about fifty years ago, Seshat had given her the address. Seshat's hopeful words–that a visit could mend their fractured past–echoed faintly in her ears. But Nuit felt the chill of his stubbornness, and it had her realizing that their relationship could never be healed. Knowing this, the courage to visit had always eluded her.

The house, a humble stone farmhouse nestled in a vibrant green valley off a gravel road, seemed harmless enough. Warm, golden sunlight from the setting sun painted the scene, yet a knot of unease tightened in her stomach. Tall grass whispered secrets in the gentle breeze, the same breeze that softly caressed her cheek while she stepped from the car, a strand of hair clinging to her skin as she brushed it behind her ear.

Nuit's hand froze inches from the weathered oak door, a cold dread seizing her, its icy grip tightening. She gulped, a dry, rasping sound, her hand trembling like a hummingbird's wing. Eyes squeezed shut, she fought the rising panic; her knuckles rapped sharply against the wood. A low, guttural grumble, like distant thunder, echoed as she shoved her shaking hands deep into her slacks' pockets. The door creaked inward, revealing Geb's towering form; Nuit's gaze shot upwards.

His jet-black hair, long and scraggly, fell like a curtain across part of his face, obscuring the sharp angles of his jaw. The glint of his black eyes, filled with disdain and mistrust, felt like an icy, hard stare. A sneer, twisting his lips into a cruel line, accompanied the harsh rasp of his voice. "Well, if it isn't my long-lost wife."

"We haven't been married in centuries, Geb," she uttered, her voice sounding meek to her own ears. "And it has been just as long since we saw each other, almost."

Her eyes focused on him—the man she once loved, the one who'd left her shattered, and the one she had not seen for centuries. He towered over her, a full foot taller, his long, lean frame familiar yet altered. His skin, once bronzed, now held a ghostly pallor, the faint scent of dust, alcohol and forgotten things clinging to him like a shroud. A chill, colder than the air itself, seemed to emanate from his very presence.

"That's true," he grumbled as his head tilted to the side. His hair fell down, giving her the full penetration of that glacial stare. "You abandoned me and our people long ago because you are weak. So why the hell are you darkening my doorstep now?"

"I'm sorry you felt abandoned," she murmured, looking down at the ground. Dirt covered the wooden floors, as if he hadn't mopped in a while. Inhaling deeply, she screwed up her courage and looked up at his face again. "I was never strong like you and could not fight. May I come in and we catch up? I wanted to check in on you."

She watched his eyes, narrowed to slits like a predator's, drift across her face. The memory of every placating trick she'd learned surged back, a bitter taste in her mouth, as her gaze dropped, her head bowing. A desperate urge to peek up, to see if her performance worked, warred within her, but she resisted. The icy weight of his disapproval, a familiar chill, settled upon her; he'd always despised her direct gaze, her slightest hint of defiance. *Is this an act or muscle memory?* The thought drifted on the wind of her mind causing a shudder to travel down her spine.

"Fine," he muttered with a sneer, shoving the door wide open and walking away.

Tentatively, she followed him into the house; a musty smell, faintly overlaid with stale alcohol, hung heavily in the air. She followed him down a dimly lit hallway. They passed by a library crammed with dust-laden books lining one wall— their spines whispering forgotten tales in the chaos of neglect. Her heart ached; she longed to explore them, rather than face her ex-husband. Clothes and trash littered the floor; peering around, she could not tell when it had last been cleaned or even had a window open for fresh air.

Sighing, she stepped into the faintly lit kitchen, a wave of stale air, heavy with the stench of mildew and mold, washing over her. Dark, dust-laden curtains hung limply before the single window above the sink. A mountain of dirty dishes loomed on the counters and sinks. She held her breath, the cloying smell thick and suffocating. The small kitchen table held the weight of numerous bottles of zythus and wine – some half-empty, most discarded and empty.

He shoved a chair out, its legs scraping harshly on the wooden floor. She snatched it before it crashed to the ground, the wood cold against her hands as she sat. A sigh escaped her lips, a soft sound in the otherwise quiet room. With a gentle push, she cleared a space on the sticky, grime-covered table.

"There she is," Geb laughed as he riffled through bottles until he found a half full bottle of zythus. "The Nuit no one would ever miss."

The words caught in her throat, a bitter taste like ash. She wanted to ask, the question a sharp, insistent sting on her tongue, but the glint in his eye, cold and knowing, told her everything. He was insinuating heavily with the accusation that she was a snob.

"How have you been?" She smiled her sweetest smile at him, hoping to disarm him.

He paused, throwing back a swig. His gaze, sharp and assessing, returned to her face. She felt the weight of his scrutiny, a silent pressure that hung thick in the air. Her smile, tight but unwavering, held firm. A fragile hope bloomed – could they, after all this time, manage a semblance of civility?

"I'm obviously fine," he grunted. "I have everything I could possibly need in life." A sardonic laugh escaped his lips as he finished the bottle off.

"Well," she sighed. "I am glad to hear you're doing good." She stopped as she had no words to further her civil attempt at a conversation.

She fought to still the roaring, echoing torrent of noises in her mind. The urge to lecture him about his drinking, his squalid lifestyle, and everything, a bitter taste on her tongue, choking her. She knew it was useless, so she bit her tongue. Their kingdom's fall had cracked him, leaving behind a hollow shell that he had filled with anger and hatred. Now, the amber liquid in the bottle seemed his only solace, a pathetic substitute for the life they might have built. She recalled the sun-drenched days, the divine glow on their skin, the adoration of their followers, a heady perfume of power. The addictive thrill of godhood, the effortless glide through life, the absence of fear— sometimes, she missed fragments of it. The anonymity gnawed at her. But more than anything, she missed the warmth of family, the comforting presence of friends, a support system that erased the chilling loneliness that had consumed her for the last hundred years. Looking at him, she understood: it wasn't just the lost power, but the lost connection that ached.

"Let's get rid of the pretense you give two shits about me," he said as he riffled through his bottles for another one. A low growl rumbled from his chest as he pushed himself up. The cupboard doors creaked loudly as he yanked them open. His search was frantic, his hands trembling slightly, each slam of the doors echoing in the still air.

"Fine," Nuit exhaled. Her gaze, like a hawk's, tracked his every subtle shift, each rustle of his clothes a faint whisper. "I wanted to borrow a book from your library."

"What?" he said, slamming a door so hard it came off the hinges and sat askew.

"A book," she said as she fell under that dark gaze. Her shoulders sagged under the weight of that glare.

"Why would I give you anything?" His harsh tone sent a trail of shivers down her spine.

"I can pay," she stated meekly.

"I don't want your money," he growled.

Taking a deep breath, she pulled the cloak of courage back on. "But you can use that money to buy the alcohol you're obviously looking for."

"Do *you* think that's all I care about?" His fist slammed onto the counter, causing her to flinch.

She paused, the oppressive darkness swirling in his eyes—a chilling, familiar shade she'd seen only once before. The acrid memory of her flight from the invasion, the searing pain of his subsequent punishment, still lingered—a phantom ache in her bones still. It had taken days of agonizing pain to mend from the beating he had given her. Even her fast healing and eternal life could not take away the shock and anguish. The silence following the beating had been deafening, heavy with unspoken accusations. The others' stony silence, a tangible weight, had pressed down on her as no one would talk to her. Though others had fled, the full force of his fury had fallen upon her alone. The suspicion, cold and sharp as shattered glass, had pricked her—he had orchestrated the campaign against her. Hundreds of years later, a few tentative family members had broken the icy silence. Yet, a question tugged at her heart: was it her actions, or the crushing loss of everything, that had ignited his relentless hatred of her?

Fingers brushed against cool, smooth metal nestled deep in her pocket; the familiar weight of the dagger, a comforting warmth against her skin. He had given it to her years ago. A bitter chuckle almost escaped her lips from the irony of returning his gift, perhaps in a deadly exchange. The thought of using it against him pierced her, a sharp, cold sensation, yet the grim determination settled in her heart; she would, if forced.

"I have no clue what you care about," she stated with what was left of her courage. "We have not spoken in eons, so it is only natural that I know nothing about the person you have become. I just wanted to buy a book from you and that is it."

He stormed towards the table, a furious red tide staining his face, yanking the edge and sending it crashing down with a deafening roar. Glass bottles exploded, a thousand icy shards glittering under the harsh light, scattering across the floor like deadly rain. She stood, eyes wide with terror, but his grip clamped around her throat, a vise of steel. She gasped, a strangled sound, her nails scraping against his skin, a desperate, futile resistance.

"You could just have stayed away," he said, splattering her face with spit.

He lifted her up; her dangling feet kicking against his leg as he swung her. The sickening thud of her back against the cabinet echoed before she landed on the cool, smooth countertop, rolling onto the gritty kitchen floor with a sharp crack. The air rushed from her lungs as she landed on the shards of broken glass, a thousand tiny pricks of pain blossoming across her skin. Pushing up, hands and knees scraping against the floor, she tasted blood. He seized her hair, yanking her head back, the rough grasp burning her scalp. Gasping for air, fear icy in her chest, she fumbled in her pocket, her heart a frantic drum against her ribs.

"I am not sure what book would be worth your life," he snorted. "You know that day I found you at the temple? You were supposed to die that day, but it looks like I've got a second chance to fix my mistake."

Chapter 13

The harsh words from Geb slammed into Nuit, each syllable a crushing blow. She knew he hated her, but at the time, she had felt that she deserved the pain and torture for not standing and fighting with her family. As soon as her mother had told her to run, she did. Even to this day, she felt the phantom sting of the explosion, the heat still radiating in her memory, and then she got separated from her daughters during the explosion. She had assumed they would head to the temple, as well. She had never realized that would be the last day she would see them. That they died at the hands of their attackers. When Geb found her weeks later and told her what happened, she did not fight even once. When his fist connected, the dull thud echoed the emptiness in her heart, a pain she thought she deserved, the taste of ashes lingering on her tongue.

Years had bled into each other, the weight of her helplessness and actions a cold stone in her gut. It had taken years to come to terms with the fact that she had never learned to fight. That even staying meant facing the inevitable storm of Roman magicals. She would have died at the tip of their swords, mirroring the countless others in her family, their ghosts whispering in the wind.

Tears welled, blurring her vision. A choked sob

escaped, a ragged sound, a tight fist, finally loosened its grip as the words she wanted to hold back escaped. But she could no longer hold them back, than she could stop the stars from shining at night. "Yet, you ran."

"What?" he screamed as he brought his face mere inches from hers.

"When our sons lay dying on the field of battle, did you stay? Did you fight to save them or did you run?" she whispered.

The rough-hewn palm slammed against her cheekbone; a searing pain shot through her jaw, her teeth chattering like ice cubes in a shaker.

But what Geb didn't know was that she'd learned to fight, and this time she would fight back. The cool, smooth metal of the hilt felt reassuringly heavy in her hand; a comforting weight against the tremor in her grip. "You think I don't know? I wouldn't find out how you ran and left them as they bleed out on the battlefield."

The acrid scent of blood filled the air as Geb's fist rose, his other hand a vise on her hair. Pulling the knife out, the cold glint of steel flashed as she struck backwards, feeling it bite into his flesh. He roared, releasing her hair; she stumbled, the shards of broken glass digging into her palms. Scrambling up the slickness of blood under her fingers, she fled down the echoing hallway, each footfall a desperate beat against the thunder of his pursuit. Panic choked her; she ran blindly, needing only distance, the icy fear a chilling weight in her chest.

Crap, I should have let Redd come with me. I don't know why I thought after all these years he would have let go of the past.

His calloused hand clamped down on her shoulder, fingers biting into her soft skin, leaving angry red marks. A jarring yank sent her reeling backward, her body slamming against the cold, unforgiving hall wall. Stars exploded behind her eyes as her head connected with the plaster, a sharp, sickening crack echoing in the sudden silence. The metallic tang of blood filled her nostrils as she swung the knife wildly, a desperate arc of steel. A guttural grunt, thick with pain, escaped his lips as the blade found its mark. His grip, like a vise, clamped down on her chin, the other hand twisting her wrist with brutal force. A searing, white-hot pain shot up her arm, bones protesting under the strain as she fought to keep her grip on the dagger. The knife slipped from her numb fingers, clattering onto the floor with a sharp, metallic clang. A final, brutal blow to her head against the unyielding wall, before he released her. She crumpled, waves of nausea and pain washing over her as she slid down the wall, her body trembling.

Bent double, he scooped up the knife; the crimson dripping from his forearm onto the floorboards, a stark contrast to the dust motes dancing in the weak sunlight. A low hiss escaped her lips as she rubbed her aching wrist, her gaze fixed on him. Through the curtain of her bangs, her eyes, wide and fearful, met his.

"I remember this," he muttered. "Was it our tenth, no thirteenth, wedding anniversary that I got you this?"

Shrugging, he twisted his wrist, bringing the knife down, its cold steel sinking into her gut with a sickening squelch. A searing, white-hot pain exploded through her, her breath catching in her throat. The coppery tang of blood filled her nostrils. She knew she only had one last weapon, a desperate gamble, and needed him impossibly close to unleash it.

"You are pathetic even after all these centuries," he growled. Gazing into those dark eyes, a chilling dread seeped into her bones; the air grew heavy, thick with the scent of fear. Her heart hammered a frantic rhythm against her ribs, deafening out her harsh breathing. She knew, with a certainty that froze her blood, that escape might be impossible. "If we had all stood and fought, our dynasty would not have fallen. You ran like the pathetic coward you are."

"You are just as blind now as you were then," she growled back as tears pricked her eyes. "The walls were crumbling around us before they invaded. If we had all ran and regrouped—"

His hand shot up, a blur of motion, slamming against the wall with a jarring thwack beside her head. She flinched, the rough plaster dust stinging as it fell around her.

"If we had stood together, we could have won," he screamed into her face. "We could have rebuilt. I sat there on the battlefield that was my throne room watching everyone I loved die and you were running away."

She wanted to defend herself, to explain the words her mother had said, the urgency in her voice ordering her to flee, to tell him how she believed she was shielding her daughters, her heart pounding as she ran with them. But instead, she sat, eyes locked on him, the air heavy with unspoken accusations. The familiar, clammy grip of guilt tightened, a stark contrast to the frantic, silent screams echoing in her mind.

I did not start that war. My only option at the time was to run and save those I could. I did not know the explosion was going to separate us, and there was no way for me to know that I would lose almost everyone I loved that day.

His hand, rough yet surprisingly gentle, stroked her cheek—a fleeting caress before a brutal fist slammed into her mouth. A sharp crack echoed, followed by the warm, metallic rush of blood filling her mouth, the coppery taste overwhelming. The impact vibrated through her jaw, a jarring shock.

"Today, I will make sure you die!" he screamed.

She reached into her pocket, feeling the slick hypodermic needle within her grasp. Pulling it out, she jabbed it into his arm. A sharp prick, then the satisfying click of the plunger as the sedative flowed. His eyes glazed over; a low moan escaped his lips. He swayed as he stumbled backward.

"What?" he gasped as he fell to his knees.

"I had a feeling you would not see reason," she whispered. "I had hoped we could put the past to rest, but it seems we never will."

Eyes blurring, she stared at the glint of steel buried in her flesh. She knew she needed to move it, but needed to staunch the crimson flow first. Each limping step echoed in the silent house. She surveyed the piles of dirty clothes in the living room—a chaotic jumble that she was not sure how long had been there. The bedroom yielded no better; another mountain of dirty garments. With a grimace, she felt the cold weight of the blade shift within her with every probing footstep. Finding a relatively clean shirt, its slightly stiff cotton a stark contrast to the slick warmth of her blood, she carefully wrapped it around the knife's blade. A deep, shuddering breath preceded the agonizing wrench. She almost dropped the blood-soaked fabric as a white-hot searing pain exploded through her. A fresh wave of nausea hit her as she frantically searched for something to bind the wound. Another shirt, hastily wrapped and painfully tightened around her waist, offered little comfort against the pulsing agony coursing through her.

Bending down, she picked up the knife. Feeling the weight of it in her hand as she saw crimson glistening on the blade and hilt, her blood. She gripped the handle; her knuckles turning white. Her breath was ragged as she walked back down the echoing hallway.

A tote bag lay crumpled up on the floor. Grabbing it, she said, "This way, I don't bleed all over the books, at least."

Walking into the hallway, she stared at his prone body.

I should stab him with the knife. She told herself, but her hands did not listen. The acrid scent of blood filled her nostrils, a stark contrast to the sweet perfume she usually wore. She saw him, his chest rising and falling shallowly, his shirt a dull grey stained with crimson, a mix of her blood and his. The icy grip of hatred still clutched at her heart for him, a phantom pain echoing the physical wounds that criss crossed her body. She felt the weight of the years, the chilling emptiness of her lost children, yet she could not bring herself to end his life, the man who'd fought so fiercely to kill her. Even if he remained trapped in the past and would continue to hunt her down until it ended in one of their deaths. She'd floated, somehow survived, drifting through time while he was mired in sorrow constantly weighted down by the past. Looking down at him, a wave of nausea threatened to overwhelm her, yet her hand remained still, unable to deliver the final blow.

Don't stand here and stare. How long will this keep him knocked out even? Get your ass to work and find the book.

Sighing, a soft, breathy sound lost in the quiet library, she walked towards the towering shelves. Her eyes, wide with a mixture of hope and despair, scanned the chaotic stacks—books overflowing from shelves onto the floor, a precarious tower on the desk, and even spilling onto the single, worn wingback chair. The sheer number of volumes, a sea of mostly brown leather spines, felt overwhelming, a suffocating weight pressing down on her as her eyes scanned.

REDD

Chapter 14

Redd, staring out the windowpane, saw the bright crescent moon hang like a silver sickle on the darkening horizon. The last fiery blush of sunset faded, leaving a cool twilight chill on his skin. Nuit's absence pressed down on him; the silence of waiting was heavy as she had not returned yet. He couldn't wait any longer. He needed to go check on his daughter, to know his family's safety. Behind him, Leo's restless pacing echoed a counterpoint to the quiet dread filling him.

A fiery anger surged through him, a hot, prickly sensation that fueled his desperate thirst. He knew it was an acquaintance of hers that held the book, but a bitter resentment simmered; he was not as uncouth as she seemed to insinuate he was. *I damn well know how to hold a civil conversation.* She had gone to an extreme to make sure that they did not help her. *Maybe it's an ex-lover or a current one.* The sharp sting of jealousy, like a wasp's bite, pierced him. His bruised ego throbbed, a dull ache mirroring the hypnotic pull of those deep, obsidian eyes, dark and gleaming like polished stones haunting him.

"Ready?" Leo snapped from behind him.

Nodding, he turned and followed Leo, the old

wooden stairs creaking under their weight. Leo's head was hunched low, a soft thud echoing as it bumped the low-hanging roof beam halfway down. A muffled snicker escaped Redd as Leo rubbed his head. Redd quickly covered his mouth, but Leo's sharp ears caught the sound, picking up the faintest trace of Redd's suppressed laughter. The glare that followed showing Leo was not happy.

As they walked towards the front door, he paused. "You know how to reverse pick a lock?"

"Reverse pick?" Leo said as he stopped.

"Yes," Redd shrugged. "You know, lock the door after we leave. Don't want anyone just walking in."

Leo stared at him, unblinking, before he shrugged. "Maybe a key is inside somewhere."

Eyes scanning, they circled the worn wooden counter, searching. A heavy metal key ring clinked as he lifted it off a hook behind the counter. The door yielded after several tries, a satisfying click echoing in the quiet space. With a decisive turn, the lock engaged, and they stepped out into the night. *I'll have to bring the keys back later.* The idea of doing the extra work feeling less like a chore and more like an adventure.

The coppery tang of human blood, thick with the cloying sweetness of alcohol, filled his nostrils as they emerged from the pub. Each unsteady footstep pulsed with the intoxicating scent, a wave of warm, alcoholic blood. His stomach growled while he tried to suppress the impulse. The urge to drink was a gnawing hunger, but he wasn't desperate yet. Not quite. Soon, though. Very soon, the craving would be unbearable, a roaring tide threatening to drown him if he didn't feed.

The agonizingly slow trip back to the manor—though realistically normal in length—ended with a jolt. He slumped into the back seat, his mind a chaotic swirl of thoughts. A low hum from the engine vibrated through the car. As the car tires crunched on the gravel drive-way, a flash of golden fur—the golden hind—leaped in front, tires screeching as Leo slammed on the brakes. He pushed down the rising frustration at the rampant wild-life taking over his lands. Ever since Alvero moved in, the manor was teeming with creatures. Aguya and Alvero's budding romance was new, but its furry, feathered, and four-legged side effects were overwhelming the property and his mood.

When he tried to drink the rabbit's blood the other day, Alvero's fury flashed—a tempest of anger he had only seen surpassed by the storm that followed Aguya's kid-napping. The sting of Alvero's lecture was a phantom burn on his skin. Usually, he supplemented between meals with the blood of small creatures. But Alvero's protectiveness had left him famished; a gnawing emptiness grew daily, a cold pressure in his gut. His own temper simmered, mir-roring the ever-present hunger raging inside him.

Leo glided the limo into the carriage house. He walked towards the house, the gnawing hunger and sim-mering rage a heavy weight in his gut. He tried to shove it away as Leo trailed next to him.

Brady was waiting in the kitchen for them, her hands wringing together. Her breathing was harsh and heartbeat erratic as she spoke, "It took you long enough to get here."

"I didn't realize there was a hurry," Redd snorted as he wondered what drama Brady was overreacting to. "Plus, I don't know if you noticed the sun just went down not too long ago."

Her smokey grey eyes glared at him as she huffed and stormed off. "Just follow me, Mr. Smarty-pants."

Glancing at Leo, he rolled his eyes, a sigh escaping his lips as he glanced at her. Whatever petty complaint she was brewing he was not prepared for; her rasping whisper already grating on his nerves. Usually, he could let what she said slide off like water, but the hunger was affecting his nerves. But lately, she had been complaining about everything from the animals to how much dust the house had. He trailed behind her; the floorboards creaking under foot as she led him to his office. *If there is some stupid animal in there, I am going to drink every ounce up, whether or not Alvero likes it.*

As his ears perked up, catching the faint thumping of hearts on the other side of the solid oak door, he realized only Feya and Aguya were there. Feya's steady heartbeat, a calm rhythm like a distant drum, contrasted sharply with Aguya's frantic pulse—a rapid, erratic tattoo, hinting at her restless pacing.

Glancing over at Brady, he watched as she hesitated before opening the heavy oak door, its varnish gleaming under the firelight. A roaring fire blazed in the hearth, casting flickering shadows that danced on Aguya's face as she looked up, worry etched deep in her golden eyes, brows furrowed as she ceased her restless pacing. Her golden blonde hair swayed gently as she tilted her head.

Feya remained still, her gaze fixed on the fire blazing. He frowned as he approached her. A chill seemed to emanate from her stillness.

"What..." Redd breathed as he knelt down. Feya's eyes, pools of misty green, unfathomable depth, seemed to see right through him as if he was not even there.

"She has been like this for the last hour," Aguya snapped. "This is what I have been trying to explain to you. She is acting... just so... weird. She is here, but... she's not."

Fingers brushing against silken strands as he tugged gently; no response. A frown etched itself onto his brow, the silence heavy and unsettling. The air hung thick with the scent of unknown magic—a strange, unfamiliar perfume. A chill prickled his skin; this was unlike any spell he'd ever encountered.

"Where are Alvero and Elwyn?" Redd asked, as his eyes darted around. Even though the boy, Elwyn, was not his favorite, he knew he would not willingly leave Feya alone.

A jolt, like ice water, snaked down his spine as he stared into those glassy, unblinking eyes. A sharp snap of his fingers echoed in the sudden silence—still, nothing.

"They left a few hours ago," Brady sighed. "I told them not to leave, but they did—"

"Shut up! You don't know what you're talking about," Aguya growled at Brady. "Alvero had a lead on getting that stupid box open, so he went to talk to someone. Elwyn hasn't gotten back from giving that fake update to the fae queen."

"Why must you always be so—" Brady started.

Redd threw his hand up and cut Brady off. "Why would Alvero leave you alone?" he snapped, his eyes meeting Aguya's.

"I told him to go, and that I'd be safe," Aguya shrugged.

"You almost died just a few weeks ago!" Redd yelled. "What the hell was he thinking?"

"I am fully healed now," Aguya growled, rolling her eyes. "I do know how to keep myself safe."

"Then how did you almost get yourself killed?" The words, rough and sharp as shattered glass, hung in the air. He instantly regretted the harshness, an icy wave washing over him, but the unspoken apology remained trapped in his throat. Heat formed on his ass as he jumped up, swatting at the fire spreading on his pants. "Dammit!"

"See, I can control my powers quite well," Aguya snickered. "Don't you think?"

"Why can you not just be normal?" Redd growled as he felt the hole burned in his pants. "Both those dumbasses should not have left you three alone. Especially with her like this." He flicked his hand at Feya. "I am not the one who knows all sorts of magic. Alvero is the one who knows magic. He should be here figuring this out."

"She wasn't like this when they left," Aguya sighed. "Plus, he was dealing with some hermit that refuses to leave his house or something."

"He said he would be back by daybreak," Brady added. "But again I told him—"

"Brady," Redd warned, his tone low. He looked at Leo for help, who just shrugged. "The commentary is not helpful right now."

"Oh, hey, you're home," Feya said as all eyes turned to her. "I see Aguya got ahold of you," the words sliced through the air, a nervous giggle, a high-pitched tremor escaping her lips.

"See what I mean, weird," Aguya said, waving her hand towards Feya.

Redd nodded slowly. He watched his daughter with a gaze both weary and intense.

"Weird?" Feya side eyed Aguya.

"Yes, I am saying you are acting weird," Aguya snorted.

"No, I am not!" Feya exclaimed.

"Aguya burnt my pants in front of you minutes ago and you did not even blink," Redd whispered, seriously. "Did you even see me arrive?"

"Wait, what?" Feya said as her eyes darted around the room.

"Did you hear the car pull up? Did you hear the door open?" Redd asked.

"No, but..." Feya trailed off.

"What's going on?" he probed. "What's the last thing you remember?"

"I was just sitting here and then..." Feya sighed as the words trailed off.

"And then?" Redd knelt down in front of her, grabbing her small little pale hand. He cradled her delicate hand in his. Remembering when she had been so tiny, and he had held that same hand.

"I heard a voice, then you were... were just in front of me," Feya said, chewing on her lip.

"What did the voice say?" Aguya asked. Sitting on the arm of the chair, she started rubbing Feya's back.

"It just said, listen," Feya said as her eyes moved to the clock.

"Alright," Aguya nodded.

"We have been so worried about you," Brady chimed in as she smoothed Feya's hair.

"It's getting worse," Feya said as she squeezed Redd's hand. "I think I had a conversation with the queen, but I am not sure. I don't even remember what it was about."

"We will find a way to get you out from under her spell," Redd whispered as he caressed his daughter's cheek. "Cass has said he knows a way out. So I am working with him on it now. We should have everything we need soon."

"Do you think it will actually work?" Feya asked as tears brimmed those misty eyes.

Nodding, a slow, hesitant bob of his head, the simple word caught in his throat. He wanted to believe the priest could help. But an icy dread had a clammy grip on his heart. It whispered of failure, of returning to the bleak, hopeless square one.

"Do you think Alvero will be back soon?" Redd asked as he looked over at Aguya.

"Yes," she said as she shrugged.

He wanted to point out the incongruity between her words and actions, but decided it was pointless.

"Perfect. Maybe he will have a good outcome and get that damned box open," Redd stated as he stood up. He weighed each word. No gentle approach presented itself. He knew coddling would be unwelcome by her. "Feya, I need to say something that's going to upset you."

"No, I will not break up with Elwyn," she grumbled as she arched a black eyebrow at him.

He could not help the smile that crept across his face. "You sure?"

"Yes, father," she laughed.

"Well, damn," he shrugged. "With all that is happening, it would be best if you are to have one of us with you at all times. And I mean *all*."

"That's—" Feya started.

"A great idea," Aguya said as she cut her off. "We can take shifts."

"What if I need to go to the bathroom?" Feya queried.

Redd frowned, debating her words. "Brady will hold your hand for that one."

"No," Feya stated as she crossed her hands in the

air. "I am fine. I don't need to have a babysitter."

"Well, obviously you do!" Redd yelled. "You randomly vanish through portals. You're losing time now."

"Do you really believe that having someone watch my every move will stop whatever the queen has planned?" Feya growled as she jumped up.

A warm flush crept up his neck as his daughter stood firm, a silent battle waged in his heart. Pride that she was finally standing up for herself mixed with knowing that it was not the time for fighting. He wished she would have waited until the oppressive weight of the celestial contract was lifted, and she obtained her freedom.

As Redd stared at his daughter, her eyes glazed over, dull and lifeless, as she stumbled past him, a faint whisper of a sigh escaped her lips. He reached out, fingers brushing against the chill of an empty space where she'd stood a moment before. A blinding flash seared his eyes, the sharp scent of ozone filling his nostrils, then silence, heavy and suffocating. She was gone, having walked through a portal.

"Fuck," he growled.

"She stepped into a portal," Aguya said as she muttered words he could not understand. Her eyes glowed with her magic as she cast the spell. He waited quietly, scared to breathe or speak. "She is at the fae portal."

"Dammit," Redd said, roughly running a hand through his hair. "We will head out now to—"

"It will do you no good," Aguya stated. "You know we will not get through the portal into the fae vale now. They have had the entrance on lock down since all this drama started."

A sharp crack echoed as his fist connected with the cold, rough brick; the sting of broken skin was immediate, a warm, coppery tang of blood filling his nostrils. "Every-

Chapter 15

one out."

Eyes scanning the dusty shelves, Nuit's breath hitched. The spines blurred, a kaleidoscope of titles assaulting her vision. Her fingers brushed the worn leather spines. Then, a sudden stillness; her heart pounded a heavy rhythm against her ribs.

"Oh," she whispered as she looked at an old copy of Alice in Wonderland. Her fingers lovingly stopped on the spine. "I haven't seen this one before."

Reaching for the book, she saw crimson staining her palm. The rough fabric of her pants absorbed the blood as she wiped it off. With a quick grab, the book disappeared into the canvas bag.

"He won't notice me taking an extra book," she muttered as her eyes continued to scan. Her ears perked, listening for any sound of him rousing.

Pausing, a leather-bound book with a tarnished gold clasp caught her eye; she shrugged, the scent of aged paper and dust filling her nostrils as she shoved it into the canvas bag. The worn cotton strained with each addition; by the time she got to the fifth shelf, the bag was overflowing. Finally, there it was: the grimoire, cool and smooth beneath her touch.

"Maybe it will confuse him that I took so many books. He won't realize which one I actually wanted," she muttered as she left the library. Pausing, she saw it. Another book she did not have. Sighing, she told herself she did not need another one as her fingers grabbed it and the two books underneath. "They are just collecting dust here. I am saving them."

Peeking from the library doorway, she saw Geb, still hunched where he'd fallen; the dust motes dancing in the sunbeam slicing through the gloom. Arms overflowing with books, she hurried out of the house. She almost dropped the books while opening the car door. She tumbled her literary loot into the passenger seat. Panic, cold and sharp, pricked her skin. He would hunt her, she knew, once he woke. The chilling thought snaked through her: *Does he know my shop's location?*

"So, I am going to go home and pack," she ticked off to herself the list of what she needed to do. "If they are at the house, I will give them the book and be done. Then I will grab my bags and run. Ugh, I felt so brave earlier and now I feel like a mouse running from a cat. Dammit!"

She whipped the car sharply around the corner, a searing pain lancing through her; a sharp gasp escaped her lips as she fought for breath. A prickly itch, the aftermath of healing magic, warred with the stabbing agony. The magical energies thrummed beneath her skin, yet the wound was slow to heal.

"Maybe I should look for a new life. Is it smart to get my passports from the same person I usually do?"

Her brain buzzed, a frantic hive of thoughts, each one a tiny, insistent drone as new questions formed.

"I don't have a choice," she muttered. "It's not like I know someone else who can do this. I will use him, then find someone new if I need to. Till then, I will just need to be extra vigilant."

Frustration warred with the pain inside her.

"Why couldn't I just kill him? I could just keep my normal life schedule. It wouldn't have been hard to stab him. Right?"

Sighing, the miles stretched as her frayed nerves continued to unravel. The sun slowly set on the horizon as she drove. Golden hills, hazy in the afternoon sun, gave way to a rising tide of brick and glass. The quiet hum of wind in the grass shifted to the low thrum of distant traffic. The scent of sycamore and earth yielded to exhaust fumes and the sharp tang of city air. Pulling into the parking lot, her eyes darted around as she searched for Geb. Every part of her body was alive with the nerves eating at her, thinking he was hiding in every shadow, in every corner. She left the stack of books in her car as she jumped out. As she ran to her house, she saw a homeless man staring at her strangely; looking down, she realized she was covered in blood. Smiling self-deprecatingly, she tried to hide as much of her clothes while rushing to her building.

The key scraped into the lock, a grating sound that echoed in the tense silence. She snatched up only the bare necessities, the rough fabric of her bag scratching against her skin. An icy dread, sharp as shattered glass, propelled her upward. Each footfall on the creaking stairs sent a jolt of pain through her. The frantic thump of her heart was the only thing that broke the silence of her apartment. Redd and Leo were nowhere to be found.

I should have known he would have left at sundown. I'll have to meet him somewhere to give him the book.

Without looking at the things her hand grabbed, she shoved clothes and toiletries into a canvas bag. The bag heavy, she raced down creaking wooden stairs, her breath coming in ragged gasps, a tense knot tightening in her stomach. She snatched her favorite books—their pages soft from countless rereadings—a comforting weight in her hands. The small shop door clicked shut behind her, the metallic sound echoing in her soul as tears sprung to the corners of her eyes. She looked at the door for a moment, as sadness washed through her. This was the place she considered home and now she feared she would not be able to come back for a very long time.

Turning away, she hobbled to her car, each footfall echoing on the pavement a shooting pain throughout her body. The bag landed with a soft thud in the backseat. Sliding behind the wheel, she fumbled for her phone, the cool glass smooth against her palm, and punched in Redd's number. She looked at her fingers, seeing her dried blood smeared across them.

Chapter 16

After a few rings, the deep baritone of his voice answered, "Hey, A mhuirnín."

Her heart pounded, a frantic drum against her ribs, urging her to ask him, the words a shimmering question in the air, what he meant. But her brain, a cold, sharp voice, commanded her to hurry. The thought, a dizzying vortex, spun in her head. A soft sigh escaped her lips as her brain's icy logic prevailed. "I have the book. Where do I drop it off at?"

"Is something wrong?" he whispered, his voice dripping with concern.

"Everything's great," she chirped, a forced brightness in her voice, the words tumbling out in a breathless rush, betraying her strained cheer. "I am just in a rush. Text me the address. Bye."

"We—" Redd started.

With a sharp click, she ended the call, silencing his voice. Her phone chirped, a tiny, bright sound, as she glanced at the address. Tapping it into the navigation app, the map's crisp voice rang through the car's speakers, guiding her.

Redd leaned back in the chair, the worn leather creaking beneath him, as the phone clicked dead. His brow furrowed, the lines etched deeper by the strained timbre of her voice; something was wrong, a disorienting chaos swirling in his mind as he debated the few words she had spoken. The last few hours had crawled by–Feya was still missing, Alvero had not returned. Brady's frantic scrubbing echoed, the sharp, sweet scent of lavender cleaning solution stinging his nostrils. Aguya's frustrated slamming of doors punctuated the silence, a rhythmic percussion through the house. From the kitchen, the tang of roasted rabbit wafted from Leo's meal.

I feel so useless. The thought, a relentless buzzing, circled his brain as memories—sharp, searing images—flooded back. The war's stench, acrid and clinging, haunted him; bloodcurdling screams, still echoing in his memories, marked the loss of his entire clan. Devastation, a cold, crushing weight, had seemed insurmountable. Holding Sophine on that battlefield all those years ago, her blood warm and slick as it flowed through his fingers, a crimson stain blooming across his hands, he'd sworn an oath—a bitter vow of solitude to never sire another or let anyone in. Then, this tiny fae, frail as a fallen leaf, dying in the dark forest, had shattered his resolve. Now, surrounded by his new family, an icy grip of despair had grabbed him in its clutches. He felt the familiar hollowness, the uselessness that gnawed at him. The path out of this mess remained obscured, a maddening labyrinth of grief and regret, each winding turn created a fresh wound to his soul. The chilling memory of Aguya, her lifeblood staining the car seat, a crimson tide, the terror etched in his mind, fueled the fear that his heart might shatter once more when he lost his family again.

A blinding flash of light momentarily stole his sight as Feya shimmered into existence, stepping through a swirling, sapphire-edged portal. The air, thick with the acrid bite of burnt ozone, smelled of singed magic; a sharp, metallic tang tingling the nostrils, a faint whisper of sulfur on the wind. He leaped to his feet and stalked towards her. He seized her, pulling her into a hug, the warmth of her body a welcome relief. Yet, a persistent, icy dread clung to him, whispering of fleeting joy and the ever present nagging fears eating him up.

How can I keep her from vanishing at the whim of that stupid fae queen? No ideas came to him.

"Dad!" Feya exclaimed as she squirmed in his arms. "I wasn't gone that long."

With a grunt, he shoved her back, his rough hands shaking her shoulders gently. "Do you know how worried we all have been? It may have been a few hours, but how were we to know you were safe?"

Redd looked down at Feya as a quiet filled the room. The squeak of the door jarring in the quiet as Leo pushed it open. Aguya and Brady followed; their footsteps created a parade of sound as they ran in. Brady moved to Feya, the soft swish of the washcloth while she gently wiped Feya's face.

"Are you hurt?" Brady asked as her grey eyes sparkled with unshed tears.

"Is that dust cleaner on that cloth?" Feya grumbled, pushing Brady's hand away.

"Leave her be," Aguya stated as she shoved Brady aside.

"Hey," Brady grumbled.

"Don't start fighting, you two," Redd said, rolling his head back and forth.

No matter what happened, these two would continue to go at each other like two old bitties, their words a sharp crackle in the tense air. Brady snorted, the sound a harsh puff of air, as she returned to tending to Feya.

"I'm fine, Brady," Feya said, pushing her hand aside once again. "Can you quit using the same rag you're dusting with on my face?"

"Tell us everything that happened," Redd grumbled, slumping back into the worn leather wingback chair. Aguya's magic sparked a sudden flash of orange light, followed by the crackle and scent of burning oak as flames danced in the hearth.

Feya nodded and settled into the chair beside him. Brady's lips parted, but a quick wave of his hand, a silencing gesture, cut her short.

"It was nothing special," Feya shrugged as she curled her legs up on the seat.

"Nothing special is a bullshit answer," Redd stated. His fingers tapped on the arm of the chair. "So, now you're going to try again and this time, the truth."

Sighing, Feya brushed a stray strand of hair from her face. "She wanted to corroborate what Elwyn had said to her. He doesn't know that I was there. She thinks we know more than we know. She knows Olette is dead, but she wouldn't say it." Feya's voice trailed off.

"The boy's not here, so tell us the rest," Redd said.

"She was happy," Feya stated as she met his eyes. "I just got the vibe she already knew, but I don't know how. That's not even the most strange part of all of this."

He waited patiently, the silence heavy and thick, for her to continue, but she didn't. A faint scent of wood smoke hung in the air. He went to open his mouth, but Aguya's sharp words beat him to it, a sudden, jarring sound.

"Are you going to tell us, or are you going to reenact it out with charades?" Aguya snapped.

"Be patient," Feya snapped, her voice like brittle

ice. His hand covered hers; a firm, warm pressure trying to squeeze the life out of her anxiety. "It's been a long day. I'm tired."

"Then tell us a condensed version and you can go to sleep," Redd said softly. "Then in the morning, you will give us the full story."

"It was Wallace," Feya said as her brow furrowed. "After the queen had finished with me, he pulled me aside. He asked about the box, but..." she trailed off as she turned her hand in his. "He asked about the box again. Concerned I would give it to the queen, he wanted to stop me from doing that. He was so very adamant that it not be given to the queen."

"Is that all that happened?" Redd asked, his eyes searching Feya's profile as she gazed into the crackling fire, its orange light painting fleeting patterns across her face. He felt the quickening of her pulse beneath his fingers. She started to speak, but he squeezed her hand. Her gaze, soft and questioning, met his. "Be careful of that lie you're thinking of saying."

"Ughh," Feya groaned. "How do you do that?"

"I know you," Redd shrugged.

"Is it my heart rate?" Feya asked.

"Don't change the subject." Redd shook his head.

"Do I have some kind of tell?"

"Answer the question. What else happened?"

A slow breath escaped her lips. Turning, she faced the crackling fire. "When I got there, there was a fea there. They had already tortured him. I'm pretty sure they had already extracted any information they needed from him. She wanted..."

A heavy silence hung in the air, thick with the

scent of wood smoke. Only the crackling and popping of the fire, a rhythmic percussion against the stillness, broke the quiet. The flames cast flickering shadows throughout the room.

"Wanted what?" Aguya murmured as she broke the silence.

Redd's eyes, blazing crimson embers, shot daggers at Aguya. The queen's intentions, he knew with a sickening certainty, were far from benevolent. A low hum of tension vibrated in the air as he'd tried to give Feya time to compose herself, but Aguya, as always, was impatient.

"She wanted me to bury him alive," Feya whispered.

His gaze searched her face, a pale canvas offering no clue to her inner turmoil, a stark contrast to the chilling stillness in her eyes. Centuries of silently guarding her felt heavy now, a physical weight in his chest, as he watched her wade into the shadowed depths of a world he was not sure she was ready for.

"She wanted to bury him so deep that no one would ever find him," Feya continued before shrugging. "Then she fed me."

"Fed you?" Brady laughed. "Did she really serve you tea and cake after asking you to bury someone alive?"

"No, she did not serve me dessert after she offered me the throat of one of her enemies and then told me to dig a hole to put him in." Feya stood up. Brady gasped, Feya waved her hand at Brady. "I am tired and ready for bed."

"Alright. You go get some rest," Redd said as he stood up. He watched, a bittersweet ache in his chest, as Feya disappeared walking through the door. "The rest of you stay."

Brady snorted, "I have too—"

"Not now," Redd growled.

"But—" Brady sighed.

"Later," Redd grunted. "Stay for now."

Amused, a sly smirk stretched Aguya's lips as her sharp gaze, like a hawk's, locked onto Brady.

"Don't start, Aguya," Redd stated as he reached towards Aguya. She smacked his hand. "Leo, I want you to stay with Feya at all times. You are not to leave her side. Aguya, stay close by so you can cast any spells to trace her down if needed. When Alvero gets back, I want him and Brady to track down Wallace. We need to get him talking about what he knows."

"No," Aguya growled. "He's not going anywhere when he gets back." A wave of heat radiated from Aguya, the air growing thick and heavy with tension. Her barely controlled fury crackled, a palpable energy in the stifling room.

"Aguya, calm down and think reasonably," Redd stated, lowering his voice, hoping to avoid her ruining another pair of pants. "They won't be gone long. We need to know what part he is playing in this game. The more information we have, the easier it is to make a plan."

Aguya mulled over the words, a frown etching itself onto her face as the silence stretched, thick and heavy. Then, a chill swept through the room, the sudden drop in temperature a tangible wave as her magic subsided, leaving a lingering whisper of ozone in the air. "Fine. I just don't like it."

Walking over, he tousled her head, his fingers ruffling her soft hair. She swatted playfully at his hand, a nervous laugh escaping her lips. He smiled, tried to put as much confidence in his voice as he could muster. "We will get back to normal soon. Then you can keep your little boyfriend close, but could you ask him to get rid of some of these animals?"

"We both know that is not going to happen," Aguya stated as she walked towards the door.

"Maybe just a few of them?" he muttered, knowing she was no longer listening.

"I'll get ready," Brady huffed as she went to leave. "I am sure that Alvero will be back soon."

"You really hate Alvero, don't you?" Leo said, while his shoulders shook.

"What do you mean?" Redd said, his eyes darting to Leo, noticing the mirth spreading across his face.

"We both know Alvero can't stand Brady just as much as Aguya can't."

Shrugging, Redd laughed. "We both know Aguya's beef with Brady is all fluster. She would hurt anyone who hurt Brady."

"But Alvero would push her off a cliff if he had a chance to. Pretty sure Aguya would just let him."

"Good thing she can fly."

Snorting Leo, shrugged. "Have you ever seen that little fae fly?"

"Just because I haven't seen it doesn't mean it can't happen."

Shaking his head, Leo turned and left the room.

Redd rolled his chair back while he sat down behind his desk, the worn leather creaking under his weight. He fished his phone from his pocket, debating texting Nuit. Frustration coiled in his gut, a knot of anger needing release. He wanted a fight. But he slumped back, staring blankly at the inky blank screen.

Nuit

Chapter 17

As Nuit drew nearer, the impending meeting loomed, a stark realization washing over her. Crimson stained her clothes, a grim reminder of her hurried departure from her apartment. Pulling onto the side of the road, she fumbled for a plastic water bottle. The cool liquid felt strangely inadequate against the sticky warmth of blood as she scrubbed frantically at her arms and hands.

She pulled the visor down and stared at her reflection. The harsh fluorescent light of the car interior glinted off a purplish bruise blooming yellow at her temple. Her swollen lip, a faded roadmap of a crimson slash, still bore a faint mark. She grabbed the concealer, dabbing it on, the cool cream a momentary relief against the throbbing pain. Even with a thick layer, the bruises stubbornly shone through, a faint lavender glow beneath the makeup. Stepping out of her car, she quickly changed, the rustling fabric a nervous symphony, her heart pounding with the fear of a passing car catching a glimpse. Before lowering the shirt, she glanced at the gash, a jagged red line across her abdomen; a dull ache throbbed beneath the surface, promising a lasting scar. With a sigh, she lowered the hem.

She drove the last few miles in a tense silence; the radio muted as the wind whistled a lonely tune through the open car window. The sun-warmed air, scented with distant roses, did little to soothe her racing nerves. Every minute, a nervous glance in the rearview mirror scanned for any sign of pursuit; the faint hum of the engine was the only sound besides the wind. Pulling into the long driveway, the manor house loomed, its windows glittering like a thousand captured sunbeams. The rich scent of roses, heavy and sweet, filled the car as she got closer. A wistful sigh escaped her lips; she knew her time here would be brief and she could not explore this enchanted place. Her fingers traced the spines of aged books until she found the grimoire. Geb's fury was a price she would need to pay one day, but she didn't care anymore. Centuries of drifting from one existence to another was ending now; she would no longer be a forgotten shadow, but a force in her own right.

"One day he will kill me," she exhaled, pulling the book to her chest. "Or maybe I'll get the nerve up to kill him. Maybe it's both of our times to go." A shiver trailed down her spine as she realized she was not ready to die.

The car door slammed shut with a metallic clang. She hopped out; the gravel crunching under her shoes as she climbed the steps. A sharp rap, rap, rap echoed against the wooden door, solid, sure, and without a tremor. *He made me feel comfortable. Even after drugging him, I know he won't hurt me. At least I hope he won't.*

The door creaked open, revealing bubbly Brady. Her vibrant red curls, a bouncing halo, spilled over her generous chest, catching the sun's warm glow. Brady, a few inches shorter than Nuit, beamed, her light gray eyes sparkling with joy, a silent chime accompanying her words. "We've been expecting you, honey. Aren't you just a sight for sore eyes?"

Brady flung open the door, a wide sweep of her hand inviting Nuit inside. Nuit stepped across the threshold, a wave of comforting warmth washing over her. Her gaze swept the foyer–dark, polished wood railings spiraling upwards to the unseen floor above, contrasting with the cool gleam of white marble underfoot and a crimson runner tracing a path. The heavy front door closed with a thud, shutting out the last vestiges of sunlight. Yet, the interior felt sun-drenched, despite the blackout curtains muffling every window. A magnificent chandelier showered the space in warm, golden light. The air hummed with a clean, fresh scent, a subtle whisper of lavender hung in the stillness. Vibrant paintings in vivid colors and snapshots of family punctuated the pristine white walls.

"Follow me," Brady guided. "I'll show you where Redd is."

Her gaze, searching, flickered from the house to

Brady. She trailed behind the fae; the floorboards groaning softly under her weight. Redd sat at a massive oak desk, the polished surface gleaming under the single lamp, his phone held rigidly in his hand. His brow was a tight furrow, his eyes glued to the screen, ignoring her presence completely.

He's probably mad at me. She pushed back the nervous flutter in her chest as she walked toward him. Brady closed the door with a solid click, leaving them alone in a silence thick with unspoken tension. Setting the book down, its smooth cover cool against her hands, she recoiled, seeing tiny, angry red cuts marring her palm. The surrounding skin, a sickly yellow, testified to a healing process already underway.

Should I ask him for cash? If I have cash, I won't leave a digital trail if he knows about my current life. Her thoughts swirled as she heard the chime of a grandfather clock in the distance. The rhythmic tick-tock of the clock inside grated on her already frayed nerves, each second amplifying her growing impatience. She waited, her gaze fixed on him, the weight of all she had not done pressing down, a physical ache in her chest. Minutes crawled by, heavy and suffocating, each one like a tiny eternity.

A nervous tremor ran through her as she gnawed on her lip, the silence stretching taut and heavy. The almost-healed wound reopened, a sharp, stinging pain, drawing his gaze at last. A single bead of crimson, warm and thick, traced a path down her lip. His eyes, dark and intense, searched her face, a slow, smoldering fire igniting within their depths.

"Who did this to you?" Redd growled.

Her lips stretched in a painful attempt at a smile, twisting instead into a grimace. "It is nothing. It looks worse than it feels. Here's your book," she muttered as she pointed to it laying on the desk.

An insatiable curiosity, a burning fire, flowed

through her, igniting a longing to read the book's secrets, explore the pages and spells hidden inside it. A pang of sadness followed as she realized her time was stolen and she would probably never have time to look through it again. The ticking clock's relentless rhythm hammered a warning in her ears; Geb, she knew, was close, his shadow a chilling breath on her neck. A week, maybe less, before the cold earth claimed her once he found her.

"You didn't answer my question." His voice, a low, gravelly whisper that scraped against her ears, sent a shiver skittering down her spine. The air grew cold, heavy with an unspoken threat. "I am going to ask you one last time. Who. Did. This. To. You?" Each word, punctuated by a sharp tap-tap-tap as his finger, bone-white against the dark wood, jabbed into the desk.

"It's alright," she whispered. "All that matters is I got the book. I took care of it and there is nothing to worry about. So, now our business is done. If I can get payment, I would appreciate it."

"The person at the dot on the map did this to you?" he said as he leaned back.

A slow breath escaped her lips, a silent sigh accompanying the slump of her shoulders. Her gaze, heavy-lidded and unfocused, rested on him. "You really are a horrible listener."

"I heard every word you said," he snorted. "You're wounded. I could smell the blood reeking off you before you entered the house."

Laughing, she shook her head. "You seemed so lost in your phone. I figured you would not notice."

"I am hungry and was trying to distract myself. You smell so... sweet."

"Oh, thank you... I think," she stated as her eyes darted around the dark room.

Her gaze drifted away, avoiding his. The firelight, a flickering dance of orange and gold, painted the room in shifting shadows. Deep, rich browns and dark woods filled the space, heavy and rather comforting. The desk before him, worn smooth in places from years of use; lighter patches gleamed where elbows had often rested.

"I have been staying in this life too long and really need to head on," she stated. "So if you could just pay my fee I would like to go."

At this point, I don't care about the money. I just need to leave. I can figure out how to get to my money later.

"But first, we celebrate," Redd growled, his eyes blazing, twin embers burning in the dusky light.

"Celebrate?" she whispered, a breathy sound barely disturbing the quiet, her brow furrowing, a delicate line etching itself between her eyes.

"Yes," he stated as he stood up. "You will have dinner with us tonight."

"I really can't."

"I insist." His voice, a low rumble, unwavering, met her gaze. The steely glint in his eyes, sharp as flint, left no room for doubt; his resolve was unyielding, as she knew he would not take a simple no.

Maybe one night won't kill me. It's not like there is any connection that Geb could find between us. At least, I hope not.

Chapter 18

Redd rose, guiding her to where Brady stood, crimson-faced, with her ear pressed close to the door. A sharp creak announced the door's opening, nearly sending Brady sprawling into the room. Redd's disapproving gaze, heavy with unspoken words, settled on Brady. *She knows better than to eavesdrop on my conversations.*

"Brady, please make sure she has a comfortable room to rest in," Redd snorted. "She will stay with us for a while. She has some wounds that need tended to, so if you could have Alvero tend to them before the two of you head out, I would appreciate it."

"Alrighty," Brady murmured, a slight bob of her head barely disturbing the curtain of red curls that fell around her face. Her gaze remained glued to the floorboards. "Aguya said Alvero called and should be back within the hour."

Turning back to Nuit, his sharp eyes searched her bruised face—a canvas of purple and yellow where her rapid healing was at work. Crimson welled anew from the split lip she'd reopened, a glistening red streak down her chin mixed with the fading bruise. The coppery tang of her blood, earthy and metallic, mingled with her natural musk, a heady scent filling his nostrils. The tang ignited a ravenous hunger, a burning in his belly. He knew now where his next meal was waiting; he only needed to wait for the cloak of night to slip out and get it.

"Follow Brady," Redd stated. His hand, warm and strong, rose, thumb brushing delicately across her lip, a feather-light touch. He brought his thumb to his mouth, the sweet nectar—a lingering taste like cold water on a scorching day—filling his mouth. A low hum vibrated in the air as his eyes, dark and intense, locked with hers. "I just wanted a little taste."

"And what do you think?" she whispered. He could hear the hitch in her breath, the unsteady cadence of her heart.

Smirking, he nodded. "Rather delicious."

"Ignore him," Brady said, her voice sharp. Her fingers grasped Nuit's arm and pulled her away.

Crimson flushed Redd's face as he considered seizing Nuit, the cotton of her shirt a phantom touch in his mind. The urge to drag her away, a wildfire of forbidden desires burning within, almost overwhelmed him. Yet, a hesitant thought breezed through him, cool against his burning skin, and stayed his hand. *She needs time to heal. I don't want to hurt her more. The scent of her fresh wounds is still lingering around her.* He took a step back, increasing the space between them. His hands plunged into his pockets. A gnawing emptiness in his belly rumbled low, a deep growl. He needed to eat; he couldn't help anyone on an empty stomach. *Plus I need to prepare for nightfall. I need to feed before I do something I'll regret.*

The tang of blood, still thick in the air, stoked a ravenous hunger, burning in his gut. He needed an escape, the claustrophobia of the house pressing in on him, but could not leave with the fiery ball still high in the sky. His gaze swept the room, assessing his limited options. *Either I go up which puts me closer to her, I stay on this floor breathing in the scent of her that lingered in the air, or...*

His contemplation ended with a heavy sigh, the sound echoing in the stillness. He turned, his gaze falling on the worn oak floorboards before locating the hidden panel. With a push, it swung open, revealing the descending staircase. The cellar's musty air, thick with the smell of damp earth and mildew, clung to him like a shroud. He hoped its earthy aroma would mask the tang of blood as he slept. A low growl rumbled in his belly.

Fingers fumbling, he set his phone alarm for sunset, the digital glow a harsh contrast to the dim room. Sleep, however, was a restless phantom. Feverish dreams, punctuated by the gnawing pang of hunger, had him tossing and turning on the lumpy cot. The jarring alarm's shrill finally broke through; wide awake, he felt a frantic pulse in his temples, hunger and a burning rage coursing through him. Leaping from the bed, he thundered up the creaking stairs, bursting through the kitchen door.

"There you are," a soft voice said.

Turning, he glimpsed Nuit. The lavender bloom of her bruises was no longer visible across her skin. The coppery tang of blood, once so sharp, was gone, replaced by the clean scent of her usual perfume—a light, sweet floral.

"You look better," he whispered as his hands trembled. The rhythmic thump-thump-thump, a soft, steady drum, filled his ears; a comforting beat, warm and alive.

"Yes, Alvero used some stinky herbs to heal me." Nuit smiled self-deprecatingly up at him. Her dark eyes shone like a thousand distant stars. "So, when are we going to eat dinner? I should get on the road soon."

"I'm going out to get a bite to drink now," he shrugged. "So you go stay inside until I get back. When I get back, I will properly thank and pay you for your services."

"I probably—" she started.

"No," he growled. "You are going to stay put. You

will not leave this house, not even to walk around the gardens. Do you understand?"

His face flushed, a hot pressure building behind his eyes. A tremor ran through his hands, the knuckles bone-white as he clenched his fists, the last threads of his control fraying like worn rope.

"I don't think–"

"You want your money?" he stated, changing tactics.

"Well, ye... ye... yes," she sputtered.

"Then stay inside the house and don't leave," he said, the sharp words echoing in the quiet. "I will be back with your money." He walked away, the slam of the door a jarring sound against the quiet.

Fingers brushing against cool metal, he snatched his keys from the hook, the familiar weight comforting in his hand. He slid into the leather of his car seat, the engine roaring to life with a guttural growl. Speeding off, the GPS's monotonous voice filled the car, a stark contrast to the whoosh of wind and a blur of green and brown. His stomach growled, a hollow ache against the vibrating hum of the car as his foot pressed hard against the accelerator.

The car slammed into park with a jarring motion. He glanced up; the moon, a spectral disc in the inky sky, cast long, eerie shadows across the valley. He knew instantly–a chilling certainty–that feeding and returning home before dawn was impossible. But the thought held no sway; a burning, visceral thirst, a metallic tang in his mouth, consumed him.

A sharp rap echoed, once, against the aged wood. He waited, the silence heavy, broken. Then a faint, rhythmic thump—a heartbeat—drew closer as he heard footsteps approaching on the other side of the door.

"I will mur..." a male started, then stopped when he

saw Redd. "Who the—"

He clamped a hand around the male's throat, lifting him off his feet. The frantic thud of the male's heart drummed in his ears, a rhythm that quickened his own pulse and made his mouth water. He shoved the struggling male into the shadowy house. With each step, something crunched underfoot—it sounded like glass—the sound a stark counterpoint to the man's ragged gasps for air. Finally, he slammed the man against the wall.

"I was going to ask nicely if you had hurt Nuit." The words felt heavy in the air, thick with unspoken accusations. "But I can smell her blood—all over this place." He inhaled sharply, the sweet scent of blood stinging his nostrils, mingling with the gritty scent of dust and the sharp, acrid bite of stale alcohol.

A guttural gurgle, like water swirling down a drain, escaped the male's lips. He loosened his grip, curiosity etched on his face as he wondered what the male had to say. He inhaled deeply the musk of his blood filling his nostrils as the male's heart raced.

"Is the bitch dead, then?" the male gasped as the corner of his lips twisted up.

A red hazy rage flooded him as his fangs pierced the male's skin, the warm nectar of life filling his mouth, a thick, hot honey flowing down his throat. The urge to prolong the kill, to inflict torture, warred with the overwhelming hunger. The coppery scent of blood filled his nostrils, overwhelming all else. His hand went up, grabbing the male's hair and contorting his head back to maximize access to his meal. Suddenly, a sharp blow to his head sent a jolt of pain through him. Trickles of warm blood slid down his face, the sticky texture clinging to his skin. He stumbled back, shaking his head, his vision blurring. Then, sharply focused: the blood-soaked candlestick, a dark, wicked glint in the male's eyes. With a snarl, he fisted his hand while swinging back as he brought his fist square on the male's jaw, the solid impact echoing through his arm. The male staggered.

The male caught himself, a grunt escaping his lips as he lunged, connecting with Redd's stomach. Redd felt a jolt from the impact; the breath whooshing from his lungs as his shoulder slammed against the hard door. He slid down, the rough wood scraping against his arms, hitting the ground with a thud. Grabbing the male, Redd tried to twist him into a headlock, the struggle a flurry of blows and grunts. Finally, with a surge of adrenaline, Redd yanked the male up by the throat, the feel of his flesh rough and yielding under his grip. His hands slick with blood, he held on to the throat. They tumbled, the ground jarring against Redd's cheek, glass shards digging into his skin. Redd pressed his hand against the man's throat, the frantic scratching of nails on his skin a sharp, burning sensation. He smelled his own coppery blood mingling with the male's as those nails dug into his flesh. He held on, the man's heartbeat growing fainter under his hand until it finally stilled, signaling unconsciousness.

With a quick twist of his hand, the limp head turned, revealing flesh to his descending fangs. The tangy juice, a warm coppery a blend of red berries and plum, flooded his mouth and nostrils, a rich scent filling his lungs. A wave of satiation washed over him as the hunger subsided. His ears pricked, followed by the slow, fading rhythm of the heart until silence.

Once the veins ran dry, a final tug freed his fangs. He looked down; crimson coated his hands, slick and warm against his skin. The male lay still, a dark pool reflecting the harsh overhead light splattered around his head. Sticky crimson stained the floor, a gruesome pattern spreading outwards.

"Well, fuck," he said as he stood up. Nudging the body, he debated how he was going to clean this mess up. "I hate having to do chores."

He shuffled through the messy house, the scent of dust motes dancing in the dim light, searching for cleaning supplies—nothing. A chill from the single-paned window snaked up his arm as he gazed out. The low-hanging moon, a pale disc, cast long shadows across the frosted glass, its silvery light barely piercing the pre-dawn gloom as it descended on the horizon. *Time to switch gears, got to block out the sun so I can make it through the day.*

Searching now, he gathered blankets and sheets. Shutting each rooms' door, then he made makeshift curtain barriers to block out as much sun as he could. He slid down a wall at the end of the hallway, watching the pale sunlight inch across the floorboards, each ray inching closer to an end he was not ready for. He made a silent prayer for nightfall's embrace to come soon.

"At least I can die full," he muttered to himself while rubbing his stomach.

He fished his phone from his pocket. The screen's blankness stared back, a shattered spider web of cracks reflecting the dim light. A helpless sigh escaped as he realized its uselessness; no calls, no games to distract. A bitter chuckle rumbled in his chest as he flung the ruined device onto the dusty ground, the dull thud echoing the emptiness he felt.

"Nothing is going to go right, is it?" he sighed.

Chapter 19

Nuit paced, the rising sun painting the walls in hues of orange and gold, a stark contrast to the icy dread gripping her heart. Silence hung heavy, broken only by the rhythmic tap-tap-tap of her shoes against the polished floor. The scent of brewing coffee, usually comforting, did nothing to soothe her anxiety as she glanced out the kitchen window again. Each unanswered text message, each unanswered call—a sharp stab of fear. The smooth surface of her phone felt cold and slick against her clammy palm as the dread deepened with the rising sun, leaving her with a chilling certainty of where he might be.

Did Geb kill him? A nauseating wave of dizziness washed over her; the thought spun sickeningly in her mind, a relentless vortex. Inhaling deeply, the crisp, clean scent of pine cleaner barely cut through the churning anxiety. A tremor ran through her, a physical manifestation of her decision. She knew what she had to do.

Fingers brushing cold metal, she snatched her car keys. The heavy silence of the house pressed in as she walked out, a chilling quiet broken only by the squeak of the door. The engine roared to life, a fierce counterpoint to the stillness she left behind. The speedometer needle climbed, each mile a frantic heartbeat against the growing dread, a knot tightening in her stomach with every passing mile. *If Geb killed him, it was my fault. He was defending me. Instead of fighting, I let him leave. I knew there was a chance he was heading to Geb's, but I did nothing to stop it. I just sat there like the coward I am.*

Pulling into the drive, the harsh glare of sunlight on Redd's car met her eyes, a searing wave of fear washing over her as she braked behind it. A cold knot tightened in her stomach as she stepped out, each footfall heavy with dread, a rising tide of panic threatening to drown her. The air hung thick and still, each nerve screaming as she approached the house. A suffocating silence pressed down, hot tears stinging her eyes, a dreadful confirmation of her worst fears. Her fingers trembled as she touched the cool metal of the doorknob. With a hesitant push, the door creaked inward; the silence amplifying her anticipation for Geb's angry shouts.

"Don't open that door too wide, a mhuirnín," a husky voice stated.

A startled gasp escaped her lips, a jump preceding the recognition of the voice—Redd. Relief washed over her as she cautiously peeked her head into the house, dust motes dancing in the sunbeams that barely touched Redd's shadowed form at the far end of the hallway. The door opened a crack, admitting her into the dimness and closed it behind her to block the sunlight. There, on the cold wooden floor, lay Geb. His usually honey-toned skin was alarmingly pale, a chilling confirmation of death, the stark sight of dried blood surrounding him a grim testament to the fight that had ensued.

"He'll never hurt you again," Redd whispered.

Her eyes darted to him, a flicker of disbelief in their depths. This wasn't the expected scene; she'd envisioned her own demise at Geb's hands, not this gruesome tableau of Geb dying at the fangs of a vampire. She had hid from Geb's wrath for eons, dreading the day he would find her. At some point, she stopped trying to hide from him and just lived her life in the shadows. The chill of fear had been a familiar companion for a million nights. The expected finality, the chilling certainty of death at his hands, had been a constant companion. Now, that fear lay shattered, as lifeless as Geb, as cold as her ex-husband's corpse, and she did not know how to feel or react.

With silent steps, she approached Redd, her eyes dark pools in the dim light, searching the shadowed contours of his face. The stillness in her heart was a counterpoint to the nervous tightening in her chest.

"Are you upset with me for not listening again? Or maybe I am not civilized enough for you? I mean, I left quite the mess over there."

"Why did you not call?" she yelled, her voice raw. A storm of emotions, hidden moments ago, now raged through her. A tempest of feelings, hot and prickly, was a roaring in her ears, and a bitter taste in her mouth.

"My phone died," he shrugged.

Tears blurred her vision, hot and salty on her skin, as she gazed at him. A choked sob escaped her lips, the sound swallowed by the lump in her throat. The rough fabric of her sleeve felt scratchy against her damp cheeks as she wiped away the evidence of her tears. "I thought you got hurt."

"You think some lush could take me down?" Laughing sardonically, he shook his head. "I've dealt with egotistical fools like that for eons. I've fought worse. But your opinion that I am so weak hurts my feelings."

Hot tears streamed down her cheeks as her eyes, wide and frantic, darted across his blood-matted face. *That's probably Geb's blood.* Her eyes scanned his skin, the pale streams of light catching the smooth surface, revealing no wounds in his flesh.

"Why didn't you come back to the house?" she whispered as her hands clutched each other. All the worries and fears, falling along with the tears.

"Have you been outside today?" he laughed.

"Of course," she hesitated.

"Then maybe you forgot that there's this fiery ball out there, a blinding menace, threatening to incinerate me at any moment." His finger stabbed at the edge of the soft, golden light, the warmth of which enveloped her as she stood in it.

"Oh, yeah," she muttered.

Her gaze fell to the ground, the small, sharp shadow a stark contrast to the sunlight streaming in. The memory of protection, of safety, felt distant, a forgotten warmth she had not felt in eons since she could not remember the last time someone had defended her so fiercely. A cold knot tightened in her stomach as unsettling thoughts swirled, her brow furrowing, a physical manifestation of her inner turmoil. *Why would he even do this for me? He risked his life for someone he barely knows. Someone he hired to find a book only.*

"Can you do me a favor?" Redd sighed.

Startled that he had dragged her from her reverie, she looked at him. "Yes."

"Could you slide a little closer and out of the light?"

Unsure, she nodded, the sun's warmth fading as she stepped into the shadows, a cool blanket replacing the heat on her skin. Kneeling, she felt the wood beneath her knees as his hand, cool and surprisingly strong, encircled her neck. A gasp escaped her lips; his touch sent a shiver down her spine, a strange warmth blooming in her chest. She didn't resist as he pulled her close, the fall onto his lap jarring but strangely comfortable. His lips found hers, metallic and strangely alluring, a taste of blood lingering.

His tongue invaded, sparking a storm within her, a raw, unfamiliar energy that consumed her completely. She surrendered, melting into him.

His tongue left her mouth as his fangs sank into her lip stopping before he drew blood. His mouth worked its way down, nibbling on her neck. His elongated fangs dragged across the delicate flesh sending shivers down her spine. His mouth came to her décolletage, his fangs sank into the delicate flesh. Where she thought she would feel pain was just pleasure. Her head spun as his mouth moved further down. He sucked her puckered nipple in the coarse fabric caught between his exploring mouth and her responsive flesh. She inhaled as her breath caught in her throat. Her nails dug into the flesh of his shoulders as the storm grew. One hand slid up guiding her shirt up as it moved. The coolness of his fingers against her flushed skin seemed to ignite the storm brewing inside her. His mouth left her sensitive nipple as he shoved her shirt overhead. His nose nuzzled her bare nipple while it reacted to the tender touch. Then he moved to the other breast, sucking her nipple in. Her back arched trying to get closer to his touch, his body.

His fingers, rough yet gentle, dug into her skin. The storm within her—a tempest of unfamiliar emotions—rolled through her, building in tempo. His calloused hands gripped her hips, lifting her up till she was standing. Her mouth opened in protest, a silent gasp, then stilled as she felt his warm breath ghosting against her stomach. All resistance melted away. His fangs, cool and sharp, grazed her skin, a thrilling pressure before the bite, a slow scrape. His firm hands tugged at her waistband, the zipper resisting for a second, then yielding with a sharp metallic zzzt. He paused as his thumb gently traced the red mark left over from the stabbing.

"It's so much worse than I thought, a mhuirnín," he whispered. His breath felt like a butterfly's wings fluttering across her skin.

He placed a soft kiss on the mark before he lifted her higher. His teeth, cool against her skin, nipped at her panties, dragging them down with a silken whisper. Looking down at the vibrant red hair, she could not resist running her fingers through the silky strands, the texture a warm caress against her fingertips. His nose nuzzled her sensitive clit; her breath hitched, a gasp escaping her lips as her fingers tightened in his hair, the strands thick and soft beneath her touch. She felt the heat bloom low in her belly, a tempest spreading throughout her core. His mouth, warm and wet, found its target, his fangs a tantalizing scrape against her clit as he rhythmically sucked and released it. Her head fell back, the rush of pleasure threatening to drown her senses.

His fingers sunk into the yielding warmth of her ass as he held her perfectly still. The rasp of his tongue and the prickle of his fangs danced on her clit, a deluge that stole her breath. Her legs, weak as water, trembled, failing to support her weight as she leaned heavily into his hands, the pressure grounding her. Her fingers tangled in his thick hair, anchoring her as an overwhelming hurricane crashed over her. She felt the phantom rumble of thunder, the electric crackle of lightning mirroring the tempest within, as he seemed to draw the very essence of her being from her core.

"God, you smell like a wet dream," he whispered as he pulled away for a moment. Her eyes locked with his as she watched his tongue flick across her bundle of nerves.

He pressed his mouth back into her core, his tongue flicking against her clit, a hot, wet sensation. He sucked her clit into his mouth, a rhythmic pull and release. Her eyes fluttered shut, her head falling back, damp hair clinging to her neck. The storm within her built a swirling vortex of pleasure with each suck and lick; a low groan escaped her lips. She shook her head, the scent of her own arousal sharp in the air. Suddenly aware of the unleashed power, a jolt of surprise shot through her as the storm raged around her, a storm in the house that she had called without thinking because she was so lost in the emotions spiraling through her. Then, another suck, obliterating thought, leaving only sensation. Her fingers slide down, digging into his tense shoulders, feeling the corded muscles beneath. The wind howled around them, mirroring the tempest within, crackling with invisible magic flowing from her. A flash of lightning illuminated the room as she climaxed, a shuddering release that left her trembling. She collapsed onto his lap, spent but exhilarated.

"That's a first," he whispered as he kissed her.

She tasted herself mixed in with the taste of blood as his tongue swirled in her mouth.

"Huh?" she murmured. The meaning of his words were not able to penetrate the haze of afterglow washing through her.

"The storm."

Laughing, she nuzzled his nose with hers. She could smell the moisture lingering from the rain. Both of them were damp. Her fingers traced the line of his cheek as she spoke. "Sorry."

"Don't apologize."

His fingers tightened on her ass, rocking her rhythmically against the firm pressure of his arousal. The rough texture of his jeans scraped against her sensitive skin, a friction that ignited a familiar tempest. A wave of desire, she thought subdued, crashed over her with each movement. Her fingers, guided by instinct, found the metal snap and zipper of his jeans, the cool metal a stark contrast to the rising heat between them. He lifted her briefly, a fleeting moment of weightlessness before the inevitable descent. She sank back down, the smooth skin of her inner thighs gliding against the rigid length of his cock, a friction that sent shivers down her spine.

"I knew you wanted me," he whispered.

Her mind screamed defiance, but her body, a traitorous accomplice, showed with him how much she wanted him. A silent nod was her only response. His hands lifted her, then plunged her down. The searing heat of his entry stole her breath; a gasp escaped as he filled her completely. She bucked, a whirlwind of sensation spiraling within. His thumb, a fiery probe, found her most sensitive point, a moan escaping her lips like a whispered prayer. His hands accelerated the rhythm, his thumb a relentless storm-chaser, igniting a hurricane within her. Each thrust felt like lightning, the roar of thunder echoing the tempest raging inside. Lightning exploded and thunder roared around them as the storm's intensity matched the one brewing inside her.

With a swift, twisting motion, he lifted her, slamming her back against the rough-textured wall as her legs instinctively wrapped around his waist. His frenzied thrusts pounded against her, a jarring rhythm. His hand, calloused yet gentle, cupped her chin, tilting her head back, exposing the delicate pulse in her neck. The sharp bite of his fangs sent a jolt of pain, quickly overtaken by a wave of intoxicating heat. A euphoric rush, like a hurricane, swept through her, mingling with the raw, physical sensations. Her fingers, trembling, dug into his back. The searing heat of his fangs left her skin as his forehead rested against hers, his breath warm on her face. She felt the sticky warmth of her blood welling from the wound, the coppery tang sharp in the air. Their eyes locked—his amber gaze intense and captivating. With each powerful thrust, she felt a deeper connection, a primal pull. A final, earth-shattering thrust consumed her, breath catching in her throat. The trembling of his release vibrated through her as her body went limp, her limbs heavy. Their ragged breaths mingled, a symphony of spent passion, the air thick with the scent of arousal and blood.

Chapter 20

Nuit sat nestled against Redd, his arm a warm weight around her shoulder as her head rested on his chest. She felt the steady rhythm of his heartbeat beneath her ear, a muted drum against the quiet hum of the house.

"Did I hurt you, a mhuirnín?" he whispered.

"No."

"I meant when I bit you."

Laughing, she replied, "The answer stays the same, no."

Thoughts flooded back, causing her to sigh. "Do you think it's a little…" she hesitated, trying to find the words to express the thoughts she was nervous to say. "A little weird that we're in my ex's house while he's…" Her voice trailed off.

"Oh, I forgot about him." He shrugged dismissively.

She shook her head, a dizzying whirl of dark hair as the absurdity of the situation crashed over her.

Golden light faded, painting the wall in fiery hues as they nestled in the deepening shadows. The whisper of a breeze that swirled around the house mingled with his low voice, recounting absurd family tales. She gently questioned him about his family's present and past. He seemed so open, but she knew there were some things he held back.

"So, what do you need the grimoire for?" she said as she realized she had never asked him what it was for. *Is there a spell in there he needs?* She wondered.

His muscles tightened beneath her, a ripple under his skin. He swallowed, a dry rasp in his throat, before the words, "Long story," escaped, tight and strained.

A ripple of laughter, bright as sunlight, escaped her lips. She pulled back, a question forming in her eyes before she spoke the words. "Is there a spell you need translated?"

He paused, his gaze a slow burn, meticulously scanning her face before gently pressing her head against his shoulder. The steady thump-thump-thump of his heart resonated against her, a calming rhythm against the frantic flutter of her own. His breath, warm and even on the top of her head, stirred the strands of her hair.

"I guess," he shrugged as her head bobbed with the motion.

Her brow furrowed, a tiny wrinkle etched above her worried eyes. A subtle tension vibrated in the air, a silent hum accompanying the sudden shift in his demeanor. A prickling unease settled on her skin. *Have I done something wrong? Is he already ready to be done with me? Am I expecting too much from him when, for all I know, this is a meaningless fling for him?* A wave of self-doubt, cold and clammy, washed over her. She struggled to find the right words, the right key to unlock his silence.

"I can help you if you want something translated from the book," she whispered. Hope, bright as a newly minted coin, resonated in her voice as her hand, cool and slightly trembling, circled his chest. His shirt, still clinging damply to his skin; the recent deluge her magic had created had washed away the caked blood, leaving only a faint, rose-tinged stain against the white fabric.

"Hmm," he hummed as his hand started stroking her arm. "So, you can go through the book and tell me what the spells are?"

"Yes, I can do that."

"Alright," he said, his hand warming her up as he continued to stroke. "I would greatly appreciate it if you tell me what spells are in the book."

He kissed her forehead as she snuggled deeper into the comforting circle of his arms. Her eyes, half-lidded, traced the sunlit dust motes dancing across the wooden floor, their slow drift mirroring the agonizing crawl of time as the sunlight slowly receded. Relief washed over her—soon, blessedly soon, they would leave this place. The cloying stench of decay, sharp and metallic, prickled her nostrils, a wave of nausea rising in her throat. She'd offered to help with... *it*, but he'd refused, his voice low and curt, promising to take care of it later.

REDD

Chapter 21

Redd's tires crunched on the gravel, his car pulling up beside Nuit's under the silvery gaze of the moon. The lingering scent of damp earth clung to him from the shallow grave he dug earlier. The ache in his muscles—a dull, throbbing reminder of the surprisingly strenuous task. A quick text to Aguya and Leo, arranging for the cleanup, brought a wave of self-disgust. Aguya's fiery magic would consume the evidence, a controlled burn, but the guilt gnawed; he hadn't been this messy since his fledgling days. The thought of them cleaning up his mess irritated him intensely.

The car door slammed as he jumped out, a sharp metallic clang in the crisp evening air. He strode ahead; the gravel crunching under his boots, Nuit trailing close, her small hand sliding into his. The contact sent a jolt of warmth through him, a stark contrast to the icy dread gnawing at his gut. His mind wondered if he should have let her into his life. His life, a chaotic mess, felt like a swamp he was sinking deeper and deeper into. He wished he could tell her he regretted what had happened at the house and send her somewhere safe, a lie, a gentle push towards safety, but the words caught in his throat. Gazing down at her flawless honey-colored skin, smooth as polished amber under the dim light, any trace of regret vanished.

His ears pricked, a faint, unfamiliar thump-thump-thump cutting through the quiet hum of the house. Someone was in the kitchen with Alvero. The rhythm resonated oddly, a ghost of a memory, yet elusive, a whisper on the edge of recognition that he could not place where he had heard it before.

"Stay behind me," he whispered as he approached the kitchen door.

"Wha–" she whispered.

His hand silenced her any further words. The steady thump of Alvero's heart reassured him there was no immediate danger. But a prickling unease on his skin still lingered. He locked eyes with her, the urgency silent in the shared gaze, a silent command to follow. A brief, delicate nod was her answer.

Turning, he walked towards the kitchen, the warm earthy scent of chamomile tea brewing hitting him. Crouching low, he peered through the kitchen window. He saw Alvero, his voice a low murmur, talking to someone obscured just out of his line of sight.

Alvero sipped the steaming cup of tea. In his other hand, the small, locked wooden box was being shaken as he made an exaggerated gesture. An intricate carving of the tree of life on the lid-the fae queen's crest-shimmered in the light. Years ago, Alvero had been called to the fae court to heal the old fae queen. When he got there, she had already passed on. The old queen's maid made Alvero swear secrecy when she gave him the box. When he got back home, because of the loss of his wife and child, he had packed the box away. The attempt to trade it for Feya's freedom had failed. The queen's fury made Feya's release from the Celestial Contract seem even more impossible. But they knew she did not want anyone to get a hold of that box or its contents.

Twisting his head, he sought a clearer view. Then, a figure stepped into sight. Wallace, opposite Alvero, maybe 5'8", his brown eyes glittering with barely contained fury. The man ran his smoothly tanned mahogany hands across his impeccable gray uniform. The badges of his years of service adorning the breast of his uniform. His black hair was slicked back and subtly gleaming. His perfectly positioned gray beret, adorned with the queen's crest, completed the image.

A long sigh escaped his lips, a puff of air in the still night air. He pushed himself up, then shoved the kitchen door wide. His gaze, sharp and cold, landed on Wallace.

"What's he want?" Redd grumbled, nodding his chin at Wallace as he turned to Alvero. "I didn't invite him into *my* home."

Nuit came up behind him, smiling at Alvero. "Hello, Alvero."

"Hey, Nuit," Alvero sighed, taking another sip of tea. "Redd, can you just relax for once? I invited him in."

"I am relaxed," Redd shrugged. "Again, what's he want?"

"He came because of the box," Alvero smirked cockily at Redd. "And you are the least patient person I know."

"Wait... What?" Redd said as he looked from one male to the other. "We said we were not giving him the box."

"Yes, we did," Alvero shrugged. "But we have figured out the mystery of the box."

"You said opening the box would trigger a spell that destroys its contents." Redd's brow furrowed, a sharp line etched above his narrowed eyes. He crossed his arms across his chest.

"Unless you opened it properly. I learned how while talking with an old friend. It was a puzzle!" Alvero said, excitement tinging his voice.

"So, did you open it?" Redd asked as he arched an eyebrow.

Alvero glared at Redd as he frowned. "Of course I did. It took us a while to solve it, but after several tries, we figured out the correct pattern. We shifted the tree branches to the proper position and viola, it opened."

"Are you going to tell me what's in it and why he has to be here to see it?" Redd jerked his head towards Wallace. Nuit pinched his side. He closed his eyes, knowing the silent message she was sending. *I already know I'm being uncouth, but I don't care and don't need to be told.*

"I can–" Wallace started.

"He is on our side," Alvero interrupted.

"How do you know for sure?" Redd said, his eyes shifting to Wallace. He studied the deep pools of Wallace's dark brown eyes, the rich chocolate swirling with unspoken depths, trying to discern friend from foe. If Alvero's conflicted feelings for his old war buddy were blocking Alvero from seeing the truth, or if Wallace would actually be of assistance. His eyes darted up and down Wallace's impeccable uniform before turning back to Alvero. "She could have sent him to spy on us."

"Redd," Alvero sighed. "He has been aiding the person who started the revolution to take the queen down after they found out the queen was trying to kill her husband. When–"

"You mean the husband that's dead already?" Redd snorted.

"Yes that one," Alvero said as he rubbed his brow. "So, as I was saying, before someone rudely interrupted me, when he found out about her plans, he tried to stop it, but it was too late. He is working with Eero, the nephew of Liyla, the first queen and the owner of the contents of this box. He has never given up on proving queen Casada had killed his aunt. They have been trying to piece together a trail of political murders. When–"

"You're over explaining it," Redd snorted. "So, the king's mistress murdered Liyla. Her nephew is trying to prove it. I got it, check. When do we get to the part where we free Feya?"

"Well, what's in this box proves Casada killed the old queen. I was–" Alvero started.

"This time I negotiate to free Feya with the box, then," Redd stated. "Problem sol–"

"No!" Wallace screamed. "Do you not understand what this could mean to our people?"

"Not my people!" Redd yelled back, slamming his fist onto the counter. "My people are in this house and one of them is constantly under threat by your people's problem."

"You think I am going to let you take something that can save hundreds of lives to save one?" Wallace yelled, spittle flying from his mouth.

Laughing, Redd said, "What you think doesn't matter, because that box won't be leaving this house with you. Even if it means I act like a piggy and have a second meal today." A low growl vibrated in his chest, and the rasp of his tongue against his fangs showed how sharp they were. A fierce glint in his eyes made his intent undeniably clear.

"Redd," Nuit gasped.

"Don't tell me to sacrifice any of my family," he growled at her.

She recoiled, her startled eyes wide and bright as a deer's, reflecting the angry expression on his face. A sharp intake of breath, a hiss of controlled frustration while he fought the urge to lash out again. He hadn't meant to snap.

"I..." he began, his gaze locked on hers, the words catching in his throat. The darkness in her eyes, deep pools reflecting a shadowed past, was haunting. He knew the brutal truth of her recent beating, yet here he was, his voice harsh when he talked to her, out of habit.

"I understand," she whispered, but as he looked into her eyes, he knew she did not mean it.

Turning back to Wallace and Alvero, he shoved thoughts of Nuit aside, a bitter taste on his tongue, knowing he would have to deal with thoughts of her later. His brow furrowed in a deep line, eyes blazing. A low hum of frustration vibrated from him as his mind raced, searching for the words to bridge the chasm of their misunderstanding about how this was going to play out. *I will not sacrifice my daughter for this fucking war.*

"Alvero," Redd stated as he stared one of his oldest friends in the eyes. "It's Feya." In his eyes and those two words he spoke, he tried to convey the profound significance of those two words.

"I know," he sighed. "I will not let anything happen to her. We need to find a way to save her and stop this war at the same time. I think if we can work together, we can find a solution. We just need to put our heads together, and then we can work this out."

"I wouldn't say that we—" Wallace started.

"As long as we know," Redd interrupted, glaring at Wallace. "Feya being released from the contract is first and foremost. I am telling you, I will not let that queen continue to use her as a weapon in this war."

"We will work on that," Wallace said, the words sharp and cold as ice, his voice a frigid whisper that mirrored the glacial stare in his eyes.

Redd glared, the fiery red of his anger a stark contrast to the icy blue glinting in Wallace's brown eyes. The chill of Wallace's ice magic was a tangible weight pressing on Redd's skin as goosebumps traveled across his arms. *I know Alvero trusts him, but I don't. He is the general of the fae queen's army. What are the odds he is here to spy on us? Probably, high.*

"Just curious." Redd smirked coolly at Wallace. "Why did you recruit Olette? Pretty stupid choice, if I say so myself. She was not the smartest of creatures."

Wallace sneered, his lip trembling. "I did not *recruit* her. That idiot Eleazer thought she would be a good choice. All the two of them did was expose our plans earlier than we were ready to. They are now trying to hunt us down, which means we have to be extra careful."

"Why would he bring that shit show into this?" Redd queried, shaking his head.

"He thought she would be some great asset or something," Wallace huffed. "I think he wanted in her pants and she was able to convince him to spill secrets to help hide her true intentions."

"Did you let her out of jail?" Redd glanced at Alvero, trying to read his thoughts. Alvero had that squinty mulling over things expression on his face, highlighting the deep lines etched around his narrowed eyes as he considered the situation.

"Yes," Wallace whispered. He paused before his voice became more steady, more sure. "I was hoping to give the queen a distraction. While also keeping Olette from being interrogated and giving away all the information that Eleazer had given her."

Redd's eyes sized up Wallace, looking for any sign-a nervous tremor in Wallace's voice or a shift in his weight-that he's telling the truth or a lie. *His heart rate leads me to believe it was the truth, but Wallace seems like a prickly son of a bitch which means that his heart beat can be deceiving.*

"Were you the one who killed Olette?" Redd asked, his thoughts swirling as they collided. *All the pieces are starting to fit. Boy, Cass will be mad if he knows I found out the truth already.*

REDD

Chapter 22

Redd's burning eyes, like embers, never left Wallace, whose gaze dropped to the floor. A heavy silence, thick with unspoken words, hung in the air, punctuated only by the hum of the fridge. The confirmation Redd sought was there in the quiet that filled the air. Now he could finally tell Elwyn the chilling truth about the assassin of his mother.

Feya slipped into the kitchen, her gaze darting around the brightly lit room. She must have felt the tension in the air. Her voice tentatively said, "What is going on here?"

"Alvero opened the box, and it proves Casada murdered the old queen," Redd sighed, running a hand through his hair. "So, we were trying to figure out how we could use the box to free you. The fae realm can be damned for all I care."

"No," Wallace growled, his brown eyes turning glacial blue, his breath puffing out in a frosty white cloud. The air crackled with his ice magic, a tangible tingle on his skin as the temperature dropped.

Crimson surged in Redd's face as a simmering rage threatened to boil over. Nuit's fingers grasped his forearm, a tentative warning that he shrugged away.

"We can stop the war if we use it properly and let the people know what she has done, you baboon," Wallace stated as he crossed his hands, clenched and unclenched. "We need to think about—"

"Get the fuck out of my house," Redd said as he raised his voice.

Redd's breath plumed out, a frosty white cloud in the frigid air that surrounded him suddenly. A bone-chilling cold, the scent of ozone sharp in the nostrils, enveloped them as Wallace's power surged. Redd's nostrils flared, a searing heat igniting in his belly; a bitter taste of fury coated his tongue. He stepped forward, amber eyes blazing like hot coals.

"Father!" Feya yelled, throwing her hands in the air. "If it stops a war, then it is worth—"

"Do you not understand what that means?" Redd slammed his fist on the counter, the impact echoing sharply. His knuckles stung from the impact.

"Fewer deaths," Feya sighed, "that's what it means. It means less people will get hurt. It means—"

"No, it doesn't mean any of that," Redd stated. "She will not go down without a fight. Do you really think the queen won't use you to fight against us? I, for one, will not stand on the other side of a battlefield from my daughter. Everyone else be damned. I'll ensure your freedom first, before anything else."

"I..." Feya whispered, her gaze drifting away, a soft sigh brushing past her lips. The silence hummed as the room grew silent.

Nuit's fingers brushed his back in a circular motion, a gentle touch meant to soothe the simmering rage within him. It did little to quell the inferno in his chest; his temper, a stubborn ember, refused to be quenched. He heard the murmur of Alvero and Wallace, their voices smooth, reasonable, prioritizing some distant, abstract "greater good" over the tangible weight of his family. A bitter taste rose in his mouth. His family—his blood and his chosen—came first.

"Nuit, you don't need to comfort that old fool," Alvero snorted as he rubbed his temples. "He's stubborn and won't listen to reason, no matter how much you try to calm him down."

Redd glared at Alvero, before speaking, "I don't appreciate you telling her what to do and remember whose house you are in."

Alvero opened his mouth to speak. Nuit's hand rose to halt him, a gesture as swift and quiet as a falling feather.

"I don't need either of you males to defend me," Nuit stated, rolling her eyes.

Redd's body shifted, a subtle twist as his arm encircled Nuit's waist; his calloused hands gripping her hip. A slow smirk stretched his lips as he glanced at Alvero. Then, a soft brush of lips against Nuit's hair, his gaze unwavering, locked on Alvero's.

"Don't be an ass," Alvero snorted. "I would never sacrifice Feya. I just think we need to find a way to help more than just ourselves. If we take the time to think about this logically, we an—"

"You think your mate, Aguya, would agree with you?" Redd asked. He knew it was a low blow; the darkening of Alvero's eyes, a sudden storm cloud in their depths, was testament to that. A muscle in Alvero's jaw clenched, the sound barely audible, yet sharp as shattered glass.

"She is not a part of this discussion." Wallace said. He cracked his neck, the cool mask settling back into place. A wave of chill, like icy breath on his skin, receded as the air warmed back up.

Redd's ears pricked up, a sharp sound against the hushed air, as he heard Wallace's erratic heartbeat—a frantic drum against his ribs. He inhaled deeply, the coppery tang of Wallace's blood filling his nostrils, a mix of sweet strawberries, jasmine, and ripe plums. A wave of heat flushed his cheeks as his mind raced, trying to decipher the secrets the male was hiding.

Maybe if I play along, I can suss out his true intentions. Is he actually a friend or a foe? Or is this self-serving so he can take the throne?

"Let's see what's in that box," Redd purred, a slow smile stretching his lips—a predatory grin like a cat about to pounce on a mouse.

REDD

Chapter 23

Redd's smile widened as Alvero let out a long, weary sigh, the sound like rustling leaves, before gently placing the worn wooden box on the marble counter. Alvero's fingers, tracing the carvings; each deliberate movement, a story Redd drank in, committing it to memory.

Once the box sprang open, the scent of aged velvet filled the air. Nestled within the plush crimson lining, he saw it: a small hand mirror, its gold frame gleaming, tiny pearls catching the light. The mirror's surface was hazy, obscuring any reflection.

Redd watched, mesmerized, as Alvero's breath fogged the mirror, a cloud against the hazy surface. Alvero muttered words in an unfamiliar tongue, vibrating in the air. The mirror swirled, a dizzying vortex of shifting colors, before resolving into the face of a blonde woman. Her hazel eyes, wide and innocent, peered out from a cherubic face framed by silken hair. A soft, lilting voice, like wind chimes in a summer breeze, startled Redd from his reverie.

"Come in," she said.

In the small mirror, he saw a door open, its hinges groaning softly. Casada entered, her footsteps barely audible on the marble floors. The blonde woman's face tightened, a subtle shift visible in the harsh light. Casada's dark eyes, large and expressive in her delicate face, demurely closed. Perfectly sculpted dark brown curls, that framed her pale skin, bounced as she walked towards the blonde woman.

"My queen," Casada breathed, the silken rustle of her gown a counterpoint to the delicate clinking of the teacup as she settled it on the polished table before the blonde woman. Redd saw then the etched lines of annoyance around the eyes of what he assumed must be the old fae queen, Liyla.

"Thank you, Casada," Liyla said, her lips turning down at the corners ever so slightly.

Liyla lifted the porcelain cup to her lips. A sip caused her face to wrinkle at the unexpected bitterness. The cup clattered to the table as Casada's fingers stroked Liyla's hair.

"Why is it so... bitter?" Liyla murmured, a barely audible breath. Her hand, slightly trembling, flew to her lips, covering a coughing fit.

"I know you found out about my affair with Buer," Casada said, laughing. "It was only a matter of time. I knew he would not leave you, but if you leave him..."

"What..." Liyla gasped, a rattling cough seizing her again.

"Are you wanting to know what I did to you?" Casada laughed, brushing hair behind Liyla's ear. "Oh, sweet Liyla. I think it's time for a new queen. Buer is rather infatuated with me. I think he might just ask me to marry him. What do you think?"

"I..." Liyla coughed. "I will make..." A harsh, rattling cough ripped through the air, the sound thick and wet, punctuated by a pained gasp. "I..." Liyla gasped, her body hitting the floor with a thud.

A tinkling giggle escaped Casada's lips as she looked down at Liyla. Casada's silk gown rustled softly as she bent over Liyla. "Soon, I will be queen." She moved to the ornately carved table, the polished wood gleaming. Opening up a jewelry box, as her fingers, adorned with glittering rings, sifted through its contents. Picking up a ruby ring, she chirped, "Oh, this is pretty." She put the ring on her finger as she admired it. "Thank you for the gift."

Casada, a smile playing on her lips, lifted the cup. With a decisive clink, she emptied its contents into the ornate garderobe. Returning the now cooled cup, she set it beside Liyla. Liyla gasped, a ragged sound, her fingers clawing at her throat. Her eyes, once bright, now dulled and glassy, glazing over with a disturbing stillness.

Casada, leaning low over Liyla, offered one last, cruel smirk before her face crumpled, a few hot tears escaping. A deep, shuddering breath preceded a scream that ripped through the air.

The vision vanished as a milky film clouded the mirror's surface. A heavy silence hung in the air, as everyone absorbed the unsettling visions reflected there.

"What was that?" Redd asked, frowning.

"It was a memory of–" Alvero started.

"That much I got," Redd huffed. "I mean, what is the mirror? How did it record..." He pointed at the mirror's foggy surface. "That."

Nodding, Alvero spoke, "This is a mirror of Vulcan. It can capture memories. So, it seems queen Liyla knew Casada was up to something and wanted to record it. Though I doubt she knew it was going to be her own death. This probably happened a few days before I got there. It was a slow acting poison. I found no trace of the poison when I arrived, so I don't know what she used. There are a few options that have these kinds of effects. From what we saw, I'd say Casada intentionally tortured

Queen Liyla."

Redd nodded, his gaze sweeping the room, a silent debate raging in his eyes. *How do I get it away from Alvero before he hands it over to Wallace? Maybe I should ask Aguya for help.*

"Now you see why we need to let our people know about this?" Wallace asked, turning to Redd.

Redd glared at Wallace. *Does he think this would really change my mind?* He wrestled with his words, the taste of bitter unshed anger thick on his tongue. His knuckles, bone-white, clenched into fists. Should he smooth things over, or let the truth, sharp and cold as a winter wind, slice through the quiet? "Do you think she won't go to war over this? That she won't make Feya fight for her? If so, then you are a bigger fool than I thought you were."

Wallace's mouth gaped, a silent O, but Alvero's hand shot up, a quick, arresting motion. "Aethelredd, do you really think that I," Alvero said, pointing at his chest. "Would sacrifice her? We will find a way to set her free and help the fae. We just need you onboard so we all can come up with a plan."

"From what I am hearing, your little friend there will sacrifice Feya at the first opportunity," Redd said, his finger jabbing towards Wallace. "So, maybe you should quit lecturing me and have a discussion with him."

Alvero squeezed his eyes shut, his fingers pressing into the bridge of his nose. A barely audible sigh escaped his lips. Redd felt a prickle of unease.

"Maybe we should talk when we've calmed down," Alvero muttered.

"Or we go with my plan," Redd smirked, the corners of his mouth twitching as he crossed his arms.

"I'm scared to ask," Alvero muttered, looking up at

the ceiling.

"Let's hear him out," Wallace sighed while his brow furrowed. "Maybe he'll surprise us."

"I take the box." Redd smiled, his eyes crinkling at the corners as he gestured towards the box. "Negotiate for Feya's freedom. Once she's free I feast on the queen's blood. She's dead. Kumbaya bitch. Problem solved."

"Is he stupid enough to think it would be that easy?" Wallace asked while looking at Alvero.

"Yep," Alvero said as he picked up the box. "Let's all go get some rest. Maybe after a good night's sleep we can come together and come up with an actual plan."

"Don't ever call me stupid again," Redd growled, his voice a low rumble that vibrated through the room, "or it'll be your neck on my plate." He gripped Nuit's hand, dragging her out of the kitchen.

He saw Brady, a shadowy figure in the corner, eavesdropping intently; the subtle creak of her shoes on the wood floor betraying her hiding spot. He glared at her, a deep frown etching itself into his brow—his only sign of frustration before the quiet thud of his footsteps echoed on the stairs.

"I'll show you to your room," Redd stated.

"She knows where her room is," Brady laughed, shaking her head. "I showed it to her yesterday."

"Well," Redd sighed. "I'll have to show her to her new room then. Go to bed Brady and butt out of everyone's business."

Leading the way down the long, dimly lit hallway, the carpet runner muffling their footsteps, he walked to his bedroom. The heavy oak door creaked open. He gazed upon the room, its shadowed corners not having seen sunlight in centuries. Long ago, he'd sealed the window, leaving only the soft, yellowish glow of the lamps on the bedside table to illuminate the space. After the searing pain he'd once endured by the morning sun, he wanted to make sure he never made that mistake again.

He dumped his pocket's contents into a copper bowl atop the rich, dark mahogany dresser. The room smelled faintly of beeswax and old wood; greys and deep browns dominated a somber palette. The four-poster bed, its mahogany spindles swirling like carved smoke, stood imposingly draped in heavy, dark grey curtains. A cool, grey duvet lay upon the bed. A subtle grey-on-grey floral pattern papered the walls.

"This will be your room while you stay here," he stated as he pulled his shirt off and threw it towards the laundry basket.

"Alright," she whispered. Walking over, she picked the shirt up and put it in the basket.

"I know I snapped at you earlier, but I'd never hurt you," he said, watching her every move. Apologies weren't his forte; a clammy sweat slicked his palms as he felt utterly adrift, like a silver fish gasping on sunbaked sand.

Chapter 24

Nuit watched, mesmerized, as Redd shed his clothes, each layer revealing corded muscles that sent shivers—a delicious flutter—through her stomach. The husky timbre of his earlier words still resonated in her ears. "I know," she whispered.

"Do you?" he whispered. He ran a hand down that muscular chest, her eyes tracing its path. His hand disappeared into his pocket. Her eyes, drawn upward, met his amber gaze–a molten intensity that burned a path straight to her core.

Her breath hitched as she opened her mouth, but no words escaped. Swallowing, she tried again. "I know you would not hurt me."

"Good," he said as he quirked an eyebrow.

Her brow furrowed, gooseflesh prickled her skin as she felt the weight of his disbelief pressing down on her. "I'm telling the truth," she said with more conviction.

"As long as you know," he whispered.

Walking over, his warm hand smoothed her hair, stroking downwards till he reached her cheek. Cupping her cheek, his thumb gently brushing her skin in circular motions, he tilted her head upward as his mouth slowly moved to hers. Gently, his tongue, a soft, intrusive pressure, slid across her bottom lip, leaving it glistening before sucking it into his mouth. As he sucked on her lip, she could feel the rough scrape of his fangs, a chilling sensation causing a shiver to course down her spine. Releasing her lip, his hand also released her cheek, leaving the faintest lingering warmth in its wake.

"I mean it," she whispered. *Although I have no reason to, I trust him.* "I know you would not hurt me."

"Good, a mhuirnín." His warm breath stirred the soft hairs at her temple as his hand, rough yet gentle, settled on her hips. His nose nuzzled hers, a soft brush of skin against skin.

She ran her hands along his muscular chest, the soft, red hair a tickle against her palms. Her fingers found his firm pecs, her thumb swirling over his nipples, sensitive peaks puckering under her touch. She dug her fingers into the yielding muscles, feeling them flex beneath. Her mouth followed, a flick of her tongue eliciting a sharp intake of breath. Bolder now, she took a nipple into her mouth, a teasing scrape of teeth before releasing it. A low groan rumbled in his chest as she gently nipped it again.

His fingers, cool and smooth, slid up, catching the soft cotton of her shirt, pulling it high. Those fingers, gliding across her warm skin, cupped her breasts, the pressure firm and exciting. He kneaded gently; she leaned in, a sigh escaping as his nipple left her mouth. The shirt, a whisper of fabric, slid over her head, discarded. Reaching up, she grasped his face, her fingers finding the sharp angles of his jaw, brushing against the stubble, pulling him down. Their mouths met in a fervent crash; the taste of him, sharp and sweet, filled her senses. The storm within her brewed, a hot, electric current with each deepening kiss. His hands, strong and warm, circled her waist, pulling her impossibly close. Her breasts pressed against his chest; the tickle of his chest hair against her skin, a thrilling contrast to the coolness of his body pressed against the warmth of hers.

His hands slid lower, sinking into the yielding curve of her ass, lifting her. She felt the insistent pressure of his hardness against her softness, her breath catching in her throat. His fingers kneaded a sensual pressure as they dug into the soft flesh. His hands moved lower, gripping her thighs, pulling them up, wrapping her legs around him as he walked. The rhythmic movement against her sent shivers through her; but his touch, grounding and intense, pulled her from the immediate sensation to an overwhelming focus on his touch alone, igniting a storm of feeling within.

A soft creak—like an old ship groaning—startled her. Her eyes snapped open. The dim, cool air of the bathroom enveloped her as the door swung inward, revealing the gleam of porcelain and the faint scent of orange cleaner. "What?" she asked, her voice low and husky.

"I didn't want to sleep on a soggy bed later," he said, pointing up.

Looking up, she saw the cloud she had called forth. "Oops." A giggle escaped her lips.

A throaty laugh vibrated against her skin as his teeth, light as a summer breeze, grazed her neck as he pulled her into the shower.

His hands, calloused yet gentle, slid her legs off his waist. The soft cotton of her slacks yielded as he unsnapped and pushed them down, the quiet snap echoing in the hushed room. Her panties followed, leaving her bare before him. She watched as those amber eyes, pools of molten honey, darkened with lust, their gaze a slow, burning caress tracing every curve, every inch of her exposed skin.

Reaching for him, her fingers tracing the warm contours of his shoulders, she moved lower, feeling the ripple of muscles beneath her touch—a thrilling firmness. The sinewy strength yielded delightfully to her pressure of her touch. With a soft click, his trousers fell open, the denim cool against her skin as she knelt. His size filled her hand, a breathtaking fullness as her fingers did not touch around him. A slow caress up and down his length drew a deep, rumbling growl from him. She flicked her tongue across his tip. The taste was electrifying, the sudden gasp at her tongue's touch sending shivers down her spine as she took control. Her mouth closed around him, a rhythmic motion mirroring the caress of her hand, the sounds blending in a symphony of pleasure.

His ragged breath became erratic as he roughly pulled her hair, dragging her up, his mouth crushing down on hers. The smooth tiles of the shower wall pressed cold against her as he spun her around, her breasts impacting the surface with a sharp sting. His hand, slick with water, found its way between her legs, his fingers circling her clit with practiced ease. She felt the hard press of his body against her, the length of him a burning presence. His other hand brushed her hair away, followed by a sharp pain, then a euphoric ache flowed through her veins, as his fangs pierced her neck; she tilted her head, offering herself to him. A wave of intense pleasure washed over her as his skilled fingers continued their dance, the rhythmic pulse a counterpoint to the low rumble of thunder echoing around them. Her heart pounded a frantic rhythm against her ribs, mirroring the storm building within her.

She felt his fangs release her neck, warm blood slick on her skin. Rain plastered her hair to her body, cool against her burning flesh. His breath rasped against her ear as his lips teased her lobe before sucking it in. A wave of a hurricane of pleasure pulsed through her as his fingers danced between her legs. She felt herself gliding on the edge of the storm, a searing pressure as he filled her, his weight heavy and warm against hers. Each slow, deliberate thrust was agony, yet exquisite. Her core clenched a tight fist around him. His thumb, a relentless drumbeat on her bundle of nerves, forced a moan from her lips.

Soon the tempo sped up, a whirlwind of motion. His thrusts, a blur, grew faster and faster, the rhythmic swirl of his thumb a dizzying counterpoint against her clit. The storm of passion intensified with each powerful thrust, a humid heat rising between them. Her breath hitched, a strangled gasp, as he pressed deeper and further, a searing pressure building within.

Icy tile pressed against her slick palms as she scrambled for purchase. The hair on her neck prickled, a buzzing sensation mirroring the storm's crackling energy swirling around them. His left hand closed over hers as his other hand, deft and knowing, strummed her clit. A gasp caught in her throat, the final thrust a searing brand. A dizzying vortex of wind and rain enveloped her insides, the world blurring into a gray, swirling chaos. The roar of the storm was deafening, a physical pressure against her ears. Muscles coiled, then unraveled as her head fell back against his shoulder as the release, a shuddering wave, washed over her. She felt his own climax, a hot rush, her body melting against his.

His warm lips brushed her skin, a feather-light touch on her neck before a deeper kiss. He murmured, his voice a low rumble against her skin, "You taste delicious."

Laughing, she replied, "Is this always going to be a thing where you *taste* me?"

"It helps me feel what you feel."

"What do you mean?" She tilted her head up to look up at him.

"I mean, it connects me to you. This way, I can get a sense of what you're feeling." His lips, soft as a feather, brushed her hair. A gentle pressure, a comforting weight, settled on her heart as he kissed her.

Chapter 25

Sitting in the kitchen, Nuit inhaled the scent of brewing Darjeeling tea that filled the air, a comforting contrast to the cacophony of shouting from down the hall. Male voices, raw with frustration, crashed against each other like waves. The rhythmic thud of her own heartbeat was a counterpoint to their escalating fury; a peaceful resolution seemed far off.

Sighing, the warmth of the steaming teacup a comfort against her fingers, she walked to Redd's office; the grimoire held firm in one hand, the fragrant steam rising around the other. Last night, before the quiet hush of sleep, Redd had explained the book's purpose, and now, nestled in the quiet of his office, she would study it. She was determined to find out why the church wanted it and if it held meaning to saving Feya.

The aged book creaked open, its yellowed pages whispering under her fingertips. Her eyes scanned the lines, a faint scent of old paper and dust filling her nostrils. The world of magic, once a distant hum, now vibrated with a newfound clarity, sharp and bright against the blurred edges of her solitary existence. The chill of years spent in self-imposed exile clung to her like a shroud, a stark contrast to the warmth blooming in her chest as she allowed these new connections to form. Fear, a chilly hand, tightened its grip as this fragile trust blossomed. *What if I open up and it's just a repeat of the past?*

Closing the book, she tried to find focus. The crackling fire roared, casting dancing shadows on the walls as she sat, the warmth a comforting blanket against her skin. A teacup warmed her hands; a subtle aroma of floral mixed with hints of fruit filled the air as she set it down on the cool, polished wood of the side table. Eyes closed, she inhaled deeply, the scent of wood smoke and tea a soothing balm against the turmoil within. *Just focus on today. Just focus on one page at a time.*

Her eyelids fluttered open, revealing the worn, leather-bound book in her hands. The supple leather, cool to the touch, yielded slightly under her fingertips, its surface worn smooth in places. Seventy-six fragile, yellowed pages lay within, the scent of aged paper and parchment filling the air. A small book, yet weighty with history. She reopened it, the brittle pages whispering softly as she searched, her gaze scanning the elegant, archaic Italian script. From nearby, she grabbed a notebook she'd placed earlier. She began to translate, painstakingly recording the spells and cryptic notes in a careful hand. The words of a long-dead witch, a woman burned at the stake, filled her with a strange fascination. A chaotic mix of rambling thoughts punctuated by moments of startling clarity; some spells were familiar, others utterly new.

Closing the book delicately with a soft thud, she heard the bickering sounds coming from the living room. The males' raised voices grated on her ears while their voices continued to echo throughout. No magical solution leaped from the pages, leaving a stark sense of frustration. Her fingers, tracing the familiar script of her notes, felt the slightly raised letters she had scribbled. Healing spells, astral projection, herbal descriptions-pages detailing poisonous and common plants and their uses–a lock in place spell, transformation spell, many other spells... yet nothing to break a celestial contract.

"Maybe I missed something," she muttered, the

words a low hum. Her fingers, tracing the worn lines, felt the rough texture of the aged paper as she flipped through the pages again.

Sighing, a sound like air leaking from a punctured tire, she finished comparing the book to her notes—a ritual repeated countless times—offering no new revelations. She softly drummed her fingers on the cover. Opening the book, she began yet another read-through. *What could the church possibly want with this book? It just seems like a normal grimoire.* Her mind whirled, a dizzying vortex of thoughts, as her eyes, wide and frantic, darted between the dense, ink-stained script of her notes and the aged, leather-bound grimoire.

A crash—the shattering of glass sent her notes scattering across the polished wood. The pungent smell of ozone filled the air as she ran, heart hammering, towards the living room. There, the window gaped open, jagged edges glinting from the overhead lighting, a massive frosted block of ice resting precariously outside, its icy surface reflecting the dim light.

The room's icy chill vanished, replaced by a wave of heat that shimmered in the air, a prickly warmth. A low hum, building to a thrumming crescendo, filled the air as Aguya's magic surged. "So much for the civilized little soldier," Aguya chided, her accent thick as her eyes flared golden.

"Aguya!" Alvero growled. "Calm down."

"He started the fight, so yell at him," Aguya stormed.

Brady came up and tucked her arm into Nuit's, whispering, "I'd say you'll get used to it, but that would be a lie."

"Why would you take that fool's side?" Redd yelled at Alvero. "Not only is he a horrible shot, but she's right, he started this."

"I wasn't aiming for you," Wallace grumbled, his voice a low growl, fingers tugging roughly at his already disheveled hair. His face, flushed and tight, spoke volumes; the air crackled with barely contained fury, a tangible tension hanging heavy.

"We were having a civilized discus–" Aguya rolled her eyes.

"You were insulting him in your native tongue." Alvero ran a hand through his hair. "So, please enlighten me on the civilized part."

"I might have something!" Nuit's cry, a sharp knife that tore through the tense silence, the sound echoing in the heavy air, thick with the smell of dust and stale sweat. Her gaze dropped to the floorboards. A wave of helplessness washed over her as the weight of her impulsive outburst settled—no plan, just a desperate plea for the brutal clashing of words to cease.

"Did you find something in the book?" Redd said, incredulously.

His words from the night before rang in her ears *'the book is probably a wild goose chase'*. She just needed time to decipher the book, then she could figure out what it was they wanted.

"Yes," she lied, smiling brightly, "But I need more time. With all this fighting, yelling, and, well... breaking windows, I am finding it hard to concentrate and get it done. So, if you guys could all go to your respective rooms and be quiet, I would greatly appreciate it."

Redd arched a crimson eyebrow, the gesture sharp against his pale skin, as she gestured towards the stairs. A tense silence hung in the air, broken only by the scrape of their shoes as the other males' eyes flickered nervously between each other before they quickly, almost silently, left the room. Aguya snorted, a sound like tearing silk, and followed, her footsteps echoing faintly. Brady trailed off towards the kitchen. Redd remained, his gaze burning into her, a palpable weight in the suddenly still air.

"Do as you're told," she hissed, her sharp voice cutting through the air, fingers like icicles stabbing towards the stairs one last time.

He nodded, his footsteps echoing softly on the stairs. Alone at last, she let out a frustrated huff. A prickling unease settled on her skin as she questioned her ability to weave truth from the elaborate tapestry of lies she'd spun. Returning to the office, the worn leather of the grimoire felt cool beneath her fingers. The blank page of her notebook seemed to mock her. She started afresh, the scratch of her pen a counterpoint to the rising tide of her anxiety. A nagging feeling, a missing piece of the puzzle, lodged itself firmly in her mind.

The arcane words swam before her eyes, blurring on the parchment's aged surface–a millionth read, and yet she felt no closer to figuring things out. Behind her, the door groaned open, its hinges sighing a soft, dusty creak. She felt the chill of the breeze from the door opening, yet knew, without turning, that Redd stood there.

"So, what's this magic cure you found?" The crackle of the fire cast dancing shadows as he walked before the hearth, stopping to stand before her.

Her eyes, the color of a moonless night, glanced up from the grimoire. A flicker of uncertainty danced in their depths before settling on his own, a silent debate playing across her features. The only sound was the soft crackle of the fire. "I'll let you know when I am done translating it."

Kneeling down, his eyes, bright and sparkling like the morning dew, met hers at eye level. "Are you going to look me in the eye and say that again?"

"I..." she paused, confusion furrowing her brow. "I don't know what you mean."

"Look me in the eye and tell me about this magical spell you found?" He raised an eyebrow.

"I am currently translating the spell," she murmured. She squinted, her eyes crinkling as she tried to decipher his expression, a faint frown etched onto his face.

"That was a pretty good lie there," he whispered.

"What do you mean?" she gasped.

"Did you really think you'd get one over on me?"

"I... I... I don't know what you mean," she stammered as the nerves took over.

"There's nothing in that book and we both know it," he growled, a fire burning in those eyes.

Eyes tracing the familiar script, she reread the spell, the faded ink slightly rough beneath her fingertips. The words leaped from the page, suddenly sharp and clear. "A lock in place spell."

"What?" He shook his head, a harsh, barking laugh rattling in his chest, the sound like dry leaves skittering across pavement.

"A spell to lock someone in place," she said with more confidence.

"And what exactly is that going to do?" His temper, a simmering volcano in the depths of those eyes, burned with a dangerous, barely contained heat. His gaze, sharp and cold, felt like a physical blow.

"It's a spell that will lock Feya in a place where not even the celestial contract can pull her from. Now, if you could please leave me alone, and stop those insinuations that I'm lying, then maybe I can see if this spell works." She shoved his shoulder—a hard, unyielding mass—and returned her gaze to the book. The effort of moving him was like trying to shift a granite boulder; he remained stubbornly rooted. She could feel the weight of his stare, hot and heavy, on the top of her head, a pressure that made concentration a near-impossible feat.

"Do you think it will work?" He whispered, his unsteady voice a breathy tremor, barely audible above the crack of the fire.

Tilting her head back, she met his gaze, the deep pools reflecting a vulnerability that tugged at her heartstrings. A silent understanding passed between them, heavy with unspoken emotions. The air crackled with a sudden warmth, a tangible shift in the atmosphere surrounding them. "I don't know, but I hope so."

Nodding, he rested his forehead on her curled knee. Reaching down, she stroked the silky red strands, feeling their satiny smoothness slide through her fingers like warm liquid. She bit her lip, the pressure a small ache, telling herself not to ask. She did not need to know, but the words, hushed and trembling, slipped out, anyway. "What made you think I was lying?"

"Your heartbeat."

"My heartbeat?" She studied his neck, her gaze lingering on two pale, raised scars tracing a path through his skin; a stark contrast against his pale complexion. Her fingers, light as butterfly wings, traced the ridges, feeling the puckered texture beneath.

"Yes," he said, the words a low rumble, "when people lie, their heart rate spikes."

His head lifted, eyes meeting hers, a spark igniting in their depths. Her fingers, cool and smooth against his hair a moment before, now lay still in her lap, a soft sigh escaping her lips.

REDD

Chapter 26

Redd stared at his phone, the harsh back-light illuminating the recently sent text to Cass. The faint scent of old paper clung to the air, a ghost of Nuit's meticulously copied lock-in-place spell, along with others scrawled in her elegant hand. The book and the spells in it had fascinated her to the point of her asking to keep the book. Nuit's obsidian eyes, dark and intense, swam before him; their silent plea almost broke his resolve. But the insistent buzz of unanswered texts and calls from Cass for the last week, a dull ache in his head, pushed him to deny her. The need to buy time, to deflect Cass's mounting pressure, felt heavy, a physical weight pressing him down. Handing over the book—his only hope for temporary peace—was a bitter pill to swallow.

A low thrum vibrated against his palm; the familiar buzz of his phone. He rolled his eyes, the light above reflecting off the screen as he saw "Cass" flash. A long sigh escaped his lips before a swipe answered the call.

"Why can't you just reply via text?" Redd growled. "Just like normal people do when someone texts."

"I needed to talk to you," Cass said, calmly. "And since you have been unable to answer my phone calls, I figured I'd try to call you again."

The male has the patience of a saint, but damned if I want to deal with it right now or to talk about whatever it is he thinks I need to learn a lesson about.

Redd stared at the ceiling, waiting for Cass's voice, a familiar rasp, to launch into another sermon. Each second ticked by with a heavy, echoing silence, broken only by the faint hum of the line.

Cass let out a dramatic exhale. "Fine. I'll bite and go first. Do you have details about the person who recruited Olette?"

"Didn't realize you were a biter," Redd snorted with laughter.

A silence buzzed as Cass did not respond.

"Come on, Cass, don't you have a sense of humor?"

"I will not discuss such things with you."

"Then I'll just make my own assumptions then."

"Can we please get back to what is most important here?"

"Which is?"

"Finding out the person who recruited Olette."

"Oh, that! I have made zero headway on there," Redd lied with ease. "But I found the book you wanted."

"Thank you. I am glad you got one thing we needed done. What kind of headway have you made on finding out who instigated this?" Cass spoke, calmly. His voice was smooth and polished, like Redd imagined it would be for one of his sermons.

"I have some feelers out," Redd stated, as if he was talking about the weather. "My contacts so far haven't been able to get any information we need. Every avenue turns out to be just another dead end. Seems whoever had pulled her into this has been very tight lipped. But, I'll keep looking. Till then you can come get your book."

"Thank you for the update," Cass sighed. "We appreciate you keeping us in the loop. I am going to need you to bring the—"

"I am too busy hunting down this lead to take the book anywhere. Come and get it," Redd growled as his patience snapped. "How am I supposed to—"

"We both know you know more than you're letting on," Cass grunted. The sound of shuffling papers came through the line, a whisper against the low rumble of Cass's voice. "Since you're not ready to tell me everything you know, then you could be nice enough to bring the book to us."

"Again, I have no additional details for you. Plus, don't I have enough vacation accrued that I can take a few days off without having to run fool's errands for you?"

"I told you we need the book and we need the person. Neither of these are fool's errands..."

"Fine. If you insist, they aren't. So when are you coming to get the book?"

"Aethelredd, you are one of the most frustrating individuals I have ever known!"

"Thank you. That's the nicest thing you've ever said to me."

"With that said. I'll text you the address to bring the book."

"The book will be here when you're ready to grab it." A sharp click echoed as Redd ended the call, cutting off Cass's reply. His thumb lingered on the cool glass of his phone, the screen's pale glow reflecting in his eyes as frustration, a hot, prickly sensation, coiled in his chest.

The phone thudded softly on the polished wood. He gazed at the worn leather of the grimoire. A chill touched his skin as Nuit's words, a low hum in his memory, echoed the quiet rustle of turning pages. 'I don't know, but I hope so.'

Could this spell actually work? Should I take the chance?

"Hello?" a sweet, tentative voice called out.

Glancing up, he saw her sweet eyes, the honey-colored skin flushed with warmth; a smile, slow and sweet as honey, bloomed across his face. *Another complication I don't need right now.*

"What do you need?" he whispered.

"I just wanted to check on how you are doing."

Looking into the depths of those eyes, he wanted to sink in and escape the world that was falling apart around him. "Maybe I'm holding on by a thread or maybe I am perfectly alright. Who knows?" He shrugged.

Chapter 27

Nuit gazed into the warm, amber depths of his eyes, the light catching flecks of gold like scattered stars. His low, melodious voice, laced with a subtle, mocking lilt, hinted at sarcasm. Yet, his eyes remained cool, distant pools reflecting an unseen depth. A strange warmth bloomed in her chest, a feeling that contradicted the playful tone and told her he meant the words more than anything. Unable to unravel the enigma that was Redd, she finally asked, her voice a quiet tremor in the stillness. "What does that mean?"

His shoulders slumped, a fleeting image of defeat, before his gaze dropped to the desk. Then, his head popped up; the carefully constructed mask was firmly in place, the cocky grin plastered on, eyes glittering with a sarcastic shine. "Nothing really," he shrugged.

"Don't do that."

"Do what?" He asked, his shoulders shaking with a tremor of laughter. One red eyebrow arched up as he tried to feign innocence.

"Retreat behind that exterior shell of sarcasm," she hissed, the words sharp as a knife's blade. Huffing a breath, wisps of her bangs tickled her forehead.

With a shrug of his broad shoulders, he turned to the crackle and snap of the small fire. "It's nothing I can't handle."

"If you wanted to push me away, I can just go," she whispered, the words barely audible. Crimson flooded her cheeks, a wave of heat mirroring the self-consciousness that washed over her, a nervous flutter in her stomach.

"You can stay," he retorted, his brow furrowing. "I've just got a lot on my plate right now."

"I can help with anything you might need or even have an ear to hear you out with."

"Not much to do right now," he said, running a hand through his hair. "When the time comes, you are going to cast that spell to keep Feya in place. That is a huge thing to be doing for us. That's all I need and can ask of you."

"I can handle more, especially if you just want to talk."

"There's nothing I need to talk about. Well, maybe one thing..." His brow furrowed, a deep crease etched between his eyes.

She waited, the silence punctuated only by the distant rumbling of footsteps in the distance. A slight shiver tracing her spine as she waited for his reply, which didn't come. "What do you need to talk about?"

He paused, before answering. "Do you need any kind of help?"

"It's nothing I can't handle," she said, her voice trembling slightly.

His eyes, narrowed to thin slits, raked over her, a slow, burning appraisal. A wave of heat, prickly and sudden, flushed her cheeks under the weight of his intense gaze.

"Are you sure you don't need help?" The doubt seeped into each word as he spoke.

Shaking her head, she met his eyes. With all the bravado she could muster, she said, "I can do this. I am just feeling nervous is all. I will make sure she stays safe"

His eyes locked on hers for a moment. She thought he was going to tell her to leave, but instead he asked, "How much space can we give her? I am not sure how long she will need to be trapped, so I don't want her to get too restless."

"I'll set it up using as much room as I can," she said. Gazing into the deep pools of his eyes, a fierce resolve ignited within her, a burning desire to be the hero, the savior of the day. But a cold tendril of self-doubt snaked around her heart. The last time she'd conjured spells of this magnitude was a faint, almost forgotten memory, echoed in her mind with a nervous tremor in her fingertips.

"Good," he said as a shadow crept across those eyes.

"Are you ready to talk about what's really bothering you?" She tilted her head, her eyes taking in every line, every crease, every freckle on his skin.

His brow furrowed, a deep crease etched above eyes that held a storm of unspoken words. His lips parted before a slow, weary shake of his head.

"I know you're worried, but I am sure everything will be alright." She smiled reassuringly.

Laughing sardonically, his eyes darkened. "Yep. I'm sure it'll all be hunky-dory."

"There's that sarcasm again," she sighed, rolling her eyes.

"What exactly are you expecting from me?" he

snapped.

"I don't know, maybe just honesty."

"Well, here's your honesty." His nostrils flared, and a fire raged in those amber eyes. "Maybe I have been through this before and the idea I might have to watch my blood, my family, those I love die again, is fucking terrifying. So, I don't always want to sit there and rehash things that could happen and instead I'll just focus on what's happening."

"We won't let anything bad happen to them," she said with as much confidence as she could muster.

"That child—" he raged as his voice grew louder.

"Woman," she stated. "That is no longer a child, but a woman. She has had a long life and—"

"No," he growled, slamming a fist on the desk. "She will always be my child. I found her dying in the forest and once I gave her my blood, she became mine. That is my blood that runs through her veins, so that is my child."

"She might be your daughter, but she is no longer a child."

He leaned back, the worn leather creaking softly beneath him as he exhaled a slow, silent breath. "You just don't seem to understand, do you?"

"Everything will work out," she soothed. Her mind, a hummingbird's wings beating against ribs, fluttered to distant memories of her own children. The same grief, a bitter, choking wave crashing against her, returned, its icy fingers reaching for her. She pushed it back, again and again, over the centuries. Her own pain—a dull ache in her chest—would not help him now. "You just need to have faith."

A harsh snort ripped through the air. His eyes, blazing with fury, snapped back to hers. The raw, animalistic rage simmered in their depths, a scorching heat she felt as a physical wave. She saw, with a jolt, the predatory male he had so carefully concealed. "I lost my faith a long time ago."

"Then there is no point, is there? We should just give up now."

"I am not up to the cryptic comments right now, so just spit out whatever the fuck you need to say."

Sighing, a soft, breathy sound lost in the crackling dance of the fire, she walked towards its warm glow. Words, a chaotic rush like pebbles tumbling in a stream, flooded her mind; she longed to offer comfort, to soothe the palpable fear and simmering anger radiating from him. Her voice, a wisp of smoke in the still air, was distant and low as she spoke, barely audible above the fire's hypnotic crackle. "Do you think you are the only one who carries grief?"

"Is this the part where we tell each other all our past traumas and then hug it out?"

"No." She shook her head. "I wish there was a window in here. Looking up at the stars is like looking at the past, did you know that?"

"Not really," he snarled.

"When you look up at the night sky, you see sparks of light from years ago. It takes eons for that speck of light to come to us. Just like life, sometimes it takes eons for it to show us where we belong. Maybe this time and this place is where you all belong. You just need to be patient and then the path will present itself." Her arms folded tight across her chest. A faint scent of wood smoke hung in the air.

Startled, she jumped as a large, calloused hand brushed her hair off her shoulder, the touch sending a shiver down her spine. The soft padding of his feet on the wooden floor had been silent as a whisper. A tender kiss, warm as the summer sun, touched her shoulder, igniting a familiar warmth that spread through her like wildfire with every touch. Glancing over her shoulder, her eyes met his; she sought to understand the powerful hold he had on her, a bond that felt stronger each day.

"I'm sorry," he breathed, the words warm against her skin as his lips, soft as a feather, brushed her neck. A shiver traced its way down her spine, the scent of his cologne filling her senses. "I'm just worried, and I didn't mean to be cruel to you."

"It's alright," she murmured breathlessly.

Chapter 28

$\mathcal{R}$edd's calloused hands, rough against Nuit's skin, gripped her hips as he spun her. The scent of him, sharp and musky, mingled with her perfume. She felt the hard press of his chest against her, a comforting weight against her yearning. His mouth, a forceful storm, claimed hers; the metallic tang of rage and the bitter taste of frustration warred on his tongue, mirroring the turmoil in her own heart. His hands tightened, a firm but tender pressure on her hips, guiding her gently as they ground against him. Instinctively, she pressed closer, the warmth of his body a haven against the chill of his emotions, her touch both desperate and soothing.

Her fingers, tracing the warm contours of his chest, snagged on the silken strands at his nape. Rising on tiptoe, a thrilling lightness in her body, she arched closer, eager for the taste of him.

Her pulse hammered a frantic rhythm against her ribs as his hands slid to her backside, pressing her hard against him. The insistent pressure of his rigid shaft against her soft flesh stole her breath, a gasp escaping her lips. His fingers kneaded the delicate skin of her buttocks, eliciting a low groan that vibrated against his mouth.

Stepping back, he left her feeling bereft as the

sound of his footsteps retreated. The sharp slam of the door echoed, a jarring counterpoint to the sudden silence before he turned. His eyes, burning with a molten heat that replaced the previous rage and sadness, glowed with a lustful intensity, making her pulse pound a frantic rhythm against her ribs. He closed the distance in a few swift strides, his breath cool, a caress against her flushed skin as he stopped before her. The scent of his breath filled her nostrils, a heady perfume. Her gaze, unwavering, locked with his, time seeming to stretch and warp as he stood before her.

Reaching up, fingers brushing his skin, she closed the last bit of distance. His lips, soft as velvet, brushed hers—a feather-light touch. She stood there, her hands cupping the strong column of his neck, a silent question hanging in the air as she anticipated his next touch. A low growl vibrated in her chest when he remained still. Then, with a fierce shove, her mouth crashed against his. The instant his lips parted, a flash of heat, her tongue darted in, tasting the familiar, electric tang that filled her mouth, a potent, intoxicating flavor.

His hands clutched her hips, fingertips pressing into the warm, yielding flesh. She swirled her tongue in his mouth. A silent moment stretched before she withdrew her tongue, its tip tracing the line of his lips; a soft sigh escaped her as she pulled his bottom lip into her mouth, tasting his salty skin. His grip tightened, a fierce pressure against her back, but he remained still. She teased his lip, a slight scrape against her teeth, a thrill of anticipation running through her. Tugging on his thick hair, she tilted his head back, her mouth trailing down the rough stubble of his chin, a prickly sensation against her lips. Her teeth grazed his skin, then sank into his neck. He still remained immobile. She bit harder, hoping for more reaction; only his death grip on her hips answered.

Pulling back slightly, she studied his neck. She saw the two tiny scars, a faint whisper of his turning. Her tongue tracing their delicate ridges. His stillness fueled her frustration; her brow furrowed in a sharp line, her glare intense.

"Let go of me," she grumbled, pulling away.

He let her go, a silent sigh escaping his lips as his fingers brushed her arm.

What is he up to? Her gaze, a silent question, drifted across his features. The faraway expression, tinged with yearning, was etched onto his face, a landscape of subtle shadows and faint lines. A chill touched her skin, mirroring the cold distance in his eyes. *Stupid male, bottling up all those emotions.*

Nuit tilted her head, brow furrowed in concentration while her eyes surveyed him. She tugged sharply on the soft cotton of his shirt, hearing the whispery sound of fabric gliding against skin as it came free. Tiptoeing, she felt the warmth of his skin beneath her fingers as she pushed the shirt over his head. Dragging her hands back down, she felt the silky smoothness of his chest hair, a soft whisper against her fingertips as she traced their path downward. There was a soft click as the pants snap yielded, the cool smoothness of his skin against her hands as she slid them down his legs. He stood before her, a proud, stiff column of flesh, the scent of him heady and strong, his arms crossed, a confident smirk playing on his lips.

The coolness of his skin, the ripple of muscles beneath her fingertips as she trailed them across his arms created a thrilling dance of sensation. She continued her exploration, the tautness of his stomach yielding to her touch, the sinewy strength a vibrant pulse beneath her fingers. A sudden hardness met her hand, throbbing with life. The thick girth filled her hand completely, causing her fingers to not meet. Kneeling, she enveloped him in her mouth, the taste of him sharp and clean, while her hand continued its rhythm. His groan, a low rumble in her ear, as his fingers tangled in her hair. Her mouth and hand worked in perfect harmony. Then, a sudden salty drop of tanginess on her tongue as he pulled her up sharply.

His rough hands tore her clothes away, the fabric ripping with a sharp sound. The cool wood of the desk pressed against her flushed skin as he turned her, her breasts tingling against its smooth surface. His fingers invaded her, eliciting a gasp; their rhythmic motion set a storm raging within. She fought to contain the magic welling up, the edges of her vision blurring as tremors wracked her body. Each thrust intensified, her heart pounding a frantic rhythm against her ribs. Then, as suddenly as they began, his fingers withdrew. A cry escaped her lips, but his hands clamped onto her hips, pulling her down as he entered. The rain she'd unintentionally conjured plastered her damp hair to her face as his relentless rhythm pushed her further and further towards the brink. With one final, deep plunge, she convulsed, her body arching, the pleasure overwhelming. Her release washed over her in a wave of pure, intense sensation.

Feeling limp, her body heavy as he slipped out of her, then gently scooped her up. The warmth of the crackling fireplace radiated against her skin as he laid her down in front of it on the rug, its soft texture malleable beneath her. He settled behind her, his chest hair a comforting brush against her back. Looking over her shoulder, she saw his face in the firelight, the flickering flames dancing in his eyes. For the first time in the last 24 hours, a calmness settled over his features, smoothing out the lines around his mouth and eyes.

"You can stop hiding who you are with me," she whispered. She was not sure where the words came from, a whisper in the echoing silence of the room, or why she said them, the taste of regret already bitter on her tongue. But it was too late; the words hung heavy in the air like smoke. She could see those eyes, once blazing embers, now icy pools reflecting the fading warmth of their tryst, the chill of disdain settling like frost.

"While this has been a nice..." he paused as he seemed to look right through her. "Distraction. I think I need to focus on something more important."

He leaped up, a flurry of motion, snatched his clothes, and stormed from the room, the door booming shut. Hot tears pricked her eyes, blurring the wood of the door.

Chapter 29

Nuit's gaze followed the fiery hues of Redd's hair on the back of his head while he stared out the moonlit window. The silence between them hung heavy, broken only by her attempts at conversation. For forty-eight hours, his responses had been guttural, rough, like stones scraping against stone doing nothing to ease the chill in her heart. She knew her words had wounded him, a sharp sting, but she couldn't comprehend why. His presence now felt icy, a wall of sarcastic indifference impervious to her touch or words.

Within an hour of the other day's debacle, he'd moved all her things back into the room where she'd first slept. She considered sneaking into his room, but the expected sting of disappointment and her own heartbreak held her back. Redd shook his head, the rustle of his shirt as he rolled his shoulders a counterpoint to the murmur of male voices. A low hum she struggled to focus on. Sleepless nights left her mind drifting off at the smallest distraction.

"I have called forth everyone to meet us," Wallace said. "We should be able to meet them tonight. They know to act with discretion till then."

"This better work," Redd grumbled.

"It will," Wallace stated.

She felt the heat of Redd's simmering anger, a palpable wave radiating outwards. He stood rigid, a statue of controlled fury, while Leo's restless pacing echoed in the tense silence. Leo only seemed to speak when he thought it was just the two of them. *I feel like a stalker since I follow him around the house, watching his every move. But instead of being a cat stalking a mouse, I'm the mouse.*

"We will set Feya free," Alvero stated, rubbing the bridge of his nose. "Redd, we need to work together to make sure everything works out."

"I can burn that queen to the ground easy enough," Aguya sighed. "It would end things faster that way."

"Cailleach Bheag" Alvero sighed. He pulled Aguya into his arms, kissing her forehead. "We still have to worry about your sister."

A sharp, icy pang of jealousy pierced Nuit as she watched the couple, the gentleness of each touch a contrast to the chill she was getting from Redd. A chill, despite the warmth from the fire, settled on her skin.

"She is not my sister," Aguya snapped, wrapping her arms around him. "Never forget that."

Alvero rested his cheek on Aguya's head. "We have word she is at the castle with the queen. We will have to fight and confront her. I don't want you to do that alone. You need to stay by Redd or myself the whole time during the fight."

The love they felt for each other was palpable.

"You are under some impression that I can't handle myself," Aguya snorted.

"I know you are quite powerful," he whispered. "I just couldn't face it if you got hurt again. Can you please just do this for me?"

"Whatever," Aguya sighed.

"Thank you," Alvero laughed.

"Alright," Redd said, rolling his shoulders. "Now that the touchy feely emotions are over, let's get back to business."

"I agree," Wallace stated. "We should go over…"

Turning, she left the room, the polished wood floor cool beneath her bare feet, the murmur of voices fading behind her. She ached to go to the battlefield to shield the stubbornly aloof male who had zero interest in her. A desperate urge to flee, to vanish into the shadows, clawed at her at the same time. She knew she needed to stay here to bind Feya with the spell to hold her here. Instead, she walked away, the silence a heavy cloak. She knew she would go along with whatever plans the males made.

Creaking wood whispered under her cautious steps, each stair a measured ascent. A chill wind rattled the windowpane as she reached her room, her heart a frantic drum. Brilliant stars pricked the velvet night, the moon, a waxing slice of silver. But nestled within its glow, a crimson ring, a horrifying halo, sent a shiver down her spine. She squeezed her eyes shut, trying to banish the dreadful sight of a bad omen.

"Everything will be fine," she muttered to herself as she turned around.

Startled, she jumped back, her hand landing with a soft thud on the cool windowsill as her legs bumped the wall. There he stood, arms akimbo, a silhouette against the dim lighting coming from the hallway. The sudden shift in the air, heavy with his presence, had been imperceptible; she hadn't even heard the quiet creak of the door.

"Talking to yourself, a mhuirnín?" he asked, tilting his head to the side. A strand of red hair fell over, obscuring one eye.

"What does that mean?" she whispered.

"What does what mean?"

"Uh-wur-neen." she said, carefully pronouncing each syllable. "You keep calling me that."

"It's a mhuirnín. It means darling." He shrugged.

"Oh."

"So," he paused, turning away. "It's just a word I use, nothing special. What is it that is going to be fine?"

"Oh, that." She shrugged, pointing towards the window. Her mind whirled, a dizzying vortex of thoughts as she searched for an answer. Turning, she saw the moon, a silvery slash hanging in the inky black. The night air, crisp and faintly sweet with the scent of roses, brushed her face. *Might as well tell the truth.* "There's a blood ring around the moon. It is an omen of bad things to come. I was just trying to reassure myself that it is nothing."

He seemed to mull over her words before he spoke. "Are you still good with doing that spell?"

As she glanced over her shoulder, she caught amber eyes, narrowed like a cat's, a silent scrutiny burning in their depths.

"Of course," she muttered.

With a few steps, he closed the distance between them. "I am starting to lose confidence in you. I can just have Alvero do it if you can't."

She inhaled deeply, the scent of his cologne filling her lungs, the little bit of confidence she had in herself shaken. Closing her eyes, she took a deep breath, the crisp air cool against her lungs. *I can't let him know he's hurt me. Obviously, I was nothing more than a distraction, as he so coldly told me. I should just take his words at face value and quit trying to make something out of my feelings alone.*

Opening her eyes up, she met his. She did not flinch or back down as she spoke. "I told you once I can do this. Once the spell is done, then we will be even. Tit for tat, if you will. I do this spell for you and you killed the man who has wanted me dead for centuries."

"Alright as long as you can do the spell," he shrugged. "What will you need to do it?"

She straightened her spine, trying to pretend the cool disdain did not mean anything to her. Even though her heart ached from the cruelty of his disinterest. "I'll get a list together for you."

"We need that list before we can go forward with any other plans. Is there anything on it that should be a concern?"

"It is all stuff that can be easily obtained." A shiver, unseen but felt, traced a path along her arm as her fingers rubbed the gooseflesh. The air hung heavy despite that a subtle coolness prickled her skin. "Is that all you need?"

He nodded, his gaze flat, unfocused, seeming to pierce right through her as if she was not there. Turning with a sigh, he left the room; the door shut with a muted thud.

Rigidly standing there, she watched the door, the faint smell of lemon and beeswax filling the air. Each second stretched, an eternity measured by the rhythmic tick-tock of a distant grandfather clock, a sound swallowed in the heavy silence. *He really meant it when he said I was just a nice distraction.* She swiped at her cheeks as she felt the dampness. Looking at the back of her hand, the sheen of tears splashed across it as she realized her heart was breaking. She could practically feel her heart sink in her chest while a maelstrom of emotions flowed throughout her.

Chapter 30

The door clicked shut, a sound swallowed by the thick silence. Redd fought back a tide of emotion, a bitter taste rising in his mouth, his chest tight. The cool air felt heavy against his skin. *I don't have any time for this shit. I need to prepare for the shit storm we are about to head into. Not prepare to slide into some female's legs, no matter how hot those legs are, those silky smooth honeyed legs.*

Shaking his head, a frustrated sigh escaping his lips, he ran his hands through his unruly hair before heading down the stairs. The door to his office slammed shut with a resounding thud, the sound echoing the turmoil in his chest; her dark, accusing eyes haunted him still. He remembered the faint glimmer of unshed tears, the glistening moisture in her eyes when he'd spoken to her—words sharp as shards of glass. He knew he'd been harsh, his voice rough as sandpaper, but her relentless pestering, her insistent need for him to dissect his emotions, pushed all the wrong buttons, igniting a fire within him. Slumping into the chair, he stared into the empty, soot-stained fireplace. His elbows rested heavily on his knees, the weight of his despair pressing down. Sighing again, a deep, shuddering breath, he buried his face in his hands.

An icy dread gripped him, a stark contrast to the

usual easy confidence that had always come so easily to him his whole life. His head throbbed, a dull, insistent pulse against his temples. The gnawing hunger, a sharp, acidic emptiness, clawed at his stomach. He'd stolen away while Alvero was momentarily distracted, snatching a meager snack, but the ravenous emptiness remained.

Maybe I should sneak off and find something to eat for the night. Maybe a little extracurricular activity afterwards. Feed both hungers, driving me mad right now. Then I can get those dark eyes and honey skin out of my mind.

Closing his eyes, he tried to find the familiar comfort in the dimly lit study. He knew he couldn't leave the urge a gnawing beast within him. He needed to pore over the invasion plans with the others—again and again. But his thoughts, like restless sprites, danced between his worry for his family, the persistent, maddeningly sweet presence of the little goddess, and a deep, visceral hunger. Alvero's demands of being nice to all the creatures and the chaos of everything else had thrown his feeding schedule off; the resulting emptiness echoed in his bones, a cold, hollow ache which translated into his mood as of late.

A soft, rhythmic thumping—a heartbeat—reached his ears. Leo. A sigh escaped his lips as he leaned back, the worn leather creaking beneath him. The door swung inward without a sound, a silent intrusion in the quiet room.

"Hey," Leo said, closing the door behind him with a soft click.

"Have a seat next to me," Redd sighed.

"That bad?"

Shrugging, Redd glanced at Leo. "We need to talk about something else."

"Am not going to like this, am I?"

"Probably not, old man."

With a groan that seemed to vibrate through the room, Leo sank into the chair, the springs protesting beneath his weight.

"I need you to stay back with the girls," Redd voiced quietly.

"I'd do better–"

"I know you would, but if anyone comes after Feya, Nuit, and Brady, they will be defenseless here alone." Redd's gaze dropped to his hands, rough-hewn and calloused, a testament to years of hard labor. He could have retired, savoring the quiet comfort of his home with his family and the warmth of the hearth. Instead of a familiar cycle of taking one job after another. He just kept going. *Would we all be in this situation if I had just stopped working?* "Nuit is going to create the spell to hold Feya here. If the spell doesn't work, I need you to let me know if the queen calls her forth. If Feya is pulled into this battle..."

Huffing, Leo said, "Alright. I will stay here and do what needs to be done."

"If I don't come back, old friend," Redd paused as the implications hit him. He'd staunchly held back the thoughts, a dam against a rising tide of despair, knowing their corrosive power. But the words, once spoken, hung heavily in the air, thick and suffocating like the scent of overripe fruit, impossible to pull back.

"You'll come back," Leo said confidently.

The confidence thrumming in Leo's voice was a stark contrast to the chill Redd felt in his own bones. A nervous tremor ran through him; he needed to finish, the words a weight in his chest, and let Leo know what he needed to say. "That's the goal, but if I don't, then take care of the girls. Sale the house and move somewhere far. Make sure they are happy. If only Aguya and Alvero would stay here, too."

Snorting, Leo shook his head. "Aguya will do as she pleases and however she pleases. You know that by now. Alvero, he is going to follow her into the fray, no matter what."

"I know," Redd said, sounding defeated. "Just make sure to keep them safe. It'd kill me if something happened to them."

"You never need to ask that of me. You can just expect it from me."

"You have always been a good friend, a good brother." Redd patted Leo's arm. "Okay, that's enough lovey dovey bullshit. I am looking forward to quite the feast." Redd could feel the grumbling, a low rumble in his stomach, a gnawing anticipation of what was to come.

"While I sit here babysitting, thanks."

"You're welcome. It does sound rather boring. Till then would you like a glass of whiskey?" Redd got up and walked over to the small bar in the corner.

Exhaling deeply, Leo nodded. He filled a single glass of whiskey and left one glass empty. Turning, he went back and set one glass on the table next to him, while holding the empty glass. He could not tell exactly when he started pretending to drink with whomever he offered a glass to, but he always brought himself a glass back so his guest did not feel like they were drinking alone.

"Do you understand the amount of meals I have missed because of Alvero's insistence to hurt no critters?" Redd uttered.

"Yet it doesn't look like you're wasting away."

"A feather could knock me over."

"Hmph," Leo snorted. "I'm pretty sure you could stand to skip a few more meals if it provides us with that sparkling personality of yours."

Laughing, Redd's shoulders shook, a tremor that sent ripples through his body, a boisterous rumble. "You should be grateful for my sparkling personality. Keeps your life interesting."

The empty glass felt cold against his palm. His emotions churned, a bitter taste mirroring the empty bottom of the glass. Obsidian eyes, shimmering with unshed tears, swam in his mind's eye; a silent scream behind a brave facade. *It's for the best. If I don't make it back, it's better she hates me now, that'll be less heartache for her later. Maybe if I am a big enough ass she'll actually be happy if I die.*

"I am fucking starving," Redd laughed, self-deprecatingly. "It seems Alvero is there every time I sneak out for a late-night snack. I've been thinking about drinking him since I'm so hungry."

"It's because the critters are gossipy little rodents," Leo laughed.

"What the hell does that mean?" Redd's head turned towards Leo, his eyes scrutinizing Leo's face.

"The rats talk to him." A sly grin stretched Leo's lips, revealing a flash of teeth as he tossed back the amber liquid. "Maybe you should drink him for your next meal, then I won't have to listen to him and Aguya fighting anymore."

Laughing, Redd's eyes locked with his friend's eyes. "That's not arguing you're always hearing."

"Ugh," Leo snorted. "Please don't say things like that."

Nuit watched as Redd opened a hidden panel in the wall, the damp smell of earth and petrichor flooding her nostrils as the door creaked open with a soft, groaning sound. Dim, yellowed light, like aged honey, barely illuminated the descending stairs, their edges swallowed by shadow. Following Redd down, Nuit felt the air grow noticeably colder, a chill clinging to her skin as the ancient, flickering lights seemed to hum with forgotten energy.

Behind her, Feya sneezed. "Oh my gods, it is dusty down here. When was the last time someone has been down here to clean? For that matter, when was the last time someone was just down here?"

"I was down here about a week ago," Redd shrugged. "It's not that bad."

"You really come down here?" Elwyn laughed. "Did you hang off the ceiling from your toes or something?"

Redd's voice, a gravelly rasp edged with annoyance, vibrated down the echoing stairwell. Each footfall on the steps added to the cacophony that echoed off the stone walls. "Some of us," he growled, his eyes narrowing. "Prefer to avoid getting a suntan. Plus, keep running that mouth and you will hang from the ceiling down here."

Over her shoulder, Nuit saw Elwyn walking close behind Feya. His hand, protectively rested on the small of her back. Elwyn's lips curled into a smirk that crinkled the corners of his eyes, retorted with a biting quip, the sharp sound cutting through the air like a well-aimed dart. "Perhaps a touch of color would do you good," he chuckled, his voice laced with a hint of mockery. "It might even improve that rather pale complexion of yours."

"I treasure the time I don't spend with you, boy. Did you know that?" Redd snorted.

"Children," Feya sighed dramatically, the sound like wind chimes in a summer breeze, a mischievous glint in her eyes. A wide grin stretched across her face, warm and inviting as a sun-drenched meadow.

Nuit longed to join the boisterous laughter and witty banter, a cacophony of merry sounds, but a knot of discomfort had tightened in her chest. The last few days had been a blur of vibrant laughter and clashing arguments, as she remained a silent observer in the corner. Her own words echoing in the hollow chambers of her heart, a chilling counterpoint to the revelry. Once the spell's magic faded, she would retreat to the quiet solitude of her home, resuming her listless existence. *It takes eons for that speck of light to come to us. Just like life, sometimes it takes eons for it to show us where we belong. Apparently, this is not where I belong. Do I belong anywhere?*

"Will this work, mhuirnín?" Redd said, his arm a blur of motion and muscle, swung wide, pulling her from her reverie.

A chill breeze stirred, raising goosebumps on her arms. Her eyes, wide and bright, darted to him, searching his face for a hint of insult. A nervous flutter stirred in her chest.

"This is a sizable space, hidden from view," Redd said, his arms crossing his broad chest, a skeptical eyebrow arching high above his intense gaze. The only sound was the faintest whisper of dust motes dancing in the lone shaft of light from the overhead lamp slicing through the gloom.

A shiver, the unsettling feeling of her thoughts laid bare, washed over her before she looked away. Impossible, she knew, yet the creeping suspicion lingered. Entering the octagonal chamber, the chill from the uneven grey stone floors seeped into her feet. An ancient wooden table and four shaky chairs dominated the center of the room, their surfaces dusted with the grime of ages of non-use. Her gaze swept across the seven windowless cells, their cold, slick metal bars a stark contrast to the rough, grey-brown stone walls, smelling faintly of damp earth and mildew. Within, cots and tiny latrines sat in the dust-laden cells, a thick smell of neglect hanging heavily.

With a subtle nod, a murmur escaped her lips, "It will do," the sound barely disturbing the quiet of the room. Her lip caught between her teeth, while her gaze, sharp and restless, swept across the dimly lit space, lingering on a dust-mote dancing in the air.

Eyes glued to the cold, grey-brown stone floor, she bent down, feeling the rough texture beneath her fingertips. She needed a clean surface; dust would ruin the chalk spell runes. To prevent the lines from being broken up, she needed a clean base for each precise rune. Fresh boot prints marred the floor, leading to the first cell. A shiver ran down her spine; what had Redd been doing in there?

"Oh my," Brady's high-pitched voice said from behind her.

Turning, she saw Brady pull out a cloth and wipe the grimy, wobbly table.

At least I will have a friendly face to help me clean up the space before tonight. She smiled at Brady, feeling thankful for at least one cheerful face in the group.

Leo dropped a worn canvas bag onto the table, the sound of a dull thud swallowed by the musty air. He retreated silently, his footsteps muffled on the stairs. Redd followed, leaving behind a silence that caused a knot to tighten in her stomach. The scent of stale dust and old wood hung thickly as she began the arduous clean-up.

They had spent the last few hours scrubbing. Nuit's aching back attested to it. The floor, though not gleaming, was finally free of the thick, gritty dust; the scent of the cleaning solution, sharp and chemical, still lingered faintly in the air.

The rasp of black chalk on stone filled the quiet space as she sketched a circle. Each Futhark rune emerged meticulously, a delicate dance of sharp angles and flowing curves. Thirteen runes etched along the outer ring.

Feya, fidgeting, stood in the center of the chalk ring. Her fingers, trembling slightly, swept her hair from her face. "How much longer will this take?"

"As long as it takes," Nuit muttered, her eyes ghosting across each stroke of charcoal as she meticulously checked her work. The dim light illuminating the swirling runes. A single misplaced line could unravel the entire spell—the weight of that possibility pressing down on her, as she knew one error and the spell would not work.

Once she was sure they were right, she turned to the walls.

"How will we know it's working?" Redd grumbled, walking around the outside of the circle. His eyes scrutinized everything.

She turned from her work to see them—the gaggle of onlookers on the stair. Their eyes felt like hot pokers on her skin as her cheeks blazed. "It will work."

Turning from the murmuring crowd, a wave of their hushed whispers brushing her skin like a chill wind, she began drawing the floor's matching chalk symbols onto the rough stone walls. With each movement of her hand, their eyes felt like a hundred needles piercing her back. Seven walls, cold beneath her fingertips, with thirteen stark black runes, her eyes traced their every slash looking for any imperfections as she stepped back.

"That did not answer my question," Redd huffed.

"Do you want me to stop what I am doing and explain it to you like you're a toddler?" The retort, sharp as a knife's blade, escaped her lips before she'd fully thought it out. A bitter-sweet ache, a war of wanting him gone yet desperately needing him near, raged within her. She didn't know which desire would win, only that she yearned for the woman she was before him—a time before the dizzying blend of agony and elation his presence ignited. The ghost of serenity haunted her, once hard-won after years of tumultuous loss and heartache.

"No," Redd dragged the word out. "I just want to know how we know it will work."

Walking into the circle, she set the chalk down on the table. "Let me begin from the start. Each rune has a special meaning and purpose. When you combine runes in a specific order—"

"Again, I just want my question answered, not a lecture on how magic works," Redd growled. His brow furrowed, as his eyes were mere slits.

"Call her name and see if she can leave the circle

when it's done. Now can I please finish without the distractions?" She huffed a warm breath as her bangs fluttered, tickling her forehead with a light, feathery touch.

Her fingers, dusty with chalk, tightened around the black stick. She stepped out of the worn chalk circle, the ground cool beneath her bare feet. Returning to her work, she fixed a few lines.

"Was that so hard to say?" Redd muttered under his breath.

A thousand fiery retorts sprang to her lips and a hundred meek apologies jostling for space on her tongue. She bit her tongue hard, the sharp pain a counterpoint to the simmering anger. Silence settled, heavy and suffocating, as she returned to the rhythmic scratch of chalk.

When she drew the last rune, chalking it onto the stones, she turned, her eyes sweeping over the intricate drawings. With each rune, a tingling warmth spread through her, a vibrant energy flowing outwards, a visible hum in the air connecting her to each rune. The pulsing energy tugged at her, a dizzying pull in multiple directions as the spell began its chaotic dance.

Tiptoeing around the chalk circle, which stood starkly against the worn stones, she reached the stairs. A hush fell; eyes, like dark stones, followed her every move. Ignoring the weight of their stares, she rummaged in the worn canvas bag, its earthy smell filling her nostrils. A tarnished copper bowl, cool to the touch, was placed inside the circle. The spring moon water, its slight silvery gleam catching the dim light, gurgled as it poured into the bowl. With a practiced hand, she added eight generous tablespoons of sea salt, the grains gritty between her fingers. Rustling through the bag, she located the dried rose petals, their delicate scent a whisper of sweetness. Crushing them gently between her palms, she sprinkled them into the bowl, their ruby dust settling on the surface.

The shuffle and murmurs behind her caused her

to lose focus for a moment; she whipped around, eyes blazing. Turning, her fingers brushed the rough canvas of the bag. Inside, thirteen sharp thorns, each a tiny glint of wicked green, awaited. One by one, she dropped them into the bowl. With the last thorn in place, she inhaled the earthy scent of dried herbs, her breath misting the surface as she blew, a tangible wave of power exhaling with the air. The words of the spell, ancient and powerful, vibrated on her tongue as she spoke them.

Spirit strong, spirit bond. I call forth to my ancestors, guiding my spell, guiding my hands, guiding my magic. I bind this creature in this circle. May no spell or power break it. Praecipe eis, alliga eos ad hanc locum.

Lifting the heavy copper bowl, now warm to the touch, above her head, she focused, feeling the familiar tingle of magic—a warm thrum—spreading from her fingertips. The copper gleamed under the dim light, acting like a conduit for her magic. Slowly, she tilted the bowl; the liquid, a molten gold, poured out with a soft whoosh. It flowed onto the dusty chalk lines, the gold shimmering, a breathtaking sight as each chalk mark glowed golden. With a soft clink, the empty bowl hit the floor.

Her fingers traced the glowing, warm lines, now infused with her energy, a faint hum vibrating through her hand, connecting her to the spell, a bond both powerful and strangely intimate.

Turning, she looked at the crowd behind her staring at them. She whispered, "It's done."

REDD

Chapter 32

Redd, clad in black from head to toe, readied himself. A dozen blades, their cold steel unseen beneath his chest protector, felt reassuringly solid. The mirror reflected his pale face, shadowed by dark circles under his eyes; weariness clung to him like the damp chill of the night. Two hidden blades pressed against his thigh, its familiar weight a slight comfort as they hid in the folds of his pants. He pushed aside the exhaustion, the bitter taste of it lingering on his tongue, and strode from the room. The scent of lemon and beeswax filled the small space.

"There is so much to do before the sun goes down," Brady sighed.

Nodding, Redd continued past her to the hidden panel.

"You and Aguya will come back fine," Brady's shaky voice announced.

Looking over his shoulder, he saw the glimmer of tears pricking Brady's eyes. "Of course. Take care of everyone until we get back."

Descending the creaking stairs, a musty scent, tinged with the sharp, clean ozone of Nuit's magic, tickled his nose. A low thrumming vibrated sound through the air—the magic's hum. Leo sat at the table, the clatter of solitaire cards a counterpoint to the hum. Feya and Elwyn huddled close, their whispers a hushed rustle. He doubted he'd ever accept his daughter's boyfriend, no matter the years. She'd never before brought a date home; this was... tolerable. Elwyn wasn't as bad as he'd feared, though he wouldn't admit it to him or anyone else. Nuit, a golden luminescence bathing her honey-toned skin, now a little paler than earlier, sat on the floor, her eyes blazing with the same golden light that had ignited the floor and wall glyphs. Her eyes met his; remorse filled him as he remembered his cruelty and her words, sharp and biting. Turning away, he sought Feya, the dark softness of her hair a comfort under his hand as he stroked it. She looked up at him, worry filled her eyes.

"How are you holding up, little one?" he asked softly.

"I'm fine, dad," Feya grumbled. Her voice dropped as it went from grumpy to worried. "Stay safe, please."

Tapping her nose, he winked as he said, "I will."

A throaty laugh escaped her lips, a jarring contrast to the tight smile that didn't quite touch her eyes. Her head rested on Elwyn's shoulder. "Take care of this idiot, too, while you're at it."

"I was going to feed him to the first creature that looks hungry, actually," Redd laughed, ruffling Elwyn's hair.

"Fuck you, Redd," Elwyn growled gently as he shoved the hand away.

"I can help you guys, you know that, right?" Feya asked. "I am not some weak little damsel in distress. I can go into the battle and—"

"No, you're not going," Elwyn stated.

"We can't take the chance of you ending up on

the other end of the battlefield." Redd stroked her cheek. "The queen can call you anytime during the fight. The best place for you is here. Finish your goodbyes, you two."

Approaching Nuit, he knelt, the rough-hewn stone cool beneath his knees. Her unsettlingly bright gold eyes met his; her skin, luminous in the dim light, radiated a faint, shimmering heat. As his fingers brushed her cheek, a wave of tingling warmth pulsed through him, a tangible current of her magic.

"We are getting ready to leave," he whispered, pulling his hand back. He looked at his fingertips as he rubbed them together.

"Oh," she whispered. His eyes, darkened and hungry, darted to her mouth, watching the way it formed that single syllable, a soft, almost imperceptible movement. The air vibrated faintly with the sound, a whisper brushing against his skin.

"Do you need anything?" he whispered. A mixture of hunger, rage and something more primal, desire, coursed through his veins.

"No." She shook her head, a cascade of raven hair shimmering, catching the light like polished obsidian.

His fingers itched to run through those thousands of velvety strands, so he fisted his hands at his side to avoid the temptation.

"If you need anything, Brady and Leo can get it," he murmured.

"Okay." The word was so soft he barely heard it.

"I mean it." His voice was rough and husky. "If you need anything, just ask. They will do or get whatever you need."

She nodded, her eyes squinting up at him.

Standing up, he looked at Leo. "Text me if there are any issues."

"You charge your phone?" Leo quirked an eyebrow at him.

"Yep," Redd snickered, patting his friend on the back before he went upstairs.

He fought back the lump in his throat, the bitter taste of finality, as he stole one last look at the four of them—their laughter echoing faintly. A silent push sent the pocket door sliding shut with a soft click, a sound swallowed by the heavy silence of the hallway.

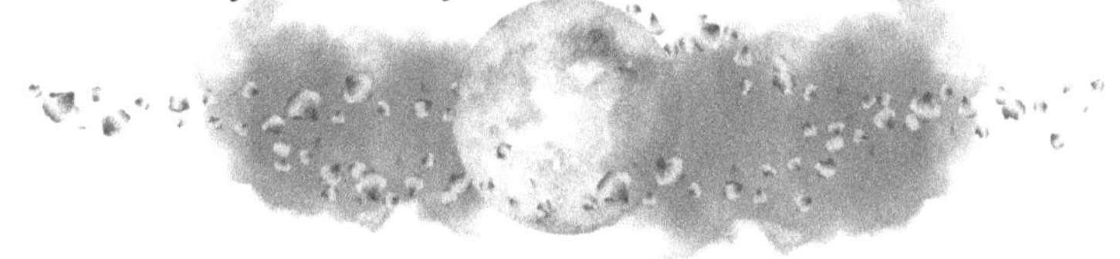

Redd stood outside the vale, the pungent smell of sweat and blood thick in the air, a thousand heartbeats, a thunderous drum. The soft, frantic thump of a thousand hearts fueled a savage thirst coursing through his veins. Aguya, Alvero, and Elwyn were beside him. Nearby, fae shimmered, their hands a blur as they worked on a portal, the air crackling with arcane energy. The chaotic sound of lightning seemed to emanate from where they were trying to pierce the vale. He scanned the bizarre, chaotic array of magical creatures—Alvero's army, a menagerie of animals, the forbidden snacks writhing amongst the fae, their fur and scales gleaming under the moonlight.

The murmur of the crowd was a tide of sound washing over him, each heartbeat a rumble in his ears. He inhaled, the coppery tang filled his nostrils as they flared, a metallic scent clinging to the sweat and dust. A burning thirst scorched his throat, mirroring the frantic pulse that hammered against his ribs. Eyes squeezed shut, he centered himself on the steady thump-thump-thump of his own heart, a lifeline until the feast began. *I don't need to go off halfcocked.*

Aguya fidgeted beside him, the rhythmic motion of her fingers a nervous counterpoint to the frantic thump of her heart. Heat shimmered visibly from her skin, a tangible wave washing over him, its intensity almost painful. He could smell the faintest acrid tang in the air, a scent always preceding her magic.

"Patience," Redd muttered, gently grabbing her arm.

"I have not tried to kill anyone yet," Aguya shrugged.

He glanced over his shoulder at Alvero and Wallace, their voices an inaudible murmur barely audible above the wind whistling through the trees and the soft sounds of the crowd. Alvero's nod was sharp, a quick jerk of his head. He wished for Leo's presence. His sharp ears could tell him what the hushed exchange was about. He trusted Alvero to do the right thing for everyone, but feared his old friend would decide that meant sacrificing his family. Looking down at Aguya, he suspected Alvero would not sacrifice her happiness for these people, but the doubt still lingered.

"Soon," Redd whispered. "We will both get our chance."

Alvero strode toward them, his boots crunching on the forest path, Bobo lumbering behind him. Bursting forward, Bobo shoved between Aguya and himself, a solid impact jarring their sides. Eyes dropping, he saw the three-foot-tall, four-legged demon dog; a low growl vibrated through the air, hot breath ghosting his face. The beast's fur, soft to the touch, glinted in the dim moonlight; a smile tugged at his lips despite the palpable menace.

"You are such a good boy," Aguya said, stroking Bobo's ruff.

"You ready to have some fun, boy?" Redd asked. Two burning coals, those red eyes, flickered up at him; a barely visible bob of the head, his reply. The soft, yielding fur of the dog felt warm beneath his hand as he turned back to Alvero. "When do we enter?"

"They should be through soon," Alvero replied. "The portal is already showing cracks through the vale. I have no doubt they know we are here, so be ready"

"Good, we can just get right to the fight soon." Redd rubbed his neck, a deep breath catching in his throat. He inhaled again, the sharp tang filling his nostrils, a primal hunger clenching his stomach. "You have something to tell us about your little convo with Wallace there?"

"Just discussing battle strategies," Alvero snorted.

Amber eyes met hazel with a sharp lift of a red eyebrow.

"Literally, he talked about his plans on entering the vale." Alvero's brow furrowed. "Quit being so distrustful. I've done nothing to deserve this."

"Quit fighting, you two," Aguya grunted. "He is worried about us all." She pointed at Redd. "He thinks he is doing what's right for everyone involved." She pointed at Alvero. "Now we can focus on ending the fight and freeing Feya."

"Look at you being the voice of reason," Alvero smirked as he brushed a kiss across the top of Aguya's head.

"Now," she snorted. "I'll make sure it never happens again after that sarcasm."

Pushing down the tremor of nerves and hunger, he watched, mesmerized, as sparks, like tiny incandescent stars, flew from the air, sizzling faintly. A small, circular blue light bloomed, a pinpoint of radiance against the dimness, then swelled, expanding with a soft hum.

Wallace turned to the murmuring crowd, the cacophony of voices a wave washing over as excitement grew. He raised his hand, a gesture that slowly stilled the sea of faces. "Soon we will be through and the fight will begin. You have all trained for this and are ready. We have justice on our sides and our people deserve to have that justice. I know some of you might have fear in your soul, butterfly wings that brush against that fear, causing it to grow. Do not let those butterflies fan the flames of fear and have it take over. When we are on that battle-field, you must all stand tall, stand brave, and fight like the devil is on your heels."

Redd turned, his eyes catching the vibrant, ex-panding blue circle, a deepening azure against the muted grey of the dark forest. An icy wave washed over him, the air growing heavy with anticipation. Growling, he said, "and some of those butterflies will be the last these sol-diers feel as they march to their deaths."

Observing Wallace's assembled soldiers, a kaleido-scope of mismatched uniforms met the eye; a ragtag army indeed. The familiar gray of the queen's army was absent, even from Wallace himself. A hopeful sigh escaped—the clash of battle might be less chaotic, a friend easily dis-tinguished from foe with the difference in uniforms.

"We're through," Wallace shouted. "Be at the ready! They know we are coming and they will fight fiercely!"

"Do you think Alse is in there?" Aguya whispered, an almost imperceptible tremor in her voice.

"I don't know," Redd replied. "But she'll be a tasty little snack."

"Have you ever met someone who wasn't a snack?" Aguya laughed softly.

"A handful of people. I've never thought you were

a snack. You, too, old friend." Redd's hand landed with a solid thwack on Alvero's back.

"Thanks, I think," Alvero sighed.

The shimmering circle expanded, a pearly gateway large enough to pass through. Fae, a blur of motion, vanished into the swirling vale. Redd inhaled the crisp, earthy scent of the air before following, the weightlessness washing over him in a dizzying rush—a sensation like soaring on unseen wings. He stumbled, knees hitting the trembling earth, a wave of nausea rising in his throat as he fought back the bile.

"Get up, old man," Alvero said, gripping his arm.

They stepped into a chaotic melee; the air filled with the screams of the dying and the clang of fighting. The earth trembled violently beneath their feet as a fireball exploded nearby, a searing heat washing over them. His heart hammered against his ribs, a frantic drum solo. He breathed deeply, the acrid tang of sweat, blood, and his next meal filling his nostrils.

Chapter 33

The strain of holding the spell sapped Nuit's energy; a dull throb echoed in her temples as she watched Feya. Sleepless nights, fueled by the new spell's volatile energy, left her achingly weary. Hours after Redd and the others departed, the queen's attempt to pull Feya to her sent a jolt through Nuit's defenses; she felt the surge in magical power, a wave of heat overwhelmed her as she had to ramp up her spell. Feya's brow glistened with sweat, her face pale, betraying the agony she fought to conceal. Nuit felt the pull, a sharp tug at the edges of her own spell, a physical sensation like being stretched taut.

Leo and Brady, oblivious, sat at the table, the rhythmic slap of cards a jarring counterpoint to the silent struggle between Nuit and Feya. Nuit's gaze returned to Feya; a single drop of sweat, glistening like a pearl, traced a path down Feya's temple.

"Is there anything I can do for you?" Nuit said, her voice hoarse as she brushed the sweat off Feya's forehead.

"Oh, I'm fine," Brady laughed, dropping a card on the table.

Nuit looked at Brady, trying to figure out why the fae thought she was talking to her, before turning back to Feya.

"Ignore her, she's not always observ..." Feya paused as she inhaled deeply and winced. After a second she finished, "observant. I am fine." A tentative smile spread across Feya's face.

"If you need something, I can help." Nuit's touch was gentle, brushing a stray strand of hair from Feya's brow.

"You're doing more than enough." Feya's eyes clouded over as another wave hit.

Nuit felt the pull on the edges of her spell, a wrenching sensation like a giant hand trying to tear the circle apart. The circle groaned and threatened to crumble under the strain; a low, guttural grinding filled the air. Her stomach churned, a nauseating twist of anxiety until the pull ceased abruptly. Wobbling on shaky legs, she fumbled for the chalk, pulling it from her pocket. Approaching the circle's edge, she reinforced the spell, drawing runes from her own heritage, her own magic. As the last symbol glowed, a wave of warmth suffused her, and the walls felt immeasurably stronger.

Rubbing her tired eyes, the room blurring, she leaned back on her heels, the rough stone digging into her skin. A low thrum vibrated through the floor, a constant, almost imperceptible hum that matched the dull ache in her head. Hours bled into each other; she wasn't sure if it would take hours, days or weeks that would be needed for her to hold the spell. Her muscles screamed in protest, each breath a labored effort, a stark contrast to the steady, unwavering pulse of magic she tried to maintain. *Maybe if I eat something. Or maybe even ask for some coffee.*

A nervous gnaw at her lip, the salty tang of blood faint. She wondered if Redd was alright. A low hum of anxiety vibrated in her chest. *Why do I care about a male who used me for sex?* The thought, a persistent fly buzzing in her mind, circled relentlessly even as a cold knot of worry constricted her chest. Closing her eyes, she pressed her knuckles hard against her temples, the pressure a dull ache against the bone. She tried to push away the image of him—that infuriating, cocky grin, the warm, amber of his eyes—but it clung to the tired landscape of her mind like a stubborn shadow.

A sharp gasp, like a knife through silence, dragged her from her reverie. A powerful tug, a wrenching sensation in her gut, ripped at the edges of her spell. Her knuckles white, she clenched her fists, muscles screaming with the effort as she channeled every ounce of magic, holding on until the pull vanished with a final, sickening pop. Dust motes danced in the weak light beams slanting through the room as she looked around; the room was strangely still, eerily quiet.

Everyone had moved, leaving her feeling isolated in the sudden hush. Leo sat on the cold stone floor, his face etched with worry as he cradled Feya. The girl trembled, a shuddering sob wracking her slight frame, hot tears streaming down her cheeks, leaving glistening trails. Brady stood over them.

Worry written across Leo's brow as he looked up. "What do we do?"

Every gaze, sharp as needles, pricked her skin. Her mind, a silent, echoing void. Her mouth, a dry, cracked desert, opened and shut, soundless as dust. *Why do they expect me to have all the answers?*

Opening it one more time, she whispered, "Sleep."

"Huh?" Brady said, her brow furrowed.

Standing, shaky legs protesting with each step, she approached them. A cool draft brushed her skin as she rubbed her fingers together, the warmth a stark contrast to the faint heat of the spell gathering. A barely audible whisper escaped her lips, a breathy incantation, as her hand touched Feya's forehead, a fleeting contact of cool skin against warm. "Naum."

Feya's eyelids fluttered, heavy as lead, before finally closing. The rhythmic rise and fall of her chest as her breathing evened out, a soft susurrus in the quiet room, was the only sound as sleep claimed her. Nuit, observing the subtle shift in Feya's brow each time the pull came – a silent, almost imperceptible twitch – felt a knot of worry tighten in her own chest. The chair creaked under her weight as she slumped into it, the rough wood digging into her aching shoulders. Her head throbbed a dull, persistent ache. The scent of dust hung in the air as she closed her eyes, the celestial contract's pull a relentless, gnawing tension at the edge of her consciousness, denying her the sweet release of sleep.

REDD

Chapter 34

The adrenaline surged through Redd—a raw, electric jolt he'd nearly forgotten. Fae blood, warm and metallic, slicked his soaked shirt. The sweet nectar's tang lingered, sweet and savory, on his tongue. He inhaled the acrid bite of smoke and scorched earth, the sharp tang of ozone from exploding spells as the scents of the war zone filled his nostrils. A gaping chasm ripped through the once-smooth grass, the earth groaning under the strain of magic. Erratic fires cast flickering shadows on the chaotic melee of magic and steel. Fists connected with bone-jarring thuds and blasts of energy tore through the air with a searing crackle. The ground bucked with a low tremor, throwing Redd off balance for a heartbeat before he regained his footing.

Grabbing the nearest fae he saw, fingers gripping the coarse gray cloth of his uniform, he hauled the fae's head sideways, the tunic rough against his palm. His other hand fisted in his hair while the fae clawed at his hand. Beneath the tan skin, a throbbing vein pulsed—a frantic rhythm of blood, fear, and adrenaline. A metallic tang of blood and sweat filled his nostrils as he paused, savoring the moment before his fangs sank in. Warm, rich fluid flooded his mouth, a delicious rush down his throat, erasing the gnawing emptiness, the hunger's claws releasing. The urge to continue was fierce, but a sharper need held him back; this soldier had other uses.

With a wet, sucking sound, he pulled his fangs free, the coppery tang of blood thick in the air. His eyes, glittering with arcane power, met the fae soldier's. A shiver, like icy fire, ran through him as the glamor magic pulsed, a tangible hum beneath his skin. "Your sole purpose in life is to keep me safe," the words hissed, the blood a tangible heat that amplified the power in his eyes, making the spell thrum with a dark, almost palpable energy.

The soldier nodded, his eyes glazed and distant. Another of the queen's grey-clad soldiers, steel gleaming, charged; a sickening thud followed as Redd's soldier spun, driving a sword through the foe's chest.

A grim smile touched Redd's lips as he pushed through the chaotic melee, the clash of steel ringing in the air, a coppery tang heavy on the breeze. While his soldier grappled with another fae, Redd spotted another soldier raising his sword, the cold steel glinting. He seized the man's sword arm, yanking him forward with brutal force. The sharp, wet sound of fangs sinking into flesh followed before the soldier even registered the attack. Using the same glamour, he now had two soldiers fighting for him, the feeling of power a cold thrill against his skin. The majority of the soldiers, despite rigorous training, were clearly inexperienced, their movements stiff and hesitant under the pressure. Two more soldiers fell victim to Redd's magic.

Spinning on the blood-soaked earth, he saw Aguya, a silhouette against the fiery inferno of her magic. The air shimmered with heat, a tangible wave washing over him.

Alvero dueled another fae, the rhythmic clang of steel on steel a deafening percussion. Alvero's sword flashed, a blur of motion surprisingly graceful for a male who hid from the world in his forest. Bobo, a blur of inky black fur, dove for the fae Alvero was fighting, his sharp teeth sinking into the fae's shoulder with a wet, tearing sound. The fae's scream, high and reedy, cut through the air, a sound of pure, agonizing pain.

Aguya's gaze flickered nervously between them, a frantic dance of golden fire.

His eyes darted around, a frantic search across the sea of faces; the queen was not visible amidst the crowd. A guttural growl ripped from his throat, directed at Aguya, the sound sharp and urgent. "We need to find the queen!"

From his perspective, the monosyllable was almost inaudible, even with his heightened hearing, but he could read the sarcastic comment on her lips. "Duh."

Rolling his eyes, *I should have remembered the cynicism was strong in this one. Why can't I just get a yes, sir?*

Scooping up Aguya, he raised her above the chaotic crowd. He balanced her on his shoulder, feeling her weight as he navigated through a slow turn. He yelled, "Do you see anything?"

Suddenly, a soldier, a blur of grey drab against the smokey landscape, crashed through the undergrowth. A frantic hand shot up, fingers outstretched towards the soldier to shield Aguya. Before Redd caught the soldier, he stumbled, a pained groan tearing through his lips, then collapsed to his knees with a thud, a wisp of grey smoke curling from his ears.

"I got you, idiot," Aguya said, patting his head. He could hear, even though he could not see from his angle, the smirk in her voice.

He continued slowly spinning as dirt flew around them. *I can't keep her up there too long, she is an easy target that high.*

A sharp tug on his hair stopped his turning. Looking up, he saw Aguya's pointing hand, a blur of motion against the dusty sky scape. Redd bent, Aguya leapt from his shoulders, landing with a soft thud on the ground. He set off at a snail's pace towards where she saw the queen. His soldiers and Aguya, a whirlwind as they followed closely. Alvero, bringing up the rear.

He watched, frowning, as a bolt of lightning flashed past him, barely missing him. The acrid bite of burnt hair filled his nostrils, a sharp, stinging smell. One of his soldiers' fell, crimson staining the ground as the lightning bolt flashed through his stomach. Stepping over the still form, a rough hand grasped another soldier's neck, yanking him from a brutal, clashing fight. The metallic tang of blood filled the air as fangs sank in; a primal pull, a relentless urge to drink, to drain, surged. A simmering rage, hot and bitter, throbbed beneath the surface, demanding release, a desperate need to sate its thirst, consequences be damned. *Who would notice or care if I drank my fill of sweet fae blood?* The taste was a sweet nectar that was like a drug. It had him in its clutches, with the last of his resolve he withdrew his fangs, casting the glamor.

The rasping of his breath, a hot, metallic tang of blood thick in the air with each ragged inhale, fueled the growing thirst. His hands, slick with sweat and blood, trembled as he navigated the crush of bodies, the cacophony of battle, a deafening roar growing ever louder. Each step brought a fresh wave of steel, soldiers pressing down with suffocating weight. His mind raced, a frantic whirlwind of strategies. Each aborted plan met with the chilling clang of swords and the sickening thud of bodies as the onslaught seemed to grow the closer they got to the queen.

A pungent, acrid cloud of emerald smoke, crackling with unseen energy, flashed past him as Alvero released one of his magical herb packets. Soldiers choked, the rasping coughs echoing, as they crumpled to their knees, their faces contorted in pain. More soldiers advanced, their boots thudding on the hard-packed earth, as a shimmering air fae, wings a blur of iridescent blue, dispersed the smoke with a gust of wind carrying the faint scent of wildflowers and ozone. Redd, his grip tight on the cool, smooth hilt of a small blade, hurled it with deadly accuracy. The blade found its mark, piercing the fae's throat with a sickening thud. She fell, a gurgling sigh escaping her lips as life ebbed away.

Another soldier approached, the glint of steel catching the dim light. There was a whistling sound as a sword sliced past his ear, a whisper of cold steel against his scalp as it shaved a bit of skin off his ear. He snatched his dagger, a familiar weight in his hand, feeling the satisfying resistance of flesh as the blade sank deep. Warm, wet blood sprayed across his face, the drug like tang filling his nostrils. Twisting it, he ripped the dagger back out.

The air crackled, a high-pitched whine preceding the jolt; his arm hairs bristled, then a searing, white-hot pain exploded through his body. He stumbled, his knees hitting the gritty earth. His vision blurred and swam with black spots. Through the haze, a woman, her hair like spun silver, stood over him. Her eyes blazed with an inner light, crackling lightning projecting from her fingers, raised high, mirroring the storm above.

Chapter 35

Nuit's eyes darted around the dimly lit room, a faint light painting shadows on the walls. Her energy was waning, leaving her restless and sleep was elusive. Soft snores, like gentle waves, washed over her from the others. Leo, slumped in his chair, his arms crossed, seemed about to topple over any second now; the squeak of his chair was barely audible. Brady sat in the other chair, her head resting heavily on her forearms, her breathing slow and even. Feya laid on the hard, cold ground; the rough texture looked uncomfortable. Brady had brought Feya a pillow and blanket, which offered a slight comfort.

Standing, her legs trembled unsteadily, as she moved towards the gleaming copper bowl. The cool glass of the spring moon water bottle felt soothing in her hand as she grabbed it; she was grateful for the extra supplies they provided her. A wave of nausea sent her rubbing her temple.

The silence pressed in—heavy, suffocating. Hours crawled by since Aguya's last text, a terse message announcing their penetration of the vale, followed by a chilling, absolute radio silence. Each tick of the unseen clock echoed the agonizing eternity of waiting.

In her bones, the rhythmic pulse of the spell, a dull

throb, eased slightly as the intense, searing pain that had accompanied their attempts to force Feya into the battle had lessened, leaving only a deep, aching weariness. The meager comfort it offered was a cool balm on her aching body, easing the searing pain that throbbed with holding the spell.

With a soft sigh, she poured the water into the ceramic bowl; the water splashed over the edge, softly hitting her hand. A wave of cool relief washed over her heated hand, the feeling gentle and soothing.

Everything will be fine, the fight will be over soon. I just need to be patient and strong. Her breath hitched, a ragged whisper against the mantra she repeated over and over in her head, a bland taste on her tongue. The thought hung hollow, mirroring the icy dread blooming in her chest. Doubt, a bitter, metallic tang, clung to the back of her throat.

With a delicate swirl of her finger in the cool water, she pictured him. Visions of his fiery red hair, those captivating amber eyes sparkling with mirth, filled her mind. She felt the phantom touch of his rough, calloused hands, the lingering scent of his cologne sharp and warm in the air. The ancient spell, a silken whisper in her native tongue, flowed from her lips.

إ ى عسأ يتلا تاباجإلا يل بلجي قمعب عطاس‌لا ءاملا. اهيلإ

Casting the spell, she watched the water swirl into a misty chaos, the scent of ozone sharp in the air as tiny, glittering lights, like captured starlight, appeared within the swirling fog. The vortex spun faster, a dizzying, blurry dance, before resolving into a vision of shocking clarity. Her breath hitched; an icy wave washed over her. Redd, eyes closed, lay still on the blood-soaked battlefield, the crimson a stark contrast against the dusty earth. The predawn chill bit at her skin. The rising sun painted the sky with ominous hues. Anger and grief, a bitter taste in her mouth, warred within her as she hurled the glass bottle across the room, the sound sharp and brittle as it shattered on the wall. Hot tears blurred her vision as she fought for control.

"What's wrong?" Leo's sleep-husky voice, a low rumble like distant thunder, grumbled.

"Oh, sweetie," Brady said, hurrying over. The rough wool of her sweater brushed against Nuit's back as Brady patted her gently, a comforting weight.

Gasping for air, a ragged breath hitching in her throat, she fought for words—to explain Redd's lifeless form, the crushing weight of lost hope. Only a silent, despairing shake of her head came. The air hung heavy with unspoken grief, a cold dread clinging to her skin.

"Why are you shaking and crying, sweetie?" Brady asked, her hand gently moved in circles on Nuit's back.

She had tried to hate him, a bitter taste clinging to the back of her throat, even knowing she meant nothing to him. She still tried to fight the emotions that built inside her heart, but now she knew she failed as a clenching fist mirroring the aching, hollow feeling in her chest built inside her core. Closing her eyes, lids heavy as wet sand, she sought the elusive calm, a fragile peace in the storm of her emotions. "It's nothing," she whispered. "I am just tired."

"Why don't you try to sleep?" Brady asked, brushing her bangs off her forehead.

"I couldn't sleep even if I wanted to," Nuit sighed, tears still streaming down her face.

"Dramatic woman," Leo muttered, under his breath barely audible.

"You shush," Brady said, waving a hand at Leo.

Nuit's throat tightened, the intended retort a bitter taste on her tongue. The cool linen against her cheeks felt strangely comforting against the hot sting of her tears;

Brady's touch gentle but firm. The hushed murmur of worried voices swirled around her, a low hum punctuated by the occasional sniffle. The sight of their anxious faces blurred through her own damp vision. *Should I share the chilling vision, or let the grim truth unfold itself later?*

"I am just tired," she whispered. "I tried to do a spell to see what was happening on the battlefield..." Her voice trailed, eyes dropping to her hands—a tremor, a frantic fluttering, like trapped birds, visible beneath the dim light. A silent swallow, and her lips clamped shut, the unspoken words a weight on her chest. *I don't think I can handle any more emotions other than my own right now. Plus, they will learn soon enough.* "I could not do the spell while holding the barrier spell."

Brady pulled Nuit's head to her chest. "We are all worried, sweetie. But we have been through this before, they will all come back fine."

"Some of us don't usually just sit at home," Leo snorted.

"He is just mad he doesn't get to go be part of the fight," Brady sighed. Nuit felt her head rise and fall with that dramatic sigh.

Nuit squeezed her eyes shut, the pressure a slight comfort against the overwhelming chaos. A low hum of anxiety vibrated in her ears, a stark contrast to the heavy scent of Brady's perfume clinging to the air. A chill prickled her skin, sending gooseflesh across her arms. *I have known him for such a short time, I should not be this torn up. He didn't even feel the same. I will not mourn someone who would not mourn me.* The insidious thoughts, even to herself, felt like lies. Hot tears streamed down her face, each drop a searing brand. She clung to Brady, a desperate anchor in the storm of her emotions.

Chapter 36

Redd jolted awake, a sharp pain shooting through his ribs as Aguya retracted her foot. Looking up, he met Aguya's furious glare, the intensity of it almost palpable. "Don't die, idiot."

Alvero hunched over, concern etched on his face as he peered down. "I don't have time to heal you, for fuck's sake."

"I don't need your help," Redd spat, the words sharp as shattered glass. He shoved Alvero's face away.

Sitting up, his muscles screamed in protest, the lingering electric shocks fading. He blinked, the gritty air thick with dust and smoke, trying to orient himself. His soldiers, a blur of motion and clashing steel, held the enemies at bay. His gaze fell upon the tiny lightning fae; her delicate form contorted in agony, smoke curling from her singed wings. A silent scream played on her lips, lost in the cacophony of battle—the clang of swords, the roar of the crowd, the guttural cries of males. The din intensified as they neared the heart of the conflict where the queen reigned.

Growling, he shouted, "She's mine."

Aguya's head bobbed, a silent acknowledgement as

the shimmering spell dissolved into the humid air, a faint scent of smoke lingering. The crackle of her magic faded for a brief moment. She spun, facing a new foe.

Jumping up on unsteady legs, he stumbled, nearly falling. His head swam, befuddled, as he tried to get his bearings. A dizzying fog clearing with a shake of his head. Shaky steps carried him the short distance. He grabbed the lightning fae's hair; coarse gray strands slipped through his fingers as wrenching her head back.

A desperate plea, "Please," escaped from her lips.

Her ragged breaths hit his face as he dragged her up, the lingering scent of burnt flesh sharp in the air. Her glowing eyes met his; he could see the sheer fear flowing from those eyes. He smiled, a cruel pleasure warming him as he anticipated the intoxicating taste. Bending, he sank his teeth into her neck, the warm, metallic tang of her blood an explosion in his mouth, a coppery peach flavor. The rich, coppery scent filled his nostrils, his vision blurring red, a burning thirst consuming him. He fought the urge, but the hunger was a wildfire, his teeth sinking deeper with each desperate claw of her hands, her pained squeal a high-pitched whine. His hands jerked her head further back, trying to get better access. Her bones felt brittle beneath his fingers. Finally, empty of fluid, he released her. She slumped, lifeless, her skin a ghastly gray. Stepping over the broken body, he wiped his mouth, a chilling resolve hardening his gaze.

Spinning, a dizzying swirl of clashing steel and desperate cries filled his ears. He scanned the chaotic battleground. He couldn't find Elwyn amidst the dust and blood, a cold knot tightening in his gut. The hope that he was safe felt fragile. The thought of Feya's wrath, should Elwyn be harmed, was a chilling weight.

The din seemed to grow louder the closer they got to the queen. The noises drowned out the sound of the heart beats around him. Thirst filled his soul as the scent of fresh blood seemed to assault him from everywhere.

Sweat dripped from his brow as Aguya burned anyone that came close to them. Steel hit steel as it clashed all over. When one of his soldiers fell, he would just create another, using his glamor to create more to fight for him. Magic collided with magic, stirring dust and smoke that permeated the air. The earth tremors seemed to grow stronger as they got to the epicenter. He could almost see the queen, almost. He could swear he could smell her blood, hear her heartbeat, but knew that was in his head.

He squinted at the fiery horizon. A canvas of crimson and gold splashed across the twilight sky. A restless feeling, a prickling urgency, told him his time here was almost over.

With a guttural snarl, he seized a soldier battling one of his glamorized minions. Sharp teeth sank into flesh, a warm wetness flooding his mouth. New droplets traced a path down his chin, joining the already crusting crimson stain. He felt the sticky warmth spreading across his shirt, a chilling contrast to the damp chill of the air. He released the limp body, its weight thudding onto the cold, hard ground.

A piercing scream—like nails on a chalkboard—jolted him from his gnawing hunger. He turned to see Alvero's face, a mask of grim displeasure etched into the lines around his mouth, the frown deep. "Huh?"

Redd's brow furrowed, a crimson line etched against his tanned skin as Alvero's rough fingers tightened on his shirt. Alvero's hot breath washed over Redd's face as their eyes locked.

"I said slow down on eating you fucking heathen," Alvero screamed.

"How else do you want me to kill them?" Redd snatched a soldier whose sword whistled down towards Alvero's head. Ignoring the burning thirst, his trembling hands snapped the soldier's neck with a sickening crack. Breath ragged, he tossed the limp body at Alvero's feet, the thud heavy and final.

"Knock them out," Alvero blustered. "These soldiers aren't all bad guys, they are just following the wrong person. Do to them what you did to them..." He flicked his hands at the glamorized soldiers. "They are blindly following based on—"

"Fine!" Redd shouted.

Redd frowned, his gaze fixed on Alvero. A pungent, acrid smell of burnt gunpowder and something metallic filled the air as Alvero exhaled a grey plume of smoke. Two soldiers crumpled to their knees, ragged coughs wracking their bodies. A cold dread, a visceral thirst for blood, clawed at Redd, but the harsh reality of Alvero's words, a chilling weight in his chest, held him back.

Then he saw her; blonde hair, shimmering like spun gold. Her blue eyes, bright and intense, locked with his. Turning to Alvero, a low growl, rough as sandpaper, vibrated in his chest, "Fuck it. Just one more meal."

Alvero's head, a quick jerk, followed his gaze. "Alright." The word, a strained whisper lost in the deafening boom that ripped the air, vibrated through the ground.

His stinging eyes smarting from the sudden flash. The force of the blast slammed against his body, a physical blow that knocked his breath away. Dirt, gritty and brown, splattered his face as he tumbled backward, landing hard on his back with a jarring thud. He shook his head, the impact ringing faintly in his ears, trying to clear the disorientation. Brushing the clinging soil from his cheeks, he pushed himself up, his muscles protesting the sudden exertion.

Scanning the chaotic scene, his eyes found her—Alse. She struggled to rise. He could see the tremor of her hand. Aguya's sister, the viper who'd nearly claimed one of his kin. He inhaled deeply, trying to catch a whiff of her blood, a prelude to his vengeance. He vowed to drain her life, and today, he would keep that vow. Retreating, he felt the icy wind increase as he distanced himself from Aguya, who was preoccupied with some fae. Alse, distracted, faced a blazing fire fae, his wings shimmering with an unearthly glow. The reason for her presence near the fae queen remained a mystery, but its relevance was insignificant now. His focus remained fixed on his task.

He wanted to savor her fear, to watch it bloom in her eyes, but the battlefield's noise—clashing steel, pained screams, and the stench of blood and ozone—was too overwhelming and time was dwindling. He circled around his prey, stopping to parry a fae's desperate strike. The whisper of steel slid past his head, ducking before he lost his head. As he rose back up, a sickening thud as his fist connected with the jaw, the fae sprawling backwards.

Over his shoulder, Alse's wide, terrified eyes met his; a slow, cruel grin stretched his lips. Her attempted retreat was clumsy as he pounced, the impact jarring. The rough ground scraped his arm as he pinned her down. He saw the desperate rise and fall of her chest as she channeled magic. His fingers circled her throat before she could cast. The frantic claw of her fingers against his wrist as he tightened his grip on her throat, the life draining from her eyes.

"Did you really think you could escape us?" he gloated.

Chapter 37

Nuit's gaze fell upon the iridescent moon water swirling in the porcelain bowl, its surface shimmering like captured starlight. Heavy eyelids fought a losing battle against the buzzing energy in her mind, a frantic symphony that drowned out the sound of Brady dusting. She wanted to fall into the oblivion of sleep, but could not. Each tug at her spell felt like a million tiny needles pricking her skin, breath catching in her throat with each assault from the pain. The silence after felt profound, heavy with the scent of lavender cleaner and exhaustion. Her shoulders slumped, a wave of bone-deep weariness washing over her. A slow, ragged exhale escaped her lips as she closed her eyes, the ache in her muscles a dull throb against the chill of the night air. She felt the weight of utter depletion settle upon her, etching lines of fatigue into her very soul.

Tears welled, blurring her vision, as a shaky whisper, thin as spun glass, escaped her lips. A chill, deeper than the autumn breeze, settled on her skin. "I don't know how much longer I can do this," she breathed, the words barely audible above the rustling leaves.

"Oh, sweetie," Brady murmured, her footsteps soft on the worn wooden floor, the warmth of her embrace a comforting weight against her. "You can do this. I have faith in you. You just need to eat. Let me go get us something to eat."

Nuit nodded, her gaze following Brady's hurried ascent up the creaking stairs, each step a muffled thud. A gnawing emptiness ached in her stomach; a stark emptiness. *When was the last time I ate? What did I eat?*

"Stay strong," Leo whispered. "They will be back soon."

Watching him, a tight smile touched her lips, eyes remaining cold and distant; a stark silence hung in the air, thick with the fact that she no longer had any words. The chill of despair settled on her, a heavy weight against her chest; only bleak, mournful thoughts echoed in her mind. She no longer had words of comfort, only words of sadness.

Turning, she looked back at the swirling water in the bowl. A hushed whisper escaped her lips, repeating the ancient words. A ghostly mist erupted, then settled, leaving the water eerily still. The silence that followed was heavy, broken only by the faint thrum of her own pulse. Tears pricked her eyes, stinging with the salt of exhaustion. The bone-deep weariness told her that she was too drained to force the battlefield's vision from the depths, but giving up felt impossible.

The cold, smooth glass of her phone pressed against her palm as she checked the time; she knew the sky was bleeding with the fiery hues of sunrise. Time was running out; he wouldn't have much time left to return. *If he gets back, which won't be happening. What if the reason the spell doesn't work is that he is dead?* She winced, a sharp intake of breath as the insidious thought burrowed deeper, its tendrils tightening around her mind. Despite the insistent whisperings of self-doubt, a dull ache pulsed in her temples. The phantom vision, blurry and incomplete, taunted her—a missing piece, a nagging itch at the edge of her awareness.

Inhaling deeply, she tried to steady her trembling hands, the cold seeping into her bones. *If I can focus on my energy, I can see if he's alive or not. I just need to focus and confirm whether or not it's true.* The cool air filled her lungs with each slow, deliberate breath. A soft sigh escaped her lips as she exhaled, the tension easing from her shoulders like melting snow. The sun warmed her face, a gentle pressure against her eyelids as she focused on the quiet rhythm of her breathing, searching for the calm within.

A single fingertip stirred the cool, shimmering water, sending ripples across the surface. She saw him again: the wry, self-deprecating curve of his lips after the brutal, bloody vengeance. The memory of his amber eyes, alight with passion, burned behind her eyelids as she recalled their lovemaking. *Was it love for him? Was it love for me?*

A soft sigh escaped her lips, a puff of warm air in the chilly room. She shook her head, the strands of her hair brushing her forehead and cheeks. With a deep breath, she cleared her mind; the silence punctuated only by the rhythmic sound of Leo's soft breathing. *Just focus on his face, nothing else. Do not think about anything else.* She pictured the curve of his lips, a sensual bow; the cat-eyed shape of his eyes, flecked with gold, the brassy red hair like spun copper as her fingertip traced its phantom texture. She recited the spell, the words a low hum.

Opening her eyes, she watched the water swirl in a dizzying vortex, a silken dance of sapphire and emerald, then fell still as glass. *Is it me or is he dead?*

Chapter 38

Twisting Alse's neck, her fingers clawing at his hands, he saw her jugular pulse throbbing violently; her ragged breaths rasping for air. The coppery tang of blood filled his mouth as his fangs sank into flesh, a wet tearing sound accompanying the searing heat of his bite. The din of battle receded as he drank deeply, the warm rush of her blood a thrilling tide against his tongue, her heart a frantic drum against his lips as it pumped the blood into his mouth faster. Her clawing ceased, her limp hand falling still as the life drained from her eyes. A brutal blow to his ribs sent him reeling, a snarl escaping his lips as blood dripped, viscous and dark, from his fangs.

"Aren't you just a scary vampire?" Aguya grunted. "She's mine. You got something on your chin, you may want to clean it off."

He nodded, pulling back, the soft fabric of Alse's shirt scraping against his fingers as he released her. Her slow, shallow breaths, a faint whisper against his ear, confirmed his grim assessment; her time was short. The battle, a dull roar punctuated by the clang of steel, was subsiding after hours of relentless fighting. The queen's grey military dress, a smudge of dull color in the dust and blood that splattered the landscape, was visible as her remaining soldiers fought desperately. He watched, his own heart heavy, as Wallace and his men relentlessly pressed their advance.

The pungent stench of burning flesh, like charred meat and singed hair, filled his nostrils. Turning, he saw Aguya; her face a mask of anguished grief contorted as she created the flames consuming her sister. Alvero, his face grim, brushed a tender kiss against her cheek, whispering words lost to Redd's ears; only the barely perceptible movement of his lips was visible amidst the flickering firelight.

"You good?" Redd said, patting her on the back.

She made a subtle nod as she turned to head towards the queen.

With the end in sight, he turned towards the horizon, the fiery orange and rose-pink of the sunrise painting the sky as the sunrays slowly stretched across the valley. He knew he did not have much longer to fight; the rising sun would soon beat down with intensity. He needed to escape before the relentless light bathed the valley.

"Time to burn them all down," Redd snapped. "Sun's going to be up soon."

Aguya stepped in front, the ground scorching beneath her feet, a fiery path blazing towards the queen. The air crackled with heat, a stench of burnt earth and smoke. He followed behind her, the infernos roar a deafening counterpoint to the clash of steel around them. His minions fought fiercely, a whirlwind of flashing blades and grunts, while behind him, Alvero's muttered complaints got lost in the din.

The clash of steel echoed as Wallace's army shattered the queen's final defense, a storm of flashing blades and desperate cries. A gritty wind whipped across the blood-soaked ground as they advanced. Wallace's roar, raw and powerful, cut through the din. "It is time you concede!"

Approaching, they positioned themselves behind Wallace.

"Never!" Casada screamed, a sharp, high-pitched sound that sliced through the air. Her brown curls, usually neat, bounced wildly around her face, now flushed and streaked with dirt. He'd never seen her so disheveled; her clothes rumpled, her eyes wide and frantic.

Two armed guards roughly grabbed Casada as she squirmed to get away. A deafening cheer, a wave of sound and motion, roared from the crowd; a vibrant sea of faces, their voices a thunderous blend of excitement and weariness.

"Let's take her inside before the sun comes up," Redd stated, his eyes going to the horizon as the ray crept closer and closer.

Wallace nodded curtly to the grim-faced soldiers gripping Casada's arms. They began dragging her away; her muffled protests swallowed by the crowd. Wallace turned to Elwyn, his voice low and sharp. "Round up the last of her followers. It's time they learned the truth."

"Will do," Elwyn nodded.

Elwyn, a grim sight caked in grime and slicked with dark blood, met his gaze. But the blood from a first glance seemed to be someone else's. He'd lost sight of him in the battle, but the relief was palpable. Feya's joy, he knew, would be immeasurable knowing he was safe. *She would probably bite my head off and bury me in a shallow grave if the boy had been hurt.*

"You did good, boy," Redd muttered before walking away. "Glad you're still alive."

"Wait," Elwyn yelled. "My ears must be deceiving me, old man. Can you repeat that?"

Elwyn's joyous laughter, like wind chimes, flowed through the air as Redd strode towards the castle, throwing a single defiant digit flipped over his shoulder. Before him lay the ravaged battlefield, a silent, grim tableau. The once-smooth ground, where grass once swayed gently, was now a brutal, uneven expanse, churned earth scarred by deep gouges, littered with the splintered remains of broken weapons and broken soldiers. The air hung heavy with the acrid smell of smoke and blood. Underfoot, the ground was uneven and yielding, a chilling reminder of the battle's destructive power; scorched, splintered tree trunks stood like skeletal sentinels against the bruised horizon.

Amidst the wreckage, fallen soldiers lay scattered—lifeless forms, like discarded dolls. The mournful wind whistling through shattered timbers pierced the oppressive silence that had fallen across those still alive.

They entered the castle, the queen screaming now and trying to break free of her captors. She twisted and contorted, but the soldiers did not give an inch.

They entered the castle; the queen's screams, sharp and piercing, echoed as she fought against her captors. Her desperate struggle—a twisting, contorting dance—was met with unwavering resolve. The soldiers did not give her an inch to fight. They entered a small, stuffy sitting room, the heavy oak door thudding shut behind them. The air was thick with tension; bodies pressed close around the queen. Alvero stood beside Aguya and Wallace. Four unfamiliar soldiers and the two guards stood in the room as well.

The muted green climbing vine pattern on the walls felt strangely cool against the fingertips as Redd absentmindedly ran a finger across it. Wallace dragged one of the green floral chairs across the dusty floorboards, a scraping sound echoing in the room. They shoved Casada into the chair with a rough thud and a soft whimper. Cold metal magic bands slapped against her wrists as they bound her to the chair. Her scream cut through the air, sharp and high-pitched. Lucky for him, the room had no windows as he looked around at the array of paintings adorning the walls.

"As I'm sure you know, these will restrict your powers," Wallace stated, a flick of his fingernail against the steel cuffs echoing faintly. He tugged at his blood-stained uniform, striving for an impeccable appearance amidst the stains riddling his uniform. Redd watched, a skeptical eyebrow arched, the crimson splatter across Wallace's once crisp uniform a stark contrast to his meticulous efforts to straighten it out.

Redd shook his head. Stepping up to the queen, he spoke to her. "It's my turn now. You're going to release the contract on Feya."

"Fuck you," Casada spat.

"Such foul language for such a dignified queen," Redd chuckled.

"You can wait—" Wallace started.

"No, can do. The sun is coming up as we speak," Redd growled. "On top of that, I have someone locking my daughter in with a spell. I am going to get her released first or I swear I will have Aguya set fire to the entire building with us all in it. We can make it a bonfire. Anyone have marshmallows?"

Shrugging, Aguya said, "I would do it. The fire won't hurt me."

"If we let you go first, will you leave sooner?" Wallace rolled his eyes, a barely audible click echoing the impatient tap-tap-tap of his foot against the marble floor.

"I make her break the contract," Redd smirked. "I go hide from the sun. As soon as that fiery ball of death goes down, I am gone for good. Then, when you have your next crisis, you can avoid involving my family and me."

"I want to know why Alse was here, also," Aguya

huffed.

Nodding, Redd looked down at his mud-caked boots, speckled with dark crimson stains and something else, a vaguely greasy smear. *I look quite the bloody mess.* A devious smile stretched across his face, a predatory glint in his eyes, as he watched Wallace futilely brush at himself. He wiped his hand across his damp, clinging shirt, the chill of the wet cotton a stark contrast to the warmth of the room. With a swift movement, he clapped Wallace on the back, the sickening thud accompanied by a spreading crimson stain.

"I will go upstairs to Elwyn's old suites and stay until nightfall," Redd said, his voice extra chipper. "Then you can beat, torture, whatever you want to this..." He flicked his hand at the queen. "Fae. I will not interfere, but..." He paused again for dramatic effect. "I will not leave until she breaks the contract holding my daughter and tells Aguya why Alse was here. But once that is done, I am out of your hair. Alright?"

"Are you really listening to this scummy blood sucker?" Casada snorted.

"Shut up, your highness," Redd said, looking down at her. "This will be the last day anyone will call you that." Redd shook his head. "Does she really think anyone cares about her opinion?"

Turning, he extended his hand, crimson-stained, towards Wallace. Wallace recoiled, his gaze fixed on the gruesome print—a stark, dark stain mirroring the one seared onto his own back—disgust twisting his features. *I don't know how this male fought and thought he wouldn't get dirty. Such a clean freak.*

Wallace tentatively reached out a hand, a sneer twisting his lips. The smooth skin felt soft against Redd's calloused hand, who responded with a bone-jarring grip as he shook it.

"It's a deal then," Redd said, before turning back to the queen.

Casada's gaze, heavy-lidded and weary, rested on him. Her hands tugged with futile efforts against her shackles. A low growl, rumbling deep in her chest, vibrated the air, a barely audible rasp. "I will not give you anything you want. So, there is no use in asking."

Bending down, he met her gaze. A moment stretched, heavy and silent, before his voice, a low rumble like distant thunder, broke the stillness. "I offer you this, your life for my daughter's freedom or I'll be damned if I care what happens next. But I will rip your fucking throat out with my teeth," he paused, licking his teeth for dramatic effect. "You will not survive the next five seconds. They can try to kill me here or hunt me down, but I'm going to have me a royal feast tonight if you don't give me what I want."

"Do you think you scare me?" Casada laughed maniacally. "There are thousands of males in line to do the same thing to me. What's one more?" With a regal shrug, her shoulders lifted, the silken rustle of her gown a whisper against the hushed air, a queen's silent command.

"Oh," Redd shook his head, a faint sigh escaping his lips. "I was not done. Every last drop of your blood will be drunk by me. I will then go after your son. Then I will go after every person in your bloodline and make sure your bloodline dies at the tip of my fangs. Your sisters, cousins, nephews, nieces, every single one will be my personal meal. So, you can hold that little contract and know that every last one of your bloodline will die."

Casada's gaze dropped, her eyelids fluttering like moth wings, a faint frown etching itself onto her brow. The silence hummed, a low thrum broken only by the rustle of her skirt.

"The clock is ticking," Redd whispered, bringing his face closer to hers. "I can hear that heart of yours racing.

The louder it beats, the stronger the sweet scent of your blood gets. Gods, your blood smells so good, a delicate little nectar to feast on. You'd think I'd have had my fill of your kind today, but turns out I haven't."

"I can just burn her from the inside out," Aguya said callously, her voice a bored monotone from behind him, a chillingly loud whisper that scraped against his ears.

Casada, her gaze glued to the floor, remained stubbornly silent. He seized her chin, a rough hand forcing her head up, the pressure a jarring physical violation. Her eyes, wide and dark with defiance, finally met his.

"You really care so little about your family..." he paused. "Your own son, Caspian? I wonder what his blood will taste like."

"Shut up!" she screamed, spittle flying out of her mouth. "You do not deserve to say his name."

"Maybe I won't drink you first," Redd whispered. "Maybe I'll start with him. Would you like to watch? Then, when I am done with him, I'll slowly work my way to you. I think I'll save you for last so you can watch your bloodline die because of your own stubbornness."

"Redd—" Wallace warned.

He raised a hand, palm outward, a silent command. Surprised him when Wallace fell silent, the cessation a contrast to what he expected.

"How about you get me out of here, then I'll release your daughter from the contract?" Casada smirked, her eyes alight with hope.

REDD

Chapter 39

Redd's sharp eyes scanned Casada's face, searching for any flicker of deceit in the darkest depths of those eyes. A doubt, cold as winter, snaked through him; was this her genuine plea, or another carefully woven snare? Glancing back, his shoulder blades prickling with unease. Aguya's loyalty was a rock, unwavering; she'd follow to the fiery depths of hell without a second thought, he knew.

"Redd," Alvero murmured, his brow furrowed.

But Alvero... the thought was a lead weight in his chest. Turning back around he looked back at Casada. *How would I get her past all the soldiers with the sun out?* With a long, weary sigh, he resolved to do what must be done; the cost be damned. *I can fix things without working with the little snotty bitch.*

"As tempting as your offer is," Redd shrugged. "It's not for me. I'd rather have a drink. I am still feeling so parched. Soooooo, should I start with your son?"

"You fool," Casada roared. "I will make you pay for this. You think—"

The shrill, grating voice finally ceased as his hand, calloused and strong, encircled her throat. He felt the yielding flesh beneath his fingers as he tightened his grip. The rough metal of her shackles bit into her wrists; a desperate, muffled struggle met his ears. Her ragged, gasping breaths were a dry, rasping sound, like the crumpling of paper. Wide, terrified eyes, magnified by fear, stared into his as he saw the chilling reality settle in: she was utterly alone.

"Do you think they are going to stop me?" Redd's laughter echoed, his face close to hers. He felt the warm, barely there brush of her breath against his cheek as her lips, turning a shocking blue, parted slightly. He pulled back as she gasped, a ragged, icy sound for air. "No one is going to save you. They all know what you did to Liyla. We got that box open with your dirty little secret. Wallace there pieced together centuries of political murders you've committed. There is not one person here that has an ounce of sympathy for you."

Her skin, already the color of moonlight on snow, paled further with each chilling word. A faint tremor ran through her, a silent response to his harsh voice.

"This," Redd said, pointing to the ground. "Is the last stand for you. There is no going back. The only question is, do you take your family with you or not? Because I am going to let you know one thing about me is when I say I will hunt them all down and drink every ounce of their blood, I damn well mean it. So, will you break the contract or not?"

His heart hammered a frantic rhythm against his ribs as he stared into her deep brown eyes. The scent of her blood, something subtly a mix of strawberries, jasmine and plums filled his senses. A thrill, cold and sharp, shot through him with each glint of amber in his own eyes; he ached to show her the extent of his cruelty, the exquisite pleasure he'd derive from draining the lifeblood of everyone she held dear.

Her throat bobbed, a dry swallow echoing the silence before her gaze darted between anxious faces. A single word, ragged and breathy, escaped her lips, "Prison," the sound heavy with the tang of fear.

"What?" Redd said, looking back at the faces behind him.

"I will release her if I am guaranteed a nice prison cell and avoid the death penalty," Casada said, her chin lifting with a defiant snap. Even in this state, amidst the harsh, chained up and filthy, there was still a regal bearing that clung to her. Her brown curls, a chaotic halo, framed a face etched with defiance. Dark brown eyes, sharp and glittering, seemed to pierce the onlookers, a silent judgment in their depths. "Caspian had nothing to do with any of this. He will be pardoned and take his rightful place. Then when my terms are agreed to," she paused. "And only then will I concede and release the contract. Do we have a deal?"

Redd turned, catching the glint of light in Wallace's dark, squinting eyes. A low grumble vibrated in the air as Wallace's brow furrowed, the lines etched deep into his skin.

"Don't take too long to figure it out there, chap." Redd quirked an eyebrow as his eyes locked with Wallace's.

"I will need–" Wallace started.

"To keep me here longer because you enjoy my company?" Redd finished with a smirk.

Wallace's frown deepened, a furrow etched between his brows as a mahogany hand once again attempted to smooth the wrinkles from his jacket.

"If I have to stay here longer than a few hours, I will start fires all over the place," Aguya snapped.

"Cailleach Bheag," Alvero sighed. "This is more complicated than—"

"Don't start," Aguya growled. "What she is asking is nothing much. You kept preaching on the field, *don't kill*, blah, blah, blah. Now you want to kill. Make up your mind."

"It is not up to us," Alvero exhaled.

"Alvero is correct, we need—" Wallace snorted.

"To concede this little thing and show the mercy she's never shown her enemies," Redd said, the words hanging heavily in the still air. He rose, his gaze settling on Wallace, a silent challenge in his steely eyes.

"Will you never let me finish a sentence?" Wallace snorted.

"There it is, see? I let you finish one." Redd smiled, a tight, strained expression that didn't quite reach his eyes. The scent of dried blood and decay hung heavily in the air, a cloying sweetness that made his stomach churn, twisting into painful knots. He longed to end this contract, to escape the oppressive serenity of the fae vale, the silence broken only by the sound of breathing. *This idiot keeps playing in charge, yet refuses to make a decision. I am tired, full, and ready to go home.*

Redd watched, a prickle of impatience rising, as Wallace's gaze swept across the four figures next to him. The crisp, identical uniforms, badges gleaming dully under the lights, created a stark visual. Three heads bobbed in quick succession; a soft, almost inaudible chorus of agreement. The fourth man, however, remained rooted, his gaze locked on Casada. Redd's eyes, narrowed in appraisal, traveled over the fae's immaculate form, noticing the rich green of his uniform. His hands, flawlessly manicured, folded precisely across his chest. Not a speck of dirt or blood on him, said he had not fought in the battle. Redd could almost feel the cool stillness emanating from him as his brown eyes narrowed, a storm brewing behind their concentrated gaze.

"Eero?" Wallace asked softly.

"I can personally make sure Caspian is put in his proper place." Eero's smile, a chilling curve of his lips, stretched taut against the backdrop of his sharp-featured face. His deep brown eyes shimmered with a chilling malice. His brown hair shaved short under his beret. The air crackled with unspoken menace, a palpable tension thick enough to taste. "I will also personally attend to your accommodations, Casada."

So this is Liyla's nephew.

A guttural gulp, thick and wet, a sound like a stone dropping into a deep well filled the air, before Casada turned back towards him.

"Looks like we have a deal, then." Redd smirked.

"You'll have to unbind me so I can break it," Casada breathed, her voice barely audible above. A cold sweat glistened on her brow, the scent of pine and dust heavy in the air. For the first time, a stark terror shone in her wide, dilated eyes as they locked onto Eero's, the fear palpable in the sudden stillness of the room.

"Alright," Eero said, walking over. "Try one thing, just one, and I will personally hand your son over to the heathen vampire here. He is already in our custody, so how you handle this situation will dictate how I handle your son."

A million emotions floated across those dark eyes before Casada nodded.

Eero's fingers tapped the bands; a soft click echoed in the quiet room. Casada sighed, a long, slow release of breath, before gently removing the necklace. It was an identical copy of Feya's—a bloodstone set in intricate silver filigree shaped like the tree of life. The stone's deep, opaque green was mottled with swirling red, like trapped drops of blood, its darkness almost tangible.

She held the necklace in her hands, closing her eyes for a moment. Then released a puff of warm breath misting the surface before her whisper, a soft hiss. "I release the spell that binds these stones."

He waited for some flash, some feeling, something to change, but none came. The necklace did not break, no thunder exploded, everything remained the same. "That's it?"

"Yes, that's it, you Neanderthal," she snorted, the sound like a released breath of icy air, dropping the necklace with a dull clink onto the ground.

He scooped it up, his fingers brushing cool silver. The stone within was chilling, utterly inert, against his palm. It felt strangely weightless, a cold emptiness in his hand. He shoved it into a pocket, not sure if keeping it would be helpful, but knew he could not leave it behind.

"Well, in that case, she's yours," Redd said, walking to the door. "Aguya, Alvero, let's go rest."

"You forgot something," Aguya frowned.

Redd stared at her, a furrow in his brow, eyes clouded with confusion.

"Alse?" Aguya rolled her eyes. "I sometimes forget what an idiot you are."

"Oh crap, yeah," Redd said, turning back to Casada. "Why the hell was there a witch named Alse fighting for you?"

Casada's jaw tightened, a storm brewing in her eyes, but Eero's deft fingers clicked the magical shackles shut.

"Just answer his question, Casada, so the vampire can leave before I grow impatient and just feed you to him," Eero sneered.

"She approached me saying she wanted to make your family pay with your lives," Casada stated, her chin lifting with a sharp click, the gesture stiff and brittle as she attempted to reclaim her regal bearing. "She said she would do whatever it took, pay whatever price if I presented your family to her. I told her when I was done with—"

"Be careful what you call her," Redd growled, his voice a low, gravelly rumble that vibrated in the air. His fingers, like steel, tightened around her throat, cutting off her breath. He didn't know who knew Feya's secret, but he wouldn't risk it spreading further. Releasing Casada, he continued, "You can finish what you were saying."

"I told her when I was done with Feya she could have whoever she wanted," Casada said, tears filling the corners of her eyes. "When the battle started, she said she was going to find you guys and kill you. That's all I know."

Redd turned to Aguya, his eyes searching her face.

"Sounds good to me," Aguya snorted with a shrug. He could see the anguish in those eyes, but knew he could do nothing to drive it away.

Nuit
Chapter 40

Nuit's shoulders slumped, the weight of exhaustion pressing her against the table. A faint tremor ran through her as the last vestiges of her spell flickered, a dying ember. The air thrummed with the fading magic, a low hum that vibrated in her bones as she clung to the last vestiges of her magic. Each muscle screamed in protest, a searing, agonizing fire that spread from her limbs to the roots of her hair, each follicle a tiny point of burning pain.

Feya lay still, breathing softly, a peaceful slumber holding her captive. The lingering echo of the tug of the celestial contract, a powerful tugging sensation, faded only about an hour past and she had not felt it since. A faint scent of smoke still clung to the air, a ghostly reminder of the near-shattering pressure she'd felt, a pressure that vibrated throughout the very bones of her body.

Digging the heels of her hands into her aching eyes, she pressed hard, hoping the sharp pain would push back the bone-deep tiredness. The untouched soup and sandwich Brady had brought mocked her lack of appetite. The coffee, long since gulped down, left only a bitter aftertaste, a flimsy bandage on a gaping wound of her tiredness.

Her eyes defocused on the rock walls as she pulled

her hands away. She felt the fragile edges of her spell cracking like brittle ice. *Just a little longer,* she thought, the thought catching in the dry, dusty air, causing a whisper of doubt to follow through her.

Her thoughts drifted back to Redd, his blood-soaked image sprawled on the ground, a gruesome tableau seared into her memory. A cold shiver, like icy fingers, traced a path down her spine as she desperately tried to banish the image. Yet, it persisted, a stubborn phantom. The deeper the exhaustion, the more it lingered in her thoughts, a swirling vortex that tore at her heart.

A high-pitched buzz, like a thousand tiny angry bees, jolted her from her daydream. She turned her head towards a slight rustle, the muscles in her neck protesting faintly, Leo withdrew his phone from his pocket.

"You can release the spell," Leo said, looking at the lit up screen of his phone. "It's done."

Pushing up, Nuit's shaky legs threatened to buckle beneath her. Her feet dragged on the floor as she stumbled to the shimmering golden circle, its surface vibrating with a low hum. Bending, she pressed her palm against the warm, pulsating line; a tingling buzz vibrated up her arm as the potent magic surged through the circle like liquid sunlight. Inhaling deeply, she felt the familiar tug as she pulled her power back, a rush of cool, clean air flooding her lungs, yet leaving her bone-deep weary. Staggering towards the nearest cold stone cell, she collapsed onto the rough spun bed.

Leo's concerned voice was a muted drone; his words lost as she plummeted into an exhausted sleep. Restless nightmares swirled, vivid and terrifying. For a fleeting moment, she soared weightlessly, then sank into the comforting softness of a downy cloud before the terrors returned.

Crimson visions of Redd, sprawled on the ground amidst the deafening boom of explosions and the ghostly vanishing of loved ones, haunted her nightmares. She jolted awake, the setting sun painting fiery streaks across the sky. Rubbing sleep from her eyes, her muddled mind struggled to recall how she'd ended up in this room. Muscles aching, she felt the grogginess cling to her as she climbed from the bed.

The hot water of the ensuite shower, a sharp contrast to the chill in the air, jolted her, a comforting warmth against her shivering skin. The faint hum of her magic felt weak, a dull thrum beneath her skin. Sleep beckoned, but the unanswered questions burned brighter, a sharp ache in her mind.

Fingers fumbling with the cool silk of her blouse, she hurried, the floorboards creaking a low protest under her feet. Reaching the door, a knot of dread tightened in her stomach. She braced herself, anticipating the harsh news to come. *I have been through this before and I can handle this too.* The thought hung hollow in her heart.

A dull ache settled in her chest as she descended the creaking wooden stairs. A ripple of laughter, bright and melodic, snagged her attention; she paused, frowning slightly. The laughter guided her down the remaining steps, each one a solid thud against the wood. Reaching the doorway, she hesitated, her gaze drawn to the warmly lit living room where he sat front and center, the source of the joyous laughter.

Redd pushed himself up from his chair. He moved with a quiet thud of boots across the floor as he walked towards her. She could smell his cologne the closer he got. "Finally, woke up, sleeping beauty."

Her head bobbed silently. A wave of disorienting relief washed over her, warm and dizzying, quickly re-placed by a chilling serpent of another feeling. *How was the vision wrong? It has never failed me before.*

She swallowed a gulp, as she fought for composure. Her gaze dropped to his scuffed boots, fingers tracing the seams of her skin-tight jeans.

"I'm glad you're safe," she whispered hoarsely. Her throat felt constricted and dry.

"Of course I was," Redd chuckled. "Don't know why you doubted me."

A cough came from Leo, making her eyes snap to his. The smirk playing on his lips felt like a tangible thing as he tried to hide it, making her roll her eyes with a sigh. She'd never spoken of the vision, yet the chill of his knowing glance, referencing that dramatic woman comment he said earlier, sent a shiver down her spine realizing he was ridiculing her.

Her gaze swept the room, settling on each face in turn—Aguya, Alvero, Brady, Feya, Elwyn, Leo, and Redd. A low hum of conversation, punctuated by laughter, filled the air, a stark contrast to the icy grip of rage clenching her heart. The scent of roses, usually comforting, now felt cloying, suffocating. She saw their relaxed smiles, felt the heat prickling her skin, a wave of furious anger surging through her. *I'm tired and hungry. The last few days have been grueling and they are just sitting here laughing like nothing happened? Making jokes at my expense since, as Leo called me, I am just a dramatic woman.*

Her gaze drifted back to the vampire, his presence a warm, unsettling weight in her heart. His amber eyes, gleaming like polished stones in the dim light, held a mocking distance, their stare cold and sharp.

"I'd... We'd like to thank you for all your help," Redd said, smirking.

Every nerve in her body blazed as she felt like she was the butt of some joke. *Is he smirking because he's making fun of me, or am I reading too much into this?* Her face flushed crimson, a hot wave spreading as her bangs, light as dandelion fluff, danced across her forehead as she released a huff. His cruel words echoed in her ears, a bitter taste lingering on her tongue, a chilling weight pressing on her chest. *While this has been a nice distraction, I think I need to focus on what's needed now.*

"You're welcome," she grunted.

His hands went up and smoothed her bangs. "Since it's over, you are free. No ex to hurt you, no war brewing in the fae community. It's all done. You are free to choose what you want to do."

"Was I not free before?" Nuit gasped, feeling the rage burning brighter. *I spent hours holding a nightmare of a spell, thinking this male was dead. I cried over him and he was just sitting here laughing while telling me I can go do whatever I want to do. Like I am some stray he rescued.* She knew the rage simmering in her was not rational, but she no longer cared.

"Don't twist my words, woman," Redd scoffed.

"I didn't twist anything. I was asking you a question," she retorted.

Redd's eyes, narrowed to thin crimson slits, scanned her; a low growl vibrated in his chest. "We both know you lived in fear of your ex coming after you. There's no use in denting the truth."

"No, I didn't," she said, folding her arms across her chest. "Did I want to see him? No. But I reached out to him on your behalf." The rage bloomed bright as she continued speaking. "He was a male hurt by a war that not only destroyed our marriage, but took the lives of our..." she paused as tears welled in her eyes. "Our children, our parents, our sisters, cousins, friends, home, you name it, we lost it. He had lived a millennium without bothering me. I knew he would leave me alone if I stayed away from him. So, excuse me if I don't feel thankful that you have given me freedom."

Redd nodded, his wide, startled eyes like saucers,

reflecting the light. "I'm sorry I disrupted your life, then."

"Yes!" Nuit yelled. "You have turned my life upside down and thrown it into some chaotic..." she paused, her hands held in fists in front of her, trying to express the words that would not leave her lips.

"Well," Redd said, running a hand through his hair while stepping back.

"Yeah, well," Nuit mumbled, looking away.

Turning on her heel, she sprinted back up the stairs, the tears now spilling down her face. She swiped at the wetness on her cheeks as it did nothing to quell the waterworks. Grabbing her luggage out of her room, she shoved her clothes into the bag, not caring if they were wrinkled or crushed.

A gentle rap on the door made her freeze. Taking a deep breath, she tried to steady her voice. "What?"

"Sweetie," Brady's voice called through the door. "Can I come in?'

"One second," she called back.

Swiping at the hot, salty tears blurring her vision, she tried to compose herself. The rasp of her breath filled the quiet room as she took deep, steadying breaths before walking to the door and pushing it open.

"Yes?" Nuit asked, her knuckles white on the door knob.

""I know you're upset, and it has been a very stressful couple of days, but," Brady sighed. "Don't let those idiots run you off. He... They say things they don't mean."

"They haven't run me off," she replied. "I just need to get back to work. My book store has been closed for days and I need to take care of what is mine."

Plus, it's not like Redd is actually interested in me. A twinge of pain shot through her heart as the words settled into her thoughts.

"You don't need to leave," Brady said, brushing Nuit's hair out of her face. "I know I am not the only one who would not want you to leave."

"I highly doubt that," Nuit laughed self-deprecatingly. "Leo thinks I am dramatic. Alvero wants to hide from the world and could care less about me. Aguya does not seem like she cares for me one way or the other. I have never had an actual conversation with Feya or Elwyn. And Redd..." she paused, debating her words. "Thinks of me as nothing more than a distraction, as he so bluntly told me."

"Sweetie," Brady huffed. "That is so far from—"

"You are too kind," Nuit cut her off. "But I want to go home."

"If you're sure then," Brady said, her eyes gazing at her with a softly pitying look.

"I am very sure."

REDD

Chapter 41

Redd stood in the shadows, watching as Nuit walked to the door. She turned her head, her eyes turning to where he stood. Tears sparkled in the corners of her eyes like little diamonds. As the door opened, a streak of light washed the hall in moonlight before it vanished and left behind nothing but darkness.

Fool, his heart told him. His heart ached, a dull throb urging him to chase after her, but a cold logic held him back. He let out a slow breath and turned toward his room. A heavy silence pressed down, broken only by the faint creak of the old house settling, each footfall echoing in the quiet as everyone else had retreated to their rooms.

His body sank into the soft mattress with a gentle thud, the cotton pillow cool against his cheek. Eyes closed, he fought the restless tide of thoughts—a cacophony in the quiet room. A sharp ache pulsed behind his eyes as he rubbed them, trying to rub the thoughts away. A low growl rumbled in his chest as a fist slammed into the yielding softness of the bed.

She deserves someone who can give her a full life. Someone who can take her out during the day, not someone who spends half his day locked away, hiding from a certain fiery death.

With a harsh snort, he rolled onto his back, the crisp cotton sheets cool against his hand. The faint, lingering scent of her perfume clung to the empty space beside him, a stark contrast to the chill of the mattress where she'd lain. *I miss her.* Realizing sleep was useless, he jumped out of the bed and headed downstairs to the gym.

The worn leather black punching bag, swaying violently from the ceiling, absorbed the furious rhythm of his fists. Each thud echoed in the musty-smelling gym, a dull percussion against the ache filling his chest. His knuckles, raw and throbbing with a dull, aching heat, pounded relentlessly, a desperate attempt to release the simmering rage within.

Her words played through his mind. *Another reason I should let her go. She was better off without me. This is for the best.*

Eyes tracing the raw, red split across his knuckle, a sharp sting met the sight. Bringing his hand to his mouth, the tang of his own blood filled his mouth, a bitter taste as he made a sour expression. It never tasted as good as the others did.

A low thrum vibrated against his thigh and he fished his phone from his pocket. Father Cass's name glowed on the screen. He hesitated, the cool glass smooth against his skin, considering sending the call to voicemail. *Maybe I need the distraction.* Clicking on the screen, he answered the phone.

"What?" Redd snapped.

"Well, hello. How are you? I am fine since you asked so nicely," Cass laughed good-naturedly.

"Get to the point, Cass," Redd growled, annoyance dripping from every syllable.

"I still need that book," Cass said, his voice a low rumble, serious and edged with urgency.

"Then come get it," Redd sighed, the sound ragged. Leaning against the wall, he slid down, he plopped on the ground.

His muscles screamed, a deep, throbbing ache; his heart, a dull, heavy knot in his chest. A bone-deep weariness settled in, a leaden weight on his soul. He knew, with a chilling certainty, that sleep wouldn't come, no matter how desperately he willed it. *Maybe I can ask Alvero for a sleeping drought.*

A deep sigh came across the line while the sound of shuffling of papers followed. "I will come get it and I have a new assignment for you. Since the fae queen is now imprisoned, I assume you were able to free your daughter?"

"Yes, Feya is free."

"Why did you decide not to report to us when you found—" Cass started.

"I told you when I got the book," Redd interjected.

"Yes, you did," Cass responded. "But, as you know, I also told you to bring the book to me. Not the other way around. We give you a lot of leeway. There was another task we asked of you. You did neither."

Redd rolled his eyes, the whites gleaming, as Cass's sharp voice, like nails on a chalkboard, began another lecture similar to so many before. He felt the familiar dull ache of boredom in his temples, a weariness born from countless repetitions of this same sermon, delivered by Cass and the priests who came before him.

"We asked you to get the information for a reason," Cass continued. "There are many magical beings involved in this, not just you. I know since it hit so close to home that you acted in a very self-serving manner. We wanted this information so we could work on a resolution that did not come with tons of upheaval..."

Redd yanked the phone from his ear. Cass's muffled voice faded as he placed the phone on the ground beside him. He squeezed his eyes shut, the pressure a physical manifestation of the world still pressing down on him. He'd believed Feya's freedom would restore normalcy in their lives, but the quiet hope was shattered. Now everything felt heavy and suffocating as the weight of her newly revealed secret pressed down on him the more people knew. Centuries of careful secrecy, crumbled by Feya's actions; the crashing sound of his carefully constructed world meant to keep her safe imploding echoed in his ears. Wallace's terse message, the single word "discuss" hanging between them like a death knell, vibrated with a chilling finality. He hadn't dared share the message; the fragile joy of Feya's liberation was still too fresh, too precious to taint.

The phone went silent, a sudden absence of Cass's voice. He pressed the receiver back against his ear. "When will you be here?" he asked, his voice an indistinct murmur against the quiet hum of the phone line.

A heavy sigh, a little shaky, drifted through the phone, a sound like air leaking from a punctured tire. "You will not bring it to me no matter what, will you?"

"No."

A pause filled the line before Cass replied, "I'll be there tomorrow evening."

"I'll see you then."

"Did you actually listen to anything I said?"

"Of course I did." Redd snorted a laugh. "You explained what a bad boy I am and how I need spankin'. Don't worry, I am sure I can find a sweet thing to spank me for you."

A harsh noise filled the line—Cass snorted.

"Are you trying to insinuate you want to spank me,

Cass?" Redd laughed harshly. "I didn't know you liked me that way."

"God, I forgot how much you never take things seriously."

"I take more things seriously than you'll ever realize."

"Do you realize the implications of you not doing what we asked of you?"

Redd leaned his head back on the wall, staring at the ceiling. "Remember always, my family will always come first."

REDD

Chapter 42

The rabbit's blood, drunk that morning before the sun dipped below the horizon, still left Redd ravenous and unprepared for this conversation with Cass he was listening to. He squeezed his eyes shut, sinking into the couch, as Cass's relentless voice, a sharp rasp, filled the room, accusing him of mishandling the information, of failing to take it to the church, and just generally never listening to orders. *Maybe Cass's lectures can put me to sleep. I can just close my eyes and drift off into the sleep that's eluded me.*

"You're not really listening, are you?" Cass grumbled.

Yawning exaggeratedly, he stretched his arms above his head. "I've totally heard every word you have spoken."

Cass stared at him, his brow furrowed in knowing disapproval, the slight frown etched deep in his brow. His foot tapped a restless rhythm on the floor, a dull thudding sound that vibrated faintly through the room.

Shrugging, Redd decided to speak up. "I am tired of you treating me like a child who always needs to be lectured at every opportunity. I'm not a school aged lad who needs Sister Cass to swat with a ruler at every opportunity."

"Then maybe you should act like an adult," Cass snorted. "Then I would treat you like one."

"No, you don't want me to act like an adult," Redd snapped, feeling the rage that had been simmering start to bubble over. "You want me to act like a mindless zombie who follows every word you speak. So, if that's what you want, you know where the door is."

Cass stared, his gaze unwavering. The blue of his eyes, bright as a summer sky, seemed to spin as he weighed his response, a silent whirring, almost audible in the tense stillness as Redd waited.

Cass's lips parted, an answer forming, only to be halted by Redd's hand, a sharp, upward gesture. "I am not in the mood. We will never see eye to eye on this, so either say what you need or leave."

Cass hesitated, a tremor in his hands gripping the worn leather grimoire before he finally nodded. "There is a vampire who stole a holy relic and we need you to get it back."

"There it is, finally the reason we're here today," Redd nodded, leaning forward, the couch creaking under his weight. A nervous tremor ran through him; the ticking of a distant clock echoed in the room, each second a hammer blow telling him any second the other shoe could drop. Around him, shadows danced in the dim light, the silence pressing down, waiting felt far more menacing than anything else. "Give me the details."

"Good," Cass stated, a slow grin warming his face as he pulled a crinkled folder from his satchel and passed it over.

Redd opened the folder, the crisp paper sighing under his fingertips as he turned the pages. A grainy image: a vial of dark, viscous liquid, like congealed

night, almost black blood. The ampoule, a rounded cru-
et of gleaming silver, topped with a tiny cross on top of
a crown, caught the light. Further images flickered—a
shadowy figure, a vampire with eyes like chips of obsidian,
gliding into a stone rectory. Another of the vampire stealing the ampoule. His gaze skimmed the report, finding
nothing of immediate note.

"That," Cass muttered, pointing at the ampoule in
the photo, "is the vial of St. Januarius's blood. It is a holy
relic that we don't want the public to know is missing."
Cass paused, flipping the page. "A vampire by the name of
Asterope. He is—"

"What's his last name?" Redd interrupted, not sure
if he wanted to hear the rest of the file read to him.

Sighing, Cass replied, "He doesn't have one."

"Ummm..." Redd paused while he processed the
information. But his mind wandered away. Figuring he
would let Cass get his rocks off by finishing telling him
what he could just read for himself. "Alright, continue."

"As I was explaining," Cass continued. "Our sources
report he is holed up in a vampire den on the outskirts of
London and is planning on selling the relic on the black
market. We need you to get the vial relic back before that
happens. The last page has where we were able to track
him to. So you and your band of merry misfits can go in
and retrieve it."

Redd's gaze locked onto Cass, the glint of sarcasm
in his eyes a stark contrast to the harsh, clipped words.
"Well, I guess us merry band of misfits will get on that
now, Sister Cass. Just don't bring your ruler out and spank
me."

"Do you even understand the headaches you cause
me?" Cass groaned.

Redd searched Cass's face, the shadowed hollows
under his eyes a stark contrast to the usual cheery fae.

Cass's mouth was a grim, thin line. Lacing his elbows on his knees, a sharp pinch to the bridge of his nose, eyes squeezed shut, he tried to quiet the hunger, rage and sadness that played havoc on his nerves. Then, a deep breath, Cass's blood, thick and warm, flooding his senses. *I need to feed again.*

A slow breath escaped his lips, a whisper of air barely disturbing the quiet. His eyes, blinking open, focused on Cass. "Have you ever had a family?"

A profound sadness, replacing the earlier weariness, clouded Cass's eyes. His voice, a low rumble, carried the weight of years as he began, "Once, a long time ago."

"Would you have done anything to keep them safe?"

Nodding, Cass's shoulders slumped, a sigh escaping his lips like a whispered secret. "I will do my best to smooth things over with the higher ups. Just please keep your heads down for a while."

"Naturally," Redd smirked, the corners of his mouth tugging upwards in a way that didn't quite reach the cynical glint in his eyes.

Rolling his eyes, Cass shook his head. "Let me know when you got the ampoule."

"Will do, boss m

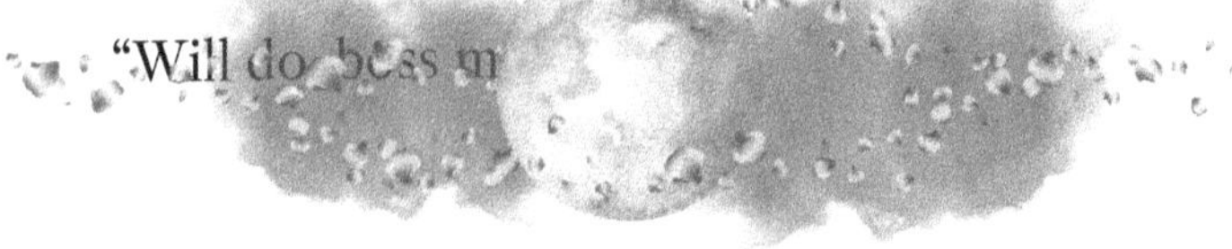

Redd waited with Leo outside the vampires' den, a nondescript brick building, its blank walls stark against the twilight. There were no windows and only two exits. The air hung heavily with the scent of exhaust fumes and damp earth. They parked a block away so no one would hear the car.

For an hour, an unnerving stillness reigned; no movement, no sound, no one coming, and no one going. Leo, sniffing around the building, while listening for the faintest whispers of movement—three vampires, perhaps, Leo has said—from what little noise he could pick up from the thick walls.

The damp chill of the alley seeped into Redd's bones while he waited. Leo circled the building, a silent shadow, one more time. The distant rumble of city traffic was a dull counterpoint to the quiet of the neighborhood. He could almost smell the lingering scent of her perfume—a ghostly whisper of lily, myrrh, and cinnamon—a cruel reminder of her. Her last, fleeting glance, a mixture of sadness and anger, burned behind his eyelids. The words, sharp and cutting, echoed in his ears, silencing the urge to text, to check if she was safe. He stood frozen, paralyzed by indecision. *Better to let her live her life than get involved in this mess that is me and my shit show.*

He jumped, startled by Leo's sudden appearance beside him, a gasp catching in his throat.

Leo's frown was a sharp line etched into his face, his brow furrowed like a stormy sky, the silence heavy with unspoken unease. Leo whispered, "Stay focused, or do you need to go home?"

"Nope," Redd murmured, a low rumble vibrating in his chest, shaking his head. "I am focused. You're just getting better at being quiet."

A barely audible hmph escaped Leo's lips before he outstretched his hand. Redd nodded, leading the way to the front door. He shoved all thoughts aside, focusing on the fight to come. With a powerful kick, the door— old wood groaning under the force—tore from its hinges, crashing to the floor with a resounding thud. Dust motes danced in the single shaft of light slicing through the gloom, revealing three vampires, their faces etched with displeasure, gathered around a scarred, ancient table.

Redd's lips curled into a devious smile, a slow, sly curve that crinkled the corners of his eyes, the glint of mischief in them like chips of amber. "Well, hello there, mates. What do we have going on here?"

"Who de foehck are you and what do you want?" a male said with a thick Irish accent.

Redd turned, his gaze a sharp appraisal, taking in the man's features—dirty blonde hair falling across one eye, obscuring the weariness in one of his brown eyes as they squinted. This was the same male in the photo Cass had provided. His gaze shifted, noting they all stood at least four inches shorter than himself. He heard Leo step up from behind him.

"I'm your local postman," Redd snorted as he walked in, stepping on the door. "I hear you have a package I need to pick up."

He sized up the two vampires, their matching blue eyes glinting under the dim lights. They seemed to be brothers' same brown hair, same blue eyes and the same scent of their blood. Something about his own kind's scent of blood always put him off, leaving him feeling slightly nauseous. He could feast on a thousand other creatures—werewolves, humans, even ghouls—but the thought of feeding on his own kind left a bitter taste.

Chapter 43

Nuit's hands, dusted with flour, plunged into the yielding dough as she kneaded the fino bread. Each push and fold, usually a meditative rhythm, felt like a physical manifestation of her turmoil; the yeasty scent intensified, almost cloying, mirroring her rising anger. The slap of dough against the board echoed her frustration. Finally, with a weary sigh, she abandoned the ruined, dense mass, its texture now as overworked as her heart felt.

She rested her face in her flour-dusted hands, feeling the cool, slightly sticky dough against her cheeks. A flash of amber eyes, cold and distant, pierced her memory—the ghost of his last look haunting her. The yeasty, slightly sweet smell of the flour filled her nostrils, a comforting counterpoint to the bitter memory. One task at a time; this bread, this meal, then the next step, then the next. *I just need to do one thing at a time, just one.*

She lifted the ceramic bowl and started over. The clatter of ingredients—flour, sugar, a whisper of salt—filled the air as she poured, the paddle whirring rhythmically against the sides as it mixed. After setting a timer, she draped a towel over the dough to let it rise. A rush of cold air brushed against her face as she opened the fridge door.

"Maybe a drink will relax me," she muttered to

herself.

Peering into the refrigerator's cool, white light, she spotted the makings of a boozy cherry Palmer. A smooth, tall glass met the ice's tinkling clatter as she filled it. The vibrant crimson cherry juice, the amber tea, and the dark bourbon swirled together as she added them, a fragrant burst of fruity sweetness and oaky spice. A quick sip sent a wave of tart cherry and warming bourbon across her tongue, a pleasant heat spreading through her chest.

The jarring ping of the timer made her jump. Gulping the last of her drink, she crossed to the bowl. The dough yielded to her touch, cool and slightly sticky against her palms. With each push and fold, worries melted away. The scent of butter enriched the air as she incorporated it, feeling the dough's satisfying resistance. She shaped the dough into logs, placing them gently on the floured tray. A soft cotton towel covered them once more, before she set the timer again for a second rising.

Walking to the sink, the warm water cascaded over her hands, dissolving the sticky, sweet dough while she washed. She mixed herself another drink. Carrying it, she settled into the embrace of her favorite chair. Picking up the book, one of the latest thrillers, off the side table, she opened it up. Words leaped from the page, sharp and clear, before blurring into a frustrating, chaotic jumble as she struggled to concentrate.

The gnawing loneliness clawed at her as she surveyed the house—once a sanctuary, now a prison of floral wallpaper and books. The faint chirp of a lone cricket outside was deafening in the stillness. She considered opening the bookstore, the imagined chatter of customers a tempting distraction from the suffocating weight of her grief. Yet, the thought of facing people felt heavier than the solitude, an emotional tax she did not know if she was up for. Each attempt to lose herself in a book since returning ended in a blur of unshed tears; focus was a distant shore she could not reach, the tide of emotion too strong.

I have spent forever living my life alone, yet never feeling alone until now. Now all I feel is an aching loneliness eating at my soul.

Closing her eyes, she tried to clear her mind, the faint scent of lavender from her vase on the coffee table failing to soothe. The rhythmic ticking of the grandfather clock in the hall, once comforting, now grated on her ears. The soft comfort of her chair felt rough against her skin. Familiar things, once sources of solace, now only brought a fresh wave of emptiness.

She sighed, as she thought of how just a few weeks ago she was going to run away and start a new life. Now she just sat here living no life, just floating in her own misery. *This is all I know. I have lived this way for centuries. Maybe it's time to start a new life, a new exploit. Then I can be free of this sadness plaguing me if I step into a new adventure.* Even as the thought drifted through her mind, she knew that running would not dilute the ache in her heart. A small part of her held hope. A hope that maybe he would come for her, and if she left he would not find her. She knew she should not foster those emotions, but they held on anyway.

The shrill clang of the doorbell downstairs jolted her from her daydream, a jarring sound that vibrated through the floorboards. Her heart leaped, a frantic bird trapped in her chest, the possibility of it being him a suffocating weight and a cloud of elation all in one beat. Inhaling deeply, cool air filling her lungs, she resolutely shook her head, a faint tremor in her hand. *There's no way it's him, it has to be a customer looking for the latest fantasy novel or something.*

The pounding of her feet on the wooden stairs echoed in her ears as she raced towards the door, desperately trying to ignore the feeling that it was him. Just steps from the door, however, her descent faltered. A shadowy figure, vaguely feminine, was visible behind the cool, frosted glass, its blurry form causing a sudden chill to run down her spine. With a deep, steadying breath, she fought down the rising anxiety, the smooth cool metal of the doorknob cold beneath her fingers as she cautiously opened it to face the mysterious visitor.

"Cousin," she gasped while seeing a familiar face from her past.

"I am sorry it took so long to come, but I wanted to check on you after our last call," Seshat said. Her long raven black hair, braided with intricate detail, cascaded over one shoulder, a silken waterfall. Her jet-black eyes, sharply lined with charcoal, sparkled with youthful energy; her honey-toned skin glowed warmly under the sun. The crisp white sundress billowed gently in the warm afternoon breeze, a soft whisper against her skin, carrying the faint scent of honeysuckle.

"Come in," Nuit said, swinging her arm wide. A strained, painted-on smile stretched her lips as she forced a brittle cheer, her eyes betraying her.

I am such an idiot. The sun is out. There is no way a vampire would come calling at noon.

The comforting weight of warm arms enveloped her, a familiar pressure against her back. She felt the soft texture of her cotton dress as she accepted the embrace, finding solace. It was a rare comfort, a precious connection with one of the few remaining threads of her family.

A faint, reedy mew reached her ears as she glanced down at the small grey animal carrier her cousin had placed on the ground. From where she stood, the interior remained a shadowed mystery, the small creature, her cousin's travel companion, within unseen.

"What's that?" Nuit asked tentatively, pointing at the case.

"Just a small surprise," Seshat smiled warmly.

"A surprise?" Nuit frowned.

"The last few times we have talked you seemed," Seshat paused, tapping a finger on her chin. Her long red nails glinted in the light. "Lonely."

"Oh," Nuit gasped, her eyes darting from the crate to her cousin's face. Uncertainty ate at her, as she was not sure she wanted whatever creature her cousin thought she might need.

"I can't stay long, but I brought you a friend," Seshat beamed. "I am meeting up with this lovely artist. For a while now, I've admired his paintings."

"Can you stay for lunch?" Nuit asked, as her eyes darted back and forth between her cousin and the case.

"Of course," Seshat chuckled, the sound like wind chimes in a summer breeze. She lifted the case and climbed the creaking wooden stairs.

Nuit locked the door, heaving a heavy sigh and followed behind.

"What are we having?" Seshat asked.

"I just started making fino bread for sandwiches," Nuit said. Her eyes darted back to the case. Whatever was in was quiet now. *Should I be worried about that case?* "I have some turkey and pepper jack cheese for it."

"Sounds yummy," Seshat softly sighed. She placed the carrier down with a gentle thud onto the floor beside the dinette. A tiny, insistent mewling emerged from within, a high-pitched sound that made Nuit's eyes flick towards it. "I haven't had home cooked bread in a while."

She turned the oven dial, its click echoing in the quiet kitchen as it heated. Pulling the towel off the dough, the yeasty scent of the bread hit her—puffed up to perfection, promising a soft interior.

"What has been going on with your life lately?" Nuit inquired.

"Just traveling," Seshat laughed. "I think I've circled the globe a million times now."

"I get the feeling. Sometimes, it's nice to have roots."

"It is," Seshat murmured. "Are you going to talk about what's bothering you, or do we need to have more small talk?"

"Small talk," Nuit replied, exhaling while she put the bread in the oven.

"Really?" A single black eyebrow shot up.

"No," Nuit grumbled as she set a timer. "I guess after all we had been through, I thought I could just float through about anything." Pausing, she walked to the fridge. "I just let the wrong one in and came crashing down to earth."

Pulling out the ingredients for the sandwiches, she decided another boozy drink was called for. "You want a mix drink?"

"Alright." A gentle quiet exuded from Seshat's voice.

Nuit's gaze met Seshat's, the warm eyes a comforting balm. The familiar scent of honeysuckle, always clinging to Seshat, soothed her frayed nerves. The soft scrape of the chair legs on the polished floor was barely audible as Nuit pulled it out. A wave of relief washed over her as she spoke, the words tumbling out like a torrent, yet a deeper ache settled in her chest, a cold weight against the warmth of Seshat's presence as if saying the words gave them actual weight.The confession, a raw, painful outpouring, exposed the truth she'd hidden, even from herself.

"I don't know why I'd fall for an arrogant, obnoxious vampire," she breathed, the words tasting like ash on her tongue. The realization slammed into her, a physical blow. A chill, despite the warmth of the room from the oven, prickled her skin.

"The heart yearns for what it covets," Seshat replied, placing her hand on top of Nuit's. "Sometimes you have to follow it, even if you end up getting hurt."

"Is this one of those times you tell me it's better to have loved and lost kind of story?" Nuit groaned.

Smiling, Seshat shook her head, the movement sending a cascade of glossy black braid swaying like a silken ribbon.

The shrill ring of the timer sliced through the air, abruptly halting her. Leaping up, a rush of warmth from the oven met her as she opened it up. The intoxicating aroma of freshly baked fino bread wafted in the air. Hot tears glistened like tiny diamonds in the corners of her eyes. With a gentle thunk, she placed the golden-brown loaves on the cooling rack.

Seshat appeared, her hands warm on her shoulders, pulling her into a comforting, enveloping hug. Tears flowed freely now, a warm torrent against Seshat's shoulder. The comforting pressure of the hug eased the tension until, finally, she pushed away, wiping her cheeks.

"Thank you," she murmured. "Let me make us lunch, then you can show me what's in the carrier."

"So, you will just hand over what you stole and we can handle this nice and easy," Redd said, while his eyes darted around the room.

The male in the pictures laughed and said, "What makes you dink we have anything we're goin' to give ye, Laddy?"

"Give," Redd shrugged while Leo snickered. "Take. Tomayto tomahto."

"Look 'ere bahys," the picture male said, his hand gesturing at Redd as they all started laughing. "We gaht ooerselves a real life comedian."

"Yep," Redd nodded. "I am quite the crack up. So, now that we have finished with pleasantries let's just hand over what you stole."

The laughter abruptly ceased, replaced by a heavy silence. Turning, their eyes fixed on Redd, the three men showed sudden awareness on their faces. The picture male spoke with a low, disgruntled voice and said, "Excuse me?"

Finally, the idiots comprehend what I am after.

"Just hand over the ampoule and you can walk away with all your limbs in place," Redd grunted. "I am feeling nice."

"I'm not," Leo muttered behind him.

He muffled a snicker, warm breath ghosting against his hand while he covered his mouth. Redd's gaze, sharp and unwavering, remained fixed on the trio. The three exchanged glances; a silent communication charged with the cold prickle of apprehension and the hot flare of rising anger.

"Do you dink you're scary ahr sahmethin?" One of the others said.

"Or something," Redd snorted, stepping further into the dimly lit room. The rough-hewn floorboards groaned under his weight. A primal itch, a thrill of anticipation, warred with a bone-deep weariness, a longing for the warmth and quiet of home so he could wallow.

A fast-flying baseball bat whizzed past his head before he even saw it coming, a blur of wood and menace. He snatched the attacker's arm, the sharp crack of breaking bone echoing as he twisted. His fist, a hard, driving weight, impacted the other male's stomach; a grunt and the sickening thud of a body hitting the ground followed. As he looked up, the picture of the charging man, a blur of motion and rage, filled his vision. A searing pain exploded in his core as the man's shoulder slammed into him, the air whooshing from his lungs as his back hit the unforgiving ground.

A knee slammed into his solar plexus, a searing, radiating pain. A fist connected with his jaw, a sickening crack echoing as his head snapped back, hitting the hard, cold floor. With a grunt, he drove his heels into his assailant's chest; the impact jarring through his legs, sending the attacker sprawling back, a muffled thud accompanying his fall. The world swam; a dizzying wave of nausea washed over him as he rolled onto his forearms, the rough grain of the wood digging into his skin.

He looked up, the sickening crack of breaking bones echoing in the air, to see Leo shifting. Soft, gray fur, like the down of a gosling, erupted from his skin. His limbs twisted and contorted with a wet, popping sound as they reshaped, the change a blur of motion. He stared at the immense gray dire wolf before him, its bright grey eyes, like chips of ice, locking onto his before turning away. In a flash of gray fur, Leo was gone, a desperate thump of paws on the wooden floor as he burst out the door. A scream, high-pitched and then abruptly cut off, filled the air, followed by a silence. A minute later, Leo returned, the scent of damp earth and wolf clinging to him, dragging the picture male, his face a mask of pain, whimpering softly, by the shoulder.

Leo trembled, his fur gleaming faintly in the meager light as he shifted, his muscles bunching and reforming into human shape. Redd pushed himself upright, his face burning with shame as he met Leo's gaze. Leo fumbled with his ragged trousers as he pulled them on. Three figures lay sprawled on the floor: one still unconscious, his shallow breaths rasping faintly; another bleeding, a crimson stain spreading across the floorboards; and the third, wincing as he cradled his broken arm.

"Where's the ampoule at?" Leo growled. Leo's eyes darted to Redd, a sheer look of disappointment radiating in that fleeting glance.

"Foehck you," the picture male said, his hand holding over the puncture wounds from Leo's fangs, trying to staunch the flow of crimson.

A coppery tang, thick and cloying, filled the air—the stench of vampire blood. His nostrils flared, wrinkling at the acrid scent; a bitter taste, ghosting the back of his throat, mingled with the sulfurous reek of brimstone.

Exhaustion etched his face as he finally stopped playing games. His fingers, calloused and strong, clamped around the picture male's throat; the cheap paper crinkled. The male's hands scrabbled, fingernails scraping against his skin. A sickening thud echoed as he slammed the male against the plaster wall, a jarring vibration shooting up his arm. He tightened his grip sliding him up the wall, the picture male's eyes widening in silent terror as their faces met, inches apart.

"Don't make us ask again," Redd whispered. He could still feel the ragged, hot breath of the picture male ghosting his burning skin. His fingers tightened, a crushing pressure against the yielding throat before releasing the slightest pressure.

"I tahld you–"

He fist, a thunderclap against the picture male's mouth, silenced the words. The crack of impact echoed in the still air.

"Let's change tactics," Redd smiled, a flash of white teeth. Fingers tightened, a harsh whisper against the male's neck, then slackened with a gush of air. "Which one of your brothers do you want to watch die first?"

The picture male's lips, a thin, white line, squeezed tight, refusing to answer. A furious glint narrowed his eyes to slits as they glared at Redd.

"Alright then," Redd nodded slowly. "We will do this your way." A hint of relief filled the male's eyes. "Leo snap one of their necks, I don't care which. You can choose which one looks most annoying."

The male's eyes widened, mirroring his rising terror. A gasp, ragged and choked, hitched in his throat.

"Fine," Leo stated. The rustle of fabric, a whisper against the rough-hewn wood of the floor, announced Leo's movement. A low groan, thick with pain, followed.

"Wait!" the picture male yelled. "We can make a deal!"

Laughing sardonically, Redd shook his head. "I don't know if you have anything worth striking a deal with."

"I 'ave a buyer fahr de ampoule," the picture male pleaded. The defiance had fled his eyes, replaced by a stark, chilling fear. He knew that feeling; a cold dread, like icy fingers gripping his heart, the same bone-deep terror that had seized him when he'd thought he might lose one of his family. "We can splet de mahney and you can say you never fooehnd oehs. We all walk away 'appy."

"What do you think about that deal?" Redd's words, sharp as shattered glass, sliced the air. He glanced back, Leo, his face grim, held the male—a whimper escaping his broken lips—the scent of sweat and fear thick in the air. The male's arm dangled at a disjointed angle.

"He hasn't told us how much money he is going to give us," Leo snorted. "You'd think if he was bargaining with us, he would say how much money we stood to gain."

"We can splet 5 mellion dahllars!" the picture male said, his voice tinged with hope. "Fifty-fifty splet."

"Woo-ee," Redd hollered. "You hear that? We can get a whole two point five mil if we betray our friend."

"Sounds a little light of funds," Leo shrugged.

"Oh, you think we could get more money?" Redd asked.

"Yep," Leo laughed. "I bet we could get $5 mil all to ourselves."

"Really?" Redd sighed, a puff of air like a whispered word in the humid stillness. He saw the male's mouth begin to open, a silent O forming with the tightening of his grip, a pressure like a vise on his arm, before the fingers loosened slightly. Leaning in closer, he felt the flutter of the male's breath on his face. "You hear that? He thinks we can get $5 mil."

"Give oehs a break, Laddy. We wahrked 'ard to steal it. Dere is a beg time vampire cahven leader who wants it and if—" The picture male gasped, his voice strained, before Redd's grip tightened on his throat. The man's eyes, wide and panicked.

"I'm tired of playing," Redd said, yawning. "I think I'm going to just keep my first deal with my..." he paused like he was choking on the word. "Friend."

"Okay," Leo said. A sickening crunch, like splintering wood, shattered the air. Turning, he saw a man, his body at a grotesque angle, collapsing in a heap at Leo's feet. "Glass jaw."

"Where is it?" Redd asked, looking back at the picture male.

"Please," the picture male pleaded.

"So, it seems we are back to who do you want to die first?" Redd queried. The room was filled with a tense atmosphere as rage simmered in those piercing amber eyes. The sound of heavy breathing and clenched fists added to the palpable tension.

A trembling hand released Redd's wrist, jerked, a shaky finger pointing. His eyes, following the direction, landed on a grey metal cabinet. With a sharp crack, his fist smashed against the male's face. The head snapped back with a sickening thud, eyes rolling up before the figure went limp. The lifeless doll slid down the wall with a soft thump, landing on the dusty floor.

Turning, he saw Leo, his worn leather boots creaking softly on the polished wood floor, approaching the dark oak cabinet. Leo's gaze met his, the skepticism etched in the lines around his sharp, grey eyes. "I can rely on you to make sure they don't jump up and get me, right?"

"What's that supposed to mean?" Redd's brow furrowed.

"It means when you said you were focused, it was a lie."

With a harsh snort, Redd glared down at the three men sprawled on the floor.

"Got it," Leo murmured, the words a low rumble as he walked towards the cabinet.

With a grunt and a kick, the stiff metal lock yielded. A brief search of the cabinet revealed the glass ampoule nestled in its cardboard box inside. The night air, cool and crisp against their skin, muffled the quiet click of the door as they slipped out into the darkness, the distant hum of city traffic a low thrum in the background, their steps silent on the pavement as they headed toward the waiting car.

"You want to talk about it?" Leo appealed.

"I don't have anything to talk about. Feya's free, Aguya's alive and everything is peachy. Though it would be nice to stop and grab a bite to eat."

With a burst of laughter, Leo's elbow jabbed into his ribs. "I have known you for centuries, and I can practically smell when you're lying."

"I'm not lying about not wanting to talk about anything," Redd said, his voice rough, a shove sending his friend stumbling.

"Want, need," Leo snorted. "Tomayto tomahto."

"Using my words against me?"

"Yep."

"Fine," Redd sighed. "I'm dreading the conversation with Wallace."

"That's not just it. We both know that's not the main thing bothering you."

A heavy silence, quiet as the moon's glow, hung between them as Redd debated his words. He looked up at the moon, a pearl in the inky, star-speckled sky, its pale light dusting the ground with silver.

"We both know you didn't want Nuit to leave," Leo murmured. "So, I don't know why you pushed her away."

Fingers tangled in the thick strands of his hair as he let out a slow breath, the scents of the city clinging to the air. "She is better off without me anyways. I am an old coot who is set in his grumpy ways."

"You're right," Leo replied, the sharp impact of his elbow a jarring thud against Redd's stomach. "She could do a hell of a lot better than you."

"Fuck off," Redd grunted.

"What woman would be interested in a loyal, strong, sarcastic, over opinionated, dumbass male like you?"

"Are you trying to cheer me up or depress me? I couldn't tell."

"I am trying to say, if you're interested, don't let her get away. She could do a helluva lot worse than you or she could do better, but do you want her to find that out on her own?"

"Remind me again why we are friends?"

"Because I tolerate you. Quit changing the subject."

Eyes fixed on Leo, Redd's weight settled into the passenger seat. Leo's face, etched with concern, was visible in the dim interior light. "She isn't interested in me."

"You're an idiot. Earlier, I should have added a blind dumbass to that list."

"She said–"

"I have heard you say a million things you didn't mean when you're mad. I watched as she sat there in that basement trying to cast spell after spell to see if you were alright. She didn't mean what she said. At least not all of it."

Redd mulled over Leo's words, a dull ache in his chest. He hadn't wanted to let her go, the thought a bitter taste on his tongue, but the gnawing feeling of unworthiness, a cold weight in his gut, persisted. *Was I wrong when I let her go? Should I have chased her down? I have fucked everything up at every turn so should I even try?* Her words and Leo's words echoed through his mind as he tried to figure out which was right. *Could she love someone who will never be able to walk in the sunlight with her?*

"Which parts do you think she didn't mean?"

"The chaotic upside down part," Leo laughed. "I'm pretty sure she was just mad at you for taking so long to finish that battle. I am too, but seeing how you fought today I can see why it took so damn long."

"How long was I supposed to be gone?"

"She probably thought for an hour. I am going to give you a little leeway, about two hours."

With a dramatic roll of his eyes, Redd glanced at Leo. "You're an idiot"

"Better an idiot than a fool like you. So, are you going to get your woman or continue to mope like a forlorn teenager?" Leo said, as he turned onto the highway.

REDD

Chapter 45

Redd, flanked by his armed escort, walked the polished white marble floors of the fae castle, the air alive with the faint scent of bluebells and poppies. Each footfall echoed subtly in the cavernous halls. He was on his way to meet Eero and Wallace; Eero, newly announced king consort, a temporary title, until the chaotic whispers of fae politics settled their plans in the wake of turmoil. Alvero had chattered on about the latest court drama, but Redd zoned out after a few seconds of listening; fae politics held no interest for him.

Everyone had clamored to go, but a firm "no" silenced them all; only Redd was who they wanted to meet with. The chill of potential betrayal snaked down Redd's spine—a trap, maybe? He should have refused, yet his better judgment had crumbled, and he had accepted. Now, the rhythmic thump-thump-thump of his boots echoed in the sterile hallway, flanked by four guards, their uniforms gleaming under the lights. *Gods only know what awaits me.*

A heavy oak door swung inward with a groan, its hinges protesting the guards' push as they ushered him through. He stepped into a room thick with the musty smell of aged paper and dust, a cacophony of shuffling papers and murmured voices assaulting his ears. The walls, lined with half-empty shelves, were in disarray. Cardboard boxes overflowed, spilling their contents—books, trinkets, and forgotten knick-knacks — in a chaotic jumble across the room. A massive, scarred wooden desk, worn smooth by years of use, dominated the space. Eero sat behind it, his expression unreadable, while Wallace leaned against a corner, his posture relaxed.

His eyes caught the relaxed slump of Wallace's shoulders as a hearty laugh rumbled from his chest, a response to whatever Eero's words were. Eero's own shoulders shook with mirth, the worn leather of his chair creaking softly under his weight as he leaned back.

"Well, hello Redd," Eero said, a warm grin stretching his face, crinkling the corners of his eyes.

"Yeah, hello to you too," Redd shrugged defensively. "Let's get this over with."

A prickly heat crawled up his neck, his heart a frantic drum against his ribs. The air tasted too sweet. His chest tightened, the air lodging in there. His palms, slick with sweat, felt clammy. *What if they issue a death warrant for Feya?* He didn't know if his legs could get them far away enough to reach safety, or if he would have to kill enough fae to protect her. Yet, he knew, with a grim certainty that chilled him to the bone, that he would do whatever it took to keep her alive and his family safe. Even if it meant facing these two alone.

"Why do you always have to be so impatient?" Wallace snorted. "Sit and have a drink. Let's relax and try to be friendly."

"I think you forget what I drink," Redd stated, the rough scrape of the chair legs on the floor a sharp counterpoint to his smooth voice. He settled into the worn chair, a tension in his muscles.

"Nope, we didn't," Wallace said, the words rough as sandpaper. He produced a bottle, the cork groaning under his thumb. Crimson liquid, thick as honey and smelling just as sweet, filled a crystal glass.

He lifted the cup, the comforting warmth radiating through the crystal, and inhaled deeply; the tang of fae blood filled his nostrils, rich and sweet. No other scent intruded as he cautiously sipped, the liquid warm against his tongue while he savored it.

"We would like to thank you for your efforts in bringing down Casada," Eero stated warmly.

Confusion etched itself into the deep lines of Redd's brow, a roadmap of worry. His eyes, darting like trapped birds, flickered between the two males. "How are you going to thank me?"

"By pardoning what you did," Eero said, the amber liquid sloshing into his glass with a soft swish as he poured. He took a long swig. Redd inhaled, catching the whiff of scotch.

Laughing, a deep, rumbling chuckle that vibrated in his chest, Redd shook his head. "I have committed no crimes by you."

"You created a halfling," Eero stated calmly, his brown eyes growing serious.

Crimson flooded Redd's vision as a million thoughts, a cacophony of whispers and shouts, roared through his mind. A cold sweat slicked his skin, his heart a frantic drum against his ribs. *Are they attacking my house as we speak? Should I have sent my family into hiding?*

"She was dying and already bitten," he growled, feeling the rage start to simmer in his guts.

"That is not consequential," Eero stated, his wrist flicking sharply. The clink of ice against glass followed as he reached for his scotch, the amber liquid catching the firelight. His brown eyes gleaming with cool amusement.

Redd frowned, the lines etching deeper into his face as he weighed his options. Could he kill them quickly in silence so he could escape? Or should he risk a text to Leo, to see if anything was going down at the place and give them a chance to run if it was not? Or would playing along be safer? "So, you're saying I should have left a child for dead? Is that what you guys would have done?"

Shrugging, Eero swirled his crystal glass. "That is a moot point, since you still broke the laws of our kind. But, since you have fought to bring peace to our kind and right the wrongs of the old regime, we are going to pardon you of your crime."

Golden light glinted in Redd's amber eyes as Eero's words, a relentless tide of sound, crashed over him. A cold dread, clammy and constricting, tightened its grip around his heart, suffocating him as the implications for his family washed over him. "And Feya?"

"As an extension of you and your hard work, we will keep her secret and allow her to live." Eero swirled the amber liquid in his glass, the ice clinking softly against the crystal.

A warm weight settled in his chest, a mixture of relief and a quiet fear. "It sounds like there is a but in there," Redd murmured. His gaze was intense on Eero's face, searching, waiting for the other shoe to drop.

"Since she has shown great restraint. If there comes a time she does not, then we will take the actions needed." Eero downed the amber liquid. He slammed the empty glass onto the desk, the sharp thud echoing in the hushed room. "The ritual is not pretty, but I will not hesitate if she shows signs of going mad or loses control."

Redd nodded, the words sifting through the smoky haze of his worry, a dull ache behind his eyes. *So, for now, we are safe, unless we piss the wrong person off.*

He debated whether to defy them with a sharp retort or to swallow his pride and accept. Swirling his drink, he stared at the twirling crimson. Eero's words echoed in his ears. Tossing back the last of his blood cocktail, both ideas warring in his head. *Telling them to fuck off would be greatly satisfying. I really don't need their approval, but it would drag out this drama. Dragging the drama out would mean more lectures from Cass. I could use a little less drama. Playing along means peace, but I need to make sure Feya keeps her head down for all eternity.* A deep, weary sigh escaped his lips as his gaze drifted, first to Wallace, then to Eero. The weight of the situation pressed down, a tangible burden on his shoulders while he decided what he was doing.

"Thanks for the pardon," Redd said, as he exhaled. "Are you going to pour me another drink?"

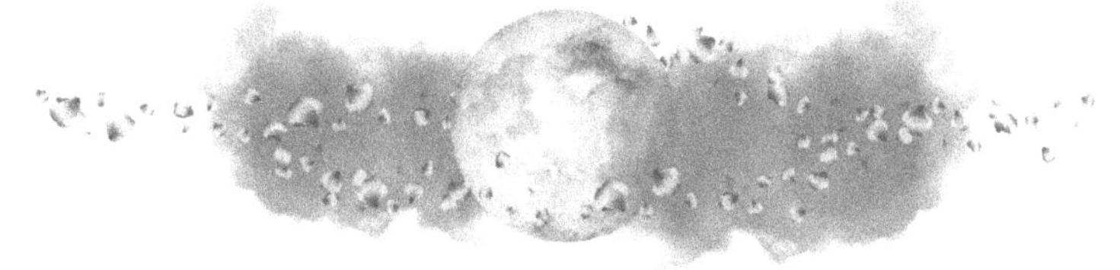

Stepping from the cool, damp shade of the forest into the road, he heard the cheerful chirping of birds, a chorus announcing the beginning of sunrise. He slid into his car, the clock glared—there was no time left. He would have to crash here until sunset. With a snap, sun blockers velcroed onto the windows, muting the harsh light. He settled into the backseat, the fabric yielding beneath him, arms behind his head, legs curled up.

He closed his eyes, but sleep evaded him; eyes as dark as a moonless night haunted his waking thoughts. The lingering scent of lily, myrrh, and cinnamon—her perfume—a phantom presence against the stale car air. He could almost feel the warmth of her skin beneath his fingertips.

Opening his eyes, he stared up at the darkened ceiling. The faint light filtering through the gap in the curtains created a lone slash of light on it. His mind, a frantic drumbeat, bounced between her comments and Leo's gruff words, a jarring contrast. *Which one should I believe? Was Leo right and she just acted out of anger? Or should I do what's right and let her live her life in the sun?*

He rubbed his chest, the friction a stark contrast to the chill that settled in his bones as her words echoed in his mind. He saw those eyes again, bright tears like glittering diamonds reflecting the dim light in their obsidian depths.

Could she be happy living in my world of darkness? Do I want to try to drag her into it?

The answer, a warm thrum in his chest, was all the confirmation he needed. He sighed, the sound a soft rustle in the still air, a sense of peace settling over him like a cool evening breeze. He knew that after sunset, he had one more stop to make before going home.

Chapter 46

Nuit's tired eyes, blurred by the dim lamplight, strained to focus on the ink of her favorite novel. The incessant chatter in her head drowned out the quiet rustle of the pages. Sighing, she gently placed the book on the coffee table. She stood, stretching her arms overhead, the movement easing her muscles. *There's no point pretending I am reading. Who am I lying to? Only myself.* She squeezed her eyelids shut, the pressure a welcome contrast to the frantic dance of thoughts behind them. The hushed silence of the room pressed in a heavy blanket against the buzzing chaos in her head.

She looked down as soft, warm fur brushed her leg—a gentle, silken touch. Cairo, her cousin's gift to her, a gift of sunshine and shadows, nuzzled her. An Abyssinian cat with short, golden-brown fur that was patterned with alternating light and dark bands. The lithe, muscular body, a warm weight, wound between her legs, a purring vibration humming against her calves, a silent demand for attention.

She had to admit, Cairo was great company. He was attentive, caring, and a great listener. A faint, musky scent of catnip clung to his fur. She felt the comforting weight of his body pressed against her leg while he rubbed up against it again. She knew he had some magical capabilities, a secret shimmering beneath his gentle exterior, but he had not shown them to her yet.

Reaching down, she scratched behind his velvety ears; a soft purr escaped him as he pressed his warm, furry body into her hand. The gentle heat radiating from his slight frame, a comforting weight against her palm, anchored her, pulling her back from her swirling thoughts.

"Oh, Cairo, are you hungry?" Her voice, a breathy whisper. She paused as if waiting for an answer she knew would not come.

His almond-shaped tawny eyes, gleaming like polished topaz, looked up at her expectantly. A soft smile touched her lips as she walked to the kitchen, the wood cool beneath her bare feet. His soft paws made no sound on the floor as he silently followed. The hiss of the can opener pierced the quiet as she pulled out his food. Dumping the contents into his bowl, a soft plop against the ceramic bowl, she set it on the floor. Cairo, a blur of fur, ran up and devoured the food with happy slurping sounds.

"It's dinner time, I guess I should make myself something as well."

Fingers brushing the fino bread, she crafted a sandwich. The clink of plate against table announced her simple meal. Looking out the window, the once monotonous gray of the cityscape changed, the lines of buildings softening and blurring as the sun dipped below the horizon. The sky transformed into a canvas of vibrant colors, fiery orange and rich red danced across the heavens, intermingling with streaks of deep purple and soft pink.

As a silvery moon climbed the inky sky, its light painting the clouds with an ethereal glow, her thoughts drifted to Redd. A gentle breeze, carrying the scent of the city through the open window, stirred her hair. *Is he staring up at the same sky as I am right now?* The moonlight streamed in through the window, dancing as clouds passed by it, a mocking distraction from the image of him. She knew she should push the thoughts away, but she could not help it. A familiar, dull ache, a throbbing rhythm like a second heartbeat, filled her chest, heavy and warm as she thought of him. The scent of rain-soaked earth did little to soothe the tightness as a soft drizzle started to come down. She had stopped fighting the feeling, the relentless tide of memory, stopped fighting her racing mind, and stopped fighting her aching heart.

She inhaled deeply, the earthy scent of petrichor filling her nostrils. A vivid memory of his hand on her cheek crowded her thoughts. His body pressed to hers left a lingering heat blooming against her skin. The clean, musky scent of his breath was a phantom touch fluttering across her skin.

Startled by the distant, resonant chime of a grandfather clock, she realized she had been lost in thought too long; her gaze fixed on the blurry city lights turned on outside the window. Soft fur brushed against her leg, grounding her. She reached down, fingers sinking into Cairo's plush fur, the silky strands cool and smooth against her skin. A gentle purr vibrated through her hand, a comforting rumble.

"You might just be my best friend, Cairo," she murmured. Those tawny eyes looked at her so knowingly, like he understood every word she said. "I need a distraction to get him out of my mind."

Standing, she placed her plate in the sink—the clatter echoing slightly in the quiet kitchen — deciding to wash it tomorrow. Walking down the hallway, she went to her room, the faint scent of lavender from her recently washed sheets filling the air. She sank into the soft, yielding comfort of her bed, the plush comforter enveloping her. The click of the remote was sharp against the silence, then the glow of the television flickered to life as she channel-surfed, finally settling on a dramatic scene unfolding. Cairo jumped up and curled on the bed by her feet.

Rich voices, warm and resonant, chased away the chilling loneliness. She was lost in the vibrant play flashing across the screen. The sudden, jarring clang of the doorbell was a shock as she let out a small squeak. A soft smile touched her lips; a sigh escaped as she pondered the unexpected nighttime visitor.

Looking down at Cairo, she smoothed his fur back. "You think it's Seshat? Two visits in such a short time is very strange for her."

The worn wooden stairs creaked under her feet as she followed Cairo. His tawny eyes, gleaming, flicked back to her as he moved with fluid grace. Each of his steps was silent, while hers thudded.

"You seem excited about having company," Nuit grumbled playfully. "Are you already bored with just talking with me? My feelings are hurt, so you know."

A tinkling laugh escaped her as her feet stumbled, when the door's frosted glass came into view. The silhouette, stark against the muted streetlight, was not Seshat. A frantic drum pounded in her ears, drowning out all other noise. Her breath hitched, a cold knot in her throat, as her trembling hand pushed open the door.

REDD

Chapter 47

Golden flecks of light glinted in Redd's intense gaze as he devoured Nuit with his eyes, a silent, scorching appraisal that traveled the length of her form. Her eyes widened, reflecting the streetlight. Her heartbeat raced while his felt like a frantic drum against his ribs, a rhythm echoing the rising self-consciousness filling him up.

"Were you really just going to leave without saying goodbye?" Redd's lips curled into a smirk. The sound was barely audible, while a low, breathy chuckle escaped those lips. *Sauvé, as always,* Redd thought sarcastically.

"That was weeks ago," she breathed, the words barely audible above the hum of the city. Frustration, a sudden, sharp storm, ignited in her dark eyes, their depths shadowed.

Shrugging, a flash of tawny fur caught his eye. He looked down at the sleek cat, a soft purring sound accompanying its sinuous dance around her ankles. The faint scent of catnip clung to its fur. A gentle warmth radiated from the cat's eyes as it rubbed against her legs. "You have company?"

"What?" she gasped before following his gaze to her legs. "Oh, that's Cairo."

"You have a cat? I didn't know that."

"I do now," she said, the crisp cotton of her shirt a cool contrast to her flushed honey skin, her arms crossing over her chest. "You obviously did not come here to meet Cairo, so why don't we get down to business and you say why you're really here."

"Can you at least invite me in? We can sit and talk. You can have some tea," Redd offered, a forced smile stretching across his face, the damp chill seeping into his soaked shirt. The drumming rain was a relentless rhythm against his skin, each drop a tiny, icy sting. He waited, the seconds stretching into an agonizing eternity, a raw, exposed feeling growing with every tick of the clock.

Shrugging, she turned and started towards the stairs. The old house creaked a silent protest. He shut the heavy oak door with a solid thunk and followed, his footsteps echoing on the aged wood above the soft whisper of her bare feet. His gaze lingered on the sway of her hips ascending the stairs while he followed her into the warm, spice-scented kitchen. A nervous flutter filled his chest as he tried to calm himself.

He sat heavily at the worn oak table, the rough grain scratching against his fingertips. Nerves tightened his throat, words catching in his dry mouth. His fingers nervously traced circles on the tabletop while she moved with a practiced grace, the rhythmic clinking of porcelain a soothing counterpoint to his inner turmoil. The kettle whistled, a sharp cry in the quiet, as she prepared two steaming mugs of tea. His eyes drank in her every move.

He mulled over his words, sleepless in the heat of the car. All those carefully crafted sentences vanished the moment he saw her, swallowed by the sudden rush of her presence; the remembered weight of his planned words were gone.

"Well?" she asked, her voice a soft chime as she walked over with the steaming cups, their warmth radiating. She placed one before him, the ceramic bright splash of color against the brown of the wood.

He stared at the porcelain cup, its warm contents swirling faintly, debating whether to feign a sip or leave it untouched. The quiet clink as he lifted it, then the soft thud of it returning to the saucer, undisturbed. *Could she have poisoned it? I watched everything she did, but she tricked me once?* He shoved the thought away, wondering what motive she had to poison him now.

"I wanted to..." he paused, a prickling unease crawling up his spine like icy fingers. The air hung heavy, silent except for the frantic thump of his own heart. He felt the weight of unseen gazes, cold and sharp. He shifted and met a pair of tawny eyes, burning like embers in the twilight, fixed on him with unnerving intensity. "I just wanted to..." Clearing his throat, he winced. "I just wanted to apologize."

"Apologize for what?" Her eyes, narrowed slits, watched him as a cat landed on her lap. Her hand, moving with a slow, deliberate rhythm, stroked the cat's back; a purr vibrated warmly, but those tawny eyes told another story.

"For just being a general ass." His smile, a flash of white teeth, felt sharp, a little cruel.

Her hand stroked the purring cat; its eyes, narrowed slits, fixed on him, its tail a rhythmic thrum. A palpable tension, a prickling coldness, emanated from the feline aimed at him. The clinking of her teacup against the saucer, a delicate chime, punctuated the silence as her gaze, sharp and intense, burned through him from above the rim of her cup. "Is that it?"

"Umm," Redd stuttered. Inhaling deeply, the crisp air filling his lungs, he sought the cool, witty persona he usually embodied so easily instead of this stuttering buffoon she was turning him into. "No... That's not everything. Umm... Maybe... We can start over."

"Why do we need to start over?"

Leaning back, he raked his gaze over her, searching for a crack in the icy facade she put up. Leaning forward, he covered her hand that cradled the warm teacup. A sharp, sudden blow grazed his hand; tiny, wicked claws tore at his skin. His own blood filled his nostrils as he recoiled.

"Oh, Cairo," Nuit scolded, leaping up with a jolt. The clatter of her bare feet on the cool tile echoed as she snatched a kitchen towel. "That was naughty."

His gaze remained fixed on the cat, its tawny eyes blazing a furious green. *Probably realizes he'll be my snack as soon as she's not looking.* Those eyes, glittering with amusement, seemed to smirk at him; a silent, knowing satisfaction.

Nuit gently wrapped a towel around his hand, the rough fibers a comforting touch to staunch the flow of blood. He felt the phantom itch of the shallow wounds, a tingling beneath the healing skin. Allowing her to tend to him, he enjoyed the gentle touch, a welcome change from her previous coldness. He was glad the icy princess was gone.

"I'm sorry," she murmured, her voice a soft rustle against the quiet air, fingers light as a feather.

His fingers, light as feathers, swept her hair from her face. Startled, her eyes, the color of a moonless night, met his.

"I missed you," he whispered.

He watched her throat bob, a delicate flutter against the creamy honeyed skin of her neck as she stared at him, her eyes wide and captivating. A nervous tremor ran through him, but he closed the distance, the scent of her perfume filling his senses. His lips brushed hers, a feather-light touch, fear a cold knot in his stomach. But her lips were soft, yielding, a warm invitation. He pressed closer, feeling the slight give of her mouth as his tongue explored, tasting the lingering earl grey tea.

"Fuck!" he yelped, pulling away. "The dumb cat is using my leg as a fucking scratching post." He shoved the cat away. *If I snap its neck now, would she be upset?*

"Cairo," Nuit yelled.

She scooped up the cat, its purr a gentle vibration showing how much he enjoyed what he did. Her steps softly padded down the hall as she walked away. He heard her soft, murmuring voice, a melodic hum fading as a door creaked shut, a muffled thud.

"Sorry," she said, rolling her eyes as she walked back into the kitchen. "Did he hurt you badly?"

"If I pull my pants down, will you administer to my wounds?" Redd said, standing up and walking towards her.

Slapping his chest with a sharp smack, she huffed, her bangs soft and wispy, fluttered. "Can you not be serious for even a moment?"

"Do you want me to be serious?" Fingers brushed against silken strands, a warm weight in his palm as he cupped the back of her head.

"Yes," she whispered. His gaze settled on her lip, a crimson bow trembling slightly. A nervous tremor ran through her as her teeth, like tiny scissors, chewed on her lower lip.

"I missed you." His fist stopped pulling her closer, her face a hair's breadth away. He felt the warm, feather-light brush of her breath. A deep inhale brought the sweet, intoxicating scent of her perfume, mingled with the essence of her.

"You did?" she said, her hand came up clutching his chest.

"Yes, I did, completely and utterly." His nose brushed hers, a feather-light touch. "Did you miss me?"

Her lips, full and trembling, hesitated. He felt their soft brush against his as they parted, then closed, a whisper of warmth. Finally, they reopened the barely audible breath of a "Yes."

His hands settled on her waist, pulling her impossibly close. She filled his senses as his lips brushed hers, a teasing pressure that begged for a response. Her mouth yielded, a soft sigh escaping as his tongue explored the sweetness within. His fingers, tracing the curve of her hips, felt the delicate warmth of her skin. The unexpected surrender surprised him; he'd envisioned a lengthy seduction, weeks of coaxing this gentle soul. But now, she pressed against him, yielding like a blossoming flower, its petals unfurling in the warmth of his embrace.

Nuit

Chapter 48

Nuit devoured his lips, a ravenous hunger filling her kiss. The faint, salty tang of his skin mingled with the sweet scent of his cologne; a heady mix that intoxicated her senses. A shiver, electric and sharp, traced its way down her spine. Weeks felt like ages since she last touched him, the memory echoing in the thrumming of her pulse against her skin.

The tug on her heart, a relentless pull she fought against, against him. When he was hurt, her brittle mask of cool indifference instantly cracked under the strain. She'd tried, desperately, to let him go, to erase him from memory. Yet, Cairo's scratch shattered her composure; the illusion vanished. She knew then, with a visceral certainty, that she could no longer pretend.

The taste of him filled her mouth as his tongue invaded, the taste of him intoxicating. His cologne swirled around her, enticing her. His hands, calloused yet gentle, clutched her hips, fingertips pressing into her skin, igniting a warmth that bloomed through her like a summer wildfire. Her mind, a hazy fog, struggled to focus as he reluctantly released her. A desperate ache pulled at her, a yearning to recapture the heat of his touch. Opening her eyes, she met his gaze—amber pools reflecting a thousand untold stories, their depths unreadable.

Thoughts tumbled back into her brain, a chaotic rush of images and half-formed ideas, like pebbles tumbling in a rushing stream. Doubt, a cold, clammy hand, crept back in with its icy grip. *What if he just wants to get laid and nothing more? What if he just needs another distraction?* She chewed her lip, eyes narrowed in thought, a soft rhythmic gnawing sound accompanying the silent debate. A slight furrow creased her brow. *Do I fight my own feelings and my own heart, or do I accept whatever is given and run with it?*

He rested his forehead on hers, the soft texture of her skin a contrast to the cool touch of his. His eyelids fluttered down as he whispered, "I don't have much to give you," as his words brushed her ear.

"I didn't ask for anything from you," she whispered tentatively. Reaching up, her fingers brushed his cheek as the coarse stubble scratched her palm like sandpaper.

Chuckling, a warm, self-deprecating sound, he shook his head. "You ask for so much more with those eyes than you realize."

A cold dread gripped her chest, silencing her heartbeat as she strained to understand his mumbled words. "What are you offering, and what is it you think I am asking for?"

His lips brushed against hers, a feather light touch. "All I offer is a life lived in darkness and you deserve a hell of a lot more. You should ask for the sun, the clouds and everything the light touches."

A renewed thump echoed in her chest, a frantic drumbeat against her ribs. Her pulse, a frantic hummingbird, vibrated beneath her skin. "Maybe I prefer the inky, star-speckled night sky over a glaring, sunbaked day," she breathed. A tense silence hung in the air, thick and heavy as the anticipation in her chest—waiting for her heart to be broken. Each second stretched, taut as a violin string, threatening to snap.

"Well, as long as you know what you're getting yourself into," he muttered, the words a warm breath ghosting against her skin as his nose nudged hers, a soft, ticklish touch.

His hands, rough yet gentle, slid to her ass, lifting her. Her legs, instinctively, wrapped tight around his waist. He twisted, the impact jarring as her ass landed with a thud on the cool, smooth surface of the dining room table. A sharp crack—the shattering of glass as cups fell to the floor—cut through the air as he pressed her back against the wood. His hands exploring, roamed her body, igniting a storm of sensations within her.

He grabbed her legs, firm hands pulling them from around his waist. A gasp escaped her lips, quickly cut short as his hands found the waistband of her pants, the cotton yielding to his touch. A giggle bubbled up as he tugged them down, the fabric rustling against his skin. Her pants sailed over his shoulder, a soft thud against the worn wood floor.

Moments ago, I was feeling lonely and sad. Now I feel like a giggling little school girl whose crush just looked at her for the first time.

"What's so funny, Mo shíorghrá?" he whispered, his mouth now a whisper away from hers. She felt each word like a caress when his lips moved against hers.

"Nothing," she murmured.

She pressed her mouth to taste him, wanting to savor the salt and subtle spice of his mouth. His tongue wet was a swirl against hers while it tangled with hers. The rough grain of the hardwood table pressed against her back, a cool contrast to the fiery heat that his body created in hers. Shivers, stormy and exquisite, danced down her spine.

His mouth, insistent, captured hers, an exploration of every contour of her mouth before releasing it. Sharp fangs pierced her skin, a chilling bite on her neck as he drank deeply. A dizzying rush, a swirling vortex of sensation, overwhelmed her before he withdrew his ivories. The metallicy tang of her blood mingled with the sharp, masculine scent of his cologne, a potent mix filling her senses.

His mouth traveled down her skin. Finding her nipple through the soft cotton of her shirt, he sucked it gently, the fabric a teasing barrier between them. His tongue lavished attention on the sensitive bud, playful exploration. Each suck created a small, almost painful pleasure, punctuated by the tantalizing scrape of his fangs. A final, tender graze of his teeth before he moved to the other side had her back arching in anticipation, a silent plea for the same delightful torture.

He moved lower, his breath ruffling the cotton of her shirt, a whisper against her skin. He paused, his breath ghosting over her most sensitive area. She inhaled sharply, air catching in her throat, anticipating the touch of his mouth. She held her breath, time stretching out before his teeth, cool and surprisingly gentle, grazed her clit. Her fingers clenched the table's edge as his fangs scraped against her again, a jarring friction. A distant rumble of thunder, a low growl, vibrated in the air. He sucked, a searing pull, her back arching, a choked moan escaping her lips. The storm intensified, mirroring the tempest within, building to a crescendo. Then, his mouth was gone, leaving a lingering heat and a tremor in its wake.

Her eyes fluttered open, a desperate need blossoming within her. His face, a looming shadow, filled her vision as he effortlessly lifted her leg, the fabric of his trousers brushing her skin as the zipper lay open. A deep, smooth thrust sent jolts of pleasure through her, a wave crashing over her as she cried out. Her body trembled, a delicate flower shaking in a storm, as he moved within her, the rhythm a pounding pulse. A guttural roar ripped through the air before he collapsed, heavy and spent, upon her.

His weight remained, a comforting pressure, as he released her leg. A slow smile bloomed on her lips, savoring the weight of him, the lingering heat within. Her fingers tangled in his hair, the silky strands soft against her skin. She closed her eyes, breathing him in. She wanted to savor the moment, no matter how long it lasted.

"I would rot in hell for all eternity if it meant one more second spent with you. Mo shíorghrá, is ceol mo chroí thú," Redd whispered, his breath warm against her ear, the words a low hum vibrating against her skin.

She paused, fingers tracing the soft strands of his hair as his words, like sunlight piercing mist, cleared her mind. A warmth bloomed in her chest, a lightness in her soul, filling her with joy. "What does that mean?" she asked, her eyes shining brightly.

"My eternal love, you're the music of my heart." His warm breath feathered against her neck, a soft tickle against her skin as his lips brushed it, a fleeting pressure like a butterfly's wing.

Hot tears welled, blurring her vision with a stinging saltiness as she spoke, her voice catching. "I think I've waited a lifetime to hear you say that."

"Not going to say some pretty little words back to me?" A smirk tugged at the corners of his mouth, a playful, yet vulnerable, glint shimmering in his eyes.

"You want pretty words?" she muttered, brushing a stray strand of hair off his forehead.

"I'd like some kind of words at least."

With a bright, melodic laugh, she tugged him closer. "I love you."

"That's better," he chuckled, the sound a warm rumble that vibrated against her chest, a sight accompanied by the bright flash of his white teeth.

She pulled him closer, her heart feeling full. Her hand stroked his back.

"Ouch!" he yelled, a raw, sharp sound tearing through the air, his body a blur as he leaped to his feet. "I am to drink every last ounce of blood from that fucking cat."

With a gasp, she watched as he, a blur of motion, dove for Cairo.

"No!" she screamed.

Then the cat vanished in a swirling puff of grey smoke, smelling faintly of wood smoke. He reappeared beside her with a soft thump, and she scooped him up, his warm, furry body a comforting weight against her. His tiny paws kneaded her arm as he curled into a purring ball. *So, he can teleport. I wonder what other powers my little friend has.*

Confusion etched itself onto Redd's face, a visible furrow in his brow as his head turned. He stared at her, his gaze a tangible question.

"Hear me out," she stated calmly. She smiled up at Redd as he came closer to her.

"He seems to think I am a scratching post," he growled.

"You'll become friends in no time," she murmured, her fingers brushing Redd's cheek—a soft touch against his stubbled face. "Just be patient. Please."

A harsh snort escaped his lips as his eyes, darting like quick sparrows, flickered between her and Cairo, whose purr vibrated faintly in the air.

"For his sake, it better be sooner or later, because I have no qualms about—"

"Please," she pleaded.

Rolling his eyes, he sighed. "What the fuck kind of cat is he?"

"Mine," she whispered, nuzzling Cairo.

Elysium Hyperionides sank into the plush navy couch, feeling the exhaustion of a long day in the Arizona sun. She and her cousins, Agatha and Mariangela Gorgo, had spent the day at Parnassica Nursery. The scent of soil and blooming flowers still clung to her clothes. By the end of the day she was drained. The constant interaction with mundies aka humans left her overwhelmed. Unfortunately, her cousins had decided that she, whom they considered the people pleaser of the group, was therefore good with the customers. So, they left her to deal with most of them. There was only so much she could take when dealing with the mundane humans before her social battery was drained.

She curled her legs up on the couch. The scent of the burning vanilla candles wafted around the room creating a relaxing atmosphere. She took a swig of cold beer as she turned the tv on. Picking a cheesy romance movie, she listened as the mundies argued.

The subtle sound of her snakes hissing whispered in her ears. Reaching up, she caressed the charm necklace hanging around her neck, a silver snake curled up into a coil. The spell carved on the back read:

Ζωγράφισέ μου ομορφιά, ζωγράφισέ μου χάρη, ενδυνάμωσε το πνεύμα μου και μάγεψε το πρόσωπό μου. Με το φως του ήλιου και τη χάρη του φεγγαριού έτσι είναι.

The charm masked her true form from the mundie world so she could blend in. With a gentle sweep, she brushed her dirty blonde hair out of her face, revealing her sharp cheekbones. Her big, round hazel eyes fixated on the flickering TV screen as the sound of the drama filled the room. The warmth of the sun had kissed her olive skin, leaving a subtle glow that complemented her rosy cheeks. Her 5'4 frame sunk back into the cushions she leaned into it.

A sudden knock on the door startled Elys, pulling her out of the captivating story she was immersed in. Assuming it was one of her cousins coming to talk to her, she sighed as she stood up. Most likely Aggie, she thought, remembering that she had taken a couple of bucks from the cash register to buy her lunch. She was going to pay it back. She just did not want to run past two customers to grab her purse.

Sighing, she stood up and walked to the door. She could hear the creaking of the wooden floors as she made her way towards it. As she reached out to grasp the doorknob, preparing for the lecture to come, she took a deep breath. When she opened the door, the sight of two males wearing masks surprised her.

Cold, muddy brown eyes, locked onto her gaze as she stared up at the taller of the two males.

Adorning his face was a mask depicting the visage of the Greek god Zeus. His scraggly brown hair cascaded in unkempt waves, framing the mask. He stood about an imposing foot taller than her, his lanky frame looming over her. The faint scent of sweat and dirt lingered in the surrounding air.

The smaller male wore a mask fashioned after Hera, the Greek Goddess. He was about five inches taller than herself, dirty blonde hair slicked back with what looked like a pound of gel gluing it to his head. He had a beefy build. As he locked his frigid, baby blue eyes onto hers, a glint of cruelty shone through them, sending a chill down her spine. The atmosphere around them was thick with tension, and she could feel her heart pounding against her chest.

"I am looking for a Gorgon named—" he said.

"You must have the wrong house," Elys said, trying to shut the door as fast as she could.

With a loud thud, the door crashed as it hit an enormous foot; the impact reverberating through her arm. Her eyes roamed up from that foot blocking her from shutting the door to the taller of the two males. As his muddy brown eyes met hers, she felt a shiver run down her spine. They were staring through her, as if they did not even see her.

The shorter male drew her attention as he moved forward. Her heart thudded in her ears as she backed up a few steps until she bumped into the couch. Her legs felt like they were made of jelly, and despite her brain urging her to flee, she remained rooted to the spot. The thudding of her heart in her ears was the only sound that could be heard. The masks hiding the faces of the two males made the scene in front of her even eerier.

"I have no money on me," she mumbled meekly.

With a forceful push, the shorter man opened the door, causing it to creak in protest as he entered her house. With his heavy footsteps echoing, the taller male followed closely behind. The living room suddenly felt cramped, as if its walls were closing in under the imposing presence of the two men.

Finding courage finally, she made a quick turn, bolting towards the kitchen, her eyes fixated on the back sliding glass door. But before she could make it to the door, a firm hand yanked her back by her hair. The pain was excruciating, as tears stung her eyes as pain flashed through her. Her snakes hissing just as loud as the pounding of her heart.

"Just come along peacefully," the shorter male laughed, twisting her hair around his fist.

"Fuck you," she said, trying to figure if she knew these males. She could tell they were eternals like herself, but that was it. No signs of recognition came to her. "What the fuck do you want?"

Her eyes darted around, tears blurring her vision, trying to focus on what she could use as a weapon. His grip on her head lessened as a bit of relief washed through her. She looked down, her eyes locked on the candles burning on the table. The pewter candle holders gleaming softly.

"That's none of your business," the shorter male said. "I am gonna just put these shackles on you. You're gonna come along peacefully or..." He shook the shackles as a cruel grin spread across his face.

Elys nodded, a small smile appearing on her lips as she tentatively showed compliance. He released her hair, and the sound of the shackles clanking rang through the room as he held them up, swaying from his hand. The cold iron sent panic coursing through her veins. As she turned, her hand brushed against the candlestick. With a swift motion, she grabbed the candlestick and swung it at the smaller male's head. The impact made a sickening cracking sound. Stepping back, Elys felt the adrenaline pumping through her veins, her heart racing with fear and determination as she turned to run. She knew she had to get to the back door, but her legs felt heavy and unresponsive. She knew she was not strong enough to defeat them both.

She felt herself fly back, as she felt the chain of her necklace dig into the delicate flesh of her throat. She could hear the snap of the chain as it broke. The charm that had been hanging from it fell to the ground, shattering the glamor spell that had been hiding her true form. She felt the shift as her hair disappeared, leaving her snakes to slither out and stretch, hissing as they did. The flicker of light glinted off their golden brown scales. As the transformation continued, her skin began to itch and crawl as scales formed randomly on her forehead and back. The pain of a migraine suddenly hit her, and she felt her hazel eyes shift and change, becoming slits like those of a snake. Her vision blurred as everything came into crystal clear focus. Finally, she completed the transformation into her true form as a gorgon.

Collapsing to the hard, unforgiving floor, a jolt of pain surged through her body as her back made brutal contact with the ground. Her teeth chattered as she crashed down. With her heart racing, her hands shook as she tightened her grip around the candlestick. A sharp, searing pain shot through her body as she tried to stand on shaky legs. A hand shot out, grabbing a handful of her tangled serpents on her head. The sensation was overwhelming, causing her vision to blur and fade to black as her breath clogged in her throat.

A blood-curdling scream pierced through

the air. The sound of her snakes' slithering and hissing filled the room. The hand released her as her snakes struck at the hand. In a panic, she crawled towards the wall, huddling under the flickering TV. Meanwhile, the shorter male stood nearby, his right hand dripping with blood from several fang bites. The metallic scent of blood mixed with the scent of the vanilla candles now snuffed out, creating a nauseating combination.

"You'll pay for that, you fucking cunt," the shorter male growled as he rubbed his hand. The towering man loomed just beyond the threshold, his eyes shrouded by a mask of Zeus. Panic seized her chest - there was no way she would make it past him if she ran for the exit. Meanwhile, the shorter male barred her way to the kitchen as he yanked a throw pillow off the couch. She winced as he ripped a strip of fabric off the cushion to bind his wounded hand. The candles' warm wax slowly congealed on the carpet. The living room was in disarray, the couch tilted at an odd angle, and the coffee table upturned, its contents strewn across the floor.

Her brain was scouring itself for an escape plan as the shorter male haphazardly wrapped his hand. Reaching up, Elys felt the cool plastic of the TV. Slowly she pulled herself up as she gently pushed up on the TV, trying to remove it from its mount. The shorter male went to the taller male to tie the wrap on his hand. The TV shifted as it finally came loose of its hooks. While they were distracted, she used her strength to push the TV up a few inches, hiding her smile. She felt the hefty weight of the tv in her arms as she twisted and threw it towards the males. It snapped to a halt, floating for a second as it hit the end of the power cord. It snapped back a bit before falling to the ground and shattering the screen.

It was just enough time for her to turn and run down the hallway. She had to get to her room, where her phone was charging on her nightstand. Her heart raced with fear as she planned to lock herself in her room and call for help. Suddenly, she felt two strong arms wrap around her chest and neck, the sound of her own attempts to scream echoing in her own ears. Her breathing became labored as she clawed at the rough forearm across her throat, feeling the heat and sweat of the attacker's skin against her own. Desperately gasping for air, she struggled to break free, but the grip only tightened around her. Her snakes were striking out desperately.

"Fuck," a howl of pain rang from behind her.

The world began to spin around her, and the smell of her attacker's body odor filled her nostrils as her vision slowly faded to black, and her body went limp.

She came to a moment later, her chest heaving as she struggled for breath. The cold, hard floor pressed against her back as she tried to remember how she ended up there. Slowly, her vision cleared to the sight of shackles encircling her wrists. Tears pricked her eyes as memories of what was happening filled her panic-stricken brain. She tried to push the shackles off her wrists. The more she tugged at the shackles, the tighter they seemed to constrict around her wrists, making her feel helpless and trapped.

"What do you want?" she screamed, locking eyes with the smaller male.

Laughing maniacally, he did not respond. Turning, he spoke to the taller male. "Pick her up while I open the trunk."

Flailing her arms wildly, she tried to fight, but the chains that bound the shackles shrunk, making movement almost impossible. The taller male picked her up and threw her over his shoulder with ease as her sobs wracked her body. Her hands were going numb from the pain of the shackles gripping them.

"Please," she begged. "Don't do this. I can get you money. My family is extremely rich."

The taller male remained silent, his long strides leading them outside. The warm summer breeze hit her like a sledgehammer. Her eyes fixated on the back of his lanky frame. She inhaled deeply before letting out a blood-curdling scream. She was flung into the trunk of a car. The impact knocked the wind out of her, and she felt a sharp pain in her head as it hit the hard metal surface. Her vision blurred, and she struggled to catch her breath. The trunk slammed shut, trapping her inside. She kicked and thrashed, trying to break free. The car sped up suddenly, and she slid across the trunk, banging her head again on the rough metal. The pain was excruciating, and she felt herself slipping away as her world went dark.

Blackberry Lavender White Chocolate Scones

Ingredients

2 ½ cups flour

1 tablespoon granulated sugar

1 tablespoon baking powder

½ tsp salt

12 tbsp cold salted butter, shredded

¾ cup buttermilk, plus more for brushing

1 large egg, beaten

1 ½ cups fresh or frozen blackberries

¾ cup white chocolate chips

Lavender Glaze

¼ cup whole milk

2 tbsp butter

1 tbsp dried lavender (adjust as needed)

1 tsp vanilla extract

1 ½ cups powdered sugar (give or take)

Instructions:

1. Preheat the oven to 375 degrees F. Line a baking sheet with parchment paper.
2. In a large mixing bowl, combine the flour, baking powder, sugar, and salt. Add the butter and toss. Add the buttermilk and egg. Mix until just combined, being careful not to over mix. Fold in the blackberries and white chocolate chips.
3. Turn the dough out onto a floured surface. Pat into a 1-inch thick square. Now cut the dough into 9 large squares or 12 smaller ones. Place on the prepared baking sheet. Brush the tops of the scones with buttermilk.
4. Transfer to the oven and bake until golden brown, approximately 20-22 minutes.
5. While scones are baking, make the lavender glaze. Warm the milk and butter in a small saucepan set over medium heat until steaming, approximately 3-5 minutes. Remove from the heat and stir in the lavender. Cover and steep for 5 minutes. Strain the milk through a fine-mesh strainer and discard the lavender. Stir in the vanilla and powdered sugar, adding more as needed.
6. Serve the scones warm, drizzle with the glaze and smeared with butter.

Egyptian Fino Bread

Ingredients

2 cup and 3 tbsp all-purpose flour

½ cup warm milk

¼ cup warm water

1 ½ tsp yeast

1 tbsp sugar

½ tsp salt

2 tbsp oil

1 tbsp butter chilled

Instructions

1. In a bowl, add milk, sugar, water and yeast. Mix and leave set aside for 10 minutes in the bowl with a towel covering it.
2. After resting, add the rest of the ingredients except for the butter. Knead for 10 minutes. The dough will be sticky but will start to come together and get firmer.
3. Now, you should have a soft, slightly sticky, smooth dough. Add the butter to the dough and knead for 5 more minutes.
4. Cover the dough in the bowl again and let it rise for one and a half to two hours. Shape the dough into six equal sized balls.
5. Roll each ball to approximately 6-inch wide and 9" long logs.
6. Cover the logs and let them rise again for one hour.
7. Preheat the oven to 400 F and bake the rolls for 10 minutes. Or until golden.

8. Place the loaves on a cooling rack.

Boozy Cherry Palmer

Ingredients

2 ½ cups fresh (pitted) or frozen cherries

Juice from 1 Lemon

½ tbsp vanilla extract

1 to 1 ½ cups sugar (to taste)

6 to 7 Lemons

10 to 12 cups boiling hot water

4 iced tea bags

1.5 oz bourbon (optional or amount as wanted)

Instructions

1. Bring water to boil, take off heat and add the iced tea bags. Let the tea bags steep. Take out the tea bags and let it cool completely.
2. While it is cooling, Squeeze the juice from all the lemons and strain the juice through the fine strainer into the pitcher.
3. Pit cherries (if using fresh) and place them into a sauce pot, heated over medium heat. Add lemon juice, vanilla, and sugar to the sauce pot with cherries. Cover, and let it simmer for about 15 minutes, stirring occasionally. Once cooked, take off heat. Strain and allow it to cool.
4. Add tea bond juice into a pitcher and stir well.
5. **Optional**: Pour into a cup with ice and add bourbon.

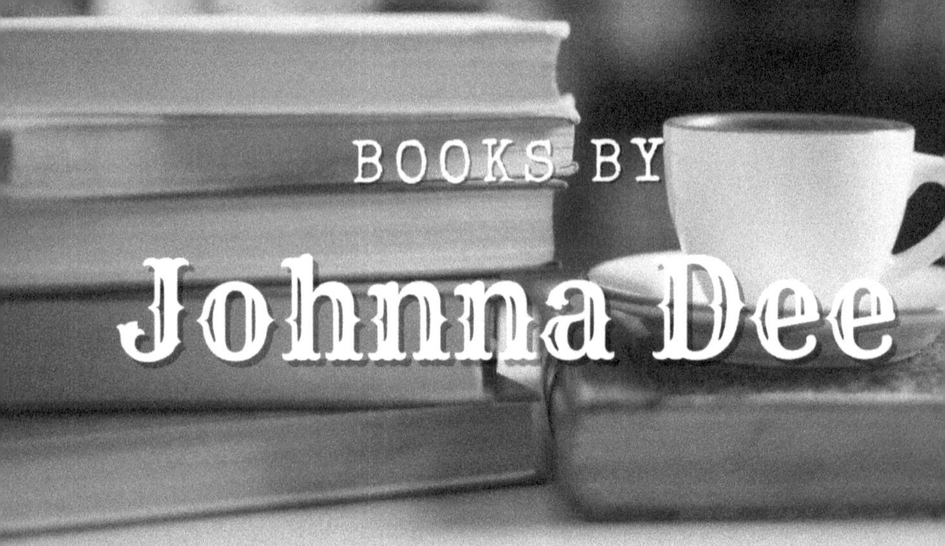

Ascelin Series:

Crest of the Fallen

Crest of the Scorned

Crest of the Forgotten

Gorgo Series:

Betrayal of the Gorgon

Ransom of the Gorgon

Immortality of the Gorgon (January 2026)

Hogsmead Series:

Shifting Sides

Johnna Dee

Magickal Morsels Series:

Cake with a Slice of Vengeance

Cake it Easy (October 2025)

Standalone Books:

The Darkside of Midnight

Calpa Series

Co-written with Fleur DeVillainy:

The Clan of Mist

The Clan of Deception

The Clan of Luna (coming 2026)

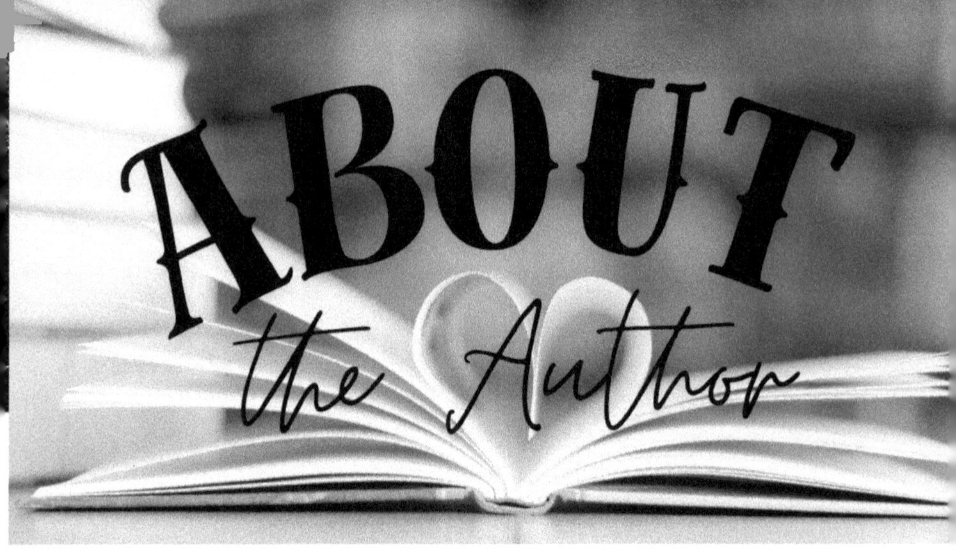

ABOUT the Author

Thank you for taking the time to read the Ascelin series by author Johnna Dee. She is a fantasy romance writer who has four series out at the time of publication. Initially, her creative journey began with poetry, where she honed her skills in crafting evocative and lyrical verses. As her passion for storytelling grew, she ventured into the realm of novels, weaving intricate plots and enchanting worlds that transport readers to extraordinary realms.

For more exclusive content and other goodies, sign-up for Johnna Dee's newsletter https://linktr.ee/johnnadee.

Subscribe to emails to get a free e-book novella, plus other free goodies!

www.ingramcontent.com/pod-product-compliance
Lightning Source LLC
Chambersburg PA
CBHW040854010826
48978CB00013BA/1013